# EXTRAORDINARY PRAISE FOR

## *BARBED WIRE HEART*

"Terrific…In infusing noir tradition with feminist resolve, BARBED WIRE HEART pulls off something rare. Harley may be ridden with guilt and overcome by the feeling that she's incapable of being loved, but in her pursuit of a life of her own, she has only begun to fight."

—*Chicago Tribune*

"Harley McKenna is possibly the most powerful, original female character we've had in decades…Masterfully constructed, BARBED WIRE HEART is an evocative work of darkness and redemption, hinting at times of Flannery O'Connor and Cormac McCarthy. An amazing debut novel. An exciting new voice in the world of books."

—*New York Journal of Books*

"[BARBED WIRE HEART] introduces a major talent…This hard-edged thriller set in the gold rush country of Northern California…has a welcome, powerful feminist sensibility and with its relentless intensity, gritty atmosphere, and compelling father-daughter psychology, this promises to be one of the best books of 2018."

—*Kirkus* (STARRED REVIEW)

"A pulsepounding thriller…masterfully written and constructed…With her powerful debut, Sharpe is definitely a name to watch."

—*Booklist* (STARRED REVIEW)

and *True Grit*, the writing is pin-sharp, with an engaging, masterfully sustained voice, and an utterly captivating story. Tess Sharpe is a writer to watch."

—Beth Lewis, author of *The Wolf Road*

"Harley McKenna is a young woman raised in a harsh world of meth and madness, a lone girl with a conscience raised by a lawless daddy. I love Tess Sharpe's clean-boned writing and tension that makes my heart gallop. Add the underdog fighting against heroic odds, and a universal cause that hits home, and I'm hooked. I am a fan!"

—Leah Weiss, bestselling author of *If the Creek Don't Rise*

"The power of her story is such that one cannot help but think that BARBED WIRE HEART is composed of equal parts fact and imagination, with perhaps a pound or two more of the former than of the latter. Those who are particularly fond of their characters shaded in deep gray, as opposed to black and white, will find much to love here, particularly with respect to the gritty protagonist."

—BookReporter.com

# BARBED WIRE HEART

# BARBED WIRE HEART

TESS SHARPE

GRAND CENTRAL
PUBLISHING

NEW YORK   BOSTON

Copyright © 2018 by Tess Sharpe
Reading Group Guide © 2019 by Tess Sharpe and Hachette Book Group, Inc.

Cover design by Ervin Serrano. Cover art by Karina Vegas/Arcangel. Cover copyright © 2019 by Hachette Book Group, Inc.

Grand Central Publishing
Hachette Book Group
1290 Avenue of the Americas, New York, NY 10104
grandcentralpublishing.com
twitter.com/grandcentralpub

Originally published in hardcover and ebook by Grand Central Publishing in March 2018
First trade paperback edition: March 2019

Grand Central Publishing is a division of Hachette Book Group, Inc. The Grand Central Publishing name and logo is a trademark of Hachette Book Group, Inc.

The Hachette Speakers Bureau provides a wide range of authors for speaking events. To find out more, go to www.hachettespeakersbureau.com or call (866) 376-6591.

Library of Congress Cataloging-in-Publication Data

Names: Sharpe, Tess, author.
Title: Barbed wire heart / Tess Sharpe.
Description: First edition. | New York : Grand Central Publishing, 2018.
Identifiers: LCCN 2017041580| ISBN 9781538744093 (hardcover) | ISBN 9781478975717 (audio download) | ISBN 9781538744109 (ebook)
Subjects: LCSH: Fathers and daughters—Fiction. | Organized crime—Fiction. | Vendetta—Fiction. | BISAC: FICTION / Suspense. | FICTION / Crime. | FICTION / Contemporary Women. | FICTION / Action & Adventure. | FICTION / Coming of Age. | GSAFD: Suspense fiction.
Classification: LCC PS3619.H356655 B37 2018 | DDC 813/.6—dc23
LC record available at https://lccn.loc.gov/2017041580

ISBNs: 978-1-5387-4411-6 (trade pbk.), 978-1-5387-4410-9 (ebook)

Printed in the United States of America

LSC-C

10 9 8 7 6 5 4 3 2 1

*For my mother,*
*who sank my roots in the red dirt.*

*And for my husband,*
*who chose to grow with me.*

# BARBED WIRE HEART

*Part One*

# THE TRAILER IN THE WOODS

# ONE

I'm eight years old the first time I watch my daddy kill a man. I'm not supposed to see. But those first few weeks after Momma died, whenever Uncle Jake isn't around, I'm just running wild.

I spend a lot of time in the woods, playing up in the deer blinds or seeing how high I can get in the trees on my own steam. Sometimes I cry over missing Momma. Sometimes I can't help it.

I try not to do it around Daddy, though.

I like the woods. They're loud and quiet at the same time, the soundtrack and lullaby of my life for as long as I can remember. When I climb the big oaks, pulling myself up with all my might, reaching and jumping and swinging my body along branch and bark like a squirrel, I have to pay attention or I might slip and fall. When I climb, I don't have to think about Momma being gone. Or about how all Daddy does now is storm around in a whiskey cloud, cleaning his guns and muttering about Springfields and blood.

Momma's been dead for three and a half weeks, and already the skin on my palms is worn rough from climbing. My knees are scabbed over from the time I fell out of the tall redwood near the creek. My fingers are stained with blackberry juice, and my arms get scratched from the thorns. My pockets bulge with the treasures I find in the forest—things she would've liked: blue jay feathers and smooth rocks perfect for skipping, a cracked acorn that looks like a face.

I stash my gifts from the forest in one of the deer blinds. Uncle Jake promised he'd take me back to Momma's grave even though Daddy glared at him when he said it. I want to bring her my presents, because Uncle Jake says she's in heaven looking down on us.

Sometimes I stare up at the sky and try to imagine it. Try to see her. But there's nothing but branches and stars.

Daddy doesn't notice how much I'm gone, warm in the forest's hold. He's got other things on his mind.

That night, after I watched the sunset, looking for a trace of Momma in the night sky, I'm still perched in the oak near the edge of the garden, the one that has a good straight branch for sitting. It's getting late and I should go inside, but I hear the sound of truck tires crunching on the gravel road that leads through the woods to our house. I tuck my feet up and out of sight before the headlights of Daddy's Chevy round the curve and flood the garden.

With my bare feet pressing up against the trunk for balance, I stretch myself belly down on the limb. I wrap my arms around it in a hug and crane my neck to get a better view.

If he's drunk again, I don't want him to see me, because I look like her. It makes him sad. Sometimes it makes him angry, but he tries to hide it.

Instead of pulling up next to the house like normal, he drives right under the tree, toward the rough road leading to the barn, parking right in front of the doors. The light on the barn flips on, the sensor detecting the movement.

I watch from a distance as he cuts the headlights and gets out. Daddy's not stumble-down drunk, but it's too far to see if he's covered in his own sick like last week. I'm about to swing down from the tree, but instead of heading toward the house, he walks over to the passenger side of the truck and pulls the door open.

I squint in the darkness. He's almost completely hidden by shadows as he drags something big out of the cab. He yanks the barn door open and the light shifts, just for a second. A beam illuminates the doorway, and I catch a glimpse of a man's feet being dragged across the barn floor before the door slams shut.

My breath comes quick and fast, so hard my belly's scraping against the rough bark. My fingers tighten on the branch as my heart hammers and the world spins. I want to dig inside the oak like the woodpeckers and squirrels do. I want to burrow and hide.

I try to tell myself my eyes are playing tricks on me.

But deep down, I know better.

A few minutes later—it seems like forever, my breath and the chirp of the crickets echoing in my ears—the outside barn light snaps off, and darkness creeps through the trees, spreading across the property.

I should climb down and run into my room and shut the door and pull my quilts over my head. I should pretend I never saw those feet being dragged across the ground.

I don't, though.

Instead I climb down the tree and head toward the barn.

I could say I regret the choice, looking back, but that's just foolishness.

I had to learn somehow. What he was. What I would be.

This was how for me.

I sneak 'round the back of the barn, where the cedar planks are pockmarked with holes. They give a terrible view into the barn, but it's the best I can do. Kneeling down in the dirt, I push my cheek against the wood, angling my head to peep through the biggest hole I can find. I'm breathing too quick still, my heart rabbit-fast under my skin, my mouth dry from the air whooshing in and out.

At first, I can't see Daddy at all. All I see is the old tractor he has stored in here, and the smashed-up quad he crashed last summer. A bare bulb strung up from an orange cord swings gently back and forth from one of the beams and that's when I hear it: his voice.

"You're going to tell me what I wanna know," Daddy says. There's a rummaging sound, like he's going through the red toolbox in the corner. And sure enough, after a few seconds pass, he finally comes into view, a screwdriver in his hand. Shadows lengthen across Daddy as he moves away from my hiding spot, turning the screwdriver in his hand over and over as he walks back behind the tractor, disappearing from view. A groaning sound fills the air.

It's not Daddy.

It's whoever he brought in here. And they're hurt.

Daddy hurt them.

It's strange to think of Daddy's hands, big and strong and calloused, so good at hugs and tugging at the end of my braid, doing that.

"You're gonna tell me what I wanna know," Daddy says. "We can do it easy or hard. Your choice, Ben."

"Fuck you," a second voice—Ben—slurs.

"Tell me," Daddy says.

"Not gonna tell you shit." There's a wet, rattling sound, like he's coughing up more than spit.

"Okay then," Daddy says. The shadows stretch above the tractor, a blurred glimpse of his arm as he shoves forward, sharp and fast. The sound that comes next, a gritted-out groan that punches out of Ben, makes the hair on the back of my neck raise.

"That's going to stay in there until you tell me what I want to know," Daddy says, and I realize he means the screwdriver.

Black spots crowd along the edges of my vision. I have to plant both palms in the dirt and concentrate, slow myself down so I don't faint. My eyes feel like they're about to pop out of my head, and my cheek presses hard against the pecky cedar siding. I want to run away. I have to stay and see what happens.

"Tell me," Daddy says.

"No."

Daddy straightens, coming back into view, and from this angle, I can see he's digging in his back pocket. He comes up with the antler-handle knife he sharpens every Sunday without fail. He flips it open, eight inches of deadly steel shining in the barn light and tests it on his thumbnail. "Let's try something different."

Daddy kneels again, disappearing; the shadowy blur of his arm comes up and then down again. Ben's sound is even worse this time, no gritted teeth, no effort to suppress the scream.

I don't close my eyes or hide my face or do anything that I should.

I keep my eyes wide open.

It feels like it's the first time they've ever been.

"Tell me," Daddy says, when Ben finally quiets to a whimper.

"I can't," Ben gasps out. "I can't. He'll kill me if I do."

"You Springfields, your momma didn't pop you out too bright, did she?" Daddy asks mockingly. "What do you think I'm gonna do if you don't tell me where he is?"

"Please. I'll do anything—money, whores, drugs, you name it, Duke, and I'll do—" His words dissolve into a yell, though I can't see what Daddy's doing to him with that knife.

I press my lips together to hold back the nausea as Daddy says, "Tell me," again, like it's the only words he knows.

"Unnggghh," Ben gurgles, panting. "Please. Please."

"Tell me."

"I can't. Carl's my brother."

Ben's left foot keeps twitching, like it's trying to make a break for it. It's the only part of him that's not blocked by the tractor, and I keep staring at his boots, because Daddy has the same pair. Momma bought them for him last year for Christmas. I'd helped her wrap them.

"Tell me where Springfield is," Daddy says. "Or I go find Caroline. How does that sound? That worth protecting your brother for? Last time I saw that wife of yours, she was looking mighty fine. Maybe I'll take my time."

I'm too young to understand what he means. Later, it'll horrify me.

Later, I'll tell myself it was a bluff. That he isn't that man.

But the possibility is there, right in front of me: He might be.

"No," Ben says weakly. "Not Caroline. Please."

"Then tell me," Daddy demands. "And I won't touch her or your boys. They'll be safe from me and mine. All I want is Springfield."

"Shit, shit…Carl's in Manton. Exit thirty-four on the old highway. House at the end of Hell's Pass. Don't you fucking touch my family!"

Daddy gets up off his knees, straightening, finally in full view. "Thank you."

He moves so fast—the motion so familiar as he reaches. His hands—and then gun—are almost a blur.

It's loud—the gunshot hammers in my ears, and there's this squishy sound that makes my stomach lurch.

I clap my hand over my mouth, but it's too late. I throw up, vomit staining my shirt, a wet splat against my skin. The smell of sour bile makes me gag as I try to get up, my legs refusing to cooperate.

I have to get into the house before he realizes what I've seen. But my legs are like rubber and there's dried salt on my cheeks when I push my messy hair out of my face.

I want Momma with an ache that never seems to get smaller, and just thinking about her makes me clumsy, stupid. When I get up, my foot hits a rock, sending it skittering against the barn, making a loud *thunk*.

I freeze on the spot.

"Who's there?" Daddy's voice thunders through the walls of the barn. I hear his footsteps, swiftly crossing the ground, and then the creak of the door opening as he peers out.

Oh no. My stomach tightens horribly. I feel like throwing up again.

"Harley, if that's you, you've got three seconds to let me know. Otherwise, I'm shooting. One…" Daddy says.

My mind's racing. I'm trying to understand.

Daddy killed him. Made it look easy. Like it doesn't matter.

Like it wasn't the first time.

"Two."

What's he going to do with the body? Will he bury it? Where? The woods?

"Th—"

"It's me!" I yell out, scrambling to my feet. My jeans are covered in dirt and my shirt's damp with vomit. My legs are still shaky, but I dart forward, around the corner and to the front of the barn.

He's standing in the entryway, the light spilling out, his arm still holding the door open.

Beyond him, in the barn, I can see the blood pooling, fast and dark on the ground next to what's left of Ben's head. It lolls to the side, his open eyes facing me. He looks confused. Like he expected Daddy to let him go.

I swallow hard.

It's way worse up close.

Daddy looks at me, his 9mm still raised. Then he looks over his shoulder at Ben and the expanding puddle of blood. Daddy steps to the side, blocking my view of Ben's face. "Baby," he starts. "How long…" He stops. "Sweetheart," he tries again. "I—"

I keep staring at the blood, because even though I've helped Daddy field-dress deer, it's never been this much. It's dark and thick, like paint. But it smells sharp, like copper, like life, soaking into the ground.

"Harley-girl," Daddy says, gentle, the voice he uses when he reads me stories in bed.

I'm going to throw up again. I grit my teeth and manage to swallow the bile down this time, my throat working furiously, sweat popping out on my face. I sway on the spot, and then Daddy's hands are picking me up around the waist and I go limp, I don't even try to fight.

I'm too scared of what this new—no, this old, *hidden*—Daddy will do if I try.

He's silent the whole time he carries me up to the house, up the stairs. He sets me on my bed and pulls my boots off, and I just sit there shaking and let him. He swaps my vomit-stained clothes for one of my sleep shirts before pushing me gently on the shoulder so I'll lie back on the bed. I think about Ben's blank eyes, and for the first time in my life, I shrink from Daddy's touch, but he doesn't notice. I expect him to leave after he tucks me in, but he stays sitting next to my bed for a long time.

It's only when he stands up after what seems like hours later when I get the nerve to say it. Daddy's silhouetted in the doorway, about to shut the door, when I blurt it out: "He told you what you wanted. You didn't have to."

I hear his sigh, but I can't see his face, hidden in shadow. He leans against the doorway, his shoulder pressing against the frame. "A life for a life," he says. "Only way, Harley-girl."

9

A life for a life. Ben's life for Momma's.

"Does that mean you're not going after Springfield?" I ask.

Daddy shifts from foot to foot in the doorway. "I have to," he says.

"But—"

"He took your momma away from us," Daddy reminds me gently. As if I could forget.

"But you said you wouldn't hurt Ben's family."

Daddy straightens, rising from the doorframe. He looks huge, like a shadow himself. I still can't see his face, but when he speaks, just two words, it's like gravel: "I lied."

# TWO

*June 6, 7 a.m.*

E ach morning, I walk the land.

I take a rifle, slung over my back, because there's always trouble of the animal or human kind brewing. I switch up my routes every few days. I can't cover all six hundred acres. Some mornings, all I do is patrol the border fences that run along the north end, the slap of canvas against my legs like a heartbeat. Duke's jacket is too big for me, but I wear it anyway, the sleeves rolled up three times so my hands are free.

This morning, I hike deep into the forest, Busy at my side. She bounds ahead of me, her whip of a tail lashing back and forth, snub nose glued to the forest floor, sniffing out the trails of deer and mountain lion.

I walk behind her, the crunching of my feet across branches and dry pine needles mingling with the squawks of the magpies waking up. The air is crisp in my lungs and the ground is steep, my foothold steady. Each step draws me closer, red dirt crumbling beneath the pressure of my boots as I climb.

When it comes to the land, to this stretch of forest, mountain, and volcanic stone I know like the back of my hand, I am Duke's daughter through and through. I know this place better than anyone but him. Its dangers and its secrets. Some of them I'll take to my grave—whether that's forty years from now or forty minutes.

"Hey!" I call, snapping my fingers when Busy wanders too far, and she skids to a stop, running downhill back to me. Her eyes shine in the early morning light, and as I scratch behind her ears, her blocky head tilts back in bliss.

"Good girl," I say. "C'mon."

By the time we get up the hill, my boots are dusty and Busy's tongue is lolling out of her mouth. As the ground levels out, she scampers after a squirrel, and I let her.

The oak's trunk is thick with age, and its branches spread out low and high, making it perfect for climbing. But that's not why I'm here.

I approach it slowly, like it's a buck I'm getting ready to take down. It's silly, but I can't help it.

Some things are sacred.

Carved over a hundred years ago, the names in the trunk start high up, faded but still legible: *Franklin + Mary Ellen. Joshua + Abigail. David + Sarah.*

I trail my fingers down, over the names—there are more than thirty of them—the great loves of the McKenna family, from the Gold Rush days to now.

There was a time I dreamed about carving my own name here. But I try not to think about Will anymore. Thinking on him takes me down the shaky path that only ever leads to *us*. And there's no us. Not anymore.

I have to be focused on other things.

Today's the day. Time's run out.

I trace the final names carved into the tree. They're down so low I have to crouch to reach them.

*Duke + Jeannie*

I press my hand over Momma's name and close my eyes. My head falls forward, forehead pressing against the rough bark. I breathe in the smell of sap from the nearby pines, and Busy rustles through the brush, searching for squirrels.

I think about Momma, of what I can remember about her. Flashes of bright dresses and cowboy boots, chunky silver-and-turquoise jewelry, the faint scent of lilies floating in the air around her. How she loved the forest and the little keepsakes she collected here: a gnarled twig that looked like a question mark, a clump of moss on a heart-shaped rock. Her smile, the way she'd wrap her arms around me and lift me off my feet.

I used to think about what it might've been like if she'd lived. But the older I get, the harder that is to do. My life is my life. My fate's been set since the day she died. And now it's time to take it back.

"I'm sorry," I say to their names. To the promise the two of them made to each other. To her, dead because of that promise. Maybe even a little to Duke, because he loved her too much to let her go, and I understand that inclination better than most.

McKennas love hard and fast and only once.

I clear my throat and get up, because crying over it's no use.

Today's the day.

*Only way, Harley-girl.*

# THREE

I'm eight years old when my momma dies in front of me.

She's been nervous since breakfast. Halfway through pancakes, she walks into the living room with the phone and leaves me alone with the syrup, which I manage to dip my braid in.

I'm trying to clean it up best I can when Momma's voice rises from the living room: "Will, no, listen—I'm coming right now. You don't need to worry. Forty minutes. Okay? I'll be right there. Don't be scared, honey. Don't let Carl in. Don't let your mom unlock the door. I'll be right there, I promise."

My hair's making a sticky puddle on my shirt when Momma comes back.

"Harley," she sighs, and wipes the ends of my hair with a wet paper towel. "Run and get dressed. We're going into town."

"It's not Wednesday." On Wednesdays, Uncle Jake drives us in his truck to grocery shop, and I sit between them on the bench seat. Momma likes to sing along to the radio, to ladies who sing about coal mining and broken hearts, and men whose deep voices remind me of Daddy's.

"I know, sweetie. Just do as I say."

She's waiting by the front door when I come back downstairs, dressed in my jeans and boots. She grabs the pink-and-black cowboy hat Uncle Jake bought me at the fair and plops it onto my head. She keeps her hand on my shoulder after we get into the Chevy, and doesn't let go until we're all the way into town.

She won't turn on the radio, and she rolls up all the windows even though it's edging into summer. Every few minutes she glances at her phone, tapping it against her leg.

"Where are we going?" I ask when she drives past the grocery store.

"To see a friend."

She turns the truck onto a street I don't recognize, with dirt and patchy grass in the yards and jacked-up, rusted-out cars without tires sitting in the driveways. The houses grow sparser until there are acres between them and the road turns to dirt. Momma keeps driving until we get to the end of the road.

She doesn't stop right in front of the rickety ranch house, spread low and sagging against the land. Instead, she turns the truck around and parks across the road. Then she leans over the seat to flip open the glove compartment. Her long hair swings across her shoulder and brushes against my arm, silky and smelling like flowers.

My eyes widen when I realize that she's got her semi-automatic in her hand. I watch as she calmly snaps the magazine into place.

"Momma—"

She smiles reassuringly at me, stroking my head with the hand that's not holding the gun. "It's fine, baby," she says. "You've gotta do something for me, okay? No matter what, you stay in the truck. A nice boy named Will is gonna come out of the house. He's ten, and he's gonna sit with you. You let him in, and then you two lock the doors. Don't let anyone but me in. You got that?"

I nod unsurely. She's smiling, but she looks weird, her eyes shiny and wet.

"Repeat it back to me," Momma directs gently.

I do, trying hard not to let my voice shake.

Momma kisses me on the forehead and stares at me for a long second. "Good girl," she says. "I love you. I'll be right back."

I watch as she strides up the road and to the house. She doesn't even knock on the door, just turns the knob and walks in, leaving it wide open.

My fingers grip the edge of the dashboard, my chin propped up between them. I scoot until my knees are jammed up against the glove compartment, my nose inches away from the windshield. It's stuffy inside the truck, and I bat at the pine-tree air freshener hanging on the mirror, watching it spin and wishing I could open a window. But I do what Momma says.

Movement in the house's front yard pulls my attention back. A black-haired boy bursts out of the house, his skinny legs narrowing into bony ankles and bare feet. He pelts across the yard toward me. Dust flies behind him, and I pull on the door handle, pushing it open as he comes running up.

"You Will?"

He nods, panting. I hold out my hand, and even though he doesn't need to, he grabs it and climbs up into the cab.

"What's going on?" I ask him as he shuts the door and slams his palm down on the lock.

"The other one locked?" he asks.

I nod.

"You got the keys?"

I hold out the set Momma had pressed into my hand before getting out of the truck.

"Good," Will says.

"What's going on? Where's my momma?"

"She's with my mom," Will says. "We're gonna wait until Carl leaves."

"Who's Carl?"

"Mom's boyfriend," Will says, but he says it like it's something dirty in his mouth. The skin below his left eye's swollen and puffy, and there's a trail of big circular scabs running up his left arm. "Don't worry. Your momma'll make him leave. She's done it before. It'll be okay."

Almost as soon as the words are out of his mouth, it happens.

There's a roar, so loud and unlike anything I've ever heard, cracking and shattering and popping all at once. I yell and clap my hands over my ears. And suddenly, the house just isn't there anymore. All I can see is fire and black smoke, bits of wood flying up to the sky and then raining down on the truck like a hailstorm.

Will's mouth moves, but I can't hear what he's saying. He's leaning over, yanking the keys away, and he jams them into the ignition.

Suddenly, it all catches up with me, like the world froze and now it's rushing forward. Fire. Smoke. Pieces of wood—pieces of the house—slamming down on the Chevy's hood and roof.

*Momma!*

I scream for her and lunge for the door, scrabbling at the handle, trying to get it to open, but it's locked. Will grabs my arm, fighting me with one hand. He yanks me toward him as he starts up the engine, stretches his long legs, and presses hard on the gas. The truck leaps backward, away from the pieces of wood, shingles, and plaster that fly everywhere, shaking the truck and cracking the windshield. Will steers one-handed as he jerks me against his side, practically pinning me there, and he doesn't let go.

We spin away from the explosion, debris flying off the hood, and it's too fast. The bed of the truck tilts off the road into a ditch with a thump, so the cab's angled up, and then we're stopped, far enough away to be safe. Will's hand is still on my arm, and mine's on his now, grabbing him back just as hard as we stare out the busted windshield.

And we watch whatever's left of our mothers burn.

# FOUR

*June 6, 8:30 a.m.*

As soon as we get back from the woods, Busy and I stop to load up my truck with what I need before we hit the road. She hops up in the cab, and we take off down the winding driveway toward the iron gates of the McKenna homestead. The tires kick up dust clouds behind us—the land's so dry this time of year, one spark could be the end of us—and Busy hangs her head out the window, drooling into the air.

I punch my code into the keypad, and the iron gates slide open. Busy barks into the wind as I switch the stations until I get more song, less static, settling on our homegrown celebrity, Merle, telling us how his momma tried. I take it as a good omen.

We live forty miles from the nearest—and biggest—town in the Dirty 530. The sky's smudged with plumes of smoke blowing in from Trinity County—the forest fires are raging toward us. But North County's always walking through fire of some kind. Our little chunk of territory should've dissolved back into wilderness, like so many of the Gold Rush towns, but somehow it survived. Folks still make their living pulling gold from the creeks—trading old-school tin pans for sluice boxes and illegal dredges. Families are still farming on land that's been in their blood for generations. We're not exactly thriving as a community, but we make do, best we can.

Busy and I drive down the mountain into forest so thick there isn't an end in sight, along red dirt cliffs and past the jagged slate crags that

18

out-of-towners like to climb. The road snakes up and down, winding through the forest, and my truck takes the curves smoothly.

When we get to Salt Creek, I take the first exit, down Vollmer's Pass. The courthouse and tiny hospital are at the top of the hill, along with the nicer houses—the ones that have been kept up. But go a few miles down the road, and you leave the neat hedges and tasteful rose gardens behind for the trailer parks, mobile homes, and motels with filled-in pools and dirty children wandering the halls.

I've got collections to make today. If I skip them, it'll look suspicious.

To most of the world, the regular folks, Duke is a businessman who ran a trucking business with his brother-in-law for years. He owns a string of motels, a bar or two, a few diners, some land here and there, until he seems almost legitimate now.

But if you step a little farther into the backwoods, where we've got our own laws and where things get real bloody real fast, you'll see who Duke McKenna really is.

For a long time, he tried to keep me away from the drug side of the business. Uncle Jake had insisted on it—it was one of the few things the two of them ever agreed on. So when I was sixteen, after I got my GED, instead of teaching me to cook or deal, Duke gave me a list of the people who owe him money and pay it back on a monthly basis.

It isn't a short list. Mainly women, business owners who haven't been able to get bank loans, so they go to Duke instead. He'd made a gamble sending out a sixteen-year-old girl to be taken seriously, but the power of the McKenna name in this town is absolute, and so far, I've had no problems.

I always start my collections at the Talbot Bakery, tucked away in one of the dingy, half-abandoned strip malls they built in the seventies, trying to pump business into the town.

I leave Busy in the car because I know Mrs. Talbot doesn't like her. When I open the glass doors, the bells attached to them tinkle, and the smell of fresh bread and chocolate surrounds me. It reminds me of when I was little, of helping Miss Lissa, our housekeeper, in the kitchen.

Mrs. Talbot looks up from the glass case, where she's arranging brownies.

"Hey, Harley," she says. Her hair is tucked underneath a green bandanna, a few stray locks curling around her face. She's got purple smudges under her eyes that come with the worry of having one kid in the Army and the other stuck in a nowhere town with too little to interest her.

Duke had been smart when he picked my collection list all those years ago. He chose women who are mothers. Who wouldn't hate me or cause trouble, but instead feel sorry for me, because they'd see their kids in me.

But I'm not like their kids. My childhood wasn't bikes and swim parties, it was full metal jackets and other men's blood crusted beneath Duke's fingernails.

"Hi," I say. "How's Jason?"

"Good. He might get some leave for Christmas." Mrs. Talbot places the final brownie in the case and slides it shut.

"And Brooke?" I ask innocently. Mrs. Talbot's never been thrilled about me being her daughter's friend. But it's not like she can do much about it now that we're grown.

She couldn't do much when we were teenagers, either.

"She's got a temp job in Burney," Mrs. Talbot says, walking over to the cash register and punching a few buttons so it opens. "They're even paying for her gas. It's leaving me short-handed here, but it's a good opportunity for her." She pulls an envelope from the cash register and hands it to me.

I take it, but I don't open it to count the money. I'm not going to insult her, not after all this time. I look down at the envelope, feeling its weight in my hand.

She probably cleared out her entire cash register to fill it.

I push down the guilt. This is my job.

"Thanks," I say, instead. "Do you want me to take the bread delivery to the diner? I'm headed that way."

Some of the tension in her face unwinds. "That would be nice of you," she says. She turns, grabs the three big paper bags on the counter full of dinner rolls and loaves of bread, and slides them toward me.

Her head tilts, her eyes narrowing as she looks me up and down. "You okay, Harley?" she asks. "You're looking kinda pale."

"I'm fine," I lie as I shove the envelope in my pocket so my hands are free. I want to give it back to her.

I want to be the kind of person who would do that. But I'm not.

I grab the bags and head toward the door. "If you don't find anyone to replace Brooke, one of the Rubies might be up for it," I say over my shoulder. "There's one lady, Sam, she's new, real nice, three kids. Her cast'll come off in a few weeks. Give me a call if you'd like her help in here."

"I appreciate that, Harley," Mrs. Talbot smiles blandly in a way that tells me she doesn't think that's the best idea. They know better than to say it to my face, but some of the locals don't exactly cotton to the women who live at the Ruby. It's bullshit, and a lot of it has to do not just with the Rubies, but with Mo, who runs the place with me. There's nothing that chaps white women's asses more around here than a Native woman having some power.

Mo protects all kinds of women at the Ruby, which makes them grit their teeth even more. The only kind of survivor in need of protection is the kind *they* deem as right and real. And most of the time, that means she needs to be white and never made a mistake in her life and whoever hurt her needs to be their idea of a predator. He can't be someone they like or go to church with or work with, because then they're uncomfortable with the idea. Then they look the other way. Then the woman is stuck without any help.

That's where the Ruby and Mo come in.

She shows up no matter what. She has the Rubies' backs, no matter what.

When I load the bread in the double cab of my truck, Busy sniffs interestedly at the bags, but I snap my fingers, and she settles down to pout.

"Brat," I tell her, pulling out of the bakery parking lot and taking a left.

The Blackberry Diner's on South Street, across the railroad tracks. There are chainsaw-cut bear statues at the entrance, jars of blackberry jam on every table, and a long counter where the regulars—old dudes with veteran's caps and bifocals—hold court. They drink black coffee by the pot and like to pretend to forget the waitresses' names. The Blackberrys—there are five spread across three counties—were diners my Granddaddy McKenna started up back in the 1950s. They were probably a way to launder money, since everything Granddaddy did was a little crooked. But these days, they manage to pull in decent business, especially the flagship diner.

"Hi, honey!" a bright voice chirps at me as I push through the double doors. "Oh, let me help you with that." Two of the bags of bread are lifted out of my hands, and Amanda, the manager, comes into view. She's tall and pretty, with tan skin and long black hair she keeps in a bun. She's always smiling—a plus in food service. Duke hired her almost ten years ago as a waitress, and she'd worked her way up. He'd given her free rein on the Salt Creek diner, and with a few changes, she'd drawn in the drivers making their way through the mountains toward Oregon. The tourists bought the homemade blackberry jam by the case just because she slapped a cute label and a square of gingham cloth on it.

"I figured I'd save Mrs. Talbot a trip on the bread delivery," I say, following Amanda behind the counter and through the kitchen doors. Heat blasts my face, and the clatter and noise of the kitchen fills my ears as the short-order cooks shout orders and sling biscuits at each other. The dishwasher hurries over to take the bread from us, disappearing into the back to put it into the warmer.

"How are you?" Amanda asks as we get out of the kitchen to give the waitresses hurrying past us some elbow room. "You want coffee?"

"Please," I say, sidestepping a busboy with a full tub. "Been busy today?"

"Got a whole load of tourists off the Five," Amanda says, grabbing a fresh pot of coffee and a to-go cup. "Nothing like four twelve-tops first thing in the morning."

I grimace in sympathy, taking the coffee cup when she offers it to me.

"Extra sugar, just how you like it."

"Thanks. So, how's Jeremy?" I ask, taking a sip of the coffee. "Is he still on that whitewater rafting trip?"

"He comes back Monday," Amanda says. "I can't believe he's almost thirteen. It's been so long since…" she trails off, her eyes growing troubled with memories.

"He was so cute when he was little," I say, trying to smooth out the moment. "Do you remember how he used to follow Busy around when we visited the Ruby? He kept trying to ride her like a horse."

She laughs. "I think I have video of that somewhere."

"Keep that for blackmail once he starts dating."

Her brown eyes soften. "Good idea."

I glance at the blackberry-shaped clock mounted on the wall. "I have to get going," I say. "I've got Busy in the truck. Thanks for the coffee."

"Say hi to Mo and the rest of the Rubies for me," Amanda says.

"I will."

"Take care, honey," I hear her call as the doors close behind me.

I will.

I have to.

# FIVE

I'm twelve the day I pull a gun on someone for the first time.

I'm in town with Uncle Jake, and we're just about ready to head home when he gets a call.

He frowns before he picks up the phone, staring at the screen and then at me for a second before raising it to his ear.

"Hey, Mo. This isn't a good—" He stops, his dark eyebrows knitting together as he listens. "Okay," he says. "Duke's not answering? Then text me the address. I'll take care of it."

When he hangs up, he looks over at me, his blue eyes worried.

"We need to go pick someone up," he says, and the way he says it, makes the hairs on the back of my neck prickle. "Can you promise me you'll do everything I say, no matter what happens?"

I nod. "Are we going to get a Ruby?" I ask.

Uncle Jake smiles, gentle, like he wants to reassure me that everything's okay, even though I know what's coming. "Yeah," he says quietly.

The house he parks in front of is nice—one of the better places in Salt Creek. The lawn is green and neat and tidy, and there's a brand-new car in the driveway.

There's a kid screaming inside. It sounds like a full-on tantrum, and it sets my teeth on edge as I get out of the truck with Uncle Jake.

"Stay close to me," he says, holding on to my arm as we walk up the path onto the porch. He knocks, but when no one answers, he just walks right in. "Amanda," he calls down the hall. "It's Jake Hawes. Mo from the Ruby told me you needed some help."

The crying stops abruptly. A hiccupping sound follows, like the kid's learned to stay quiet when a man speaks.

We step into the kitchen. The dishwasher is wide open. My heart starts hammering as Jake walks down the hall.

And there she is, in the master bedroom, throwing things into a suitcase. Her kid—a little boy with dark hair who looks about three—is sitting on the edge of the bed, a fresh bruise fanning across his forehead.

She looks up, and I see a matching, older bruise on her cheek. "Jake," she says, and her entire body relaxes with that one word. "You came."

"Of course," he says, stepping into the room. "When did he leave?"

"A half hour ago. He was so mad—I forgot his lunch and Jeremy was crying, and he…" She takes a deep breath, her fingers clenching around the shirt in her hands. "I called Mo," she says.

"You did the right thing calling her," Jake says. "Let's get your stuff together and I'll take you to her."

Amanda looks around the room, tears in her eyes that don't ever fall. "I got Jeremy's stuff. I have money; I've been saving up."

"Take what you need now. You don't have to come back," Jake says gently.

She nods. "I don't have to come back," she repeats.

Then I hear a car door slamming, and my head jerks toward the sound, primed as I am by Daddy to identify anything new in my vicinity.

"Uncle Jake," I say.

Before I can get out another word, the front door is opening and slamming so hard, the walls shake. Amanda's eyes widen with terror and she steps toward her kid, an instinctive movement that's all about protection.

"He's back," she whispers.

"Harley, take Jeremy," Jake orders, grabbing the toddler and thrusting him into my arms. The kid clings to me, burying his wet face in my neck, and I grab him back, because I know what's coming down the hallway.

I know what men are capable of when it comes to women. The proof is right in front of me, all over Amanda's face.

"Go," Jake says, pushing me down the hall toward the kitchen and the back door. I hear footsteps that aren't Jake's coming toward the bedroom from the living room, and a deep voice yelling Amanda's name.

Jeremy's legs wrap around my waist, and I hurry down the hall, single-minded. I have to get him out. Keep him safe.

The back door's right there; my hand closes around the knob.

"What the hell is going on?" the voice booms out, echoing down the hall.

He's reached the bedroom.

I hesitate at the back door. I love Uncle Jake, but I've never seen him throw a punch in my life. What if...

Jeremy's face is still buried in my neck, and his little fingers wrap tight around my braid.

I have to get him out of here.

I jerk the back door open and run down the steps, through the yard, to Uncle Jake's truck. I lift Jeremy into the cab, looking over my shoulder.

The house is quiet.

Too quiet.

I flip open Uncle Jake's glove box, take out the pistol, and check the rounds. "Hey," I turn to Jeremy, smiling really wide. "I'll be right back. You stay in the truck. Don't move, no matter what you hear. If you stay, you get all the cookies you want. Okay?"

"Okay," he says softly, his eyes wide.

I get out and make sure the windows are rolled down enough, but not too much; then I lock him inside. It'll be safer for him that way.

I force myself not to think about when I was locked in a truck while my momma faced down a bad man, and how that ended.

It won't end that way for Jeremy.

I run back through the backyard toward the house, this time as quietly as I can. The gun is a familiar weight in my hand, but now, in this moment, suddenly it's very different.

Now it's not just target shooting. It's not just Daddy throwing discs in the air for me to shoot holes through. It's not squirrels or deer or bears or even a mountain lion.

It's a man.

Can I shoot a man?

Am I about to find out?

There are voices—now muffled and tense—coming from the hallway as I creep back into the kitchen, holding the pistol tight. My palms are sweating, but I can't let go to wipe them off, so I tighten my grip.

*Breathe, Harley-girl.*

I flatten myself against the wall that turns into the hallway, peering around it.

His back's to me in the hallway. A big, burly guy with a massive neck and fists the size of forty-pound dumbbells. He's facing Jake, who's standing in front of Amanda, shielding her.

Mr. Big and Burly has a gun. I can't see it, but I know it. I can feel it in the air. I can see it in her face, the terror, the resignation in her face that says *He really is going to kill me this time.*

"Where is my kid?" he growls.

"This is a bad idea, Hunter," Jake says. "You let us go, you won't have any trouble. But you do something to Amanda? To me? You've got McKenna on your ass."

"Bullshit," Hunter says. "McKenna's not gonna care about this stupid slut."

"She's a Ruby now," Jake says. "You know what that means."

"You've got no right messing in my marriage. This is between us."

"It's up to you, Hunter," Amanda says, and her voice shakes, but she stands tall. Strength shimmers off her like the air above a bonfire. "You've got the gun. So do I leave this house in a body bag? An ambulance? Or do you let me go? Because one way or another, I'm leaving. I won't live like this anymore. Not with Jeremy."

"Honey, I didn't mean—" he started.

*"You hit him,"* she cuts into his sentence viciously.

"Your wife's leaving you," Jake says. "So either you put down the gun like a real man. Or you shoot. But you can't hit both of us at once."

His arm shifts; he's raising his gun hand. "I can try," he says.

I move, my steps smooth and silent, all the training that Daddy's drilled into my head there in a flash as I close the space between us. Jake's eyes widen when he sees me, but he stays still; he doesn't give it away.

I press the barrel into Hunter's back. He stiffens, his head twists, and Jake takes advantage of the diversion I've created. He lashes out so fast his hands are a blur as he grabs the gun in Hunter's hand, jerking it toward him, wrenching his fingers to the side.

Hunter howls, stepping back, so the barrel of my pistol digs deeper into his back as Jake yanks the gun out of his hand and then points it at him.

"Out of the way, Harley," Jake orders, and I duck beneath his arm, coming to stand next to Amanda as Jake advances on Hunter. She puts her arm around me, smoothing the hair out of my face. "Where's Jeremy? Are you okay, honey?" she asks.

I nod. "Jeremy's in the truck. He's fine."

Jake tucks the gun in the back of his jeans and rounds on Hunter. His first blow lands on Hunter's jaw, the next breaks his nose, and the third, to the solar plexus, puts him on the floor.

Jake stands over him, his fist still clenched, the gun in his other hand, like he wants to do more.

"Uncle Jake," I say.

He turns to me, like he's just remembered where we are. The look on his face—the wildness in his eyes, the anger that's so out of character it makes my stomach twist—fades in an instant. Hunter's head thunks against the carpet as he sputters, blood from his nose dripping into his mouth.

"You don't touch her again," Jake says, his voice low, the promise of hurt in every word. "You don't come near either of them. If you do, I'll send McKenna for you. There'll be nothing left but your teeth, and I'll grind those into dust personally."

He grabs Amanda's suitcase from the bedroom, stepping around Hunter to get it.

"Let's go," he says.

Amanda starts running the second she gets to the porch, running to Jeremy, who's still sitting quietly in the truck. Jake unlocks the door, and she jumps in, gathering the boy in her arms, hugging him tight.

It's a squeeze to fit in the cab, but we make do as Jake drives us all to the Ruby. A skinny woman's waiting at the entrance for us, cigarette in her hand, glasses looped around her neck on a chunky beaded chain. When Amanda gets out of the car, Mo envelops her in a smoky hug.

"You're safe now," Mo tells her in a gravelly voice, smiling down at Jeremy. "C'mon, I've got a cottage all ready for you two."

I start to follow them, but Jake holds me back. "Not today," he tells me.

He doesn't drive me home, though. Instead, we go to a spot by the river, where he parks the truck and just sits still in the driver's seat for a long time, looking out at the water.

"You okay?" he asks.

I shrug. "Is she?"

"She will be. With time," Jake says.

"And him?"

"He'll stay away," Jake says. But the way his fingers clench around the steering wheel makes me wonder if he believes it.

"They don't always stay away," I say. I know this, for a fact, because there have been nights when Daddy disappears after getting a call from Mo, and when he comes back, he's got that light in his eyes that tells me he's shed some blood.

"They follow the rules if they know what's good for them," Jake says.

"And if they break the rules?"

He pauses. "Well, there are consequences."

"Would you have killed him?" I persist.

Jake looks away and doesn't say anything.

"Have you…" I don't finish the question. I can't, not when he looks at me with those eyes that are so much like Momma's, begging me not to go there.

"Your momma loved the Ruby," Jake says. "When she inherited the motel, I was worried. I didn't think she could pull it off. And then she told me what she intended to do with it, offering it up as a safe haven for women. I thought she was crazy. Thought it was too dangerous. But there was no stopping your momma when she got something in her head." He smiles at the memory.

"Like me," I say.

"Like you," he agrees. And he smiles again.

He rubs a hand over his face. Even after all these years, he won't grow a beard. It's the one thing that sets him apart, these days. "What your momma and Mo did for all those women, what the Ruby means to the women of this county? Apart from you, the Ruby was how she made her mark on the world. It was her way to give back. And someday, it'll be yours to run with Mo."

"I know," I say.

I don't know if I'll ever be ready, though. If I'll ever be able to harden my heart enough for it not to break when I see bruises around throats, around wrists, on tiny rib cages that haven't finished growing.

Sometimes, when I'm with Uncle Jake or Mo, I start to question things. I start to wonder if maybe hardness isn't the answer. Maybe the horror, fresh and present with each woman, with each bruise and tear, is what I should feel.

Maybe hardening a heart is the problem. Not the solution.

# SIX

After I leave the diner, I make two more collections at the top of the hill before beginning my descent into the guts of town. Along the pass near the bottom of the hill, there's a line of motels that Duke owns. Five of them, side by side. They're pay-by-the-month or hourly types, breeding grounds for drugs and trouble.

You want to control your customer base, you keep them in one place.

But the Ruby, the last motel at the very bottom of the hill, is different. The Ruby had belonged to Momma, and it's the one safe place in North County where a woman can go if she's in trouble.

Momma had a soft heart for strays. That's the way people always put it, with this rueful smile. Like she was silly for caring. Like what she and Mo did wasn't fierce, protective, womanly instinct.

Momma's parents owned the Ruby, forty A-frame cottages near the river, all painted bright red. She took charge of it after she married Duke, but instead of renting out rooms, she opened the Ruby free to the women who need it the most. Women on the run from their husbands, their boyfriends, their fathers. Women who want to get clean or sober or just plain out. Pregnant girls with nowhere else to go. Momma sheltered all of them at the Ruby, and no man dared defy a woman who carried a twelve gauge just as surely as she carried the McKenna name.

Mo came down from Montgomery Creek, a tiny town on the way to

31

Burney. She belonged to the Pit River Tribe up there and she'd come to work the second year after Momma took it over.

I'd asked her once, what had drawn her to work at the Ruby, and she'd raised her eyebrow and asked me if she needed a tragic backstory to do the right thing. I'd turned red at being called out and apologized, because it was where my mind had gone.

*I believe in this,* she had told me, sitting in the Ruby's lobby. *I believe in them.*

Without Mo, the Ruby wouldn't have survived after Momma died. The motel got handed over to Uncle Jake until I was old enough to inherit it, and Mo convinced him to keep it running instead of selling it or turning it back into a regular motel. Jake did his best, provided the muscle, but Mo nurtured the heart of the place. The Ruby would be a shit-show without her.

The Rubies are part of the McKenna family, and if anyone messes with them or their children, that man has to answer to me and Mo, then to Duke. Not that I could guarantee there'd be much left to hand over to him.

The Ruby is mine and Mo's now. We're partners. The day after I inherited it, I had the paperwork drawn up so Mo owned fifty percent of the land and buildings and would get all of it if anything ever happened to me.

I'll never be as good as Momma, who women all over the county still talk about in hushed, reverent tones, and I'll never be as smart as Mo, but I do the best I can. My name keeps everyone safe. I make sure the tweekers stay clean and the kids are getting everything they need.

As I pull up, kids are splashing in the pool I had put in a few years ago. I park the truck and open the door, letting Busy hop out and follow me up the walk.

"Puppy!" A little girl toddles up to Busy and me at full speed, her mom following close behind.

"Sit, Busy," I say quietly. Busy obeys, tail wagging, and licks Jackie's face when she throws her arms around her neck. "How you doing, Sam?" I ask her mom.

"We're good, Harley," Sam says. Her arm's still in the sling, and I can see her kids' signatures all over the cast. "The boys love the pool."

"Glad you're settling in." Out of the corner of my eye, I can see someone peek out the door of one of the cottages and close it fast. I frown. That's Jessa's cabin.

"You seen Jessa around?" I ask Sam.

"The woman in number eight?"

I nod.

"No, not for a few days. I think she works nights, though."

"Yeah, she does. I should check in on her. You let me know if you need anything, okay? Mo has my number posted in the office."

I'm about to turn away when she grabs my hand.

"Thank you, Harley," she says. "What you did—"

"It's fine," I interrupt her. "I just do what I can."

"You made him stay away, and that—" Sam's eyes fill, but she doesn't let the tears fall. She picks up Jackie, cradling her close. Jackie squawks in protest, struggling to get back down on the ground with Busy. "He's never stayed away before," Sam says.

"He'll stay away this time," I promise. If he doesn't, I'll set his truck on fire. Maybe with him in it. I told him that much when he'd tried to muscle in my way as I took Sam and the kids out of the house last month. "You don't have to worry anymore."

There's movement at the window of Jessa's cottage, and after I say goodbye to Sam, I head across the driveway and knock on the door of number eight.

I wait a long time before it opens. Jayden, Jessa's nine-year-old, stares up at me. Her hair is in crooked braids, and her pink shirt's on inside out.

"Hi, Harley," she says.

"Hi, Jayden," I peer inside the cottage. "Where's your mom?"

Jayden shrugs and opens the door wider to let Busy and me in. I snap my fingers and point. Busy plants herself in the open doorway, keeping watch.

I look around the room. It's clean, but when I flip open the fridge, there's a bunch of labeled tupperware. I recognize the handwriting. It's Mo's, not Jessa's.

When did I last see Jessa? Last week when I visited? Did she look strung out? My mind races, trying to think of something I overlooked. Goddammit, how did I miss it?

"How long has she been gone?" I ask Jayden.

"I saw her on Tuesday. We'd be fine, Harley, promise. But she took the EBT card."

I have to clamp down on the anger—I've given Jessa chance after chance to clean up, and now she leaves the kids without enough food?—but Jayden sees it anyway.

"Mo's been having us eat with her, and she's been staying over each night. You gonna call CPS?" she asks, her face tight with worry.

I smile at her, trying to be reassuring, sad that she knows too much. "'Course not," I say, even though that depends on what I find once I track Jessa down. If she's using again…

I reach into my back pocket, coming up with my money clip. I peel off one of the hundreds I collected from Mrs. Talbot and hand it to Jayden.

"You go get Jamie and order a pizza. Get a salad, too. When you guys are done eating, I'll have Mo drive you to the grocery store. I'm gonna go find your mom."

Jayden looks down at the money, and I know the private war going on inside her. You're not supposed to take too much charity. You're supposed to hold your head high. Stay proud.

It's bullshit, those lines our parents fed us.

You survive. Any way you can.

Jayden had to become a survivor, for better or worse.

"I'll pay you back," she mutters, her cheeks turning red as she stuffs the money in her pocket.

"And you gotta promise me something," I say, kneeling down so I'm eye to eye with her. I put my hands on her shoulders. "If this happens again, you call me. Okay? That's why I'm here. To make sure nothing happens to you and Jamie. And your mom."

"I promise, Harley." The relief in Jayden's eyes makes me wonder if she's lying. If Jessa's been gone longer than two days.

I take a deep breath. Getting angry in front of Jayden is no use; it'll just make her more upset. I knew when I let Jessa in that there might be consequences. She's stubborn as a mule and wild as a bobcat. Trying to help her has never been easy, but I hoped it would be worth it. I check my watch. It's quarter past eleven.

I've got to find her fast. I need to be at the Tropics for collection count by one.

"Go find your brother and get some food now," I tell Jayden. "And remember what I said."

She hugs me, quick, like she expects me to pull away instead of hold her tight. I hug her back, letting it last as long as she wants.

I wait until she's walked down the drive to the enclosure surrounding the pool before I grab a carton of cigarettes from my truck. I let Busy hop up inside the truck cab and switch the AC on before I walk over to the largest of the A-frame cabins, where the office is.

Mo's got a Camel Light in one hand, a cup of coffee in another. She looks up when she hears the door open.

When I was younger, she'd worn her hair long, but a few years back, she'd hacked it all off, muttering about how she was too damn old to bother with it anymore. I like that about her, how she has no tolerance for time wasting.

She's a woman who gets shit done. I've learned more from her than any other woman in my life.

"Hey," she says. "I was about to call you."

"About Jessa?" I ask.

Mo's lips press together as she takes a long drag. "Yep," she says.

"How long has she been gone?" I ask again. I don't have to hide how worried I am with Mo. She never lets stuff fall through the cracks like this.

But it's Jessa, which is why I get it. Jessa's charming and manipulative, and she knows how to sweet-talk anyone—man or woman. It's why, despite all the using, all the bad behavior, she's never lost her kids, unlike some of the other ex-tweekers at the Ruby.

"I wish you had called me."

Mo looks down, stubbing out the butt in the chipped cup she's using

35

as an ashtray and lighting another before answering. "I was going to if she didn't come home tonight. Wanted to give her some time before the warden came sniffing around."

"Is that my new nickname?"

Mo grins. She's never had a drug problem, unlike a majority of the people in my life. Her teeth are straight, white, and perfect. "It's what they called your momma."

"Do I even want to know what they call you?"

Her grin widens. "Doubt it."

"Have you called Centerfolds?" I ask. "Has she at least been showing up for work?"

Mo's eyebrows scrunch up. "She lost her job there last month. Jayden let it slip today, which is another reason I was about to call."

Goddammit. I slam my hand against the wall, and Mo frowns at me. "So she's using again," I say.

"I don't think so." Mo shakes her head. "I've heard some rumors. About her going across the river."

My stomach sinks and twists all at once. I can feel color rising in my cheeks, hot anger rising and seeping through my skin.

I don't have a lot of rules for the Rubies. Stay clean. No booze on the property. Keep your kids fed and in school. Get a job—I don't care what—and keep it. No male visitors unless they've been checked out first.

And no going across the river. That rule is more for their safety than anything. In the world that men like my daddy and Carl Springfield run, the Rubies are mine. An extension of me, a legacy from Momma. They're all McKennas, in a way. Crossing over the river is too much of a risk. They could get hurt.

I learned the hard way that Springfield's always looking to hurt me.

"What the fuck is she doing across the river?" I ask Mo.

"I don't know," Mo shrugs, "but I think she has a boyfriend."

"Jesus Christ." I want to punch the wall again. "Okay, keep calling her for me. Can you or one of the other women take the kids to the grocery store? I gave Jayden money."

"I'll take them," Mo says, nodding. "What are you going to do?"

"I'm gonna find Jessa," I say. I set the carton of cigarettes I brought her down on the counter. "Let's hope it's before she fucks her life up again, chasing the high. I wish you would've told me sooner, Mo."

She raises an eyebrow. "Sometimes we do things my way," she says. "And if it doesn't work…"

I sigh. "We do it my way," I finish for her. It's our agreement. Our vow to each other. And it means something. Everything.

"It's not like *you* don't keep things from *me*," she says pointedly.

I bite my lip, trying to ignore the look in her eye. She knows me. Probably better than any of the adults who watched me grow up. She's the only woman in my life I haven't lost somehow. And I can't lie to her.

"It's safer if you don't know," I say, because I'm not going to disrespect her by denying it.

"I never really cared for safe," Mo says. "You be careful out there, Harley."

# SEVEN

I'm sixteen the first time I learn what fearless looks like.

After my birthday, I have the kind of freedom I've only dreamed about. I'm grown. And finally, Daddy's hold lessens just a sliver from the death grip he's always had on me.

I spend a lot of time at the Ruby with Mo, as she teaches me what it means to run the place, to protect it, to live and be and breathe it.

The day everything goes to shit, it's pouring down rain. It's probably a sign or something, but I don't take it as one when I arrive. A bunch of the kids are having a mud fight in the greenbelt behind the cottages, and Mo's standing under a big umbrella, watching them with Amanda. They smile when they see me, waving me over, and I join them. The kids shriek and shout, stomping in puddles, flinging mud in every direction, reveling in the mess.

"You ever do this when you were a kid, Harley?" Amanda asks. "My momma would've yelled her head off if I got so dirty."

I laugh. "I always got the better of Will during our mud fights. Or maybe he let me get the better of him."

"That boy," Mo says, shaking her head affectionately. "He's not with you today?"

"He's working for the Sons today."

Mo's mouth flattens, and she doesn't say anything, but I know what she's thinking. She doesn't like Will working on the grow. She says it's too dangerous, and she's right. Pot is a white man's game, because they don't get busted as easy. The cops don't need a reason to go after a Native man—they just do it. It makes everything Will does, every step he makes, a risk. And I can't do a goddamn thing about it but watch as Daddy does the same thing Miss Lissa does: ignore that the rules are different for Will. That the stakes are higher. That the risks go deeper.

I try to think of something to say to Mo, but I know it'll fall short. There's no comfort to give. There's just the reality that he's stuck.

"We'll both come by later this week and barbecue," I promise, and Mo gives me a fleeting smile that fades quickly when the children's shrieking is drowned out by a loud crashing sound, the scrape of metal against metal filling the air.

All three of us whirl around as one, eyes wide. The umbrella falls to the ground, Mo's hand going to her waist.

"Amanda, get the kids inside," Mo orders. "Tell the women. Take cover. Harley, come."

I obey, falling into step next to her as Amanda runs out into the field, yelling for the kids. We move behind the cottages, blocked from view.

"Amanda's got the kids. Get inside. Like we practiced!" Mo calls as women begin to peek their heads out of their back doors. They disappear at her calm orders, and we round the corner past the last cottage, the front of the property coming into view.

The gate that guards the Ruby's entrance is down, busted off its hinges by a red F-150 with a now-crumpled, smoking hood.

The driver is nowhere to be seen.

"We need guns," I say.

"Office," Mo replies.

Swift and steady, we move through the rain. My heart's pounding in my throat. I feel naked without a gun, my fingers twitching, restless and eager for a trigger.

I yank the lobby door open and we hurry to the back office. Mo's phone buzzes, and she pulls it out.

"Amanda's got the kids secure in Katie's cottage," she tells me. "She's got everyone on that text chain she started. Everyone's in touch and safe."

"So far," I say grimly, keying in the code to the gun safe tucked in the corner of the room. I pull out two shotguns and a box of shells, handing one of the guns to Mo. "Who do you think it is?"

"I don't know," Mo says, opening the box and loading the gun. "We don't have anyone new. There haven't been any problems."

"He was probably lying low. Waiting for the right time." I grab the .45 out of the safe, holstering it on my waist.

"You ready?" Mo asks.

My fingers curl around the shotgun. My hands are sweaty. I nod.

We walk back into the main lobby, armed and ready. With each step, dread builds in me.

This isn't like anything I've ever had to do.

This may be the day I have to kill. Because I will lay a man down before I let him destroy the safety Mo and the Rubies have built.

I peer out the lobby window, squinting through the sheets of rain. And there he is, standing in the middle of the parking lot. He's not moving. He's just standing there.

Like he's waiting.

"You see him?"

Mo nods, stepping forward.

"You know him?"

"That's Katie's father," she says.

"Shit."

Katie left her daddy's house the day she turned eighteen and never looked back. She came from one of those super-fundie families, where the women aren't much more than baby makers. They homeschool them and marry them off young and keep them pregnant. When Katie ran, her daddy had been setting up a courtship with a boy there'd been rumors about—rumors that he'd forced himself on another girl. Katie hadn't even been able to use the word *rape* back when she told Mo. Forgiveness was paramount in those sorts of families—when it came to the men, at least. Man rapes a girl, all they've got to do is repent, and all is well in their version of God's eyes…women are such terrible temptations, after all. They just sweep it under the rug, blame the woman, and then it happens over and over and over again.

So Katie ran. And we sheltered her. It'd been a full year. She's been talking about going to cosmetology school ever since she got that job sweeping up at the beauty shop. She does the prettiest braids for all the little girls at the Ruby. They follow her around like they're her ducklings. It's cute as hell. Katie's sweet as hell.

"I'm gonna have to kill him," I declare, and I'm already reaching for the door. My mind's already made up.

"Wait," Mo says. "Stay here."

"But—"

"Stay."

So few people are willing to give me orders, I'm half startled into obeying for a second.

She strides out into the open. Her gun's not even raised. I dash out behind her, but it's too late. So I hang back, wary, watchful. I want to raise my own gun, but I don't see one on him. That doesn't mean he doesn't have one, but if it's not out, I'm not gonna escalate the situation.

I have to trust Mo. She's done this way more than me.

Mo walks right up to him, fucking fearless. Rain pounds down on them, plastering her hair to her head.

"You're not welcome here, Aaron," she says.

"I'm here for my girl," he says.

"She's not yours," Mo says, still keeping her gun down. "She's a grown woman. She gets to live where she wants, work where she wants, and do whatever the fuck she wants. You've already destroyed property, and now you're trespassing. So you better go. Or I'll give you a look at what hell's really like."

"Hell is what's waiting for you," he says, like it's some sort of condemnation, coming from him.

"Any heaven that lets in men like you, I don't want anything to do with," Mo says. "If you don't go, we're going to have a big problem."

"McKenna's not in town," he says. "I made sure."

I have to lock my arms, every muscle in them tense, to keep myself from raising the shotgun at his smile after those words.

But then Mo smiles too.

"You think that I need to call McKenna every time some pitiful piece of shit like you comes crashing through *my* gates?"

His mouth twists meanly, condescension dripping from his words as he says, "I won't hurt anyone if you just give me Katie."

"Harley," Mo calls. "How many cottages do we have?"

"Forty," I answer.

"Forty," Mo repeats, jerking her thumb back at the cottages behind her. "Forty cottages. Forty doors. Forty women behind them. With forty guns in their hands." She pauses deliberately. "Harley, would you want to play those odds?"

"Nope," I say, staring at Aaron hard. "That would be downright foolish of me, Mo."

"You're a smart girl," Mo says, never taking her eyes off him. "Are *you* smart, Aaron?" she asks. "Or do you have a death wish? Because it takes just one word from me, and they come out shooting."

"I want my girl," he repeats, like a broken record.

"You're never getting Katie," Mo says. "It's not just me or Harley or McKenna or Hawes standing in your way. To get to her, you will have to go through every single woman living here. And if by some miracle, you manage that, and Katie's left standing? *She'll* take you out. Because you may not have taught her how to defend herself, but I did."

She still doesn't raise her gun. She doesn't need to. She just stands there, staring him down like he's a speck of dirt on her shoe. "Get out. Or we will come for you. And we will not be kind or gentle."

I'm tensed, poised for the second he moves. He's going to lunge or reach or punch any second. I know it.

But then, he steps away. He spits on the ground near Mo's feet, and his voice full of disgust, says, "She's not worth it, anyway. She's not pure anymore."

Mo shifts as he backs up toward his truck. She waits as he gets inside, the hood still smoking as he starts it up. As he throws the car into reverse and heads out, she follows, until he's driven off the property, heading toward the main road.

She stands at the entrance of the Ruby where the gate used to be, and I join her, watching as his taillights fade in the rain.

"He might come back," I say. It's not an accusation, but Mo raises her eyebrow at my words.

"Sometimes, we have to do things my way," she says. "He comes back, we'll do things your way. Agreed?"

I nod.

We walk back to the cottages, and Mo pounds on the door of the nearest one. "All clear!" she shouts.

The doors open slowly, and the women come out, pulling on jackets and opening umbrellas. Katie runs down the path past the rest of them. Her dark hair streams behind her, and she throws herself into Mo's arms.

Mo holds her tight, cradling the back of her head. "It's okay, honey," she assures her. "I wasn't gonna let him near you."

"Everyone okay?" I ask, looking over to the women who've gathered around the two of them. They nod, but I can feel it in the air, the spark of fear. "I'll get the gate fixed tomorrow," I promise. "And I'll stay tonight. No one will bother us."

"You did good," Mo says, addressing all of them. "Just like everyone practiced. Are the kids okay?"

"Amanda's playing with them," Katie says, wiping at her eyes.

"Good," Mo says, and I watch as she takes a breath, her eyes closing for a second. I want to reach forward, to steady her, but I don't.

She doesn't need me to.

"Let's get the gate moved and out of the way," she says, clapping her hands together. "And after, we'll get pizza for the kids. Do a movie night in the game room."

I join them as we move the busted gate to the side. It takes half of us to drag it out of the way, but we manage. Glass from Aaron's truck crunches underneath my feet, but I ignore it.

Later, in the game room, while the kids eat pizza and the cupcakes that Amanda had brought over from the diner, I watch as Mo moves from woman to woman, talking, listening, checking in with each one. I watch as some of the worry drains from their faces, replaced by smiles, laughter, and fondness as they watch the children.

Mo knows every story, every detail, every bruise and broken bone on every woman's who's ever lived here's body. Sometimes I think I understand, and then something happens, like today, and I realize I've just scraped the surface. Of the evil in the world. Of the good.

Of the strength in every woman.

My daddy may have taught me who I have to be to rule.

But Mo is the woman who teaches me who I have to be to lead.

# EIGHT

*June 6, 10:30 a.m.*

Now that I need to track down Jessa, I can't avoid being late for my meeting at the Tropics. I flip open my glove compartment, where I have three phones stashed. I grab mine, leaving the burner and the black one inside, and text Cooper that I'm stuck doing some business.

I crank the AC up high in my truck before driving the six miles west leading to the riverfront. If anyone's gonna give me information about the happenings on the other side, it's the people who live by the east bank.

The river cuts through North County like a warning. Deadly in places if you don't know how to handle the rapids, and home to the salmon the Wintu pull from the water every summer.

Salt Creek's on one side, as well as three-quarters of North County.

Blue Basin's on the other. Springfield territory.

Carl Springfield never should've survived the explosion that killed Momma and Desirée, Will's mother. But he's always wiggling out from whatever tight spot he's got himself into. Explosions, prison, even Duke's vengeance—he's always slipping free.

It took me months after Momma died before I got the full story, pieced together in snatches of conversations and arguments between Duke and Uncle Jake. But when Miss Lissa and Will came to live with us, it was Will, whispering in my ear, high up in the deer blinds as we played, who truly filled in the blanks.

45

nd Desi had been together for about a year, and he'd been hit-
er almost as long. It took him a while to start beating on Will, and
t's when Desi started calling Momma. They'd all gone to school together, and Momma was a peacemaker—she always got Carl to leave.
When Will told me that, there was a note of awe in his voice, like he
couldn't quite understand, still, how she'd managed it.

Carl would storm out, and Desi would hold strong for a few days—
sometimes a few weeks—but the pull of him, the pull of the drugs, it
was always too much. She'd call him or he'd show up with beers and
drugs, and it'd be fine and meth-bright for a few weeks until he lost his
temper again or Will spilled a glass of milk or Desi didn't cook the eggs
right.

That day, Momma kicked Carl out, putting herself between his fists
and Desi's already beaten face like she'd done before. But instead of
driving away, pissed-off and drunk like he'd done so many times before, he decided to circle 'round and set a fucking fire in the garage he'd
turned into a meth lab.

He managed to get far enough away from the house before the
flames reached the chemicals and blew the whole place to kingdom
come. Supposedly, he was badly burned, but I've never seen the marks
myself.

Was the fire supposed to just scare them? Or did he mean to kill
them?

Those questions, they used to bother me. They'd circle in my head
like a pair of crows around a deer carcass. It took a long time—years—
to realize that it didn't matter if he meant it. He did it.

And he needed to pay.

For two years, Duke hunted Carl. Two long years when I wasn't allowed off our property without Duke because it wasn't safe. But in the
end, it wasn't Duke who got Carl. It was the police.

Sometimes I wonder if he let himself get caught, because prison's
certainly safer than running from my father. It's what I'd do if a man
like Duke was hunting me.

Carl did seven years in the federal pen for possession with intent to sell. He should've done longer, but he turned snitch or something, and they let him out.

When Carl was sent up, Duke made a deal with Caroline Springfield. A truce. As long as she handed over the Springfield customer base and stopped cooking, she could stay in North County with the boys Duke had orphaned by killing her husband. He wouldn't bother her. Not as long as she gave him the business and stayed quiet and on her side of the river. It must not have been easy—the Springfields have been cooking for as long as meth's been around, and they've been slinging other shit for even longer. But Caroline's smart enough to know cowering is lot safer than trying to rise up against him.

When Carl was released, the truce held. That surprised everyone. Even me. I wondered if maybe Duke was just getting too old for a war. Maybe he'd finally realized it wasn't what Momma would have wanted.

Or maybe he was playing the long game, and I just couldn't see it.

It's been almost six years since Carl got out. We stay on our side of the river, and the Springfields stay on theirs.

But if something's happened to Jessa…

I can't even think about it.

I turn right at an oak tree with a wooden cross nailed to it, my tires skating over the tight-packed dirt road. The long, flat building in front of me isn't much of a building anymore, long fallen to ruin, the tin roof half collapsed now. There's a battered wooden sign made out of split log leaning against one wall, reading HAWES LUMBER MILL EST. 1905.

Momma was a Hawes before she married Duke. The mill was owned by Grandfather Hawes—a man I never met—and then Uncle Jake, but now what's left of it's mine. Seems everything I have comes from somebody being killed. I try not to think about that too much, but sometimes it's hard not to.

The Hawes family was an old one, like the McKennas. There's always been some of us here, way back before there were even county lines. But the Haweses are, or were, legit. And the McKennas never have been.

Momma's life wasn't supposed to follow the path it did. If her parents hadn't died, it probably would've gone a lot different. Jake tried his best, loved her fiercely, but he hadn't been able to control her. She'd been wild, searching for the kind of free most girls never even touch. She was sixteen when she met Duke. Ten years her senior, he was all wrong for a girl like her. But I guess that's what she was after, because she married him the day she turned eighteen, and I came along six months later.

But now she's gone and so is Jake, and I'm the only Hawes left.

I park the Chevy behind the sagging building near a pile of rusty equipment. The teeth of the big table saw are chipped and missing, and stacks of rotted lumber are scattered around.

Uncle Jake sold most of the mill equipment when he and Duke went into the trucking business together. He got offers on the land all the time, being right near the river like it is, but he wouldn't sell. He wanted it to stay in the family.

So I never sold it, either. A few years ago, I was driving by when I noticed the tents set up by the river. Decent but down-on-their-luck people. I brought some supplies over the next day, and as the years passed, the little community grew. There's twenty or so people living by the banks now. The people across the water, with their vacation houses and river views, aren't too thrilled about it, but Sheriff Harris isn't about to tell me no.

I honk a few times, not getting out until I see a figure in the distance, walking up the slope that leads to the river. Dust clouds the air, kicked up by the breeze, and his thinning hair flaps against his bald spot.

When he's near, I slip out of the truck, waving. Busy scrambles out next to me, watching Ray carefully, but sticking to me.

"Hey, Ray," I say, when he gets close enough.

"Harley." He nods. His sad beagle eyes are puffy with age, his skin drooping from too many hard years, sleeping rough wherever he could find a safe spot. "I was hoping you'd come by."

My eyes narrow in the sunlight. "What's up?"

"You missing a Ruby?" he asks.

"Yeah. Jessa Parker. Have you seen her?"

Ray looks toward the riverbank, half hidden by the sloped yellowing hills and the old-growth oaks. "You better come see," he says.

I follow him, careful to watch my feet as I go. There are gopher holes everywhere, weakening the clay soil, ready to break an ankle.

Ahead of us is an encampment, a cluster of tents and tarps set near the river. There are men and women moving around inside and out of the tents, twenty or so all told, last time I did a head count.

Ray leads Busy and me down the main path between the tents to one made out of green tarps. He pulls back the flap, gesturing to me. I duck inside, and the only reason I don't gag is because this isn't even close to the worst thing I've ever seen.

Jessa's lying on top of a sleeping bag, her right eye swollen shut, her left cheek bruised so bad it looks black, her bottom lip split, and finger marks on her throat and thighs. Her skirt's torn and her shirt's stained, reddened with what might be clay or blood. Hell, it might be both.

I take a deep breath.

I do not flinch.

But I shake when I kneel down beside her. When my hand hovers over her shoulder and finally makes contact, I want to hug her, but I'm no good at that sort of thing, even when someone's not messed up.

"Jessa?" My voice cracks on her name. It's not fair to have favorites among the Rubies. But Jessa reminds me of Momma, that wild streak in her a mile wide, and her eyes blue and laughing, like she has a secret.

Jessa's head turns a little at the sound. "Harley," she breathes, wincing as soon as the sound's out of her bleeding lips.

I'm going to end the man who did this.

"Who?" I ask.

She takes in a rattling breath, her throat catching. And then one name falls from her lips, the name that dominated my childhood in mutters and curses, the name that makes the gnawing in my gut sharpen to a knifepoint.

"Springfield," Jessa says.

# NINE

I'm seventeen the first time I come face to face with Carl Springfield. It's a sunny day in March. Will's in the feed store and I'm outside in the truck. I have Busy with me—I'm not allowed in town without her. Daddy's got her trained to stick to me like a burr.

Sometimes I watch him working with her from the deck, teaching her how to protect me, making her more deadly—and it's hard not to compare.

He trained me, too.

The cracked vinyl of the Ford's bench seat makes the back of my thighs sweat, so I get out and pull the tailgate down. I leave Busy in the cab with the air conditioning on, because she's panting and I forgot to bring any water.

"Well, look at you."

I spin around from my spot on the tailgate and look over my shoulder.

When I see him, when I finally connect a voice to the face that's been lurking in the back of my head since I was eight, I go completely still. Rigid like a deer caught in a hunter's sight.

Carl Springfield strolls around the truck and up to me, his head tilted as he takes me in.

*If you ever see him, you run, Harley-girl.*

I should run. Yell for Will. Yank the truck door open and let Busy at his throat.

But that reckless part of me, that part of me that's pure McKenna and all Daddy, makes me want to stay right here.

I want to see what the bogeyman's made of.

I've been waiting.

He's short and stocky, a redneck peacock of a man in a dirty wifebeater and Wranglers with oily stains on the pockets. Slicked-back hair just starting to go gray, and the kind of sunken cheeks and jutting bones that come only from years of tweeking.

I know how to spot them.

He walks with his chest thrust out, so you don't miss the swastika inked on his sternum. I'd heard he'd gotten even more into that sick neo-Nazi shit inside the pen. It makes me want to vomit, especially when I think about how he'd treated Will as a kid.

I can't see the burns—the scars he got in the explosion that killed Momma and Desi—but I know they're there, hidden by his clothes.

I pray they hurt. That they pull and ache with every move he makes.

"You know who I am?" He grins, his Skoal-stained teeth bared at me. "Course you do. Bet your daddy's got a target with my face on it."

I stare straight back at him. I don't move. And before I speak, I wait until I'm sure my voice is level.

"I'm surprised they let you out of prison. You turn snitch or something?"

He rocks back on his heels, sticking his thumbs in his belt loops. He grins, eyes sweeping up and down me in a way that makes me want to take ten hot showers, one right after the other.

"You're taller than your momma," he says, and my stomach clenches because it sounds almost like an accusation. Like I've done something very wrong. "God, you've got the look of her, though."

He reaches forward, and I pull back, but there's nowhere to go. Busy barks in the cab as Springfield strokes one dirty finger up the length of my hair. His hand closes around my braid where it starts at my neck, and suddenly he jerks my head back, his fingers digging into the base of my skull.

I can't stop the breath that wrenches out of me, almost a whimper as he leans in close. I can smell the minty tobacco from his chew. Tears trickle down my cheeks from how hard he's pulling my braid, and his eyes map all over my face like he's looking for something. "You favor her, but they say you're all McKenna on the inside." His hand tightens in my hair, and I can feel strands tearing out of my scalp.

"Oh, yeah?" I hate how the words come out in a strangled gasp when he yanks forward, dragging me off the tailgate by my braid. My feet leave the ground, and I scramble to regain my footing as he crowds me against the truck so close that it would make Daddy gut him if he saw. I choke, blinking furiously as he pulls and pulls my hair like it's gonna achieve something, like it'll crack me open wide enough to give him what he wants.

Busy's freaking out. Pawing at the windows, barking in short, furious bursts. She can't get out, and she knows I need her.

"I'm wondering," he hisses, "if you aren't your daddy's girl at all. Maybe you're a devious little bitch like your momma was."

I gasp and lunge. A chunk of my hair tears off in his hand as I knee that fucker right in the crotch. He's close enough and I'm mad enough that I get him good and hard, my hands slamming down on his shoulders like I've been taught, so I have leverage. For a split second he gasps for air, then the pain hits him.

It doubles him over, and I dart out of his reach, yanking the door open.

Busy snarls, leaping out of the cab and toward Springfield. Her teeth sink into his leg, and he yells, trying to kick her off, but she holds on with a ruthless determination, clamping her jaws down harder.

I let it go on for a good long while before I say, "Busy! Off!"

She lets go immediately, looking over her shoulder at me.

There's blood all over her snout.

I take a few steps closer to Springfield. Busy growls low in her throat as he slowly rises to his feet.

He's smiling.

I just kneed him in the nads, there's blood running down his calf, my dog's seconds away from tearing out his throat—and he's smiling, still clutching that handful of my hair like it's a prize.

"Oh, baby girl," he says. "I'm gonna have so much *fun* with you."

I go white; I can't control it. He sees it and laughs as he limps away. I don't try to stop him.

For a moment, I think about it: grabbing the Glock I know is stashed in the toolbox. It'd be so easy: His back's to me, and the wind's perfect today, barely any breeze. I'd just raise, aim, and then...

I shake my head.

Carl Springfield's not gonna turn me into a killer.

After he drives away, I bend down and clean Busy's snout off the best I can. Then I wipe down the back of my neck at the hairline, where the blood's oozing. He tore a huge chunk of my hair out and my braid's coming loose. I unravel the strands completely, arranging them to hide the red marks and raw skin.

Ten minutes later, when Will comes out of Jones Feed and Farm Supply, Busy and I are back inside the cab of the Chevy like nothing's happened.

# TEN

By the time Doc comes, Jessa's passed out. He checks her pupils and her pulse, and then unfolds the stretcher next to her. Doc's short and tidy. His thin gray hair is always neatly parted to the side, never a strand out of place, and his pink fingernails are always spotless. He's the kind of alcoholic that manages to hide it—most of the time. Despite being a drunk, Doc's good at his job—he hardly ever loses a patient. I trust him as much as you can any man who makes his living fishing out bullets and stitching up wounds that'd call unwanted attention in an emergency room.

"I gave her four ibuprofen," I tell him as I grab under Jessa's shoulders, and together we roll her onto the stretcher.

"Let's get her in the van," he says.

I take one end of the stretcher, he takes the other, and we carry Jessa down the main path through the tents. Ray follows us, reassuring people who've come out of their tents that everything's okay.

Doc and I load Jessa in the back of the van, onto the inflatable mattress he's set up.

"Gonna ride with her?" he asks.

I check my watch. "I've gotta get to the bar," I say. "Call me as soon as she wakes up. And you take good care of her."

"Not gonna let one of your soiled doves die, Harley," he says with a grin. "Don't worry."

I shoot him a look. "Don't be an asshole."

Sobering, he looks down at Jessa, then up at me. "You gonna get the son of a bitch who did this?"

Springfield. My heart races just thinking about what I'm gonna do to him.

"Yeah," I say, and my voice is steady. "He's done for."

They all are.


I get to the Tropics later than I'd like, but I still take the time to throw on a long-sleeved plaid shirt over my tank top and shorts before I climb out of the truck. I pat my side pocket, the weight of my hunting knife comforting against my hip.

Though it's just early afternoon, the parking lot's already starting to fill up with bikes and trucks. Behind the bar I can see Lassen Peak, dark and oddly bald because the drought's fucked with the rain and snow levels. The lakes in Shasta County are so low it's starting to mess with the wildlife—and the tourist trade.

The bar's squat cement block walls can't muffle the sound of Merle belting from the speakers inside. Above my head, the neon outline of a palm tree flickers, the words THE TROPICS buzzing steadily in green and pink.

The steel door's scuffed from years of dragging across concrete, and its blood-red paint peels off as I pull it open. Inside, it smells like beer, sweat, leather, and a hint of motor oil. Long before Duke's organization took over the place as home base, the Tropics was a biker bar, home to the Sons of Jefferson. And for the fifteen years since, an uneasy alliance between the two groups has kept things from getting ugly, because Duke started using the trucking business to run the Sons of Jefferson's weed down south. They'll drink side by side without bloodshed and they'll do business with us, but it's a wary sort of peace.

I'm lucky—Paul, the president of the Sons, likes me. He's provided muscle a few times when I needed it at the Ruby.

I nod to him as I come in. He's at the end of the bar, his braid longer than mine and a greasy bandanna knotted tightly over his head. He tilts his beer toward me in greeting before going back to his conversation with the skinny guy next to him; obviously a new pledge. I can practically see the green behind his ears.

A short, middle-aged woman with thin, peach-colored hair down to her waist and a black leather vest slung over her shoulders comes ducking through the wooden beads strung up in the doorway leading to the storeroom. "Hey, Sal," I say.

She looks up from her clipboard and smiles. "Harley, how you doing?"

"Good. You?"

"Can't complain."

"Boys in the back?" I ask.

"They are."

"I'll be joining them."

I'm almost home free, halfway across the room, when Sal calls out. "Hey, have your daddy give me a ring, will ya? Haven't heard from him since he went down south, and that damn swamp cooler's leaking like crazy."

I flash a smile over my shoulder. "I'll do that, Sal."

The back room's door is always shut tight, and everyone knows better than to try to get in. The conversations that go on inside are drowned out by the honky-tonk on the jukebox, the click of pool balls being racked, the crash and slosh that always goes along with Southern Comfort and Jack and Jim.

I tap on the door lightly before swinging it open. It's even darker in the room than the bar, most of the light coming from the neon Budweiser and Coors Light signs flickering on the walls. Posters of half-naked women beam down at me from the ceiling, beer bottles clutched in their hands, logos arranged carefully not to cover up the important parts.

There are only two men still in the room—the others have already left. I'm that late. Fuck.

Buck looks up from his seat at the end of the table, his greasy dark hair plastered against his bulbous forehead. "Nice of you to finally show," he growls.

Buck pretty much hates me, and as long as Duke's gone, he doesn't make much effort to hide it. The last few years, Duke's been spending more and more time in Mexico, and it's been making Buck bold and me uneasy.

If I wasn't around, he'd truly be Duke's second-in-command, in charge of everything in his absence. But I'm almost twenty-three, and every year, Duke gives me more responsibility. When Duke drives down to Mexico, Buck's in charge of the cooking and the protection, but I'm the only one allowed to touch the money—or the guns. It chaps Buck's ass something awful, but he has to deal.

"I had some shit to do," I say, closing the door behind me. "I texted Cooper."

"I told him," Cooper says. Cooper, who used to run guns with Duke and went with him when he expanded to cooking meth after Momma died, is at Buck's left. Of all Duke's men, Cooper's the closest thing I have to family. There are parts of me he knows even better than Will does.

It's never a good idea to entrust your secrets to a man who can kill a person seven ways to Sunday, but sometimes it's necessary.

"Hey, honey," Cooper smiles, craning his neck to look at me. "Come give me a kiss."

I walk over and peck him on the cheek obediently. His white curls are soft around his face, making him look sweet, even grandfatherly, until you notice the five blue notches tattooed underneath his right eye. Prison tats. "A notch for each one I got away with in there," he'd once confided in me with a wink.

"You have the cash?" Buck demands.

I hand over the envelope, still looking at Cooper. "How are your plants?" I ask him. Cooper and Wayne grow some of the best pot in the mountains. But it's a hobby, not a business, since the Sons have the weed trade covered.

Cooper nods. "Looking good," he says with a smile. "Trying out a nice new strain. It's—"

"This is short," Buck interrupts, looking up from the cash he'd been counting. "You run out of nail polish or something?"

"Yes, that's exactly what happened," I sneer, turning to him. "I spent a grand on nail polish. Fuck you, Buck. While you were sitting on your ass, Springfield attacked one of the Rubies. I needed the money so her kids could buy food and I could pay Doc to fix Jessa. Carl broke some of her ribs and maybe her jaw. So you gonna keep riding me? 'Cause it looks like we've got a Springfield problem on our hands while Duke's away. Good to know you've got a hold on the situation."

I shake my head in disgust and double down. "I told Duke you'd be shit at running things this summer. He should've put me in charge of everything. I'm a better shot than you, anyway."

Buck jerks out of his chair so hard it falls over. "You little cu—"

"Buck," Cooper growls. "That's my goddaughter you're talking to. Watch your tongue."

But Buck's on a roll. "Harley spends all that money on some stupid whore who's probably working for Springfield and you're telling *me* to watch my tongue?" He slams his hand on the table, and the beer bottles rattle.

"Call Jessa a whore again, and you won't have a tongue," I say flatly. "You show the Rubies the respect they deserve or you get the fuck out of here." Cooper stands up behind me.

Buck shifts a little, just a touch away from the table.

Away from me.

He has good reason to be nervous, and not just because of Duke's wrath or Cooper's backup.

I've been deadly since I was eight. From the first time Duke put that gun in my hand. When my fingers closed around it, when I raised it to aim at the target, everything else falling away until it was just me and the pistol and the clear red circle ahead, it was like finding the first real part of myself.

There's being a good shot. And then there's being me.

I don't miss. If I'd been a boy or born to different parents, I'd probably be a special-ops sniper right now.

Duke recognized my talent. Honed it and me. And he made sure every man in my life knows exactly what I'm capable of with a gun in my hands. It was part pride, part protection.

"Fuck this," Buck says, knocking over his beer bottle on the table, where it bubbles out across the scarred redwood. "I'm going to the warehouse." He stands up and glares at me before he kicks his chair away and turns to the door.

"Great to know you're on top of that Springfield thing," I call after him.

He storms out without saying another word, and I sit down next to Cooper, who holds the chair out for me before taking his own seat again.

"You sure your Ruby was beat up by Springfield?" he asks.

"Yes," I say.

Cooper leans back in his chair and shakes his head. "Shit. Duke's gonna lose it."

"I called him," I say. The lie is easy, because all I do is lie nowadays. "He told me he can't get away and that I should take care of it."

Cooper's bushy eyebrows rise up so high they almost disappear under his white curls. "Honey, no. You must've misunderstood him."

"I didn't," I say, my heart beating fast against the lie. I need Cooper to believe me. If he doesn't, my whole plan's screwed. "The Rubies are my responsibility, and I'm grown. If Duke thinks I can handle it, I can handle it."

"I'm gonna call your father." He's already reaching for his phone, but I stop him with a question.

"Do you remember that night out on Route Twenty-Three, Cooper?"

"Harley—" His face changes, darkens. A half minute ticks by. "We're not talking about that," he says finally.

I see the weakness and push it. "After that, are you really gonna bet against me?"

He looks away and shakes his head. "Springfield's a grown man. We have a truce."

"Which he broke the second he hurt Jessa." I can't believe he's arguing with me about this. I thought that out of all of them, Cooper would understand. Buck hadn't been around when Springfield was at his worst, but Cooper was. He had known my momma. Hell, he'd been Duke's best man at their wedding.

"What kind of woman would I be if I let that go unpunished? My momma wouldn't have allowed any man to get away with hurting one of the Rubies. Neither would Mo. And neither will I. Especially that man."

Cooper looks up, and I see he's wavering. He sighs. "At least give me a day to get Wayne, and we'll track him down and go with you," he says.

I let the anger melt off me, and I smile. "You're right, that's a better idea," I say. "I'll wait until you get Wayne. You'll call me? Tomorrow morning?"

"Of course," Cooper says, and probably he really means it. He doesn't like to lie to me—but he'll lie *for* me.

"I'll go to the nursing home then," I say, standing up and walking to the door. "I'm late to see Miss Lissa anyway."

"How's she doing?" Cooper asks.

"Okay," I say. "She misses Will…when she can remember him."

"You be careful out there," Cooper warns. He looks troubled, and for a moment I feel bad for conning him. But I push it down.

I'm doing this to save people. And Cooper's one of them.

Sometimes you've got to save people from themselves. Even if they don't want it or know it.

"I always am."

I wave goodbye and head to the end of the bar, where Paul the biker is still sitting with the new pledge.

"Hey, darlin'," he says, and nudges the new pledge out of his stool so I can take it, jerking his chin at the man to move away so we can have some privacy. "How are things?"

I hop up and lean forward to say quietly, "I need a favor."

Paul looks back at me, unmoved. "Well, seems to me that I don't owe you one," he finally says—but I know his weak spot.

"You'll want to do this. One of the Rubies got beat up real bad. Springfield fucked her up. I was wondering if you could send a few of your boys over there, keep watch until I've got it sorted out?"

Paul's grizzled goatee twitches. "Which Ruby?" he asks, trying to sound unconcerned and failing.

"Jessa."

A little too quickly, he asks, "Mo's okay then?"

I don't smile, but I know I've got him on the hook. "Mo is fine. She's watching Jessa's kids for me."

Paul loves Mo, but she refuses to become his old lady. So he pines and presses me for bits of information instead. And I'm not afraid to use that. "I bet if you sent some protection to the Rubies, she'd be mighty happy."

Paul grins and holds out his hand. "Consider it done."

We shake on it, and I get up off my stool.

"You watch your back, sweetheart," Paul warns me. "If Springfield's causing trouble, you know there's more coming."

"I'll be fine." I hope my voice has more confidence than I feel.

On my way out, when Sal's back is turned at the bar, I reach over it and grab a half-empty bottle of vodka, slipping it inside my plaid over-shirt.

Trouble's coming, all right.

# ELEVEN

Two months after our mothers die, Will and his grandma move into the guest cabin a mile south of the main house. Miss Lissa's short and baby-powder soft, fond of needlework, brightly colored sweatsuits, and revolvers over semi-automatics. I come by to watch Daddy's men hauling in their furniture and boxes of belongings while I hang back, uncertain of this new woman in my life.

But when she sees me, she walks up and wraps me up in a hug that goes on so long I'm wiggling, uncomfortable, and prickly hot against her. She smells flowery—not the right flower, not the way Momma did, but it reminds me just the same.

One afternoon not long after they're settled in, Daddy tells me to come along, and we walk across the meadow to the cabin.

He doesn't tell me why or what we're doing here, but he walks up and knocks on the door. Miss Lissa answers it like she's expecting us, and she and Daddy send Will outside where I'm waiting on the deck to keep us out of their hair so they can talk.

It's the first time since that day that Will and I are alone together. We stand on opposite sides of the back deck, the cedar planks distancing us like some kind of border under our feet. I scuff the toe of my boot into the wood. I don't want to look up at him.

If I do, I'll remember.

He's the first to give in. "You okay?"

I shrug. "You?"

He shrugs too, and I can't tell if he's making fun of me or if it's something else. My shoulders rising off the railing, I step forward without thinking. Will stays very still, watching me carefully as he lets me come close, until we're just a few inches apart.

Will looks nothing like Miss Lissa or the pictures I saw of his mom in the newspaper. She was pale and blond, but he has dark hair and eyes and skin. The black eye from that day has long since faded, and the burnt circles on his left arm have healed to lumpy pink messes stretching from wrist to elbow.

I reach out and run my finger over the rough edges.

Will doesn't jerk his arm away. His breath puffs over the top of my head as he looks down at me and lets me do as I wish.

"Do they still hurt?" I ask softly.

"Sometimes."

"Carl Springfield," I say. "He did this?"

Will nods.

My thumb presses into the edge of a scar and it fades pale from the light pressure. "Why?"

"I disobeyed."

"That's a shitty reason," I say.

"I know."

"He's mean, isn't he? Springfield?" I don't really have to ask; the proof is right there in front of me. But all I have is a picture and Daddy's orders: *Just follow the lessons, Harley-girl, and stop asking so many questions.*

I can't help but be curious.

"When he's high," Will says. "Or drunk." He snorts, but his eyes aren't laughing. "Or breathing."

That day, when the fire department and the sheriff came and broke the truck windows after Will and I refused to let them inside, he didn't let go of me the whole time. Not even when they tried to pull us apart.

He held on, like if we stuck together that tight, we'd be safe. I felt like that too.

"You gave me bruises that day," I say.

Will's eyes flicker to my arm and then down to his where we're still touching. "I didn't mean to. I was just—I was scared you were gonna get out of the truck. Your momma told me to watch you."

"I'm not a baby!" My temper flares and my thumb accidentally presses down too hard on the still-healing part of his arm. He tenses, but doesn't pull out of my grasp. He's stronger than me, so much bigger, he could easily break free, but he doesn't. He stays.

"Sorry," I mutter, my cheeks going red.

"I'm older," he counters. "I wouldn't hurt you," he says after a while. "I don't—I'm not like that."

I nod. "He's not your daddy?" I say. "Springfield, I mean?" I know he can't be, because Springfield's white, and Will looks like his daddy isn't.

He shakes his head quickly, but a second later it looks like all the air's gone out of him, and he says in a small voice, "No. But he partied with my mom when things were good. And when things were bad..." He trails off. Will twists his arm under my grip so his hand cups my wrist. "He's bad," he says. "He's really bad. But you shouldn't worry."

"Daddy says he killed our mommas. And he wants to kill me," I whisper. I haven't said it out loud ever, not in the two months since Daddy told me.

Will squeezes my wrist gently. "Your momma was nice to me," he says. "I promised her I'd watch you."

"She didn't mean—"

"I know you're not a baby. But I promised." He stares at me, looking more serious than a kid should.

There's something behind those words I can't figure out. A question I'm not sure of, but I nod anyway. "Okay," I say. "Then I promise to watch you, too."

He smiles, and it's not mean or anything like the way boys usually look at me, with my skinned knees and dirty hands. Instead it makes me feel taller than I am, steadier and strong.

"Never had anyone watch my back before," he says thoughtfully. "Gonna be my sidekick?"

I smile, and it's maybe the first time in months I've done that. "You can be *my* sidekick."

Will's smile grows wider. "We could flip on it," he suggests, pulling a quarter out of his pocket. "Call it," he says, and tosses it high in the air, so high it glints in the sun.

I reach out, lightning fast, catching it before he can. But I don't look at it yet. That'd be cheating, and I don't want to cheat with Will.

His mouth drops open in surprise, and I beam. I've always been quick. Daddy says I have a good eye.

"Heads," I say.

I uncurl my fingers, and George Washington's profile shines up at me.

"Looks like you win," he says, smiling even bigger.

"McKennas always win," I tell him solemnly.

I don't know why that makes his smile disappear for a second, but it does.

# TWELVE

Fir Hill Nursing Home is just a few blocks from the bar. I take a minute to pull over and pick a few wildflowers in one of the empty lots. They aren't much, just a scraggly collection of lupine and California poppies, but Miss Lissa has always liked wildflowers over fancy ones.

"Be back in a little bit," I tell Busy, patting her on the head, leaving the AC on and making sure the water bowl I keep in the car is filled.

Inside, the nursing home's quiet. I smile at an older man in a robe shuffling down the hall on his walker and turn left at the activity center, past the group of ladies who are watching an old black-and-white movie on the flat screen.

I walk past the ALZHEIMER CARE WING sign and stop in front of the lavender-and-white-striped nursing station. There are bouquets lining the counter, and a few stuffed teddy bears placed on top of the computer monitor.

A curly-haired brunette looks up when she hears my footsteps. "Harley." She smiles. "I was wondering if you were coming."

"I'm sorry I'm late, Becky," I say. "I got hung up on an errand. Is she awake? Has she been asking for me?"

"She's been a little distracted today," Becky says. "In a good way. Go on in."

I'm already halfway inside the room before I realize I should've asked Becky why Miss Lissa was distracted. Because the answer to that question is sitting right next to the bed, talking to her in a low voice.

There are already wildflowers on the side table. He must have brought them. The blue tin vase they're in is set beneath a poster board that has photos of me and Will as kids taped to it, the words WE LOVE YOU in glitter glue scrawled across the top.

I make a noise, I must have, because Will's head snaps up.

I haven't seen him in over a year. When he came home that first Christmas, we fought—the kind of fight you don't recover from, the kind that changes everything and you can't take any of it back.

Some things—the memory of angry words turned soft and then silent—I don't want to forget. But the look on his face when I told him to go, that hurt. It's branded on my mind.

He left, and he didn't come home again. Next year, whenever he visited Miss Lissa, he stayed in a motel. I know he called Duke, because occasionally Duke would mention him, but when it came to him and me, it was silence.

Like right now, as we stare at each other.

Before he can say anything, before I can do anything, Miss Lissa's smiling from her place in bed, looking cozy and warm under the blue-and-lavender wedding-ring quilts she stitched herself.

"Jeannie!" She beams up at me. Her hair is neatly combed; the dark-blue bed jacket she has on is probably from the sixties, but it looks brand new. The nurses here take good care of her. It helps that I come twice a week to keep tabs and give Christmas bonuses large enough to ensure she wants for nothing.

"Look, Will, Jeannie's come to visit! How's that baby girl of yours? Harley must be getting so big."

I smile back at Miss Lissa as she reaches up for a hug, and fold her gently in my arms. She smells like her favorite lilac talcum powder. It's gone out of production, but I've managed to track down a container of the brand she likes each year for her birthday.

Now that I'm grown, she mixes me up with my momma more and more. I've stopped correcting her—there's no use in it.

"Harley's doing real good." I smile as she leans back into the crisp white pillowcase she made and embroidered decades ago. I stand up and step aside, unsure, because Will hasn't said a word, though he's staring at me.

What is he doing here? He's supposed to be away at college. He has summer classes. I checked. I made sure.

He can't be here right now. Not today.

He'll ruin everything.

"I was just telling Will about Duke and the bear." When Miss Lissa smiles, it's like sunlight pouring down from cracks in the clouds. It comes from every inch of her, and I reach out and squeeze her hand. Her tiny fingers, gnarled from arthritis and age, curl around mine, cool to the touch.

She's lost a lot of weight in the past year. On bad days the nurses have a hard time getting her to eat. So I bring her the things she taught me to make: meatloaf and scalloped potatoes, roast chicken with delicate white pearl onions simmered in cream and nutmeg, cheesecake rich enough to stick to the roof of your mouth. I wrap the food on the golden poppy dishes she left with me, and I bring along pieces of my grandmother's heavy silver that I still polish every few months, even though Miss Lissa is the only person left to appreciate it, and she won't remember.

Sometimes I can get her to eat.

Sometimes she doesn't recognize me at all. I'm not Harley or Jeannie—I'm a stranger, and on those days, the fear that mixes with the confusion in her face makes the back of my throat burn.

Will hasn't taken his eyes off me. He seems relaxed, leaning over Miss Lissa's bed, his elbows resting near her feet like he needs to stand guard. I almost laugh when I see we've both automatically picked the two points in the room where our backs are to the wall, with clear views of the door and window.

Duke trained us well.

I clear my throat. "I wanted to bring you these, Miss Lissa. I can't stay today, I'm sorry." I place the flowers next to her on the bed. I hate that I have to leave, because today's obviously a good one, but Will's her actual family, her blood, and he doesn't see her twice a week like I do.

"Going so soon?" Miss Lissa drops my hand and plucks at the quilt, her face falling.

I lean forward and kiss her on the forehead, resisting the urge to run my hand through her frizzed silver curls. "I'll be back on Friday, like always. Promise."

I can't think about not being able to keep that promise. I have to get out of here.

"I love you lots," I tell her. "See you on Friday."

I leave the room without a word to Will and hurry down the hallway. I'm turning the corner that leads off the Alzheimer wing when I hear it: his voice, calling my name.

I speed up. He follows.

All he ever does is chase. And all I ever do is run.

I keep walking until I hit the doors, until we're outside in the fresh air, standing next to the circle of fir trees the home's named for. I feel calmer here, beneath the shadowy patterns of needles soothing my skin, reminding me of my forest, of home.

But thinking about home always brings me back to him.

"Harley."

It takes me a second to get a hold of myself enough to turn around and look at him. His black hair's longer than I've ever seen it, gathered at the back of his neck, a few shorter strands dipping into his hazel eyes.

He's been the most solid thing in my life for as long as I can remember. He'd had it so much harder than me, the half-Native boy raised by a white tweeker momma, his dad long gone before he was even born, probably not even knowing he existed, because Desi was such a mess. Will never knew his tribe or a whole side of his family. He couldn't mix with the redneck boys, so he was always on the outskirts instead. With me.

I had the kind of protection he didn't when we were kids. I was a

69

McKenna, so everyone feared Duke. I was a girl, so everyone underestimated me. I was white, so I was trusted on sight.

He had none of those things as we grew up. Will had Duke's protection, but he didn't have his name. And even Duke's name didn't
keep some assholes from messing with him or from them making
their fucking "jokes" about firewater and calling him Chief and other
racist bullshit over and over, year after year. Even the bikers did it,
when Will was grown and working for them. They thought it was
funny.

It wasn't. I'd watch as his mouth would flatten every time, but he always stopped me from saying anything.

He's twenty-five now. Last month, I spent his birthday staring at my
phone, unable to press *Call*, but now that I'm a few inches away, I want
nothing more than to grab him.

It hurts not to touch him. It's not even an itch or an urge or a want—
it hurts like someone's dragging the edge of a hunting knife up my
belly.

"What are you doing home?" I blurt out. My voice is angry, but I'm
not.

"Visiting Gran," Will says. "I had some free time."

"You have classes." I sound like I'm accusing him of some crime. Jesus. I need to keep it together.

His mouth quirks up, higher on the right than the left. "You keeping
tabs on me?"

I refuse to blush. "When are you going back?"

"It's nice to see you too, Harley." His mouth smiles again, but his eyes
don't.

"Will." I glare at him. I don't need to be teased.

He needs to be away from here. I can't have him around right now.

I am not letting him get hurt again. I promised myself, never again.
That's why I forced Duke to let him go. College gave Will some sort of
legit life away from all this.

Away from me.

He leans back on his heels. He's wearing the leather motorcycle boots I bought him for his twentieth birthday, and I study them for a second, noticing that the left toe is scuffed.

"Can you please just tell me how long you're staying?" I ask, addressing his feet.

"Hey." He reaches underneath my chin, gentle, tilting my face up. My stomach swoops down, an endless drop of *missed you, missed you, missed you*. I need to pull away. I have to.

I don't.

"What's going on?" Will asks.

I lick my lips, and for one glorious second, I think about how it'd feel to tell him. Not to be alone in this, because he'd take it on for me, he'd share it—that's who he is.

Which is why I can't.

This has always been my fight, never his. One of us has to get away from all this, and it was always going to be him.

There is too much of me rooted here to ever leave.

I step back so his fingers slip away from my skin. It's easier to think if I don't touch him. "Nothing's going on."

He shoves his hands in the pockets of his leather jacket, and I fist mine so I can't reach out for him. I can sense it in the air, pulsing off the both of us, and I feel greedy in that *want* and *need* and *now* way. I remember what it was like, him and me, and it makes my blood beat too fast under my skin.

But if I want him to survive long enough to have the normal life he worked so hard to get, I have to stay strong.

"Duke hasn't called me in a few months, so I stopped by the truck yard when I got into town last night. Wanted to see him. He wasn't there, though," Will says. He's staring down at me, hard, searching.

I go ice cold, but I use it, freeze out the pain and nervousness. Make my voice level. "Duke's away. Down south."

Will frowns. "Kinda early," he remarks, a little too casually. "Crop's not in yet."

"He's been spending a lot of time in Mexico, last few years," I say. "Expanding the business."

"Right," Will responds, a strange, sharp edge to his voice. "Gotta build his girl a bigger empire."

I stiffen, the bitterness in his words singeing the edges of me. "Go back to school, Will," I say. "Everything's fine here."

But he doesn't turn away. Instead, he keeps his gaze on me, looking so close I feel caught—not stripped bare, no, worse: It makes me feel *known*.

"I know what you look like when you're lying," he says, quiet, even though there's no one around to overhear. "You gonna tell me? Or do I have to find out myself?"

"There's nothing to find out," I say. And I tell myself it's the truth.

At least for the next few hours.

"I've gotta go," I say. "Collection day, you know. I hope you're liking school. It was nice to see you. Have a safe drive back."

I walk past him, toward the parking lot. The sun's starting to head west toward the mountains. I only have a few hours of light left. I need to move.

"I'm gonna find out," he calls after me. "And I'm not leaving until I do."

To anyone else, it'd sound like a threat. But I recognize it for what it is: a promise.

A promise from him is worse than any threat—he's the kind who keeps them.

# THIRTEEN

When I'm fourteen, Bennet Springfield breaks my nose.

Every Sunday, after church, Miss Lissa visits with the other ladies, and Will and I are supposed to go to youth group, but most of the time I slip out without anyone noticing—or maybe they do, but they don't want to bring it up to Daddy.

It's only three blocks and across the street to the graveyard. Daddy doesn't visit Momma's grave, and whenever I go with Uncle Jake, he ends up drinking afterward, so I've stopped asking. I'd rather go alone anyway, just Momma and me.

The graveyard's old as California, there are stones that say nothing more than RAILROAD WORKER, and in the Wilson Tomb, four cracked and ancient graves labeled INFANT are dated ten to twelve months right after the other.

I slip between the iron gates and make my way up the grassy hill, toward the west end where the McKenna plot is.

Momma's family is buried here too. They're on the south side of the graveyard. Uncle Jake had wanted her with them, but Daddy was having none of that. She died a McKenna, in a McKenna's death, and she'd be buried as one, next to all the others.

The grass is wet from the sprinklers, slippery as I trudge up the slope. The plot's one of the biggest, edged by redwood fencing and a neatly carved gate that has the family name burnt into the wood. I push it open and step inside.

Momma's headstone is at the end of the long line that starts with the first McKenna, Franklin, his wife Mary Ellen, and their five children. I kneel down, brushing off the yellowing leaves that speckle the green grass.

Talking always feels silly, even though I've seen Uncle Jake do it, so mostly I sit instead. When I can, I bring her things from the forest. This time it's an arrowhead I found last week when Will and I went fishing. Before I get up to go, I place it on top of her headstone, which is scattered with my other gifts: blue-jay feathers pinned beneath river rocks, a vial of gold flakes I'd panned from the stream under Uncle Jake's careful instruction, a dried hornet's nest she would've shrieked at and dropped if I'd put it in her living hands.

As I leave, I pass by the two spaces next to her.

They're unmarked. For now. But I know who they belong to.

One is Daddy's.

The other is mine.

I cut across the graveyard with the intention of going out the back exit. Will knows to meet me there. Even though Carl Springfield's been locked up for years, I'm not allowed anywhere in town by myself, but when I'm on Will's watch, he looks the other way.

As I make my way down the hill, I realize I'm not alone. About fifty feet ahead of me, a boy's standing near a grave. Even in the shade of the great oak looming over him, his red hair shines bright.

I should stop. I should back away right now.

I know whose empty grave he's standing over, and I know who's responsible for that empty grave.

We both know.

Which is why I should go the way I came. Get out of here before he sees me.

*You ever see one of those Springfield boys outside of church, Harley-girl, you back away fast.*

I walk forward instead.

When he hears my footsteps, Bennet looks up. His lips press together and disappear into his pale skin. His freckles and pimples are like flashing lights against it.

"What the fuck are you doing here?"

I keep walking. All I want to do is get to the back gate.

"Bitch, I'm talking to you."

I pause. I dig my heel in the hard red dirt and turn. He's right up close, trying to use the few inches he has on me to his advantage.

"You're not the only person who has family here, Bennet." I turn back around, but he lurches in front of me, blocking my way. I fold my arms and try to look as bored as possible. He lays a hand on me, and all bets are off. But I'll wait for that moment.

I'm not gonna throw the first punch.

"My dad would still be around if it weren't for yours," Bennet says in an icy voice, his words slurred a bit, and the scent of beer wafts over me.

Great. He's drunk and angry.

He's also fiddling with something in his pocket.

So: drunk, angry, and possibly armed.

"Lots of people would still be around if it weren't for either of them," I say carefully.

His face twists in pain, pure and simple, when he says, "We couldn't even bury him."

Later on, I'll kick myself for that second when I lower my guard because I know what it's like, visiting an empty grave.

There hadn't been enough left of Momma to bury.

Bennet's fist smashes into my nose. My head pops back, pain explodes underneath my eyes, and I can taste blood in my mouth, running down my chin, at the back of my throat. I stagger, losing my balance and catching my hip hard against a grave marker.

I gasp, but I force myself to ignore the pain. He's coming at me again, and this time I need to be ready.

I sidestep his angry half-tackle, grabbing one of his outstretched arms with both hands. I knee him in the crotch to get him to behave before yanking his left arm out, getting him by the elbow. I should twist it up and take him down to pin him safely.

Cooper taught me how to fight. But Daddy taught me how to brawl. I shouldn't hurt Bennet bad.

"Cunt," he snarls at me, finally finding his voice.

My fingers tighten on his arm. I pull, hard and fast, knocking him off balance enough to slam his palm to the ground and step down hard on it with my boot.

He gasps as his fingers crunch underneath it.

And then he screams when my other boot slams down onto his elbow, once. Twice.

There's a horrible snap. The sound of a branch cracking, a gun going off, a bone breaking—they aren't much different. It makes your stomach drop, just the same.

Bennet sags on the ground, dirt smearing against his forehead as garbled sounds come out of his mouth. Tears streaking down his face, he cradles his broken arm to his chest.

I wipe away the blood dripping from my nose, flicking it onto the dirt. It's swelling up already. Daddy's gonna rage when he sees me.

"I'll do more than break your arm next time," I growl at Bennet, my throat clogged with blood and what would've been tears if I hadn't been trained out of crying years ago.

I leave him there at the foot of his daddy's grave, and as I pass the headstone, I press my hand against it.

A taunt?

No.

An apology.

# FOURTEEN

*June 6, 2:45 p.m.*

I screech out of the nursing home parking lot. A part of me's afraid of Will jumping on his bike and following. But after a few minutes with my eyes on the rearview, I relax. I manage to get through town, almost to the highway, before Busy's whining makes me pull over.

"It's okay," I tell her as she butts her wet nose against my arm in worry. "It's okay," I say again, trying to convince myself.

Everything is going wrong. Jessa is hurt. Will is supposed to be three hundred miles away. But I can't let it fuck me over. I need to adapt. Keep going.

"Okay," I repeat.

*Breathe, Harley-girl.*

I can hear Duke's voice, clear as day. It's probably a sign I'm losing my goddamn mind.

I press my hand against my mouth, trying to keep everything I'm feeling from bubbling up. I can't focus on Will and what seeing him does to me. I have priorities.

I push him out of my mind, ignoring the ache, like an open wound that won't heal. I'll deal with him later. I need to focus.

My plan's always involved baiting the Springfield boys—I need the men on both sides not knowing what end's up, because men on the edge make bad decisions, and that makes them easier to take down. But I'd planned on doing this a lot later. Jessa getting roughed up means I have to move up my timeline. But I can make this work—I have to. And if I push the right buttons, I might get some useful information out of them. Carl Springfield is a hard man to find—those years of running from Duke taught him well. I haven't been able to pin down his exact location even though I've tried. The houses on the other side of the river are set deep in the wilderness, off old dirt roads that are kept in disrepair for a reason. You don't want to drive down them unless you live there. You might not come back.

There's a buzz coming from my glove compartment. I flip it open, pull out the black phone, and key in the code.

It's a text from Buck: T and D headed to Jackson.

I have to text back, or he's going to suspect something. I need him as oblivious as possible for as long as I can so he'll just stroll right into my trap, none the wiser.

I memorized the codes Duke used with the men a long time ago, even though he didn't realize it. It's a mix of numbers to spell out words and Johnny Cash lyrics to mean certain things. Nothing genius, really, but no one's ever caught on. Not that anyone's really looking. Having the sheriff in our pocket is something of a family tradition for us McKennas.

I punch out 65 and press *Send*, then toss the phone back into the glove compartment.

I have an hour, and I'm going to make the most of it. For Jessa.

Blue Basin's not much more than a truck stop straddling the county line. A place to fuel up for folks on their way to Shasta or Weed. It's right off the old highway, the skeleton of an old silver mine, the last relic of what was a flourishing town back in the Gold Rush days, now a scant handful of buildings: a crumbling RV park, a tiny post office with a trailer behind it where the postmaster lives, an abandoned feed store—and Springfield's gas station.

This is where they've been banished. Driven to a town whose population is less than a hundred. Stripped of any power or influence their family once held.

Duke and Caroline's truce sent Springfield here, and for the most part, he keeps to the deal his brother's widow made.

But sometimes he just can't help himself. And now he's gone after Jessa.

Did he think I would let it go? That she wouldn't tell?

Did he mean to kill her, and she got lucky and ran?

It doesn't matter, I decide as I approach the exit. No matter what, he's going to pay.

I've driven past Blue Basin many times, probably too many, but I've never stopped. I know better than to cross that invisible line between them and us.

But now I don't think twice when I flip my turn signal and pull off the highway onto the potholed road that leads into town.

I stop across from it, the only gas station in fifty miles, just a few pumps in front of a dingy building with a sign on the roof that says SPRINGFIELD GAS & MINIMART in big rusty tin letters. I turn my key in the ignition, the radio cuts off, and I sit back and wait.

I stare at the station, cataloguing the people going in and out—the girl in Hello Kitty pajama pants and yesterday's eyeliner, the old-school rancher driving a cherry 1930s Chevy, the obvious tweeker who comes out of the store with a paper bag instead of a plastic one like the other customers. The building's windows are tinted, so I can't see through them, but I know they're inside.

My phone rings. Still watching the building, I answer.

"It's Mo."

"I was just about to call you," I say.

"Paul and the Sons showed up. They've got a patrol going. Should I be worried?"

"I sent them just in case," I say. "I found Jessa."

"And…?" Mo asks, but with that one word, I can hear the dread in her voice.

"She's beat up pretty bad," I say. "She's with Doc now. I'm going to need you to watch the kids."

"Done," Mo says. "You wanna tell me who I need to go after for hurting her?"

I smile at Mo's fierceness as a dusty truck pulls up to the pumps. "I'm taking care of it," I promise. "Just keep the women and kids calm. There's nothing to worry about." I watch as a rail-thin girl jumps out of the truck and walks into the mini-mart.

"It's under control," I say, keeping my eyes on the store. "I gotta go. I'll call as soon as I've got news on Jessa."

"Take care of yourself," she orders.

"Yeah, yeah," I say.

Before she can issue any more orders, I hang up.

The girl in the truck hasn't come out of the mini-mart yet, so I figure I have enough time. I dial Doc's number, and he answers after the fifth ring.

"It's Harley," I say. "How's Jessa?"

"Six broken ribs. He busted all the toes on her right foot, too, for good measure." His disgust radiates through the phone. He'll be hitting the bottle tonight for sure, trying to drown out the blood and the bad. "Her jaw's bruised all to hell, but it's not broken, so that's a small mercy. But she's got a concussion. I'm keeping her here until tomorrow. You got someone to watch her kids?"

"Yeah," I say. "Be careful with the pain pills, okay? She's got a problem."

"The teeth and the shitty veins clued me in, Harley," Doc says. He sounds offended that I even bothered to point it out.

The skinny girl comes out of the mini-mart and hops into her truck. The store's empty now, and there's no one around.

"Hey, I gotta go," I say. "Call me if anything changes."

The girl drives away, leaving the parking lot empty.

I get out of my truck with Busy at my side. We cross the street and the parking lot. My hands don't shake, but my heart skips in that bad way as I open the grubby glass door and step inside.

The little store's rickety aisles are stocked with the basics. Despite Springfield's jacked-up prices, the people who live in the woods around the Basin don't like to drive all the way down the mountain whenever they need a box of tampons or stuffing mix.

Bobby's behind the counter in his wifebeater and sagging camo pants. He's older than me, around Will's age, with a shaved head and full sleeves and neck tats on display. As I walk in, he's leaning down to grab a pack of cigarettes, but when I reach over and lock the door behind me, the click makes him jump and look up.

He freezes.

I don't.

Before he can lunge for the shotgun I'm sure he's got stashed, I pull my .45. "Don't even think about it, Bobby," I say, pointing it at his chest.

His eyes widen, and he stays frozen.

"Bennet," I call. "I know you're in the back. You come out, nice and slow. Hands where I can see them. Or I blast a hole in your brother."

There's a pause, tense and thick, and for a second I'm sure he's gonna come out shooting. I breathe deep, trying to stay calm. I need a steady hand.

There's a shuffling sound, the door behind the counter slowly creaks open, and Bennet emerges from the back room, hands up, his right elbow permanently bent at an odd angle. His red hair glints in the weak fluorescent light

He looks just like his daddy.

"Hi, boys," I say.

"You fucking bitch," Bennet replies. But his hands stay up, where they should be.

"Yeah, yeah." I keep them both in my sight. They know better than to charge. Not with Busy next to me, growling low in her throat. "I'm looking for your uncle. So tell me where he is."

"Fuck you," Bobby hisses. He's sweating bullets. "We're not telling you shit."

Most of the contact I've had with the Springfield boys is at church—one of the few places that's considered neutral territory by both our families. Bennet is my age, so we would've been in the same grade, but Duke never let me go to school.

Still, these past fifteen years, I've learned a lot just from watching them across the pews. Bobby talks big, and he likes the fear his name makes people feel because it doesn't take much effort on his part. He resents his momma, treats her pretty shitty, even in church, which is just the cherry on top of the asshole sundae.

And he's not very smart.

But Bennet is. Bobby hates me because it's simple. Because that's what he's been taught to do. He doesn't put much thought into it because he doesn't put much thought into anything. He's a follower. That's why he latched onto Carl's neo-Nazi shit in a way Bennet never seemed to.

Bennet hates me because he sees how we're alike. How we've been marked by men with bloody hands and shady hearts. How we've already lost more than we've ever been willing to give up to this world we were born into.

He sees himself in me the way I see myself in him. The difference between us? He's been raised up with a grudge hanging over his head.

I've been raised up with a mission hanging over mine.

"Tell me where Carl is," I say.

"Harley—" Bennet starts, stepping forward.

Busy barks in warning, the sound echoing through the store.

I point the gun at him. "Stay where you are. And tell me where your goddamn uncle is."

"Look—" Bennet starts again, staying where he is this time. Busy snaps her teeth in the air and bares them at him. Her growl is a continuous, present thing that comforts me like a cat purring. "You're—what the fuck are you doing, Harley?"

"I'm looking for Carl. Seems that trailer he had near Castella's been moved. Where is he living now?"

"You're breaking the rules," Bennet says, like he can't quite believe it.

He's clearly decided to try to appeal to my sense of reason. Well, it's too fucking late for that. It was too late for that months ago.

He doesn't know what I know. And he won't until this is all over and I'm home free.

I've made a plan. It's going to work. I just need to figure out what the fuck happened to Jessa first. If I get Carl's address out of them, well, that's even better.

"Your uncle already broke the rules, Bennet," I say. "He fucked up one of the Rubies. So you're going to tell me where he is. And he's going to pay for what he did."

"What?" Red splotches rise in his freckled cheeks. "Wait—which Ruby?"

I frown, but I keep my gun steady. "Jessa," I say, watching him closely.

His color deepens—but it's not guilt, it's anger.

"What?" He spins around to stare at Bobby. "Did you know about this?" he demands.

"Shut up," Bobby growls, looking away.

"What did he do to her? Did you help him?"

Bobby doesn't say anything.

"Answer me, Bobby!"

"Bennet!" Bobby hisses, a warning.

But it's too late. I've figured it out.

"You're the guy she's been fucking."

"Harley…" Bennet licks his lips, the guilt pouring off him. I want to take him down. He's the reason she's in this mess. "Jessa—is she okay?" he asks in a voice I've never heard him use before, soft and worried. Oh, Jesus Christ. I can see it clearly now. He's totally gone on her. Razzled by Jessa's spark. It makes me angrier. It makes me reconsider my previous thinking: Bobby's stupid, but clearly Bennet is a fucking moron.

"No, she's not okay," I snap. "She's got broken ribs and broken toes because that's what happens when a man twice your size stomps on your feet while the other guy holds you down." My gaze flicks to Bobby and I can see in his eyes that's exactly how it went down. My finger twitches. I want to shoot him so fucking bad. "My guess is that Bobby did the holding down. Carl did the stomping." I shake my head. "Jesus Christ, Bennet—what were you thinking? You both knew what would happen if you two were found out."

"I met her when she was dancing at the club, and I just—"

"Bennet!" Bobby yells again, and this time, he moves. Not toward me, but toward his brother.

"Busy, get him!" I tell her. She leaps forward, sinking her teeth into Bobby as he reaches for his brother, right arm raised to punch him into submission and silence. He howls, trying to shake her off, but it's no use. Once Busy's got her teeth in you, she doesn't let go unless she's ordered.

It's one of my favorite things about her.

Busy puts Bobby on the ground fast, and I walk forward, calling her off after I plant my boot on his chest. "Stay down," I order him. "Your brother and I are talking."

He spits at me, which is the stupidest fucking thing in the world to do because he's on his back and it ends up in his face. I roll my eyes in disgust.

Like I said, not a ton of brains rolling around in Bobby's skull.

I look up at Bennet. "How long?" I ask him.

"A few months," he says, not looking down at his brother. "But only at the club. I'd just buy dances. But she finally agreed to see me outside of the club, and I just—I love her, Harley. We love each other."

That tone in his voice again. Fucking shit. Love. Like that matters. Like that's going to help the hell he just brought down on them.

"She has kids, Bennet," I say. "She hasn't even been clean for two years yet. She doesn't have a job anymore, and I'm betting that's because of you."

The red in his face rises higher and higher until it almost blends with his hair. "I want to take care of her. I don't want her to dance at that club, guys looking at her all the time. I don't like it." His eyes scrunch up in pain just like they did when I broke his arm more than a decade ago in the graveyard. He really has it bad for Jessa. Fucking moron.

"That's not your choice to make," I say, the anger rising in my throat. "And you're not taking very good care of her—you didn't even know your uncle beat the shit out of her!" My voice rises to a shout, fury filling the space between us. "She's been missing for three days now. If you're so hell bent on taking care of her, how the fuck could you not notice?"

"I—"

"No more bullshit, Bennet," I interrupt viciously, snapping my fingers for Busy. She growls once more in Bobby's face and then trots back to my side. I bring my attention back to Bennet, who shrinks behind the counter, looking nervously at Busy.

"You stay the fuck away from Jessa. If you come across the river, if you even come near the Ruby, I'm going to blow your big *and* your little head off." To drive in the point, I lower my gun eight inches, pointing it right at his crotch. He gulps nervously and stays silent.

I turn and unlock the door, jerking it open. I have places to be. I don't have the time it would take to beat an answer out of them.

"You two aren't doing anyone any favors not telling me where Carl is," I say, the .45 still trained on them both. "When I find him, I'm going to tear that fucker apart. You tell him that. You tell him I'm coming."

I duck through the open door and run. I can hear Bobby shouting, "Get the shotgun, you stupid bastard!" and Bennet swearing back at him as Busy and I race across the parking lot and jump into my Chevy. I pull an illegal U as both of them come running out. Bobby's got a sawed-off shotgun in his hand, and a second later the sound of buckshot pinging against pavement fills the air behind me.

But I'm already out of range.

It's time.

# FIFTEEN

I'm almost eighteen when I break Bobby Springfield's nose.

I'm at the Shasta County Fair with Uncle Jake. It's this tradition of ours. He's been taking me every year for as long as I can remember. When Momma was alive, she'd come with us, but she hated heights, so it'd be Uncle Jake and me on the Ferris wheel, high as the clouds. When I was little, I always wanted to go around and around until I was almost sick with it. Hell, a few times I think I did get sick.

I still love going with him, after all these years. We play the rigged carnival games, and he stands back, smiling, as I draw a crowd at the shooting booth. I hit target after target, even though the toy gun's so off balance it's hard to shoot straight, and I end up winning a stuffed bear the size of a toddler.

"What are you going to do with that?" Uncle Jake asks as we lug it away from the shooting stand, toward the food booths, where fried Snickers bars and other horrors wait.

I look down at the bear. It's kind of heavy. "I dunno. Give it to one of the kids at the Ruby, probably."

"You remember that stuffed bear you used to carry around as a kid?" Jake asks as we weave through the stream of people. Cowboy hats bob along the top of the crowd, the smell of cheap beer and fried food thick in the air.

I shake my head and he seems surprised. "Really? You were always carrying that thing around. Your momma couldn't even get it away from you long enough to wash it."

I don't want to say it, but sometimes, those years before, the ones where Momma was alive are hard to remember. The older I get, the fuzzier they are. It's strange to think of a world before I knew what Daddy was. What I was expected to be.

"I bet I'd remember if I saw it," I say as we fall into the line for burgers and fries smothered with melted cheese and grilled onions. "It's probably up in the attic."

"We should go through all the stuff up there sometime," Jake says, and he says it carefully, like he's not sure how I'll react. "All your baby clothes are saved. And your momma's jewelry. I think your grandma's china's somewhere up there. That's yours, for when you get married."

I snort. "I don't think that's ever gonna happen."

Uncle Jake smiles. "You never know."

I shift from foot to foot. The line is long, and it's moved slow since we got in it. "I'm gonna run to the bathroom," I tell him. I take the bear with me, so Uncle Jake doesn't have to juggle it and the food.

The bathrooms are set at the very end of the double aisle that makes up the food section of the fair. The lights from the rides dance across the ground, the beeps and whirls and bells mixing with the hum of voices and laughter. Children run past me, fistfuls of red tickets in their hands.

I go inside the restroom and pee, washing my hands one by one awkwardly because I've still got the bear to hold. The bathrooms are on the edge of the fairgrounds. They're isolated. And this late at night, as the night begins to wind down, pretty much abandoned.

I'm about to turn and head back to Jake when a movement out of the corner of my eye makes me freeze.

"Thought it was you," a voice says behind me. "I smelled bitch in the air."

The bear drops to the ground as I turn.

Bobby Springfield pushes off the tree he'd been lounging against.

He takes after his momma—dark hair, big eyes—but his are mean. Bulging. His hair slicks across his forehead, dipping into his eyes.

"You grew up," Bobby says, and his gaze settles on my chest. My skin prickles in that dreadful way all women know as he looks at me.

Bobby is way bigger than I am. Last time I came up against Bennet, we were around the same size. But Bobby?

Bobby's going to be harder to take.

I square my shoulders and meet his eyes head-on. "We doing this?"

There's no point in trying to sweet-talk my way out or running. I'm no coward, and this is one of those inevitable things—it was just a matter of time. I can't back down.

I don't really want to.

"Oh yeah." He lunges, telegraphing his hit with his entire body. He's big and he's dangerous, but I'm fast. You have to be when you're as skinny as me. The muscle I've got is hard-won, but I'm quick and I'm smart.

I go low, landing a solid blow to his diaphragm. He staggers back, but recovers almost immediately. This time I'm not fast enough.

His fist crashes into my jaw and my teeth clack together. It's a bone-shaking hit that leaves blood bursting in my mouth. He lands another, a fist to my shoulder that sends me spinning. Then he grabs me around the waist, yanking me into him, right off my feet. I kick out, but I've got nothing.

I jerk when I feel his lips graze my ear, something dark and feral curling inside me when he whispers, "When I'm done with you, you're going to be bloody inside and out."

I grit my teeth and jerk my head back—hard. The back of my skull crashes into his face, I hear the crunch of bone, and then he's howling, his hands falling from their grip on me. My ears ring, my head throbs, and my mouth's full of blood as I wriggle free.

I can't wait to recover, even though my head's spinning. I just round on him while he's distracted. One precise kick to his crotch while he's still clutching his bleeding, broken nose, and he's down.

I spit out a mouthful of blood on the grass. "That was the wrong thing to say to me," I tell him, drawing my foot back and slamming it into his ribs. He lets out a choking gasp, blood pouring down his face as he curls into a fetal position. I kick him again, hard enough to fracture. He screams. Steel-toed boots come in handy.

I'm circling around him, ready to deliver the same treatment to his back when a clapping sound jerks my attention up.

I freeze, scanning the area, and then my eyes settle.

I haven't seen Carl since that day six months ago in the feed store parking lot when I set Busy on him.

He stops clapping. "He raised you into a vicious little thing, didn't he?" he asks.

Any other time, I'd be scared. But my body's full of adrenaline and my mouth's full of blood and I am fucking game to take him on.

"I'm not little," I say, stepping over Bobby's groaning body, heading toward Carl, fists curling. "And I'm not a thing."

He smiles, a delighted leer that makes my stomach turn. "Gonna fight me, too? I thought shooting was more your thing. I watched you. At the shooting gallery. That's quite a talent you got."

For some reason, it makes me feel naked that he was there, watching me do the thing I do best. Like he's intruded on something sacred.

I'm almost to him, just three more steps…

"Harley!"

Uncle Jake's voice rings out, making me stop in my tracks. A shadow falls across Springfield, and Jake's there, looming over him like a Reaper, putting his body between the two of us.

"Get the fuck away from my niece."

"It's free territory," Carl says.

"You go nowhere she does," Jake says, and his blue eyes glitter. The anger coiled in his body, in the ropy strands of muscles in his neck that tense with each breath, is frightening.

But I understand it.

I feel it too.

I hate him too.

"Well, I don't know the girl, do I?" Carl asks. "Couldn't predict she'd be here. I was just enjoying the fair with my nephew. Who's bleeding on the ground over there, if you didn't notice. Because of *your* girl."

"He deserved it. And you were watching me," I hiss.

"You draw the eye, darling," Carl drawls. "Just like your momma."

Jake leans forward, so he's nose to nose with Carl. "I'm going to say this once," he says. "She does not exist to you. And if I ever see you near her again…"

"What?" Carl laughs. "You gonna kill me, Jake? I've known you my whole life. You wouldn't even go hunting when we were kids. You couldn't pull the trigger on a man to save her life or yours. You're a fucking pussy."

Jake backs away, grabbing my hand, pulling me closer to him. "Things change," he says. "You've been warned. Obey the fucking rules."

Springfield doesn't follow as Jake yanks me down the main drag of the fair, his grasp on my hand so tight that it smashes my fingers together.

"Are you okay?" he keeps asking, his eyes tracking ahead of us and his head turning to check behind us every few seconds.

"I'm fine," I say, tugging at his hand, trying to lessen the pressure. I'm not, really. My face is starting to swell, and when I run my tongue along my teeth, I realize there's one missing.

That fucking bastard knocked one of them out. It hurts like hell.

"Jesus Christ," Jake swears, pushing through a crowd of rodeo clowns. "What the hell happened?"

"It's fine, Uncle Jake," I say. "I got the better of Bobby."

We hit the exit gate, following the stream of people heading to the parking lot. Once he's got us in his truck, safe in the cab, the doors locked, Jake doesn't start the engine. Instead, he turns to me, his face serious.

"Tell me what happened."

"It's not a big deal," I say, even though I still feel shaky from the adrenaline. "Bobby was just being a shit. He's an asshole. In church, he likes to mouth swear words instead of singing."

"What did Carl say to you?" Jake asks, his voice intense, and his hand suddenly on my arm.

I pull away from him, frowning. "He was barely there. He came along after I got Bobby on the ground. All he said was he was watching me shoot earlier."

"I should have noticed him," Jake says instantly. "Shit." He closes his eyes, pushing his black cowboy hat back off his head. His thick brown hair—the feature we share—flops across his forehead, and he runs his hand through it, resignation settling over his face.

"I have to talk to your father," he says.

*"No,"* I say. Daddy's out of town, and I probably have enough time to get my tooth fixed and for the bruises to fade before he's back. If Uncle Jake tells him, then I'm screwed.

"Harley—" Uncle Jake starts.

"You can't. It's a miracle Daddy didn't put me on house arrest when Springfield got out of prison. If you tell, he won't let me leave the property anymore."

"You don't know that," Uncle Jake says, but even he can't keep the doubt from his voice.

"I am not ten anymore," I say. "I'm grown. I work. I have the Ruby. He'll keep me from all of that if you tell him."

"Carl was watching you, Harley. You said it yourself."

"Yeah, he was watching me," I say. "He was watching me *shoot.* Something everyone made damn sure I was near perfect at. In a gunfight, you don't think I could take Springfield down? I can outshoot and outdraw anyone around here."

"There are more ways of fighting than shooting guns," Jake says. "It's a miracle you got the better of Bobby."

"I got the better of Bobby because I am *better than Bobby,*" I snap, my pride bristling. "I got the better of him because no man threatens to rape me or any woman and walks away unhurt."

Jake's eyes widen and I refuse to look away. I am not backing down. Not when it comes to this.

I've seen what some of the women at the Ruby have had to survive. And I'll do anything to spare any woman in this county from that.

"You shouldn't have to fight," Jake says.

I bite my lip, looking out the truck window. "Neither of us should have to do a lot of things."

He sighs, staring at the steering wheel. "Duke will lose his mind if he finds out I've kept this from him."

"He won't find out." I pause, and then I add the one thing I know will clinch it for Jake. "It'd start another war."

I don't know if it's the truth; probably. Duke's a fearsome man when it comes to me. And Springfield's return has put him on edge.

I'm not gonna do anything to push him over that edge.

"Fine," Jake says, finally. "We'll keep this between us."

I let out a long breath. "Thank you."

I think I'm doing the right thing.

Later, I'll realize I'm not.

Later, it'll haunt me, because if I had let Jake tell Daddy, maybe we would've been ready.

Maybe Uncle Jake wouldn't have died for me.

Because of me.

In front of me.

# SIXTEEN

*June 6, 5:00 p.m.*

It's pretty easy to blow up a meth lab. One spark in the right place, and you're golden.

The problem is, there are usually people inside. Sometimes it's just the cooks. Sometimes they deserve it. Sometimes they don't.

But sometimes it's their wives. Their kids. Their clientele. Tweekers who're so lost in it they can't do anything but swirl down that drain.

Innocent people. Maybe messed up, maybe not good, not all the way through, but who the hell is, really, if you get down to it? We've all got grit buried deep. Dirty secrets and big mistakes.

This is gonna be secret, but it can't be a mistake.

If you don't want to hurt the innocents, you have to be careful. But if you don't want to hurt anyone at all, you have to be perfect.

I was lucky. I've had to time plan it all out. Obsessively. Step by step. Plan A. Plan B. Plan C.

But time's run out. No more planning. Just action.

Today, the trailer. Tomorrow, the warehouse. And then…

Then the house on Shasta Street.

A new pink bike with training wheels is parked in the house's front yard, just the right size for a six-year-old.

I wonder if she knows, the little girl who rides that bike. What her daddy does.

At six, I didn't.

But things change.

The cooks don't know about the old mining road, but I do. It's washed out in places, but I manage. I flagged the path to the clearing weeks ago.

I scale a tree and wait for dark. I feel numb instead of scared, and I think that's for the best. My hands need to be steady. My mind needs to be quick. I can be scared later. It's easier to go through with something when you don't think too much about the consequences.

This is going to work. No one is going to die. And no one will catch me.

After the moon rises and the stars soar across the sky, sparkling like creek water on a sunny day, I slip down from my perch and keep hidden along the timberline as I head north. I set my trap and hurry back to the tree and climb it again. I need the vantage point.

I need to watch them.

The trailer—a seventies fifth wheel with blacked-out windows and ventilation fans punched in the roof—is sitting just a hundred feet away in a clearing cut hastily out of the forest, just big enough for it and a few pickups.

The harder it is to get to a lab, the smaller the chance of getting it jacked.

I shift down the branch with one hand, my night vision scope in the other. My shoulders smack against the trunk, the rough surface pressing through the thin cotton of my T-shirt. Leaves brush the top of my head, my silhouette blending into the thick forest shadow.

I grip the branch tight with my thighs, balancing as I raise the scope to my eye. The paint's peeling in big patches off the trailer roof, and I see vapor from the fans swirling up into the air and vanishing.

I'm just waiting now. Waiting for the sound that will draw them out. I tilt my watch closer, the numbers on the dial gleaming in the darkness. A quarter mile away, I've set my trap—a small, contained fire. Any second, the flames'll reach the small mound of ammunition I've put in its path.

Simple. Easy. Classic.

It begins with the bullets bursting in the fire. The *pop-pop-pop* fills the air, echoing through the clearing. Birds rustle in the trees close to me, and deeper in the forest something four-legged—mountain lion, probably—dashes through the brush, away from the noise.

The trailer door swings open. A skinny guy in overalls—that's Dale—steps out, twelve-gauge firmly in hand as he scans the clearing.

I'm waiting, breathless. He could just dismiss the sound as hunters, though most of them know better than to poach around here. Or he could call for Troy.

I need him to call for Troy and for both of them to get away from the trailer. Fast.

Dale lowers his shotgun slowly and is turning to go back inside the trailer when he sees the smoke rising in the distance.

I smile. Got him.

"Hey! *HEY!* Troy! Get the extinguishers! Smoke! There's a fire! Shit!"

He nearly falls ass over ankles, the straps of his overalls slipping off as he scrambles back toward the trailer. Another guy, balding and husky, runs out, red extinguisher clutched in one hand, a pile of blankets thrown over his shoulder.

I watch as Dale points to the smoke in the distance, and the two of them take off.

This is it. My heart thumps in my ears, and my fingers clench tight around the scope. I wait until they've disappeared down the side of the hill.

Then I scramble down the tree, bark scraping against my stomach, and I vault the last four feet to the ground. I grab my rucksack and drop my scope inside, where it knocks against the can of spray paint. After making sure the area's clear, I race toward the trailer.

I've got only so much time.

I yank the bandanna out of my pocket and tie it over my nose and mouth. Taking a deep breath, I fill my lungs the best I can and dash up the steps into the fifth wheel.

It's trashed inside, gutted to accommodate the lab, with a mix of coffee filters, matches, and empty bottles of rubbing alcohol strewn across the ratty brown carpet. I pick my way through the mess quickly, my lungs burning with the effort not to breathe in the toxic air.

Where is it? It has to be here. I checked the warehouse—they haven't had a chance to deliver the batch. I use the edge of my shirt to flip open the round cooler stashed in one corner behind a pile of dirty clothes.

*Yes.*

I load the plastic baggies of meth double-time into my rucksack, so roughly I can hear the pieces breaking as they hit the canvas. I want to stamp the crystals down to powder, cut it with so much shit that even the most desperate tweeker won't touch it. No time for that—my head's throbbing and light. I need to get out.

But I can't hold my breath any longer. I inhale, my lungs shuddering in relief, only to recoil from the all-too-familiar burn of ammonia and phosphorus through the bandanna.

My lungs sting as I throw the bag over my shoulder and run, gasping in fresher air as I burst out of the fifth wheel and race away into the clearing.

Smoke's pillaring thick over the ridge to the south. I've gotta hurry.

I make sure I'm far enough away that the message will be clear. Rummaging in the rucksack, I pull out the can. On the ground, in long careful strokes where they can't miss it, I spray-paint in bright red: DEATH TO MCKENNA.

Tearing the bandanna off my face, I dig in the bag again to grab the half-full bottle of vodka I stole from the Tropics earlier. I feed the end of the cloth into the neck of the bottle, making sure it's soaking up the alcohol.

For a long moment, I stare at the trailer, my heart beating so fast it feels like it's the only part of me that's working. In one hand, I have the bottle. In the other, I have a lighter.

It's time.

I light the end of bandanna, take aim, and throw the bottle hard, back through the open door of the fifth wheel. Then I run like hell.

The explosion rips through the clearing, knocking me off my feet onto my stomach.

The sound roars in my ears and heat washes over my back, and I lie there dazed for a second before rolling over. Acrid black smoke curls up from what was once the fifth wheel, blending into the dark sky at the top of the pines.

My ears still ringing from the blast, I force myself to my feet—I have to get away, they have to believe it's Springfield's doing—and stumble toward the woods.

Right before I disappear into the pines, I turn back, just once.

The inferno looks like hell on earth, the charred, twisted remains of the fifth wheel burping out chemicals that'd sear the skin right off you.

But it's not hell. Not even close.

Hell's what's waiting for me if any part of my plan fails.

One down. Two to go.

# SEVENTEEN

When I'm ten years old, Carl Springfield is sent to prison.
It's what I've been waiting for, and it's supposed to change everything. But it doesn't. Daddy still drinks too much and takes too many risks, and sometimes when he looks at me, I know he's seeing Momma and it hurts him.

I want to go to school with Will. But whenever I bring it up, all hopeful he'll say yes because Springfield's behind bars now and I'm safe, Daddy just shakes his head.

"You stay with me, Harley-girl. You have different things to learn. Useful things."

So I'm locked in a six-hundred-acre cage, and I'm starting to see the tall trees and winding creeks I used to love as the bars. No matter how far I climb or swim, I'm stuck here.

I think Daddy worries about it because he starts taking me places. Now I go along with him on his rounds, meeting with people, collecting money, checking in at the truck yard. He even takes me to the Ruby, where I hang out with Mo. Daddy thinks my hero worship of her is cute. He doesn't have the foresight to see that Mo's way of thinking might make more sense to me than his.

One day, before we have to pick Will up at school, Daddy takes me out all the way to Pollard Flat, down a dirt road where the houses are set deep in the woods, rusty tin roofs glinting through the pines the only hint of their presence.

We pull up to a house where a man's waiting on the porch. Dogs bark all around us, and two big pit bulls gallop up to the Chevy, but the man calls them off.

"Mr. McKenna." He takes off his dirty baseball cap. "Wasn't expecting you today."

"I bet," Daddy says. "But it's time we talk, Gary."

Gary swallows, his Adam's apple bobbing. "My boys are 'round back with the dogs, if your girl wants to join them," he says.

Daddy nods at me.

I don't really want to, but I hear some yipping behind the house—what sounds like puppies. So I go.

There's a tangle of baby pit bulls in a kennel set in the yard that's mostly gravel, red dirt, and pines so tall and old that I have to crane my neck to look at the tops. I make a beeline for the puppies, their gray-and-white wiggling bodies calling to me. But then I notice Gary's sons on the other side of the yard.

For a second, I think they're tossing a baseball back and forth. And then a frightened whine shatters the silence.

They're throwing a puppy back and forth. A little white ball of fur, smaller than the others.

The runt of the litter.

"Hey!" I shout, running forward. "Stop it!" I grab at the puppy, but the taller boy laughs and lobs it back to his brother, high over my head.

"Stop!" I shriek. I yank at the taller boy's arm, but he shakes me off like I'm nothing.

"Leave us alone," warns the younger one with a snarl. He catches the puppy and is swinging it by the scruff of his neck as it whines and wriggles, trying to get away.

"Give her to me," I demand.

The taller boy laughs, his thin lips in a nasty twist. "It's just the runt. We're gonna drown her anyway."

"No, you aren't," I hiss. "Give her!"

The younger boy tosses her again, high above my head so I can't reach her. But this time when his brother catches her, I'm ready. I lunge forward, my fingers skating across soft fur—almost grabbing her, but then pain bursts below my eye like a water balloon popping.

For a second, I don't realize what's happened. No one's ever hit me before.

No one would dare.

I stagger backward, losing my grip on the puppy, gasping for breath as tears start to form in my eyes.

I can't cry. I don't cry anymore.

Instead, I ram forward like a goat, my head bent, my mouth howling. I hit him directly in the stomach and I don't stop. I won't go down.

As we roll around in the dirt, the puppies go crazy, barking loudly, scrabbling at the kennel fence with their paws. I can't see where the runt is—I'm too busy punching any body part I can reach. My fists smash into the boy's neck and then his cheek, my knuckles glancing across his cheekbone sharply, splitting it open.

"Hey, *HEY!*" A hand grabs my shirt collar, hauling me off my feet. I kick out furiously, and my fists punch the air.

I want to hurt that boy. I've never wanted to hurt anyone so bad before. It's an alien feeling, bubbling inside me, hot and thick.

But I remember the runt, and suddenly the feeling seems right, a surge of emotion ripping through me, making me something new. I turn to my captor, swinging wildly in the air.

"What is going on?"

It's Daddy. His voice is low and deadly, and it makes all the fight flow out of me, rushing out of my body like a river, replaced by prickly fear. I go limp as he sets me down.

"Th-they were hurting the puppy," I stutter. "They wouldn't stop, so I had to..."

Daddy bends down, gently gripping my chin with his fingers. There's something wet and warm running down my face, I realize too late.

Blood.

The boy made me bleed.

*Blood for blood, Harley-girl.*

Panic shoots through me like a bullet. "Daddy—" I start.

But he's already looking at the boy on the ground, his dark eyes glimmering. "Did you hit her?"

"Mr. McKenna. Please." Gary's standing behind his son, fear written on every line in his pale face. "They're just kids."

He knows what's coming.

"Daddy," I say again. "I hit him first."

But he doesn't even seem to hear me. He turns away and steps forward, towering over the boy. "A real man doesn't hit a girl," he says. "And no man hits *my* girl. Looks like I'm going to have to teach you a lesson your father didn't bother to."

"Daddy, no," I say, because I'm the only person who can say that word to him. I'm the only one who won't suffer the consequences.

"Go to the truck, Harley-girl," he says.

"The puppy—" I look around. Where is she?

"Go to the truck," he grits out, in that scary low voice that means business. It sends shivers down my back.

I need to do as he tells me, because I'm scared of what he'll do if I refuse.

He's already killed in front of me. I don't ever want to see that again.

I hesitate, biting my lip, and for a moment, the boy and I look at each other. I want to tell him I'm sorry.

I want to tell him he deserves it. The warring parts of me—the one that belongs to Momma and the one that belongs to Daddy—twist and turn inside my brain.

"*Now*, Harley!" Daddy orders.

I go.

"Mr. McKenna, that's my boy!" Gary shouts behind me, his voice breaking with terror. "Please!"

Holding my hands over my ears, I break into a run back toward the truck. My right eye throbs, and my nose is still bleeding. I wipe my face with my sleeve, but it just makes more of a mess.

I climb into the cab like a good girl. I put my hands over my ears again and close my eyes. And I wait.

It's muffled, but I can hear it: a high-pitched scream echoing from the backyard, breaking through the dog's howling. A scream that starts off as *No, no, nooo!* fading into one long vowel.

My stomach churns, sick and glad all at once. It's warm outside, but I start shivering and I can't stop.

It seems like forever before Daddy comes back. He gets into the truck without a word, shoving something wrapped in his flannel shirt at me.

It's the runt. She's alive.

I take her in my arms, a warm, wiggling mess. She's dirty and smells like pee, but I couldn't care less—she's alive. Her little claws snag in my shirt and she whimpers against my chest, shaking like me, still terrified, but somehow unhurt. I can feel her heartbeat, thumping against mine, like she's another part of me that's just been waiting to be found.

"It's okay," I whisper against the top of her head. "It's okay now."

Daddy wipes his hunting knife on his jeans before putting it back in its sheath. As the dark stain spreads on the denim, I clutch the puppy tighter.

Daddy takes his phone out, dialing a number. "Cooper, you and the boys get over to Gary Hunt's place. Take the dogs—yes, all of them. Bring a kennel; you'll be picking up a litter of pups, and you'll need to find them good homes. And send Doc over. He's got some stitching to do."

When he hangs up, he looks over at me. "You all right, baby?"

I nod and take another deep breath, but it comes out like a shudder.

Daddy reaches over, gently touching my cheek. I flinch, not only because it hurts.

"He got you good," he says.

"I got him back," I say. And it makes him smile.

"Damn right," he says, staring at me with an odd expression I suddenly recognize as respect. "You did me proud."

I hold the puppy closer to me. I don't want to think about the boy. I don't want to know what happened—if he's alive, if he's dead.

Since Ben, I understand that a lot of the time, not knowing is best.

"Can we find somebody nice to take her?" I ask, stroking the silky fur as she roots around in my shirt, not shaking anymore. I don't know what Daddy might do, so I have to think of options. "Wayne might want her. Or Cooper. I know she's small, but she'll get bigger fast."

"I think she likes you," Daddy says, his smile broadening. "And you fought for her. You saved her. So she should stay with you."

My heart leaps. I can barely believe it. "Really?"

"I'll train her up," he says. "You need a guard dog. But she has to go everywhere with you. So she can protect you."

I nod, but it hurts my head, so I stop. "I promise."

He reaches out and gently squeezes my shoulder. "You've got a good heart, Harley-girl. Just like your momma. It's gonna get you hurt unless I surround you with things that can hurt back."

I swallow. "But Carl Springfield's in prison." Why is Daddy so scared still, when Springfield's gone?

"There'll always be people who want to hurt you," he explains solemnly, smoothing back my bloody bangs, the lines around his mouth turned down in concern. "Just because of who you are. Look at what that boy did to you."

"I wanted to hurt him," I say. A quiet confession, spoken in the safety of the truck cab, to the only person I knew who would understand that feeling.

Daddy looks over at me, surprised. I look back, solemn, the puppy's heart beating against my chest, because of him. She's safe now, because of him.

Just like me.

He smiles.

"That's my girl."

I look down. The puppy's paws are damp with the boy's blood.

I wipe them off, best I can.

# EIGHTEEN

*June 6, 10:00 p.m.*

I snap the red tie off the tree branch. Flagging my way was smart. I can't waste any time getting lost in this thicket.

Right now, speed's essential. I need to get into range to call Fire Watch.

I don't sprint, but I move quick and low through the forest, a blur of brown hair and camo. It's two miles of rocky cliffs and thick pines to make it to the old mining road where my truck's parked. Awkward in the dark, I trip a few times, but I keep going—I have to.

I'm sweaty beneath the reek of char and chemicals that clings to my skin. By the time I finally make it to the crude dirt road and uncover my truck, carefully concealed with branches, I'm coughing hard into my sleeve.

Busy barks, just once, when she sees me coming. After stashing the bag of meth in the toolbox in the bed of my truck, I climb into the cab and drive. She sniffs at me and sneezes, backing up along the bench seat.

"Sorry," I tell her. "I'll smell better soon."

One hand on the steering wheel, I roll down the windows as I navigate the narrow dirt road, weaving through the trees until we hit mountain. The red clay cliffs, studded with roots and slate rock, sprinkled with lupine and redbud, loom above me on the left.

When I was really little, Momma used to scoop the clay right from the ground, wetting it down and forming it into balls for me to play with. When I was older, after she died, I used to get into clay fights with Will until we were streaked with it. It would dry and crack under the sun until we jumped into the creek to wash it away.

I try to think about that, trying to forget the smell sticking to me and the heat I can still feel on my skin. But it creeps back in: The weight of what I've done, what I've started, it settles on me as my truck bounces down the uneven road. I breathe through it because I can't afford to pass out or pull over. I have to get out of the woods and onto the highway.

I need to call Fire Watch. The last thing I want is to be the cause of a forest fire.

It'll be fine. I just have to stick to the plan.

By the time Busy and I are out of the forest and into range on the highway, it's nearly eight. The fire's been burning for over an hour. I grab the prepaid phone from the glove compartment and punch in a number.

"North County Fire Watch. How may I help you?" asks a woman's voice.

"Hi, me and my friends were camping near Route 43." I pitch my voice high and shrill. "Right around Castella Road. We heard, like, an explosion or something. And there was all this black smoke. I think something bad happened. Someone should check it out."

"Can you tell me—" starts the operator.

I roll down my window and pitch the burner cell out the window. In the rearview I can see it hit the pavement, shattering into pieces that bounce into the brush. Slamming down on the accelerator, I reach over to the glove compartment and pull out the two remaining phones. The black one has no missed calls or texts—yet, but it's just a matter of time.

They'll call Buck first, as soon as they give up fighting the fire and get into range. And then Buck will call Duke. When Buck can't get a hold of him, he'll call me.

And then the real work starts. My plan. My con. My performance of a lifetime.

I drive like hell.

Busy and I make it to exit 34 later than I'd like, but I'm not out of time yet. I take a right at the off-ramp, following the rusted sign pointing toward a campground. Busy's edged away, leaning against the passenger door, the stink coming off me offending her nose.

I drive past the happy couples out enjoying nature, the grandparents tucked safely in their RVs, and the hippie kids roughing it in tents until they can get trimmigrant jobs on all the grows come harvest time. The Sons will probably hire half of them; they've got to get the bud trimmed, dried, and cured in record time these days to stay competitive. Parking next to one of the log-cabin-kit bathrooms, I grab my big duffel from the truck bed and whistle for Busy to follow me.

The showers are set up in individual rooms. I dump my bag on the side of the wall farthest away from the spray and feed some quarters into the coin drop on the wall. Busy watches me carefully, sitting next to the door, not startling even when the water comes on.

I strip off my camo pants and army-green shirt and shove them in a plastic trash bag. I reek—the acrid chemicals and smoke have sunk deep into my pores and all through my hair.

I wash my hair twice, then soap and scrub myself down three times until my skin feels stretched too tight over my bones. From my bag, I take out the pair of cutoffs and slip them on, along with a clean tank top and one of the flannel shirts Will left behind.

Sometimes I can trick myself into thinking it still smells like him.

On my way out, I dump the plastic bag holding my toxic clothes in the trash, and Busy and I drive out of the campground, no one the wiser.

It's begun: Now the black phone is buzzing constantly, filling up with texts, so I find a place to park on the side of the road, hidden from view, and grab it, keying in the code.

There are twenty text messages. The same one, over and over again: 5 feet high and rising. Call me. Now.

Duke's code for a blown lab. Buck knows.

I swallow, trying to keep my hands from shaking. Soon, Buck's going to give up texting him and call me.

*Make a plan and stick with it, Harley-girl.*

I turn the phone off and drive.

When I don't pick up, Buck will send someone by the house. He won't do it himself, because he'll be too busy giving orders and panicking. When whoever he sends—probably Troy—can't get past the gate, Buck will really freak out. He'll think Springfield got me. Then Cooper will come. He and Wayne will go out looking, but they won't find me. Not until I want them to.

Buck will go for the warehouse next. He'll be looking for all the gunpower he can find, preparing for a war.

But I'm a step ahead of him. I'll hit the warehouse later, but I know Buck's likely to stop there before me. So I spent an afternoon taking every gun in the warehouse apart and putting them back together—with a few vital parts missing. They look normal, but they won't get him anywhere. Not that he'll have a chance to use them. I'll have taken care of him before it comes to that. But I need him to collect the guns and take them to his house. And he will. He's predictable—they all are. I've been watching them all for years, and now all that time will pay off.

He'll want in Duke's shed next, because Buck's trigger happy as hell and there's just a handful of guns at the warehouse. Duke's shed is where the real arsenal is. An armory with enough ammunition and guns to wage ten turf wars.

I won't let him near it.

It'll start to really sink in then. The helplessness. The fear. He'll be in over his head. No clue. No guidance.

No Duke telling him what to do.

Buck will be desperate for someone to come in with a plan. Because he'll think that Carl Springfield is coming; that he's finally broken the truce, plotting to destroy everything. And Carl will be on edge now, since Bobby and Bennet will have told him I crossed the river, looking for him.

And so the McKennas and Springfields will start running around, preparing for the coming war they both think the other side started, and they'll all be too busy to see the real threat coming: Me.

They think the only power I've got comes from Duke.

They're wrong.

I smile.

Everything's going according to plan.

# NINETEEN

I'm fifteen when Brooke Talbot and I become friends.

It's kind of funny, because apart from Will, she's my first friend. But before I decided to take a walk on the riverbank that day, we were straight-up enemies, forced to interact only when one of us managed to get roped into youth group before slipping free. Most of the time, we ended up circling, snarling, but never lashing out. Will pulled me back each time, and it's a good thing he did, because I'd have put her down in ten seconds flat.

It's not like I can really blame her for hating me. Daddy backed her mom's bakery when she was just starting up. When I was twelve, Mrs. Talbot got a few months behind on her payments. I remember the baseball bat smashing into the cash register, how wide and scared Mrs. Talbot's eyes were when Daddy told her that next time it wouldn't be the only thing he broke. How he'd swung the bat back and forth in the direction of the kitchen as he said it, where I knew Brooke and her big brother were cowering underneath the prep table.

The money was paid the next day and was never late again, because that's what a mother does when the meanest son of a bitch you ever did see threatens your kids.

When I see her ahead of me on the river trail that day, I almost turn back. I'm walking along the east bank with Busy, waiting for Will to finish up at the hardware store and drive us home. Busy's sniffing her way through the pines, and when we round the bend, there's Brooke, twenty feet ahead of me, gesturing wildly at a guy I don't recognize.

The last thing I want to see is Brooke's angry, red-splotched face, and I definitely don't want it to devolve into hair pulling, like it did the one time Will wasn't there to get between us, so I've already turned away when I hear her cry out.

I whirl back around. I know that sound.

The guy's hands are gripping her upper arm and shaking her hard every few words he speaks. When she tries to pull away, one of his hands drops, not down, but back.

"Hey!" I shout.

It's too late.

Smack. Open-handed, hard across her cheek, leaving a bright red imprint. She crumples onto the ground, her bare knees scraping against the pavement as her denim miniskirt hikes up a few inches.

Busy snarls, straining at her leash.

I take long, sure strides toward the guy until I'm close enough to hear Brooke sniffling, close enough to hear the shit he's saying to her.

"Hey, asshole," I call out. I don't go for my knife yet—its weight against my leg in my pocket is enough.

At least for now.

The guy's attention finally snaps to me, and I recognize him: It's Tripp Hughes, the son of one of the sheriff's deputies. Daddy has them all in his pocket.

Perfect.

He scowls at me. "This is none of your business, Harley. It's between me and Brooke."

I stare hard at him and let everything I'm feeling—how I want to slice him up with my knife, to keep going until there's nothing left but innards—show on my face. His eyes flicker—there's fear there, but it's tamped down by male ego.

He's gotta prove himself. They almost always do.

"You want me to go, Brooke?" I ask, not looking away from Tripp.

Nothing but sniffling.

Tripp smiles, smug, like he's got her trained good.

"See?" he says. "There isn't any problem here. Leave us alone." There's a threat in his voice, and that makes me even angrier. What an idiot.

My hand closes around Busy's collar. "Brooke," I say again, and this time, I'm not asking.

I'm warning.

She understands and crawls away out of the line of fire right before I let go of Busy's collar.

Busy leaps, knocking Tripp off his feet and flattening him on the ground. I'm pleased to hear his choked groan as the impact knocks the wind out of him. She plants herself on his chest, pinning him, and bares her teeth in his face.

"Good girl," I coo, moving forward so I can loom over him, too. I'm not scared. I'll never be scared of someone like him.

"Wh-what the fuck, Harley?!" Tripp gasps. "Call off your dog!"

"Why would I do that?" I bend down, unsheathing my knife right in front of his face.

His eyes widen. It's like watching a cartoon—any second, they'll pop out. "My dad—"

"Is owned by mine," I finish.

Tripp struggles to sit up, but Busy snaps her teeth an inch away from his nose. He freezes. First smart move he's made.

"Leave it, Busy." She pushes off him, digging in her claws, and trots over to Brooke, circling her like she's a puppy needing protection. Every time Tripp even glances Brooke's way, Busy growls.

For a second, he looks relieved that I've called Busy off, but then I lay my knife against his stomach, pressing hard enough for him to understand I'm serious, and his eyes go wide again. Now I've got him right where he should be: scared shitless.

"I could cut you," I tell him. "I go deep enough, I'll probably nick your spleen. You might bleed out before the next jogger comes by and calls 911. Or you might not."

I drag the knife up his chest to his throat. "Now here…" I tap the blade against his neck. His Adam's apple bobs frantically as his breath stutters in the back of his throat. "Here's the sweet spot. Fast, efficient. You drown in your own blood for a little while, but it doesn't hurt as much as, say, getting gutted." I smile at him, my sweet smile, like I'm handing him some lemonade at Youth Group. "So which one is it gonna be, Tripp?"

"Please," he whimpers. "Please don't."

I press harder, to the point of almost breaking the skin. I lean forward, so I'm whispering in his ear. "I'm feeling generous today, so I'll let you go this one time. But if I see you near Brooke or any girl ever again, I'll cut off your dick and feed it to my dog."

He lets out a gasp, and a wet spot spreads down his leg.

I look meaningfully at the stain. "Might want to go take care of that. Down at the QuikStop, they've got some diapers."

I step back, and he scrambles away, swearing under his breath. I don't sheathe my knife until he's well down the river trail, until I'm sure his pride's not gonna get the better of his survival instinct.

On the side of the trail, Brooke sobs and Busy noses at her face, trying to make her feel better. Her mascara and eyeliner are black smears down her cheeks, but I can already see the bruise forming beneath the streaks.

"Hey, it's okay," I say, gentle as I can. "He's gone. But we should move. Just in case he's stupid enough to call his dad."

I offer her my hand and she grabs it, holding it a bit too tight. She lets me pull her up and follows obediently behind Busy and me.

This time of day, it's so hot there aren't many people out. Joggers pound the winding trail in the early morning, hopping over the cracks in the pavement where the tree roots break through. Bikers take the evening hours if it's cooled down enough.

I walk Brooke up the river trail to the little rest area with a bathroom and a water fountain.

"Stay right there." I leave her by the door with Busy and go inside, banging open both stall doors to make sure it's empty. I peer back outside. "Okay, all clear. Come on."

I get her to sit down on one of the toilets while I soak a handful of paper towels. She sniffles as I try to clean her up, flinching when I press too hard on the cheek where the bruise is already rising.

"Sorry," I say.

This entire time, she hasn't met my eyes. She's focused on her folded hands as tears keep running down her face. But when I pull away to get some clean towels, she grabs my hand and stares at me, confused and demanding.

"Why are you helping me?" she asks, her voice choked and rusty. I look down automatically, to her throat. Bruises there, too. A few days old, from the color of them. They're badly covered with foundation; it's starting to flake off.

I should've stabbed the asshole.

I shrug, fiddling with the makeup-smeared towels in my hands. "You needed help."

She narrows her eyes. "But you hate me."

"No, I don't."

"I hate you. And your dad." She glares at me like she's daring me to do something about it.

"So?"

I don't wait for an answer. I walk back to the sink, pull a bunch of clean towels out of the dispenser, wet them down, and come back to kneel in front of her. I press them against her swelling cheek. "We should get some ice for that."

She holds the makeshift compress to her cheek, and I pull away, standing up. She follows me, and we walk outside to sit on top of the cement picnic table.

For a long time, Brooke and I don't talk or even move much. We just sit there, side by side on the table, and I watch her out of the corner of my eye, waiting.

She holds out longer than I expect. She fights it hard, the rush of emotion that comes from getting the shit beaten out of you by someone you love. Her lips press together, a thin line of determination. She blinks furiously, curling her fingers tight around the concrete edge of the table.

But it's impossible to fight it forever.

Tears leak out of the corner of her eyes, her shoulders start heaving, and she breaks down into sobs, bowing her head, her bleached hair falling like a white curtain to cover her face.

I try to figure out what to do. The only thing I can come up with is to put my arm around her, like I've seen Mo do. I cup my hand over her shaking shoulders and pull her against me awkwardly. To my surprise, she leans into it, kind of collapses into me like she's been waiting for something to fall on.

"That wasn't the first time he hit you, was it?"

I can feel her shake her head against my shoulder before she huffs out, "No."

I squeeze her shoulder, thinking.

"Want it to be the last?"

She tilts her head up. Looks at me through swollen, curious eyes.

I smile.

It takes a few moments, but there it is, through the tears and bruises: She smiles back.

# TWENTY

*June 6, 11:30 p.m.*

Around the time I hit Burney, the small town southeast of us, the black phone finally stops buzzing.

Momma brought me here a few times because there's a waterfall and she loved taking me on nature expeditions. I remember us picking our way down the steep, winding trail to the base of the falls, her hand firmly gripping mine to keep me on dry land. I kept trying to jump into the water because it was so blue and bottomless.

But today I'm not here to enjoy the scenery.

I drive to the edge of the town, taking a left. As I pull into the small parking lot, the exhaustion starts to catch up with me. I can feel the heaviness in every part of my body. But I force myself to get out and walk up to the rock fountain, the water splashing cheerfully in the darkness.

Brooke's waiting for me there, sitting on the wooden bench. Her bleach-blond hair is like a beacon in the night, and the heavy kohl around her eyes makes them look huge and dark. She has a silver stud in her nose, a pink crystal flirting above her lip, and a guilty look on her face.

"What happened?" I turn to the building's frosted glass doors. "Did—"

"No, no." Brooke's eyes, if possible, get wider. "Today was a good day. Everything's fine."

My shoulders sag and my legs want to do the same, but I lock them.

It takes me a second to gather myself, heart thumping too fast for my liking, gripping Busy's leash tight. When I do, I realize Brooke's biting her lip and staring at me like I'm a handful of words away from shooting her.

"Just tell me."

"Run into anyone today?"

"*You* called Will?" I stare at her in disbelief.

"I had to," Brooke says. "I was worried."

"You promised you'd help me."

"I did," she insists. "And I *am*. I'm here every day, Harley. I've done everything you've asked of me."

"I didn't ask you to call him. Brooke, if he—" I stop. "I need you both to be okay."

"And we both need *you* to be okay," she snaps.

"This isn't about me," I say. Because it isn't. This is about the Rubies. This is about the town. This is about Brooke's mother and the waitresses at the Blackberry Diner and the guys at the trucking yard. This is about the little girl in the house on Shasta Street.

This is about Springfield, and how he needs to pay for all he's done.

"I had to call Will," Brooke says. "You know I did."

"You're such an asshole," I say, because there isn't anything else to say.

After a long pause, she asks in a hesitant voice, "Did it go okay?"

I nod, short and jerky.

"And now?" Brooke asks, like she doesn't know.

"Now you've got to do what you promised."

She makes a face. Scrunches up her eyebrows and nose, like she's smelling something bad.

"We have to get out of sight." I grab her arm and walk her over to the side of the building, looking up at the windows, all the blinds shut.

I stand across from her, planting my feet hip-width apart. "I need it to look real."

Tears start to swim in her brown eyes. Goddammit. She can't chicken out now.

"Brooke, *please*," I insist. "If you don't, they're not going to believe me."

She rocks back and forth on her heels. "I don't know why being beat up helps you."

"It's the final nail in the coffin," I say. "They're going to assume Springfield blew the lab, but if he doesn't make another move, they'll start getting suspicious. If I walk into the Tropics black and blue and tell them one of the Springfield boys did it, then *that's* a real declaration of war. Once they're in defense mode, I can get what I need from all of them."

"I want to go on record, again, and say this plan is shitty as hell." Brooke sighs.

"It's the only one I've got," I say. "Come on. Hit me."

Her mouth twists, her fingers flexing. "I don't know if I can."

"Bitch, there were a good ten years when you'd do *anything* for a chance to hit me," I say. "Just...just be twelve-year-old Brooke."

Her eyes narrow. "You can be such an asshole sometimes," she says. And then she throws a perfect right hook, smashing into my cheekbone. Pain surges across my face, and I gasp.

I've taught her well.

She doesn't even let me gather my breath. She punches me again, hard, in the nose this time. Blood spurts down my lips, and my head snaps back with the impact. For such a small person, she's strong. I take a deep breath.

"More," I say in a choked voice.

She splits my lip. Perfect. The key here is to make me look bad, but I need to be able to move.

I need to be able to run.

"Okay," she says, stepping back, her hands up. "Okay, Harley. That's enough."

I spit out a mouthful of blood. Had she managed to knock some of my teeth loose? I feel strangely proud. Any man who tangles with her is gonna regret it. We've made sure of that.

My stomach's throbbing, and blood's rising beneath my skin, I can feel a bruise forming on my cheekbone. Soon, I'll have one hell of a black eye.

Perfect.

"Thanks," I say. "Ow."

Brooke's glaring at me.

"I'm sorry," I shrug, because what else can I say? Who else could I have asked?

I trust three people—that's it. She's one of them. And she's the only one I've told.

"Here." She rummages in her purse and thrusts a tissue at me. I dab at my nose. It's not broken, but it's gonna swell like a bitch.

"This is so stupid," she says.

"I'm doing what I have to do," I reply, my words clogged and muffled.

Brooke shakes her head. "You're a fearless, scary bitch. But I love you."

"I know," I say, because saying that back, well, I don't do that.

"I have to go," Brooke says. "And you have to get inside. There's an icepack waiting for you in the room."

She always thinks of everything.

"I left some books," Brooke says. "The doctors want to talk to you tomorrow. Three o'clock."

As if I don't have enough to do—to get back here by three, I'll have to find a way to slip away from the mess I've started.

She heads toward the parking lot, pausing on the curb at the edge of the path.

"Harley," she says. "Don't die on me, okay?"

I smile at her, but I don't say anything. I can't make that promise, not anymore. Not ever. It isn't the kind of life I lead. It isn't the kind of vow I can give.

I wait until she's in her car, pulling out of the parking lot, safe on the road and heading home, before I breathe easy. Then I stand up, wincing from the pain in my stomach, and walk to my truck, letting Busy out and snapping her into her service-dog vest so I can take her inside.

I run my hand through the strands of hair that got loose from my braid, pushing it off my forehead. I wince when it pulls at my skin, making my soon-to-be black eye throb.

At least I look adequately beat up. The second he sees me, Cooper will be so mad, he won't be able to concentrate on anything else. And I can send him on a wild goose chase—a crucial distraction.

Buck isn't stupid, but if I'm careful, I can con him. Cooper's another thing, though—not only smart, but he *knows* me. He's been around my entire life. He was there the day I was born, waiting with Duke in the lobby. He knows things about me that even Will doesn't. He's seen through me before.

So unless I keep him angry and running around, looking for my "attackers" in all the wrong places, he might see through me again.

I want nothing more than to collapse onto the bench here for a few hours, but the glass doors beckon. So I untangle my braid and arrange my hair around my face, hiding my injuries. I take a deep breath and head on through. The silver handle is cold and smooth in my hand. It reminds me of the barrel of a gun.

It's dim inside, the waiting room's tasteful table lamps turned low now that night's fallen. This late, there's no one sitting on the plush crimson couches, just the night nurse sitting at the station far in the back, under a sign with the words PATHWAYS—TAKING THE JOURNEY TO-GETHER. Busy's nails click against the tiles, the only sound in the room.

I nod to the nurse as I pass, flashing my plastic badge but keeping my swollen face hidden. She smiles briefly, her attention sliding back to her computer.

The hall's lined with more tasteful lamps, vases, and prints of those lily pictures that look like they're sponge-painted. The door of the room at the end is closed, and when I open it, I'm greeted by the rhythmic beeping of the monitor and his quiet breathing.

I shut the door behind me and take a few seconds to let my eyes adjust to the darkness. When I'm sure I can move forward without bumping into anything, I make my way to the end of the hospital bed, where Busy's already settled herself on the shiny linoleum floor.

"Hey," I whisper, stroking his arm, bony and still under one of Miss Lissa's quilts.

There's no answer. I don't expect one.

I sit down in the chair next to the bed after picking up the crocheted blanket that's folded in it—more of Miss Lissa's handiwork from better days. Then I grab the ice pack Brooke's placed on the table, pressing it gently against my cheek. The cold makes me wince, but I grit my teeth and press harder.

I turn on the burlwood lamp, casting a warm yellow light across the room. I'd brought it from home, along with the quilts and the photos that are laid out along the window. I've done the best I could to make his room homey, like Will and I did for Miss Lissa at Fir Hill.

The difference is, we decorated Miss Lissa's room for her to live in.

But Duke isn't here to live.

He's here to die.

# TWENTY-ONE

I'm twenty-two when Duke gets diagnosed.

Five months ago, we're halfway into our camping trip on the coast when Duke's skin turns a weird shade of yellow. He argues with me for two straight days about seeing a doctor. But on the third day, he's throwing up too much to stop me from taking him in.

There's no one to call, even if he'd let me. It's just the two of us now: Uncle Jake's dead, Will's at school, Miss Lissa's in Fir Hill. So I sit in the ER waiting room by myself and work hard at not being scared.

Two days later, test after test, scan after scan, and suddenly it's a brand new world: *stage four, spread to the liver, a year, maybe less.*

We're quiet for a long time after the oncologist leaves, the surgery scheduled for the next morning. It's no cure, just hoping to buy some time: some sort of stent thing so the stuff that's turning him yellow will stop. Jaundice caused by bile or something? I don't understand half of the words the doctor uses.

A part of me has always been prepared for losing him. Nights when I thought he wouldn't make it home alive. Days when I was sure he'd die on me like Uncle Jake or go up in flames like Momma. There were times I thought he'd end up in prison, his doings finally catching up to him.

But in the end, Duke McKenna's greatest enemy is his own damn body.

121

I'd never even thought of cancer bringing a man like him down.

We're still not talking when the nurse comes and checks on him, fiddling with his IV drip to up the dose. But when she leaves, his eyes drift open, hazy from the morphine.

"Gotta promise me something, sweetheart," he mumbles.

I squeeze his hand. "Anything."

"Gottadoitforme." His words slur together as the morphine kicks in.

"Do what?" I stroke his upper arm, where there aren't as many tubes and needles sticking into him.

"Gotta..." His eyelids droop, and his head sinks deeper into the pillow, but his hand reaches out and grasps mine with surprising strength. "He'll get you. Gotta kill Springfield. Gottaendit. Gotta do it for me. Gotta kill him. Only way...only way, Harley-girl." His voice trails off to a whisper, his eyes close, and his grip loosens, his hand dropping onto the quilt again.

"Shh," I say, brushing his wiry hair off his forehead. "Don't you worry about that. Get some rest."

I wait until I'm sure he's asleep before I stand up and make my way back through the quiet halls. It's late, one or two in the morning by now, and I can smell salt and fish in the crisp ocean air as I walk out the sliding doors.

I cross the parking lot to the smoking area set far from the ER entrance. It's empty of people, but I'm not surprised to see roaches mixed with cigarette butts in the overflowing ashtray. We are smack dab in the middle of the Emerald Triangle.

I sit down on the redwood bench and pull my hoodie tighter around me as the wind whips at my braid. I bend at the waist, my head hanging low, my forehead pressed into my hands.

*Stage four, spread to the liver, a year, maybe less.*

My hands shake.

I can't stop it.

Duke's going to die. He's going to die, and I can't stop it.

My chest tightens like someone's pushing with both palms against it, pressing me against a wall. My toes curl inside my boots. I haven't changed my clothes or showered since we got here. All I've done is drink crappy coffee from the cafeteria and wait for the biopsy to confirm what we've known since the first night: Duke's got pancreatic cancer, that it's spread, it's everywhere now.

He's gonna be gone soon.

"Fuck," I whisper. "Fuck. Fuck. Fuck. *Fuck*."

I won't cry. I won't. I breathe in and out through my nose, biting the inside of my cheek...fighting, fighting...

Failing.

# TWENTY-TWO

*June 7, Past Midnight*

After Duke got diagnosed, life went on like everything was normal, even though it was anything but. He went to the Tropics, he took care of business, and no one caught on, even if he did look a little rough.

But then he started losing weight, fast. Somebody was going to notice.

He trusted no one but me. And that made it easy.

He always took an annual trip down south, stopping first in L.A. to sell the pot Paul and the Sons had grown and then heading down to Mexico to make whatever connections he needed to. When I turned twenty, he started taking more trips down there—not just at harvest time. He'd disappear into some hole in the wall and he wouldn't come out for a month or two. It was his version of a vacation.

And now it was his saving grace. The cooks didn't even blink when he told them he was going down south for a while. Then he retreated to the house and ordered me to not let anyone past the gate.

He wanted to die at home. I wanted that for him, too. For three months, I fought for it. I bathed him. I fed him. I helped him to and from the toilet dozens of times a day. I cleaned up puke and shit and drool and blood.

I tried. But I couldn't bring in a nurse—there was no one I could trust—and soon, he couldn't get out of bed anymore, and I wasn't strong enough to lift him. So for a week, I fed and cared for him in his bed.

Then he stopped eating. For months, it'd been a struggle to get anything down him, but one afternoon, he just turned his head when I tried to get him to eat or drink anything: rice pudding, those instant breakfast drinks that have become a staple, watermelon, which I read on the cancer sites online was good. But he wouldn't take anything, no matter what I offered or how often I asked.

He slept most of the time, and when he was awake, he talked mostly nonsense: to Momma like she was here; to me like I was a baby still. He'd even call out for his daddy in a voice that sounded so young it made my stomach hurt.

So a month ago, I put him in hospice care in Burney. I knew, then, that this was the beginning.

The beginning of the end. And the beginning of my plan.

When he died, everything would go to hell. Chaos would reign, the cooks would fight it out with each other, with Springfield, and probably with the Sons of Jefferson, too. Everyone would be fighting for a piece of North County.

Unless someone already had control, before Duke died.

I had to watch him walk that tightrope between life and death for weeks, waiting until he was close enough for me to start destroying what he built.

Then, a week ago, he fell into a light coma, his body too weak to even stay conscious.

When the nurses told me it wouldn't be long, I knew it was now or never. I had to act and clear the playing field before anyone knew Duke was going—or gone.

Duke's orders were to let him die at home in secret, and then I was to deliver a box he kept under his bed to Cooper—and "things will be handled so you can take over."

But I have other plans. The older I got, the more I lost, and the more

I saw, the more sure I was that the only way to break free was to burn it all to the ground. And that I was the only one who could do it.

So I smiled when he told me what I had to do and I nodded and I told him I'd do anything he asked. I lied—I had to.

I knew what would happen if I did it Duke's way. If I waited and did nothing until he died, and then just sprang it all on them.

Buck would turn on me the second he knew Duke was gone. He'd take all the product and all the cooks, and he'd spend the next few months, maybe years, pumping more poison into our county before he screwed up and got caught. Cooper would be on my side, but Cooper's old. He's tired.

Buck would kill him.

Buck will try to kill me. He won't succeed.

But Carl Springfield might.

Mo is the reason the Ruby is still a haven, but fear of my family helps keeps them safe. If Carl Springfield kills me, Mo and the Rubies would end up going down, fighting every step of the way. If Buck took over and I managed to live, all the power to protect them would be gone. Being a McKenna would mean nothing.

Being a McKenna had to keep meaning something.

To protect the Rubies, to protect myself, the McKenna family has to continue to rule North County. The only way we all survive is if I take Buck and Springfield both out, one after the other, before anyone knows what's happening.

The trailer in the woods. The warehouse. And the house on Shasta Street. All the blame on Springfield, Buck out of my way, and me slipping free of all of it.

My plan hinges on hitting each target before Duke's death forces my hand. Now it's in motion, and I can't turn back—not that I want to.

Sometimes I wonder what Duke would think if he knew what I've done. The steps I'm taking to destroy his empire and to protect the people who looked to me first and him second. I'm using everything he taught me, but I've turned the lesson upside down.

Would a part of him be proud?

Or, given the chance, would he just shoot me where I stand?

I'll never know. Soon he'll be dead, and I'll be alone.

I spend each night here, watching and waiting for him to stop breathing. It's fucked up, but it's the truth. I'm terrified it'll happen during the day, when I'm not here. When I'm out tearing down everything he built up.

But he holds on. He's stubborn, my father.

I tug the quilt higher on his chest, smoothing down the sheet. I push the sleep chair the hospice nurses were nice enough to find me close to the side of his bed and fold my hand into his.

Duke doesn't stir. His skin's dark and getting darker as his liver tries to work and can't, choked by the cancer. When I look at him now, a hollow-cheeked shell of a man wasting away in the hospital bed, I can't help but think back on the strong, stocky, robust father who could gallop up a steep hillside like a mountain goat and lift me high in the air, balanced on one hand. Of the man who taught me to shoot, hunt, punch, kill.

I lay my head on the edge of his bed, finally giving in to the exhaustion.

No one but Brooke knows I'm here. Busy is by the door. My knife's in my boot. My phone is off until tomorrow.

I'm as safe as I'll ever be.

I fall asleep to the beep and whir of the oxygen machine.

The next thing I know, a hand's on my shoulder, shaking me awake. I'm slumped over the bed, my head pillowed in my arms, my butt half out of the chair. My throat's so dry I can hardly swallow, there's a crick in my neck and dried spit on my cheek, and I jerk up, blinking a few times before Brooke's face comes into focus.

"You look awful," she says. "Jesus."

I stand up, still groggy, my head pounding, and stumble over to the mirror above the sink. My right eye is purple and my nose is swollen so badly it's hard to breathe.

"Here." She holds out a travel mug and four pills. "It's aspirin."

"What time is it?" I mumble, taking the coffee and pills. I down half of it in one gulp, soothed by the bitter heat. Brooke did a number on me; my face is aching all over.

"Almost six. How was the night shift?" Brooke pulls up the rolling chair on the other side of Duke's bed, setting her bag on the floor next to the oxygen machine.

"Okay, I think," I say. "Doesn't seem like he was in much pain at all."

I can barely make out the curve of Brooke's small smile in the early morning light seeping in through the blinds. "That's good."

"Yeah." I stretch slowly, muscles stiff. Busy snaps to attention, trotting over to me from her place next to the door. I fasten the leash onto her collar. "I've gotta go." My hand strokes Duke's shoulder compulsively, and it takes more effort than I'd like to pull away.

"The doctors want to talk to you this afternoon," Brooke reminds me. "Three o'clock."

"I know. I'll be back by then."

I tug on the leash, and I'm almost at the door when it gets the better of me. "Brooke," I turn around. "What do you do all day in here with him?"

"Mostly I play the music you left me," Brooke says. "I think he likes the Johnny Cash and Townes best. And I remembered you saying once that your momma loved Loretta Lynn, so I downloaded her greatest hits. I thought maybe if he heard it, it'd remind him of her."

I hold back a smile—I'm afraid if I move any part of my face, I'll break completely. I'll be across the room in a few steps, hugging the life out of her, and I can't handle that right now. Also, it'd hurt like a bitch.

"I've gotta go," I say again, hoping she knows all the things I'm not saying, all the thank-yous and the apologies I owe her. She hates him. She always will, with good reason. But she's doing this for me, and I'm so grateful for it, for her, that it chokes me.

"Remember, three o'clock."

"I'll be here." I look over at him. He's still breathing, still being stubborn, still hanging on.

You could never say Duke McKenna didn't go down fighting. Even if he's just fighting himself now.

Every time I leave I wonder if it's the last time I'll see him alive. If he'll finally give up and I'll be alone.

"I have to go," I say. But my feet won't move. I keep looking at his chest, rising and falling. It's a slow up and down, but it's there.

He's still here.

But I have to go.

"Harley, do you need to stay?" Brooke asks gently.

"No," I say. "No…I can't. I have a plan."

I force myself to walk out the door and down the hall, nearly plowing down the early-morning nurse. Busy barks, and I don't even stop to say sorry.

# TWENTY-THREE

I'm fifteen when I find the box of Momma's old dresses in the attic. I'm looking for Christmas decorations, and I discover it stuffed in a far corner, dusty and forgotten. I recognize her handwriting on the side, so I bring it down to my room.

When I tear off the tape and push up the cardboard flaps, I'm flooded with the smell of lilies. Unexpected, not forgotten, but *missed*, and it makes my fingers curl, my nails press into my palms.

I lift out the dresses, one by one: the mustard-yellow fringed one she used to wear with cowboy boots, the white cotton sundress with black buttons running down the front, the purple stretchy one with long sleeves that fell to her ankles, but probably would only reach my knees.

I'm much taller than her now. It's a startling thought, something that's never crossed my mind. I'm always looking up at her in my memories.

I touch the edges of the yellow dress, letting the fringe slip through my fingers.

I haven't worn a dress since Momma's funeral. Back then, Miss Lissa tried her hardest to get me out of my jeans and boots, but Daddy didn't give her much help.

Sometimes I wonder if Daddy would've liked it better if I'd been born a boy. If he'd treat me any different. Or if he'd be rougher, like sometimes I catch him being with Will.

Daddy handles me differently because I'm a girl. He'd never admit it, but as proud as he is, he underestimates me. Mo says he can't help it. That it's the way fathers are.

Sometimes I think it's just the way men are.

It used to annoy me. But then I realized it was a weakness.

And I've been taught to exploit weaknesses.

I tug off my shirt and jeans, slip the yellow dress over my head. The fabric settles against my legs, cool against my skin, the fringe dancing above my knees. I walk over to the mirror, staring at myself.

There's a long scrape running up my leg from where I bark-burned it climbing, bruises dot my shins, as usual...and for some reason that comforts me.

The girl looking back at me reminds me of Momma, but my marks make me *me*.

There's a light knock on my door. "Harley? You ready to—" Will opens the door before I can stop him. I whirl around, seconds away from diving behind the bed.

My hands fly up defensively to my chest instead, covering myself like I'm naked.

Will's face splits into a smile, and my stomach twists when I realize it's not mocking. It's all sharp fondness that is anything but brotherly, because he's never been my brother, and we both know that. It's more and more obvious as we get older. I worry that Daddy will notice the way we're becoming, *what* we're becoming, and that scares me...or maybe he has already, and is making plans...that might be even scarier.

Which is why most of the time, I pretend it's not what it is. I pretend I don't want to chase Will down, kiss him, do everything with him.

Daddy loves Will, but he loves me a lot more. And he's sliced fingers off men who looked at me the wrong way.

So if Daddy's making plans, I'm making them, too. I resist, and I plan, and I try not to think about what happens when I finally give in.

Love always makes you give in.

"Don't look at me like that!" I hiss.

Will shrugs, rubbing the back of his neck, still smiling. "How am I looking at you?"

"Like you've never seen a girl in a dress before."

"I've never seen *you* in a dress before," he points out.

I roll my eyes. "I need to change."

Will frowns. "Why? You look fine."

I'm too focused on him to notice the footsteps in the hall, and I hear Daddy's voice before I see him: "You two are gonna be late."

"We were just going," Will calls out. "Come on, Harley."

"What are you wearing?" Daddy looms over Will's shoulder, and then he's pushing him out of the way and striding into my bedroom.

"She looks pretty, doesn't she?" Will asks, and I wonder if the last time he fell out of a tree he hit his head too hard, because Daddy's face is anything but pleased.

I back away from him.

"Will, go wait in the truck," Daddy says.

Will doesn't move.

Daddy shoots him a look over his shoulder that would make most men run, but Will meets his gaze steadily for a moment before very deliberately looking at me.

I nod, barely, and Daddy's nostrils flare as Will nods back and only then leaves the room. Even though I can hear his footsteps, I know he won't go downstairs. He'll position himself somewhere in the hall, where Daddy can't see him, but close enough to hear me call out.

Will's loyalty has always been to me, not him.

"Where did you get these?" Daddy demands.

"They were in a box in the attic." I hate how small my voice sounds, how small I feel. The fabric that had moved free and loose against my skin feels hot and scratchy now.

Daddy grabs the two other dresses on my bed, his fingers bunching up the material like he wants to rip it apart.

"Don't!" I reach for them, and he jerks backward. "Give me those!"

"You don't need things like this," Daddy says. "Take that one off. Give it to me."

"They're Momma's. They should be mine."

Daddy's bushy eyebrows draw together in a pained line. "Harley Jean..." he sighs.

I wilt beneath his broken gentleness. His voice is like it was the first nights after she died, when he wouldn't meet my eyes in daylight but would come into my room, reeking of whiskey, when he thought I was asleep and stroke my hair. Then he'd whisper drunken apologies, to me, to Momma, that he didn't think I could hear.

I'm almost as old as she was when he met her. In her clothes, with my hair long and loose instead of braided like usual, the resemblance must be disturbing. Enough people tell me I look like her.

He misses her. I can see it in his face. In the way he can't quite look at me.

I think I understand. Or I'm on the edge of understanding, with Will.

McKennas love hard and fast and only once.

"I'll take it off," I say, because I know what happens when he gets sad about Momma. He starts drinking and starts muttering about Springfield and then someone ends up dead, and it's never the right person. "I won't wear them. But, please, let me keep them."

Daddy looks down at the dresses in his hands and drops them hastily on the bed, rubbing a hand over his beard. "Harley-girl," he starts. "I'm sor—"

"It's fine," I interrupt. I grab the dresses off the bed before he changes his mind, along with my discarded jeans and T-shirt, and hurry into the bathroom.

I stay in there a long time, pressing the dresses against my face, breathing in the lilies, staring in the mirror, looking for traces of her.

When I finally get the nerve to go back to my room, changed into my jeans, Daddy's long gone.

# TWENTY-FOUR

*June 7, 7:15 a.m.*

I pull over at a gas station halfway home to fill up my tank, feed Busy, and grab another cup of coffee. I've long since finished off the one Brooke brought.

I linger at the coffee area inside the empty mini-mart, my cup filling slowly. The lights flicker, and the Christian music station wails praises in His name, heavy-metal style.

The painkillers Brooke gave me are working a little. Even though I look it, I don't feel too busted up. I keep running my tongue over my teeth. I need to brush them. I need a shower. I need to stash the drugs somewhere safe. I need to sleep for about a month.

I need Duke not to be dying.

Hot liquid bubbles over my fingers, and I hiss, snatching them away from the cup. I dump out some of the coffee, snap the lid on it, and take a long sip.

Sleep isn't on the agenda today. Caffeine is.

I pay for my gas, coffee, and the cinnamon roll I grab at the last minute. The sun's rising high as I navigate the curves that hug the mountains. Sometimes I think I could drive this road in my sleep.

Right now, I'm close to it. I take another gulp of coffee as I weave the truck back and forth along the twisty road.

Red and blue lights flash behind me. I swear, spilling coffee on my

134

jeans, and squint as the car behind me flashes its brights and sounds the siren.

Fuck.

It's never a good idea to get pulled over. Especially when you have a shitload of meth stashed in your truck's toolbox.

It's not Highway Patrol—that'd make my life easy. I slow to a crawl and drive a quarter of a mile with my turn signal on until I come across a shoulder wide enough to pull over. My heart beating faster, I get my license and registration out of the glove compartment and roll the window down, then put my hands back firmly on the wheel, in plain sight. The early morning air floods into the truck, carrying with it the damp piney smell that rises in waves off the trees this time of year.

I look in my mirror, groaning when I see the deputy getting out of the car. "You be chill," I tell Busy, who's growling low in her throat at the flashing lights. I feel like growling, too. Snapping my teeth, punching the accelerator, melting into the forest.

I stay still. Calm.

I'm wearing sunglasses, which covers most of the black eye, but my nose is unmistakably swollen. I push my hair into my face, trying to mask it.

Deputy Daniels strolls up to the driver's side and leans against my window. Her blond ponytail is deceptively bouncy—the woman's tougher than a pack of wild pigs. Her khaki uniform is wrinkled— she's coming off shift, probably. They always give her the shit ones— graveyards no one else wants.

Frankie Daniels has been on my ass since I was sixteen. Always pulling me over, messing with me, trying to get me to talk. It's never worked. But she keeps trying.

She'd known my momma—back in Momma's good-girl days, before she went wild. Frankie's the sentimental type. She's still attached to this idea of the girl she knew instead of the woman Momma grew into. Maybe she mourns both of them, or just the possibility of Momma's life before Duke came around.

"Harley," she says. "What a surprise, finding you here."

"Huge surprise, considering I live off this road. Wanna tell me why you pulled me over, deputy?"

She frowns. "What's wrong with your face?"

I sigh, taking off the sunglasses slowly and pushing my hair off my cheeks.

Frankie's eyes go steely and all business. "Who did that?"

"Kickboxing class," I say. "You know how I like to keep fit. Why did you pull me over?"

I've thrown her, and she doesn't like it.

"There was a fire yesterday afternoon," she says. "Out in Viola. Looks like a lab blew. You wouldn't know anything about that, would you?"

"Great to know you and the sheriff's boys are so on top of the meth problem you're pulling over random people for questioning," I say.

"You and I both know who's on top of the meth problem," Deputy Daniels says through her teeth.

I don't say anything. Duke has most of the sheriff's department and five different town councils in his pocket, but you can't buy a woman like Frankie Daniels. Which is why she's still doing the scut work, even though she's the smartest person in that group of easily bought morons down at the station.

"Someone called it in to Fire Watch. A young woman, the operator said."

I stare straight ahead, my hands still placed unthreateningly on the wheel. I smile blandly. "That's nice."

Daniels drums her fingers on the roof of my S10, *tap tap tap*. "You wanna tell me where I can find your father?"

"He's away."

"Right," Daniels says, her sharp blue eyes flashing at me. "And the fact that you're beat up all to hell has nothing to do with that fire."

I raise my eyebrows. "I don't see how my accident in kickboxing class and some fire have anything to do with each other."

Frankie's fingers grip the edge of my window, flexing in frustration. "I made a promise, Harley," she begins.

I've heard this all before. How she wants to help. How she wants to whisk me away from the life I lead.

She's been trying to work me since I was a teenager. It's never stuck, and it never will. It's not just that her meddling would get her killed; it's that I don't need saving. I am who I am. I'm what Duke made me. There's no running from it. There's only facing it.

"My momma's been dead for a long time," I tell her. "I don't think she's gonna be rolling over in her grave 'cause of any old promise you might break."

"She wanted me to look out for you," Frankie says, going for the gut. She ought to know by now it won't work.

"She wanted a lot of things," I say. "I don't think she wanted to get blown up, but she was. If I can get the hell over that, you should, too."

I'm so worn out, she's rattled me; I barely manage to keep my voice from shaking. But I force myself to meet her gaze, staring her down, because I have to. It's the only thing I know how to do.

Frankie looks away first, shaking her head like she still can't believe I'm such a hard-ass.

I don't know why she's always so damn hopeful.

"Drive slower, Harley," she says quietly. "And you know you can call me anytime."

"Right. Thanks."

Daniels sighs and turns back to her patrol car, muttering under her breath. She'll probably end up out at my momma's headstone tomorrow, genuflecting and apologizing to an empty grave.

My fingers clench the steering wheel tight as Daniels turns her patrol car around and drives back toward town. I turn the key in the ignition and pull back onto the highway. There's a wet patch on my jeans where I spilled my coffee that's gone cold and uncomfortable, and I shift in my seat, starting the engine.

I speed, mostly to disobey Daniels. But when I get near home, I don't drive all the way to the front gate. Cooper might be waiting for me outside—or worse, Buck. I'm not ready yet. I have to get the drugs out of my truck.

Instead, I take the third dirt road before our main one. A road that's hidden high up on the mountain. After a half mile and a few hard turns, it fades into a rough-cut path through the pines and oaks—not really even a road, steep and tricky with winter rockslides and fallen branches, but I shift the Chevy into four-wheel, and I manage.

I need to drop off the drugs here before I go to the Tropics to show off my black eye and tell the sad tale of my attack. That's when the frenzy will set in. Buck's first instinct will be to go balls out: arm as many people as he can and jump in, guns blazing. He'll probably have hit the warehouse by now, which meant he had the useless guns on him. He'll take them to his place for safekeeping, because he's a paranoid bastard who doesn't trust anyone. Which is exactly what I want.

I reach the clearing, driving up to the back entrance through a large field that my great-granddaddy used for cattle, and the tight, hard knot inside my stomach begins to unravel.

When I kill the engine, open the door, and my boots hit gravel, relief swamps me. I made it. I'm home.

For the first time in days, the moment I turn the key, I take a deep breath. Busy trots ahead of me, heading toward her water bowl. I fill it with some fresh water and toss the bag of meth on the kitchen counter.

Dried blood flakes off my face as I rub my cheek. I walk over to the big mirror in the hallway, wincing when I get a good look. My nose looks a lot worse than it feels, thankfully. But my eye is still throbbing like a bitch. I head upstairs to shower.

Generations of McKennas line the wall along the stairs, from my mutton-chopped great-great-great-great-granddaddy Franklin, who settled the land after conning some miners out of it like the crooked asshole he was, to Momma and Duke on their wedding day. At the landing is a timeline of pictures of Will and me, gangly kids growing inch by inch, the awkwardness fading from our faces. The last picture is from the day he left for college, his arm around my shoulders, our smiles fake and wide, hiding the hurt. There's dust gathering on the top of the frames, but I'm too tired to beat myself up for not keeping house.

I've been busy.

I toe my boots off at my bedroom door and strip off my clothes, leaving them in a heap on the floor, and head into the bathroom, where I turn on the shower faucet. The water's hot and perfect, and I stand under the spray for a long time, letting it beat down on my sensitive cheek. The pinpricks of pain spread down my face, and I picture them swirling down the drain with the pinkish water, but no such luck.

Busy's still downstairs when I get out and dry myself off. As I walk back into my room to pull on a clean pair of cutoffs and a tank top, my wet hair drips down my back. I'm just about to twist it up when I hear a thump downstairs.

I freeze, and my heartbeat thunders in my ears.

Busy's not barking—that's my first thought.

I need my gun—that's my second.

There's a .22 under my bed and a .45 in the bedside table. I grab the .45.

Busy should be barking. She should be attacking. I should be hearing screams of pain. Growling. Whining. *Something.*

But there's nothing but silence.

My fingers curl tight around my gun. I pad across the bedroom in bare feet, curving my body around and out the door. Rounding the corners, I lead with the .45, keeping my back tight to the wall, just like Duke taught me. Every step is steady and silent, but my heartbeat's anything but. As I clear the rooms on the second floor methodically, it hammers in my ears so loud I'm afraid I'll miss something—the squeak of a floorboard behind me, the snick of a door shutting. With each breath, each step, my mind's racing, panic rising. *How'd they get in? Is it Buck? Where's Busy? If they hurt my dog, I'll slit their throats. Then I'll have to deal with a body dump. Where the hell am I going to get enough lye this early in the morning?*

Shit. Shit. Shit.

I might have to kill them no matter what. Anyone who trespasses on McKenna land is out of their mind. Or here to kill me.

Possibly both.

*When they invade your turf, shoot first, ask questions later, Harley-girl.*

I step down the stairs with my back to the wall, my shoulders brushing against the photos, making them rattle against the plaster. I have to bite down my urge to call for Busy as I reach the bottom.

The light's on in the kitchen. My .45 raised and ready, I step forward into the line of sight.

And then I see why Busy's not barking.

Will is standing there, the bag of meth I jacked from the trailer sitting open on the kitchen island in front of him. His gaze rises to meet mine. His arms are crossed, and every line of his body tenses—but not because I've got a gun pointed at him. No, he's *furious*. It radiates off him in ripples, like air wiggling in a heat wave.

My stomach sinks as I lower the gun and thumb the safety back on. I walk into the kitchen, placing it on the island next to the drugs. Busy's sitting next to Will, gazing up him adoringly like the traitor she is.

He's the one person she's no use against.

"So," Will says, gesturing at the bag. "Want to tell me again how nothing's going on?"

# TWENTY-FIVE

I'm almost eleven years old when I wake up inside a car trunk.

At first, I don't know what the hell is going on. I remember being in my bed. And then...nothing. When I open my eyes, it's all darkness tinted red, the tang of gas strong in the stuffy air.

The car's moving. I've been taken.

I keep my eyes closed, because if they're closed, I can pretend that's why it's dark. I can pretend I'm not locked in here. I tuck my knees into my chest and wrap my arms around them tight, curling myself into a ball.

I'm not here. I'm not here. I'm somewhere light. Somewhere it never gets dark. I'm just gonna wait this out.

I suck in a mouthful of musty air that smells of gasoline and rubber. Breathe in, breathe out. But no matter how hard I try, I can't pretend any longer. I can smell the exhaust, feel the spare tire underneath the lumpy carpeting, rubbing against my belly.

It's so dark.

I concentrate again on my breath huffing in and out.

Suddenly, the driver guns the engine. I don't have time to grab hold of anything—my body's tossed to the side, slamming hard into the back of the trunk as the car gains speed. I'm rocked back and forth. All I can do is clamp my arms over my head, trying to protect it as I try to jam my legs up against something, anything for leverage.

Warmth trickles down my face, and I don't know if it's sweat or tears or blood until it leaks into my mouth.

Blood.

The taste of it centers me. Clears the fog and loosens the tight feeling in my chest.

I've been taken. I don't know who did it. I have to concentrate.

*What do you do, Harley-girl? What do you do when someone takes you from me?*

Be calm. Find a weapon. Run at the first chance. Kill if you have to. And never, ever stop trying to get free.

I have to get out.

The brake light. I need to smash it.

I take a quick breath in and slam my palms up, scrambling for a hold. My fingers scrape smooth metal, catching on a loop of wiring that leads to the locking mechanism. I grip it like it's my lifeline, swinging my legs down so they're braced against the bottom of the trunk where the bumper must be.

I need to get to the brake light.

The next second, the car chassis scrapes against the blacktop and the back end flies up—we hit a big bump. I grit my teeth and hang on, my legs smacking hard against the side of the trunk as the driver takes a sharp right.

More blood trickles down my cheek. I tilt my head, wiping it away with my shoulder as I squinch down onto my hands and knees and angle my foot down, stretching it toward the brake light. My feet are bare, but it doesn't matter.

*You do anything it takes to get back to me, Harley-girl. Anything.*

I smash my heel against the plastic, hard, ignoring the pain that shoots up my foot. Sweat or maybe it's blood gathers at the small of my back and my thighs tremble from the effort. I kick and kick and kick again, ignoring the pain, ignoring the blood.

I have to get out.

I finally burst through, the cracked plastic slicing my ankle, but I can feel cool air against the torn sole of my foot.

Okay. Okay. Now I just need to get my hand through and pray someone will see. I pull my foot free, whimpering as it scrapes against the broken plastic and glass. Blood trickles down my toes, drying in the spaces between.

I wiggle toward the busted brake light, and poke my hand into the space I broke through. I wave frantically, just like Daddy taught me to.

The car comes to a sudden, shuddering halt, and all the panic I've managed to push down rises up inside me.

*Run. Find a weapon. Aim for the crotch or the head. Kill if you have to, Harley-girl.*

The trunk pops, and sunlight bores into my eyes. I blink, tearing up, trying to make out the blurry person in front of me.

I need to come out fighting. I need to do anything I have to so I can get away.

But then my eyes clear. It isn't Carl Springfield in front of me. And it isn't some strung-out tweaker.

It's Daddy.

For a second, my mind just does this loop-de-loop. Like I'm on a roller coaster and my stomach hasn't quite caught up with the rest of me. And then I realize: This is a test.

Another lesson for me to learn. Just teaching me theory isn't enough.

No, Daddy has to know his lessons are sticking.

"Under twenty minutes," he says, nodding. "Not bad."

Then he reaches down, not to grab me, but to flip up the carpeting covering the spare tire. He pulls out a tire iron and places it in my hands.

"Next time, think before you panic," he orders. His mouth is a determined line, but there's something lurking in his face, hiding beneath the beard, maybe, that looks like regret. "You could've gotten free a lot sooner if you'd thought for a second and used the tire iron. Then when they come for you, you'll be ready for them—you'll be armed. You've got to stay cool and be smart. You can't panic, Harley. Panicking will get you killed."

I lick my lips. They're raw—I must have chewed them bloody without knowing it. I want to scream at him. I want to swing the tire iron and smash his face in with it.

I want him to hug me and promise me he'll never do this again.

But Daddy never makes promises he can't keep.

"Do you understand?" he asks me, when I don't say anything.

I look up, and it's the closest I've ever come to hating him. But there's nothing I can do, nothing I can say. His crooked world is my school, and it's been that way forever...will be that way forever.

I am my daddy's girl, and I do not flinch. Not even in front of him.

But it takes me two tries to say, "Yes, sir," in a hoarse voice.

Daddy grabs me beneath the arms, heaving me out of the trunk and setting me on my feet. We're still on the property, but now we're a long way from the house, near the western part that sinks into nothing but forest for acres. My head's spinning, and so's my stomach. I want to puke, but I breathe hard through my nose, a long, shuddering gasp, and hold it in.

"Are we done?" I ask Daddy, clenching my teeth. I won't throw up. I won't.

"We'll go back to the house," Daddy says. "Clean you up. Your head—" He reaches forward, and I finally flinch.

"Sweetheart," Daddy sighs. "I know this is hard—"

"Are we done?" I ask again.

We're at a standstill for a long moment, when all I can feel is the blood trickling down my face, and something else, something deep inside me that hurts more than my foot or lips ever could.

Then he looks down. "We're done...for today."

I nod, just once, my chin jutting out. And I turn and walk away, ignoring him when he calls out for me. The world starts spinning beneath my feet, my arms feel wobbly and my legs tremble, but I stagger forward, aiming for the splash of dark green ahead of me.

I barely make into the forest before I collapse onto my knees, vomiting helplessly into a fern bed.

Eventually, seeking solitude like a wounded animal, I get up and stumble deeper into the woods until I end up in one of my favorite spots, the ruins of the stone house, the one that my great-times-a-bunch-grand-daddy built. Only two walls and the river-rock chimney still stand, overgrown with manzanita and blackberry bushes. I'm sitting with my back up against what's left of the chimney, fiddling with a loop of barbed wire I've picked up along the way, when Will finds me.

He doesn't say anything, just drops down next to me onto the ground, his legs stretched out in front of him. I know there's blood on my face, so I don't look up, but after a few minutes of silence he holds out the paper bag he brought.

I scoot until I'm sitting cross-legged in front of him. Will sets the bag down between us, grabbing a washcloth and bottle of water from it. He wipes my cheek, dabbing gently at my temple where the gash is.

Will's good at patching me up. I suck at doing the same for him, but I'm teaching him how to climb trees right to make up for the last time, when I accidentally elbowed him in his fresh black eye when I tried to clean it. He'd been really nice about that. He's really nice about everything. Sometimes I wish I was, too, but I don't think I'm built that way.

I don't think Daddy built me like that.

"You hurt anywhere else?" Will asks, pressing a bandage onto my cheek with his thumb. His eyes scan up and down me, checking.

I start to shake my head, but stop halfway into it, closing my eyes, because my brain feels swollen and sore inside my skull. I can't help it and it shames me, but I can feel a tear sliding down my cheek. I raise my fist and wipe it away furiously.

Will shoves the box of Band-Aids back into the bag a little too hard. It rips, the contents of his makeshift first-aid kit scattering onto the forest floor.

"He shouldn't have done that," he says quietly, like he's expecting Daddy to be looming, listening. Ready to teach me another lesson.

I shrug, unable to meet his steady gaze. But I can feel the sobs rising in my throat. So I swallow them down and go back to fiddling with the barbed wire again, twirling it back and forth between my fingers.

"Hey," Will says, and I finally look up. He tries to smile at me, but it doesn't reach his eyes. "It's okay. You got through it. Maybe he won't make you do it again."

We both know he's lying through his teeth. If Daddy doesn't do this again, he'll do something worse.

"You can get through anything," Will says.

"You don't know that," I say, because the years have taught me that sometimes people don't. Sometimes houses blow up. Sometimes mommas die. Sometimes daddies are something that shouldn't live in the same skin as the man who tucks you in at night.

"I believe it." Will tugs at the wire in my hands. "Look," he says, running his finger down the barb. "You gotta be like barbed wire. Tough no matter what, ready to tangle with anyone who gets too close. If you stay like that, you'll be too strong for anyone to hurt you. Not inside. Not where it counts."

He grabs my hand and loops the wire around my wrist. Digging in his pocket, he comes up with his hunting knife and uses it to twist the ends together to form a bracelet. Then he presses the flat of the blade against the barbs, bending them inward so they can't scrape me. When he's done, he looks up and smiles, this time for real.

"So you don't forget," he tells me.

I smile back. My stomach's tight, there's the taste of blood in my mouth, and barbed wire wrapped around my wrist, like a gauntlet, a badge of honor, a tie that binds him and me.

I'm too young for this feeling and too old and too scared and a little happy, and it's years till I realize this is where I start turning away from Daddy and toward Will instead.

# TWENTY-SIX

*June 7, 9:55 a.m.*

For a long moment, Will and I just stare at each other from across the kitchen island. I want to say something—anything—but I don't know where to start.

"What the fuck happened to your face?" he demands, and then he moves forward. He's touching me, light and careful, always so careful. I want to lean into it, but I force myself to stay still. "Jesus," he says. "Who did this?"

"You wouldn't believe me if I told you," I answer, pulling away. I back up and put the kitchen island between us, like that'll help me. I should know better.

When it comes to him, I do know better.

Will glares at me. "You need to start explaining. Now. Because the last time I checked, you never handled the product. You gonna tell me Duke changed his mind about you cooking? Or have you developed a habit the size of Texas?"

"If you're gonna be nasty—"

"Then tell me what's going on!" Will demands. It takes a lot to get him this angry, but I reckon he has reason, so I hear him out. "What the fuck, Harley? Where's Duke? Don't tell me he's away in Mexico like you've been saying around town. I talked with Mo. She hasn't seen him for months. His guns are still in their hiding places downstairs. I checked. No way in hell he goes any distance unarmed—"

147

"He bought some new guns—"

*"Harley!"* He cuts me off with my name.

I flinch, too worn down to hide it. Busy's ears perk up; she rises and moves to my side, nosing at my hand.

A flush rises on the dark curve of Will's cheekbones. "You're lying," he says. "Stop it."

I shrug.

"Please, just tell me what's going on," he begs, quieter.

He steps forward, and when I don't step back, he comes even closer.

"Brooke's worried about you," he says.

"Brooke worries too much."

"I didn't start worrying until I saw what you've set up in the attic."

He's found my perch. Fuck. Heat crawls inside my chest, an anger and embarrassment that's hard to define. It's almost unbearably intimate that he's been up there, that he's walked around my nest of blankets and pillows. That he's seen what I've been doing. How I've been living when I'm not in Burney.

"You've got a sniper rifle trained on the driveway." Will takes another step forward, slow and steady so I don't run. "With enough ammo to take down a small army. From the looks of it, you've been sleeping up there. Makes sense: easily defensible space, hard to reach, single entry point, only one window."

He ticks off the attributes dispassionately, because that's the way Daddy taught us to be. *Analyze the situation. Protect your back. Never let go of your gun. And if you draw it, you best be ready to kill, Harley-girl.*

I lock my knees as he takes the final step forward. Now we're closer to each other than we've been in more than a year, and it's playing tricks on my resolve.

"Something is very wrong. This is overboard, even for you. So let me help. Tell me what's going on."

I stare up into his face. He is my first, only, forever love. I can't shake him even when I try my hardest. And I want. It swells inside me. I want so badly to tell him, and right now, with him so close, so pleading and willing, that I betray my name. I crumble.

Duke would be ashamed.

"Duke's sick," I blurt out.

Will's eyebrows snap together. "Sick," he repeats. "How sick?"

"He has pancreatic cancer. Stage four. They diagnosed him five months ago. He won't let me tell anyone." My heart pounds just thinking about the betrayal in my words, and the truth in them.

It's like watching a war go on in Will's face—his eyes sharpen and glint, but then he clears his throat and presses his lips together, keeping it in.

"Where is he?" he asks, his voice tight and strangled.

"He's in Burney...in hospice care. He's—he's—" I shake my head. I can't say it. I can't think it. I promised myself.

"Oh, Jesus, Harley," he breathes. He wraps me up in his arms, and I grab his shoulders and hold on. His hands are warm and strong around me, and I want to sink into him, let him soothe away everything else. It feels right, like he fits with me and doesn't belong anywhere else.

But he doesn't belong with me or to me. He belongs back in college, where he won't get shot or arrested or end up dead in the woods where no one'll ever find him. There's no place for me in his new life, and the sooner he gets back to it, the safer he'll be.

I pull away, cross my arms, and grit my teeth.

"You didn't have to come all this way. It's not your job to worry about me. No matter what Brooke said, I'll be fine."

"Bullshit," Will says. "You're telling me Duke's *dying*, and you're fine? Are you kidding me?"

"It's my problem, Will. My family. Not yours."

"*You're* my family," he says.

It's like getting punched in the gut, those three words. They mean so much more than just love or blood. It's the two of us and how we grew up and why: bonded together by circumstance, until it didn't matter how we came together, only that we did.

"What are you up to?" He bends down so he's looking down right into my face, like the answer's blinking on my forehead.

I make sure my face is as blank as it gets when I mumble, "Don't know what you're talking about."

"You're not running," he explains patiently. "You know the second the cooks find out Duke's dying, Buck'll take over. Cooper's too old and tired of the game to stop him. When the Springfields find out, it's gonna be a bloodbath. They will kill you. It'll be at the top of his list to snuff you out. But you're not running."

"I'm not running," I confirm, holding his gaze.

He cocks his head and narrows his eyes, staring through me so hard I want to run. When we were kids, he'd get like this when I didn't want to talk about one of Duke's lessons. He'd stare until I wore down and spilled it in halting bursts.

It always made me feel better, after.

"The fire out in Viola yesterday," Will says slowly. "That was a hit on a lab, wasn't it?"

I don't say anything, but he knows; oh, he knows.

"You hit a lab," he says slowly, his eyes drilling into mine. "You hit one of Duke's labs." He's saying it like it's fact, but the way he's looking at me is all searching, like he hopes he's wrong.

But he knows me better than that.

"That's where you got all the drugs," Will goes on. "You—did you kill anyone?" he whispers, and I want to grab his arm, pull him close, because his voice cracks on *kill*.

I shake my head. "I was careful."

"You *did* do it," Will breathes. His eyes widen and his hands clench at his sides. "Holy fuck, Harley! What were you thinking? There's no *careful* in blowing a lab. You of all people know that."

My palms itch, my body instinctively aligning for a fight. "Don't you dare bring them into this."

"Do you really think your mom would want you doing this shit?" Will demands.

I may love him with whatever's good left in me, but he's on dangerous ground. One more word, and I'll snap.

"Momma would've wanted me to survive," I say, with ice in my voice. "And that's what I plan on doing."

"If survival was on your mind, you would've run the second Duke got sick," Will says. "You wouldn't be blowing up his meth labs. You wouldn't have an Army-issue sniper rifle locked and loaded in your attic. You wouldn't be all beat up by whoever did that to you. You'd be in Mexico, where no one can touch you."

"I'm a McKenna," I say. "We don't run."

"Bullshit," he snaps. "This is more than that. This is about *him*."

Almost fifteen years have passed, and Will hates saying his name.

"Fine," I say. "It's about him. Is that what you want to hear?"

"Revenge isn't gonna bring her back."

I look at him, and I can't stop the disgust from curling my lips. Who the fuck does he take me for?

"I'm not some little girl on the deck waiting to be saved anymore," I hiss at him. "I'm a grown-ass woman and I am taking care of business. *My* business."

"I know that—" he begins.

"You obviously don't," I say. "There is no fucking way I'm letting Carl Springfield drive me from the only home I've ever known just because he had a hard-on for Momma and Duke got her. I'm not running because of him. I have the Rubies to think of. And I can't let Buck take over the trade—he'll start selling to kids and pregnant women before Duke's cold in his grave.

"Duke's a rotten man, Will. We both know what he's done. But he never sells to kids or knocked-up tweekers. He has my back when it comes to the Rubies. His honor's shot to hell, but at least he's got some kind of a code. Buck's got nothing, and you know it."

I look in his eyes, searching for a flicker of understanding, but he's staring me down, resolute.

"So, yes, I blew the lab. I have a plan. I'm done with all of this. I'm sick of truces and territory lines and bodies in the woods. Grown men running around, playing at war. Well, I'm putting an end to their fucking war."

Will steps forward and then back. He can't decide what to do. For once, I've thrown him, and his hands clench and his jaw twitches as he tries to figure out a way to talk me out of this.

But he knows it's a losing battle.

*I'm* a losing battle.

"They'll come for you," he says quietly. "The second they find out."

"Good," I say, and I mean it more than anything I've ever said in my life, feel it with a surety that walks hand in hand with the snake-handling, crazed kind of faith. "I'm ready for them."

*Part Two*

# THE WAREHOUSE

# TWENTY-SEVEN

I'm nine years old when Uncle Jake tries to take me from Daddy.

Jake's smart about it, because by then, Daddy's got me trained. He's got me scared and already on the path to dangerous, his lessons drilled into body and mind. The moment I walk into a room, I look for the escape routes. I can load a rifle in the pitch dark. I can shoot any gun I'm strong enough to lift. I can throw a knife and hit a bull's-eye at twenty feet.

Uncle Jake waits. He lets Daddy grow distracted, obsessed with getting Carl Springfield. And when the moment's right, Jake makes his move.

Daddy and Cooper have been gone on business for almost a week. Miss Lissa's busy that day, because Will got into a fight at school. I'm bored and trapped at home, going stir crazy, and it's been like that for over a year, so when Jake suggests we take a drive, I leap at the opportunity.

The only time I'm ever let off the property is with him or Daddy, so I don't think much of it at first. He tells me we're going to the feed store. But then we don't take the right exit off the highway—we just keep going, heading south. The alarm bells that Daddy's worked so hard to hardwire into my head start to ring.

"Where are we going?"

"I've got an errand to run," Jake says.

He's never been a good liar, and I've been taught to spot even good lies. But I want to believe him. I tell myself to, because if I don't...

As we drive down the highway, I start to sweat. Uncle Jake doesn't say anything, but he lets me play with the radio. I switch back and forth between the oldies and the country station, my nervousness showing, filling up the cab of the truck like smoke.

I look out the window, turning in my seat to look behind me. That's when I see the suitcases in the bed of the truck.

My stomach twists and turns like the road cut through the mountains.

We pass Salt Creek, heading over the lake and down toward Shasta County, and I know what's going on now, but I don't want to voice it. If I say it, if I ask him, if he confirms it, then it's real.

Then I have to run.

*If anyone tries to take you away from me, Harley-girl, you run. Never stop trying to run.*

My mind's blank with panic, because it's Uncle Jake. He loves me. He wouldn't...

He would. Of course he would. I see how he looks at Daddy when he thinks I'm not paying attention. I see how Daddy looks at him.

They don't like each other. Uncle Jake's legit. That's what Daddy says, and when he does, his lip curls.

McKennas aren't legit.

We're criminals. I know this. I understand it better than Daddy thinks.

Uncle Jake sticks around; he skates the line between good and bad...only because of me. He loves me. And Daddy tolerates it, to a degree. He allows it in a way he wouldn't with anyone else because of Momma.

Uncle Jake and Daddy have two things in common: They love her and they want what's best for me.

Problem is, they have very different ideas of what that means.

I let it go for another hour. I stay quiet and I pretend I haven't noticed. But once we've passed Red Bluff and the shadows lengthen, I start to worry he's heading to Sacramento. That he's going to put me on a plane.

"This is a bad idea," I say. I croak it out, my throat dry with anxiety, with fear, with a shred of hope that I try to ignore, because it's not right. It's not.

I belong to Daddy.

*You run, Harley-girl. Never stop trying to run.*

Jake's fingers tighten around the steering wheel. He pushes harder on the gas pedal, and the truck speeds up. "What is, baby?"

Irritation prickles through me. I'm not a baby. He treats me like one.

Daddy doesn't. He puts guns in my hands and steel-toed boots on my feet and tells me that one day, I'll have to use both.

"I'm not stupid. I know what you're doing."

He glances over at me, his face showing the guilt. He knows it's wrong.

He knows it's dangerous.

"Harley," he says, and then he presses his lips together, shaking his head. "I'm getting you out of there."

I can't stop my eyes from skittering over to the door. My mind's already twisting through it: a way out. The door's unlocked, but the truck's moving too fast. If I tried to roll out, I'd go splat.

I could just be patient and wait. Daddy will find me.

But it might take him a while. And the longer it takes, the madder he'll be.

My heart thuds in my ears. He wouldn't kill Uncle Jake.

Would he?

Maybe not when Momma was alive. But now...

It's a new world. A new Daddy. He left the cloud of whiskey and grief behind for the hot spur of the hunt. Seeking out Springfield, destroying Springfield's business, killing Springfield's men—it's filled him up and buried his mourning of Momma deep.

I lick my dry lips, trying to think.

I need a phone. If I call Daddy and keep him from getting too mad, he might let Uncle Jake live.

I need information, so that means I have to play along. "Where are we going?"

It's the only way to save him.

"Far away," Uncle Jake says vaguely, his eyes on the highway ahead.

"Yeah, but where? What's the plan?"

Does he even have one?

"You don't have to worry, honey," he says. "You're never going to have to worry again," he adds under his breath, like he needs the reminder to believe it.

But deep down, he has to know it's a lie.

"Everything's going to be okay," he says, and he smiles like he isn't putting his life on the line.

I go quiet, because bugging him isn't gonna work. I look out the window, at the acres of crops—sunflowers and corn—that blur as we speed by. The sun will go down soon.

I'll wait him out. He has to stop eventually—even if it's just for gas. And then I'll make my move.

The first time he pulls off the highway, he won't even let me out of the truck cab. He pays for his gas at the pump and jumps right back into the driver's seat, his head down and his baseball cap pulled down firmly over his eyes. We drive on.

We're about two hours north of Los Angeles when he finally stops for the night. It's past two a.m., and I'm nodding off, my head bumping against the window.

"C'mon, honey," he says, pulling me gently from the cab and leading me into a motel room. It's got these big pictures of flowers all over the walls and flowers on the blankets and hell, even flowers on the carpet. I crawl into one of the beds and pull the blankets over myself, my eyes drifting shut.

I keep them shut until I hear his gentle snoring. Then I can't help but look over at him and think *Stupid*. Because Daddy would never have stopped. Daddy would never have fallen asleep. And neither would I.

I swipe his car keys and the motel key and slip out of the room. The parking lot's quiet; everyone's asleep but me. His cell phone's in the glove compartment, and I turn it on, watching as the screen fills with missed call alerts from Miss Lissa and Daddy.

My finger hovers over Daddy's name. I need to call. But I don't know what to say to keep him from killing Jake.

I'm supposed to run. I'm supposed to call him. *You run, Harley-girl. Never stop trying to run.*

I take a deep breath and press my finger down, bringing the phone to my ear. Two rings, and then he picks up: "Where the fuck have you taken my daughter?" he yells into the phone, and my shoulders hunch, my stomach freezes at the snarl in his voice.

"It's me."

*"Harley,"* he breathes, like a prayer, like I'm the best thing he's ever heard. "Where are you?"

"At a motel in Lost Hills."

"Are you okay?" he asks.

"I'm fine."

"I'm coming to get you," he says. "You stay right where you are."

I look over to the motel room. The window is still dark, but Jake will wake up before Daddy gets here.

Jake will have me in Mexico before Daddy gets here.

"That's gonna be hard," I say.

"Harley, you find somewhere to hide," Daddy orders. "Somewhere Jake can't find you. You take the phone and you stay there until I come for you."

I shake my head. I bite my lips as I think, the chapped skin breaking under the pressure.

"I don't want you to kill him," I say.

"You don't—" Daddy chokes on his anger. I can almost hear his fists clenching. "Harley Jean McKenna," he says, his voice low and menacing. It sends chills down my spine. I look over my shoulder, even though I know we're hundreds of miles apart. "You will hide. *Now.*"

Momma wouldn't let him touch Jake. She would understand where Jake was coming from.

But Daddy can't. Because when a person takes someone he loves, he only knows how to hurt and kill.

And I am the only person left that Daddy loves.

"When you get here, I can make sure I'm still in Lost Hills," I say. "But I'm not gonna tell you exactly where I am until you promise me you won't kill him."

"He took you from me!" Daddy thunders, so loud it makes my ear hurt. "I thought Springfield had got you! That bastard is gonna pay."

I swallow, my heart beating so fast I'm afraid it'll jump out of my chest. "You promise me you won't kill him, Daddy," I say. "You swear on Momma."

It's a terrible silence that swirls around me. I feel light-headed as he draws it out, lets me stew, lets me soak in the fact that I'm defying him.

That I've broken the rules.

That I've brought Momma into this.

But he's not the only one she's haunting. Her ghost may fit into the curve of Daddy's smile and the blue of Uncle Jake's eyes, but it's my face that's the mirror, the constant reminder to the men she left behind.

She would want me to keep Jake safe.

The silence stretches on for what seems like forever. I've never done this before, never defied him, and I'm scared. Not just of what he'll do to Uncle Jake, but what he'll do to me. But I have to keep Uncle Jake safe...for Momma's sake and for mine.

So I wait. And then it happens. Daddy clears his throat, and after a few more long seconds of silence, he says it. "I swear on your mother I won't kill him," he chokes out the words. Finally.

I take a deep breath and close my eyes in the relief that washes over me. "We're at the Vanguard Motel. Room 208."

"I'm on my way," he says. "You best be hiding, Harley-girl."

"I have a better idea."

When Uncle Jake wakes up, I'm back in bed and his keys are long gone, flushed down the toilet. His tires are slashed, and I even tossed out the spark plugs for good measure. At first, he looks around, fumbling in the blankets and looking on the bedside table sleepily for the keys, and as his eyes clear, he gets more frantic. Then he stares at me, and the look of betrayal in his eyes makes my stomach sour, like I've drunk bad milk.

"Is he on his way?" Uncle Jake asks.

I nod.

"When?" he asks.

I look at the clock on the bedside table. "Half hour. Maybe less."

"Did you fuck up my truck too much?"

"You're gonna need new tires," I say.

He sighs, burying his face in his hands. His shoulders slump, defeated.

"Your mother didn't want this for you," he says.

"That doesn't mean it's wrong."

"Oh, honey." He lifts his face from his palms. His blue eyes—so much like Momma's—are wet. "It's all wrong."

"He's trying to keep me safe."

"He's the reason you *aren't* safe, Harley," Jake says quietly.

I glare at him. "Springfield killed Momma. He started it."

"Yes," Jake says. "He did. But there are ways of making him pay that don't involve killing."

"Is that what you want?" I ask. Uncle Jake loved Momma, too. I know he did. How can he not want Springfield dead?

*I* want him dead. I know what he looks like now. Daddy showed me pictures, because I need to know. At night, I picture him with a bullet hole between his eyes. Or covered in cigar burns, like the ones he pressed into Will's arm.

"What I want doesn't matter," Jake says. "Not when your safety is at risk. Your daddy can't see that."

"Daddy sees everything," I say.

He lets out a tight breath, despair all over his face. I hate that I'm making him feel this way, but he has to know. He thinks he can talk his way out of stuff. He can't, not unless he can back up his words with his fists and bullets and blood.

There's a banging on the door. I jump, and so does Jake.

*"Open the fucking door!"*

"Stay there," I tell Jake when he starts to get up.

I unlock the door, cracking it open a sliver. Daddy grabs it, wrenching it open. He glances at me, a quick up and down like he's making sure I'm not missing any fingers or something. Then he reaches out, grabbing me and drawing me to him, tight against his chest in a half hug, half shielding movement. As soon as I'm in his arms, in his grasp, all his attention goes to Jake.

"You goddamn son of a bitch," he says, and I've never seen him so angry. Even when he killed Ben Springfield, there was a calm over him. Carefulness. Control.

There's none of that now. His hair is sticking up in the back and his beard looks bushier, uncombed, his eyes glittering with a murderous anger. He looks like he hasn't slept in days. Like he's just spent the last eight hours speeding down the highway and pissing in a bottle to get here in time to claim what's his. To claim me.

Jake gets to his feet, his eyes hard. "I did what I thought was right."

"It doesn't matter what *you* think is right," Daddy hisses. "She's *my* kid."

Jake's chin tilts up. He's one of the only men I know who's clean-shaven. It makes him look younger, weaker.

Like something smooth and soft and easy to cut.

"She should go sit in the truck," Jake tells Daddy. "Before anything happens."

Daddy looks from Jake to me, still clutched to his chest like I might fly away. "What do you think, Harley-girl?" he asks me. "Should you go sit in the truck while I teach your uncle a lesson?"

I swallow hard, but it does nothing to stop the fear rising in me. He'd sworn on Momma.

He wouldn't break that kind of promise.

I want to believe that, but I'm not sure I can.

Which means I have to stay.

"I'm not going anywhere," I say, and my throat feels like it's on fire, like I'm gonna shrivel in the heat of Daddy's anger.

"Harley," Jake says. *"Please."*

I pull away from Daddy, and it takes a good, hard tug to get him to let me go. I look up at him, wary. "You promised," I say.

"I did," Daddy says, fishing into the pocket of his shirt, pulling out a set of brass knuckles. He slips them over his fingers. "You stay right there," he orders.

He's across the room and on Jake in just a few steps. And Jake just…takes it. He doesn't fight back. He doesn't even try to guard his face.

The crunch of brass against bone fills my ears, the splash of blood muffled by the cheap motel carpet, the low growl in the back of Daddy's throat.

I stay rooted to the spot and I keep my eyes open. I force myself to watch, because I did this. I called him, knowing that this would happen.

I'm responsible.

I wait until he's got Jake on the ground, curled in a barely conscious ball, before I move.

"Daddy, stop!" I say, but he doesn't.

I reach out with both my hands, grabbing under his elbow, and I *pull*.

Though I'm strong for my age, I'm nothing to him.

But I have nails. Chipped and dirty, but they'll do. I dig them deep into his skin, and he grunts, his head finally swiveling to me.

"No more," I say.

His eyes narrow, dark flecks in his red face. "Harley…" he says in that way that makes it a warning.

I look down at Jake. His eyes are already swollen and just half open, his face a mess of blood, his mouth an open wound.

Jake's eyes meet mine as he pants, "Look away, baby. Please, look away."

But I'm not something sweet and breakable like Jake thinks. I am my daddy's girl, and I did this.

I'll make myself watch, even if it kills me.

I turn to Daddy. "You *promised*," I say.

Daddy glances over at Jake and then back at me. His fingers clench around the brass knuckles.

They're shiny with Jake's blood.

"He took you," Daddy says, and there's so much in his words, so much in his face.

Jake scared him. More than anyone's done in years.

"He's my family," I tell him, because it's the only defense I have. That Uncle Jake and I, we share blood. That he's a part of me, a part of Momma.

That means Daddy has to love him, too. Jake is part of us. And he has to love all of us. That's how it works.

Daddy sighs. The brass knuckles slip off his fingers, landing with a thud on the carpet. I want to scramble to the ground, to grab them and hide them away. But they're just a tool.

Daddy is the weapon.

"Okay, Jake," he says, bending down and grabbing him by the shoulders. I step forward, afraid that it's the end, but Daddy's just propping him up against the bed. With a great effort, Uncle Jake raises his head.

Daddy crouches down next to him, staring into his eyes.

"I once told Jeannie I'd never hurt you," he says.

Jake laughs, a weak movement that makes blood spill from his lips. "Guess you fucked that one up."

Daddy smiles, a bitter twist to his lips. "Yeah, guess I did. But you deserve it."

"She's a kid, Duke," Jake says.

I hate being talked about like I'm not in the room. Daddy doesn't do that. He talks *to* me, not at me or about me.

Daddy draws his knife out of his pocket, flicking it open. He glances at me, warning me not to move with just a look.

"She's my heir," Duke says. "And we're at war."

Jake shakes his head. "You and Springfield and your fucking war." He coughs, wincing and grabbing his ribs.

Daddy's mouth flattens in anger. "He killed your little sister," he says. "Doesn't that spark up anything in that pussy-boy brain of yours? God, what a waste you are." He places the flat of his knife against Jake's busted cheek. "You should be frothing like a bitch in heat to get to that bastard. I should have you by my side instead of trying to snatch my daughter."

"Jeannie is gone," Jake says, not flinching, even though I know the steel must be cold against his cheek.

"And Springfield's gonna pay for that," Daddy spits out.

"Then what?" Jake asks. "Say you get him tomorrow—then what? Are you still gonna keep Harley penned up in the woods? She should be in school. She should have more friends than just Will. She should be learning things."

"I teach her just fine," Daddy says.

"You're teaching her she isn't safe," Jake says.

Daddy draws the knife away from Jake's swollen cheek, pulling out his silver lighter that's engraved with a wolf's head. "And you'd teach her to think she was," he says scornfully. "That kind of thinking would get her killed."

"You're teaching her there's no safety to be found *anywhere*," Jake insists.

"That's because there isn't," Daddy says flatly. I know this like I know my last name. Like I know Daddy loves me. Like I know the sky is blue.

It will never be safe.

But Daddy didn't teach me this.

Carl Springfield did.

"I am who I am," Daddy says. "That won't change. But it means Harley's a target. So I'm raising her up to be the kind of woman who doesn't just survive—she'll be the kind of woman who can rule what I've built for her. A woman no man can hurt. And if you were smart, Jake, that's what you'd want for her, too."

Daddy thumbs open the lighter, flicking it on and running it along the blade of his knife. I watch as it blackens, not understanding what he's up to. I can't tear my eyes off the knife.

Is he going to stab Uncle Jake?

Will he break his promise?

"My girl," Daddy says, "she loves you. And Jeannie loved you. But I don't love you, Jake. I don't even like you. Frankly, you've been nothing but a pain in my ass since the day I met you."

"You think you haven't been a pain in mine?" Jake sneers. "You're a career criminal who knocked up my teenage sister. You're a decade older. You should have known better. Instead, you ruined her life."

Daddy's eyes flicker like the flame from the lighter. There's a dangerous edge to them that should make Jake stop. But maybe he figures he's dead already.

Maybe he just doesn't care.

"I loved that woman more than you will ever know," Daddy says. "She gave me my child. She was a fucking angel."

"She deserved better than you."

Daddy stares at him, grim and cold. "That we can agree on," he says. "But she wanted me. She chose me. She was too damned good for me and too damned good for this world. And now she's gone and here we are."

Jake pushes up on his elbows. His bloody chin trembles almost as much as his hands as he says, "Go ahead, Duke. Do it. But make her leave first."

"I'm not gonna kill you, Jake," Daddy says. "I made a promise."

Jake glances at me, licking his lips and wincing at the taste of blood.

"What's going to happen is simple," Daddy says. He flicks the lighter again, running it along the blade of the knife. It's gone from black to a ruddy orange, and I suddenly realize what he's going to do.

He's going to brand Uncle Jake.

My stomach flips in a sick, slow somersault. I can't stop this.

It's the price Jake has to pay to live.

"You and I," Daddy explains, "we're going into business together."

"We…?" Jake trails off, his eyes widening in horror. "No!"

"Yes," Daddy says. "You're gonna sign the trucking business over to me. You'll still run it. But some of the product is gonna be different."

"You want me to traffic." Jake says it like it's a curse.

"Such a dirty word," Daddy says. "We're businessmen, Jake. Doing business. Transporting product. Widening our customer base."

Jake looks at me, and I look back, pleading, begging with my eyes. *This is the only way. The only way he won't kill you.*

He looks back at Daddy. "And if I say no?"

"You won't," Daddy says, all surety. He knows he has all the cards. He has *me*.

"No," Jake says. "I won't."

Daddy smiles and holds out the red-hot knife. "You're gonna need a reminder, then," he says.

Jake stiffens, eyes fixed on the knife.

I know he's heard the rumors. Everyone has.

"I don't want her to see," he says.

Daddy looks over to me. "Go outside, Harley-girl."

"But—" I want to be there for Uncle Jake. I don't want to see, but I want to be there. I want to help him.

I did this. I need to stop it.

*"Outside!"* Daddy says, and something in his voice scares me so much I jump up and back out of the room, fast.

I obey because I have no choice. My stomach hurts as I stand outside the closed door, frozen. I wait, my heart thundering in me like a hammer. I tell myself not to listen, but I can't help it. Every part of my body is tensed, waiting, waiting, waiting...

When Uncle Jake's scream breaks the air, all the hairs on my arms stand up and my knees give out. I crumple onto the rough concrete as I listen to Jake scream again as Daddy uses his pocketknife on his chest.

And then there's silence. A terrible silence that creeps in and takes hold of me. It ticks by for such an impossibly long time I can barely stand it.

The motel door jerks open. Daddy is standing there, and Uncle Jake's on his feet, buttoning up his shirt.

"It's time to go," Daddy says. He looks over to Jake. "Cooper's waiting to drive you home," he says, gesturing across the parking lot where a weathered blue Dodge is parked.

Jake nods. His face is swollen and battered almost beyond recognition, and I see that his shirt has soaked up thin trails of blood in the shape of the letter *M*.

He can't look at me when he walks past, but for a second, he squeezes my shoulder with a shaky hand. I want to lean into him, but I know better.

Daddy waits until Cooper and Jake pull out of the motel parking lot and are a good way down the road before turning to me.

Feeling like I want to bolt, I look back at him, because I know that's what he expects.

*Never flinch, Harley-girl.*

"What's the lesson here, Harley Jean?" he barks.

I let out a little huff of breath, holding his gaze with shock and disgust that I can't tamp down fast enough to hide. His eyes narrow.

"There's always a lesson," he says. "What is it?"

I don't respond. I can't. I just turn, walk away, and hop up in his truck without a word, leaving him and his knife behind.

We drive all the way back home in silence. I just stare straight ahead, barely seeing anything. I won't even eat when he stops for food.

When I get home, Miss Lissa hugs me hard and offers me some fresh-baked snickerdoodles. To please her, I take one, but it tastes like dust in my mouth, and I spit it out when she isn't looking. His face busted seven ways to Sunday, Jake is already home, crumpled up in a chair in his bloody shirt with Cooper standing guard. His nose will hang to the right forever after this, and whenever I look at it, I'll think of his screams, and how I was responsible for them.

Daddy looks at him, nods, and disappears into his office.

I hover in the doorway of the living room, wanting to say something, anything, but no words will come.

Uncle Jake looks up at me and manages a weak smile. "It's okay, sweetheart," he slurs, his swollen eyes gentle in his ravaged face.

But it's not. And it never will be again.

I've learned the lesson. It's not the one that Daddy meant to teach, but it's the one that's branded on my heart, just like that *M* is branded on Uncle Jake.

The price of loving me is pain.

# TWENTY-EIGHT

*June 7, 10:00 a.m.*

You're out of your goddamn mind," Will says.

He stalks over to the cupboard above the fridge, grabbing the first aid kit. "Sit down."

He has his doctor voice on. It's so familiar that I obey before I can think it through. I sit down on one of the wine-barrel stools at the kitchen island, and he drags another one in front of me. After washing his hands, he sets the kit on the butcher-block counter and opens it, selecting an alcohol wipe.

"Wanna tell me why your knuckles aren't bruised?" he asks.

My eyes narrow. "What do you mean?"

"Your fingers aren't busted up," he says. "Which means you didn't fight back. But you always fight back."

He's right. Fuck! It's a detail I forgot.

"So...who'd you get to hit you?" he asks, almost conversationally. He wipes the gauze against the cut on my lip. It stings, and my tongue goes to the spot automatically, trying to soothe the burn.

"Brooke," I say finally.

"Figures." He presses around my nose with his fingertips. Pain flares through my sinuses. His movements are gentle, but his anger fills the air between us. He takes out a tube of arnica gel, squirts it on his fingers, and spreads it beneath my eye where the bruising's the worst. "She'd do anything for you."

"And I'd do anything for her," I say. I've done things for her even Will doesn't know. That he's better off not knowing.

There's a certain kind of trouble that men have no business meddling in. Usually because one of them is the cause of it.

He roots around in the kit until he comes up with a bottle of ibuprofen. He puts four tablets on the counter and gets up to fill a glass with water.

When he sets it down in front of me, I can't help but smile. "You're always patching me up."

"Somebody has to," he says, and there it is—the pity. I hear it in his voice.

"I really need you to go back to school," I whisper.

"And I really need you to stay alive," he snaps.

"I'll be fine. As long as you're not around to distract me."

"Distract you from what, exactly?" Will spits out. I've hardly ever seen him this mad, and it makes me worry. "What have you got planned next? Are you going to shoot Buck? Nail Springfield dead between the eyes with your sniper rifle? How the fuck do you expect to get away with this? What are you thinking, Harley?"

Heat crawls up my neck. I hate that he underestimates me like this. I was never going to end up in college like him, but I'm not stupid. I've thought this through from all sides. I have a goddamn plan.

"Do you remember the last time a lab blew?" I ask.

He frowns, thinking back. I was twelve, and he was fourteen. It was summer, and I remember it vividly. The dry heat made the air shimmer in waves around us on the porch. Uncle Jake drove up reeking of sour meth smoke and Daddy had burns so bad I had to call Doc to come quick.

"Everything got shut down for months," he says slowly, remembering. "And Duke brought all the remaining product onto the property. I helped him and Jake load it into the shed."

"Exactly."

"So…you're just gonna sit on a shitload of meth?"

"No."

"Are you gonna kill him, Harley?"

That's the question, isn't it? I'd like to say I have an answer, but I don't.

When it comes down to it, I'm not sure I trust myself *not* to kill Springfield.

"If he could, Springfield would kill *me*," I say.

"You're not him."

I smile, a bitter twist. "No," I say.

Will folds his arms, staring me down as he thinks. I can practically see the wheels turning in his brain, sifting through all that he knows. "If killing him is what you're after, you'd just take a rifle, find a perch, and blow his head off."

"That's one approach."

Will looks at the bag of drugs on the counter. "You could've left this inside the trailer…burned it up with the rest of it. But you didn't. That means you have a plan for it."

I love him and this game we're playing. It's a part of him and me, sorely missed. Finally, someone who will meet me step for step. Who understands all of me—the good parts, the bad parts, the parts that belong to Momma, to Duke, to him.

"You're setting Springfield up," Will says slowly, putting it all together. "The lab getting blown must've spooked the cooks," he goes on. "How'd you make them think it was him?"

"You know Springfield would be flashy as fuck if he finally decided to take us down. I played into their expectations. This"—I gesture to my face—"will just seal the deal."

"Smart." Will nods in reluctant approval. "Let them draw their own conclusions first. Makes them more sure when you come along, confirming it."

"Makes them easier to deal with," I agree.

"So you let them fight it out and hopefully destroy each other—then you get away clean," he says. "But what happens if Buck turns on you? Figures it out and sides with Springfield?"

It's a possibility, because Buck doesn't have a loyal bone in his body.

He obeys Duke because Duke terrifies him. I'll never inspire that kind of fear because I'm a woman.

That's a blessing and a curse. But it's the main reason I think my plan will work. They all underestimate me. Most of the cooks, they like me. Cooper loves me. But to them, I'm twelve years old and trembling at best and a pair of brainless tits at worst.

*Always take advantage of weakness, Harley-girl.*

"I don't want to kill anyone," I say, and it's the truth. "But I will if I have to." That's the truth, too.

Will looks away from me, like my honesty is too much. "You sound like him," he says softly.

I can feel the blood draining out of my face, and when Will catches sight of it, his mouth twists in apology. "Harley—"

"Don't say you're sorry." He's not. He's being the honest one now—I do sound like Duke. I know it.

Do I have to become him to survive? To keep everyone safe? It's the question that burrows in the back of my head, and I do my best to keep it there, but the answer's waiting for me at the end of all this.

But Will draws things out of me that no one else can—the deep kind of love, the protective kind of violence, and the hurtful kind of truth.

He leans against the counter like someone punched him. "I'm too late, aren't I?"

I close my eyes against tears that stopped coming years ago. "What were you gonna do?" I ask shakily. "Save me? Snatch me? Take me away to Humboldt so I could go to class and live in the dorms with you?"

"Yes," he says.

I turn red, and it's not out of embarrassment or girlish satisfaction. It's at the realization that he means it. That maybe he even planned it.

It's not something he would do. Taking me against my will, getting me away from Duke.

It's something I would do.

Hell, it's kind of what I *did*. I forced Duke's hand and made him let Will go once he got into college.

"Will…" I say. I want to step closer to him. I want to yell at him for even thinking he could get me to leave…get the best of me.

He can't. Not unless I let him.

And I never would.

I can't leave the Rubies unprotected. I can't leave the county to Springfield and Buck.

"What am I supposed to do?" he asks. "In the two years I've been gone, he's dragged you further and further into the business. Yes, I want to get you the fuck away from him."

"Well, you don't have to worry about Duke," I blurt out. "He can't hurt anyone. He's not even conscious anymore. The nurses say it won't be long."

"Jesus," Will says hoarsely, like I've sucker-punched him.

I forget sometimes, that this is what he wants to do with the rest of his life: be around sick people. I thought I understood it when he left. It made sense, him becoming a nurse. He was good at taking care of people. I was basically his test dummy when we were kids.

But when Duke got sick, when my days became nothing but vomit and sweat-stained sheets, muddled morphine moans and bruises from his flailing, I realized I didn't understand this part of Will at all. How could he want to do this for someone he didn't even know? Didn't even love? Did it hurt less when you didn't love them?

"I didn't realize…he's that close…" Will's eyes go bright again.

I'm going to lose it if I keep having to look at him fight against grieving over Duke. It's too much like what I'm doing myself.

"I don't want to talk about it." My voice is so close to pleading, it fights against my nature, against the whisper inside me: *McKennas never beg, Harley-girl.*

"You've gotta let me take you away, Harley," he says. "Especially now."

I look at him…really look at him.

I love him. For his goodness and his strength and caring. For his ability to forgive and for the scars he bears, the ones that are my fault, that are Springfield's, that are Duke's, that are his mother's…but never Will's.

174

I love him. I'd kill for him. Die for him. But I won't leave for him.

"This is my *home!*" It comes out fierce and loud—as it should. He should know this about me. "Do you know what happens if you take the McKenna out of North County? Think about it for a second. Think about what would happen if I just up and left. The sheriff can be bought off, no problem. The city council's as corrupt as they come, and you've got a whole county's worth of tweekers and junkies running loose, throwing around whatever money they've got, stealing stuff to get the cash they need. Prime ground for a cartel or the Aryans to come in, if Buck and Springfield don't kill each other first.

"And what about the Rubies? What's gonna happen to them if I'm not there to put a gun between them and the men they ran from? What about Mo? What about the diners? The trucking company? All the people who work for Duke's businesses? What about them? You take the McKenna out of this county, Will, and there's no county left."

"So *you're* gonna take all this on?"

"Someone has to," I grit out.

"Jesus," he says, shaking his head. "Jesus fucking Christ." He stares up at the ceiling, like an angel's gonna fly down and hand him some magic key that would change my mind. A minute ticks by.

"Okay," he says finally. He pushes off the counter, turning to face me. "Okay, then. If you're in this, then so am I. You need someone to have your back."

"No, I don't," I insist. "If you're at my back, you'll get me killed or caught. This is a one-woman job. If I take one wrong step, I'm dead. I can't be looking out for myself *and* you."

"You can't go in alone."

"Think for a second," I tell him. "If I go to the Tropics with you, they're going to want to know why you didn't stop whoever did this." I gesture to my face. "You'd mess up my plan from the get-go. You're a distraction. And you're not part of the business—you left. He let you go. There's no way they're letting you back inside. Especially when they think Springfield's gonna attack at any moment."

There's anger behind his eyes, but he doesn't allow it reach the rest of his face. He knows deep down that I'm right. His heart's just got to fight with his head a while before he admits it.

"What's Brooke doing, then?"

"She stays with Duke during the day. The hospice thinks she's my cousin."

"What about Gran?"

"I paid the security guards at Fir Hill extra to keep a close eye on her. And the nurses know that only the people on her guest list are allowed in the wing. You think Springfield wants to mess with an angry nurse?"

His mouth twitches, stifling a smile. "And the Rubies?"

"The Sons of Jefferson are guarding them. I have a deal with Paul. I've got everyone covered but you."

"I'm not going back to school. Not if he's dying, Harley, I'm not going anywhere."

"You were just talking about taking me away from him," I say. "And now what? You want to stick around to say goodbye?"

It's a low blow, one I regret the second it's out of my mouth. Will's eyes narrow, the hurt plain on his face.

"Don't pretend I didn't spend all those years at your side, under his hand," he says. "He's the only man who's ever given a shit about me. He's the man who rolled up my sleeves and saw my scars and told me he'd kill anyone who did that to me again. And I believed him, not just because he's the scariest motherfucker I've ever met, but because I knew he meant it. I didn't know what safe *was* until him."

I suck in a shaky breath, too sharp and quick. Then I reach out, compelled by more than want, by a need that's been so ignored and goes so deep that it hurts when I touch him. I don't push back the sleeve of his flannel shirt; instead, I wrap my fingers around each of his wrists, my thumb resting on the inside.

I can't feel it through the flannel, but I know it's there. The first in a series of scars, round and puckered, burned into his skin by a vicious man.

"I get to say goodbye to him," he says, softer now. Not as angry, because he feels my apology in the curl of my fingers, in the brush of my hip against his as I step closer.

It's so much easier without words, when the person can just read you in breath and body.

"Duke took Gran and me in," Will whispers, his eyes not quite meeting mine. "He saved me...and taught me...and he loves me, I think."

"Of course he does," I say, and the truth of that goes deeper than he'll ever know.

"So I'm staying," Will says.

From years of experience, I know there's no pushing him. Not without hurting him. Or knocking him out and dragging him over the county line...which I consider for a moment before folding my arms and gritting my teeth.

"Fine," I say. "But stay out of my way. And lay low."

"And I want to see him," Will adds, an urgent note in his voice.

I expected this, but still, something sick curls in my stomach. It's childish, but powerful, this leftover fear that's ingrained in me.

*Don't break the rules, Harley-girl.*

"I need to see him," Will says.

*No one can see me like this. Please, Harley Jean.*

"Please, Harley," Will says.

"Of course," I say, and my betrayal is complete.

I've broken every rule.

Every promise.

Every vow.

I really am his daughter.

# TWENTY-NINE

I'm twenty-one when Will and I stop talking.

After almost a year away at college, he comes home for Christmas. He's visited a few times, but never for long.

We call and we text, but it's not the same.

I can't picture how he spends his day, his life at college. And the way he looks at me tells me that how I'm spending my time these days is all he's thinking about.

With every month that passes, Duke gives me more responsibility. I can see how it pisses Buck off, how it makes Cooper proud, and how it makes the fear in Will spark quick and hot.

*I don't want this for you,* his eyes say. They follow me around the kitchen as I bake the snowball cookies Miss Lissa always made for Christmas.

I keep quiet. I don't bring it up. I'm scared of what might happen if I do.

Our worlds are separating, piece by painful piece, and if we speak on it, then it's real. Then it's something I have to deal with. Then I lose him for good.

My plan, to keep my mouth shut and not ripple the waters, is working. And then it isn't.

He'd been staying up at the main house with us instead of the little cabin where he grew up with Miss Lissa. But the night before he had to go back to school, I wake up. When I walk downstairs to get water, I see a light across the meadow and I go, drawn to it—to him.

The little cabin is sweet and cozy. Duke built it himself when he was a teenager, back when Granddaddy McKenna was still alive and living in the big house. From all accounts, my Granddaddy was a mean son of a bitch, and Duke had the scars to prove it. Moving out—even if it was just across the meadow—was probably a relief.

The cabin's still decorated the way Miss Lissa left it, with the pictures and photos that I didn't bring to Fir Hill still on the walls and the crystal vase her momma had passed down to her on the mantel above the woodstove.

I hear a rustling sound in the back bedroom, and that's where I find him, sitting on his childhood bed, a cigar box he must've swiped from Duke in front of him.

"You smoking cigars now?" I ask, coming to sit next to him.

He shakes his head, flipping the box open. There are some old black-and-white photos of Miss Lissa when she was young and baby pictures of Will with her, but none with his mother. A worn Bible with a white leather cover, an old gold ring on a chain—Miss Lissa used to wear it around her neck, her late husband's wedding band— and then I see it at the bottom of the box: a loop of barbed wire, fashioned into a bracelet.

"Remember this?" he asks quietly. He runs his index finger lightly over the bent barbs.

I have to grip the edges of the bed to keep from snatching the wire away. I want it back with me, in *my* hands, around my wrist, even though it's too small. It's been too small for years, shaped for me before I hit my growth spurt.

"Of course," I say. My voice is hoarse. It doesn't sound like me.

"Here." He moves closer, his knee brushing my thigh. With a deft movement, he untwists the wire. "Give me your wrist."

His fingers slide against my pulse point, and I wonder if he can feel it speed up. He closes the bracelet around my wrist, reshaping it to fit me again.

My wrist's still clasped between his fingers and I stare hard at his hand beneath the barbed wire.

"I remember when I made this for you. You were what—nine…ten, maybe? You were still on house arrest back then. There were times I thought he'd never let you off the property. I'd think about it, how to sneak you out…run away."

"Even then?"

He's looking down at his hand, just like I am. But I can feel his gaze all the same when he says, "Always," and my heart stutters inside my chest.

His head tilts up; I feel it more than see it. "Do you know how much I've missed you?" he asks, and my head jerks up; I'm startled into looking at him because of the pain in his voice.

It makes me want to crawl out of my skin into his. To do anything to erase how he's looking at me right now, raw and hurt.

"I missed you, too," I say. "But you have school. And I have…" I don't finish. I don't need to, because we both know. I have Duke. I have the business. I have the Rubies.

I don't have him.

All that openness in his face shuts in a second. His fingers twist in mine, and the movement tugs the sleeve of his Henley up. When I see the flash of black ink, everything inside me locks up. He drops my wrist instantly, pulling down his sleeve.

But it's too late.

I've seen it.

I grab his wrist, but he jerks it away from me.

"Harley…" he says, like he's going to explain or something.

I don't want an explanation. It's not going to stop me. I'll pin him to the bed if I have to.

"Let me see," I say.

"Look—"

"Let. Me. See."

Will grits his teeth, staring up at the ceiling. Then he raises his left arm and pulls up the sleeve to his elbow to expose the scars Springfield burned into him.

One for every year he'd been alive, he'd told me years ago, with a sad, crooked smile. Ten circles, second-degree burns that didn't get treated right, because Desi didn't want CPS coming around.

But now they're transformed. He's had thick lines tattooed up the arm, lines that curve and twist into ten perfect barbs to cover the scars.

Barbed wire, like the bracelet he just put on my wrist, inked into his skin.

My mouth's dry and my heart thumps in my chest, because I know what this means.

A declaration that goes beyond promises or rings or even vows before God.

This is blood and ink and forever. Something inside me falls into place when I see it on his skin, like the turn of a bullet in the chamber. The rightness of it settles over me, pouring into my heart. It should make me happy, but it doesn't. Instead, cold dread grows inside me like moss on a tree, in all the little cracks and hollows.

*Loving that boy will get him killed, Harley-girl.*

"Say something," Will says.

But I can't. That'd be me being brave. And when it comes to him, I'm a coward.

So I run. I spring up off that bed and I walk out of the cabin and off the porch, heading across the meadow to the trees, to anywhere but him.

And he chases after me, because that's what he does. I run. He chases.

But if he catches me this time...

The grass swishes against my ankles. I don't turn around when his footsteps join mine, but I keep walking to the edge of the meadow where it fades into forest, far from both of the houses, hidden from view. He follows.

"Harley, please."

He isn't playing fair. I close my eyes, trying to breathe, trying to do anything that doesn't involve turning and facing him.

"You were supposed to have a life," I say, halting, the words rusty in my throat.

"I do have a life," he says. "I have friends. I have school. But I don't have you."

I turn around then. It's dark outside, but the moon's high, and I can see his face clearly. "You never had me."

"Bullshit," he grinds out, his arms tensing under his shirt.

"We haven't ever—" I start, but then he reaches out, and I fall silent as he pulls me forward, until I'm looking up at him and he's just inches away, and our hips are pressed together.

He's never even tried to kiss me. There have been moments where I've known exactly what he was thinking and feeling because I was feeling it too, but he's never pushed across that invisible line in the dirt that no one drew, but exists all the same.

"Did you think I was gonna just forget you? Start dating some girl at college?"

"Why not?" He pulls me closer, so now there's no space between us. With each breath, I can feel his chest against mine. It's a strange thing to focus on, but it's all I can think of, all I can feel.

"You know why," he says. "It wouldn't be fair. I'm not doing that to you or to me or to any other girl."

Of course he wouldn't. Because he's honest and good.

If I was good, I would walk away.

I would let him go.

But I am not good. And I'm so sick of wanting and never getting.

So it's me who crosses that line. Me who leans up and presses my lips against his.

It is gentle and it is sweet, until it's not. Until all those years of longing finally catch up to us. Soft like silk turns deep and reverent in the time it takes to catch a breath, and his hands are under my shirt, and mine are on his belt.

Soon it's all skin and glory, the meadow grass against my back, his mouth on mine, my fingers tracking down his chest, over his heart, like I need to mark the spot.

When it happens, when it's me and him and then suddenly it's this long, slow, slide into *us*, the feeling's almost too much. Unbearable in its closeness. Overwhelming. Wonderful and on the edge of perfect, and it's my shuddery breath against his ear and his body pressed into mine, and I want with a fierceness I never knew I had.

I *want*.

He gives, thinking it's the start.

I take, knowing it's the end.

# THIRTY

*June 7, 10:20 a.m.*

I should get going," Will says, but he doesn't get up, and neither do I.
We sit across from each other, our knees brushing, and it's familiar and strange at the same time.

He's been gone for two years, but that first year, he called, he visited.

Until I screwed it all up at Christmas.

And now he's here and I don't want him to go, even though I need him to for his own sake.

The buzzer on the gate goes off, saving me from having to make a decision. My head whips toward the sound and I'm up off my feet and dashing for the monitor set in the hallway before Will even reacts.

I flip the monitor on, the black-and-white feed from the security cameras flicking on the screen.

Cooper and Wayne are outside. I can see Wayne riding shotgun. Cooper's out of the truck, staring directly into the camera and pressing on the *Call* button.

"Shit." I look over to Will, who's followed me into the hall. "We've got to take the back way out."

He sighed. "Can't we just wait for them to leave?"

"You think Cooper's gonna let a gate stop him?" I ask. "I don't know if Duke ever told him about the back ways. Let's go."

I whistle for Busy and grab the bag of meth on the counter, heading for the door. "I need to lock this in the shed; give me a minute."

184

I jog through the garden—which is overgrown and weedy since Will left—weaving through the raised beds Duke built Momma the first year they were married. I duck underneath the clothesline. I'd forgotten to bring the wash in, and the oversized plaid shirts that I've claimed as mine, but used to belong to Will, brush over my shoulder as I make my way down the well-worn dirt path. Dust covers my boots as I tramp down the yellowing hills that roll over the east end of the property, patches of scrub oaks the only green in sight.

Daddy's shed is set at the base of the third hill, tucked out of sight of the path and driveway. It's a little two-room, windowless log cabin built from a kit. It has enough locks to deter even the most determined man and a generator whirring in the back to keep the room temperature regulated. Duke's got some antique guns that cost a lot of money, on top of the arsenal that actually still works.

We've hit the point in summer where it never stops getting hotter, and I'm sweating by the time I scale the third hill, my feet slippery in my hiking boots as I swish through knee-high foxtails and star thistle. I can smell the faintest smudge of smoke in the air.

There's a digital key pad and a padlock on the shed—Duke didn't like taking chances. I type in the code and pull out the key. I unbolt the steel doors on the shed, pulling them open. They swing shut behind me with a bang. Inside it's dark and quiet, like I've stepped into some underground shrine, untouched, as close to holy as someone like me gets.

I close my eyes and breathe for a second, letting it sink in.

I'm safe here. Even if it's just for a minute.

I flip the light on, a bare bulb swinging from the ceiling that casts a weak light across the room. Every available inch of the wall has been taken up by row after row of guns in steel, padlocked cages. Hunting rifles, sniper rifles, assault rifles, handguns, machine guns, pistols, revolvers.

I know every model, every make. I can take each one of them apart and put them back together blindfolded if need be. This place had been my schoolroom as a kid; my math papers and science textbooks smudged with gunpowder from the ammo Daddy made himself and taught me to do in turn.

There are crates in the corner—the guns Daddy runs up and down California through the trucking business. I have plans for those, but not now.

I scrub my hands over my face. I need to get moving. I pick up the bag of meth and walk briskly toward the steel cage covering the back wall. I get it open, tossing the bag inside before locking it all back up again. The drugs will be safest in here. Until I need them.

I have enough guns up at the main house. I don't need an M-16 to take down Buck or any of the Springfields.

My plan's enough. I'm enough.

I've gotta be.

Will's already loaded his bike into the back of my truck, strapped and secure by the time I get back. He's got Busy rolling around, baring her belly in delight as he rubs it. When she sees me, she scrambles to her feet, looking guilty.

"Traitor," I tell her and she trots over to me, nudging my knee with her nose.

"She looks good," Will says.

I nod. Busy's getting old, and I can see it sometimes, in the way she takes longer to get up in the morning. The vet gave me some pills to make her bones strong that I shove in her food every day, but I can't even think about what happens when she gets too old to follow me everywhere.

She's the only one who's never left me.

"We need to go," I say. "Is the bike secure?"

"Yep." He walks over to the passenger side, opening the door for Busy to hop up and getting in after her. I take one last look down the driveway—I can't see the gate from here, it's half a mile down the twisty road, but I know Cooper and Wayne are standing outside it, wondering what to do.

I climb into the truck and start the engine. Busy's got her head on

Will's knee, drooling happily between us. I roll my eyes. "You spoil my dog."

"She just likes me more because I used to let her lick the dinner plates when you weren't looking," Will says as I drive down the old access road, toward the trees that hide the back way into the homestead. In minutes, the world darkens, the trees blocking out big chunks of the sun as we follow the path deeper into the forest.

I'm quiet, concentrating on the road, and I can feel him looking at me, wanting to say something. He's got to know I'm beyond convincing now.

Or at least I hope he knows. It's too late to back out.

"How's school?" I ask, because it takes almost twenty minutes to get to the road from the back way and I'm not gonna sit in silence that whole time.

"Good," he says. "I'm taking lots of science courses. But mostly..." He hesitates.

"But mostly?" I prompt.

He pauses, long enough that I glance over at him. He looks nervous for the first time. "I did something," he says.

"Okay," I say, looking back at the road, wondering if I should pull over. "What?"

"I went looking."

My eyes widen and my foot presses down on the brake, the truck coming to a halt. I pull the emergency brake and turn to face him fully. "You mean..."

"Yeah," he says.

I lick my lips, hope for him twisting like vines inside me. "How did you even start?"

"I still had a few boxes of stuff she'd left at Gran's. There was an address book. I just kept calling people and asking if they knew anything until I finally found someone who knew someone who knew someone."

"You found him?" I ask. The thought even makes me a little breathless. His mom had never given him any information about his dad—

he hadn't been on Will's birth certificate, and Miss Lissa had never met him. When Desi died, there was no way to search for him. Not that I'm sure Miss Lissa would've tried even if she had the information. She and Mo were always clashing when Will and I were kids, because Mo would let him hang out with the boys in her family when they visited the Ruby. That always made Miss Lissa nervous. She was always pushing him toward white boys instead, like they were better or something, and she hated that he and Mo got along so well. The only time I'd ever seen Miss Lissa fight with Duke was the day he let Mo take Will to the annual Pit River Pow Wow in Burney.

I could be stupid and excuse her, thinking that it was just fear of losing him that motivated her, but I'm not stupid, and I can't excuse her. Miss Lissa raised Will to be one of the best men I'd ever known, but she'd raised him up while casually denying and trying to push down half of him. It wasn't fair or right.

"I found a cousin. Liana," Will says. "She lives in Hoopa. I messaged her with what I knew, and she brought it to her grandma—well, *our* grandma—and she helped put the pieces together."

"You have another grandma," I say, and the feeling blooming inside me is all happiness tinged with dreadful selfishness, because if he's finally found his place, his real family, that means he can leave us behind for good.

"My dad…his name was Allen," Will says.

The happiness in my chest stutters. "Was?"

Will looks down. "He was a fisherman. He drowned."

"Shit." I don't know what else to say.

"Yeah," Will says, staring out the window, his jaw doing that clenching thing it does when he's trying not to be emotional. "But I've got two aunts and an uncle," he says. "And eight cousins."

"Wow." I hate that they've been out there this entire time, everyone not knowing what they were missing. "What are they like?"

"Great," he says, and his eyes shine in that happy way I rarely saw when we were kids. "Liana and her brother Shane are closest in age to me. Liana graduated from Humboldt a few years ago; she's a social worker. And the little cousins are cute; Katrina's just learning to walk, and she's falling all over."

He'd always been so good with the kids at the Ruby. A big family was exactly where he always belonged. I used to think maybe that family would be with me, but this was so much better. This was his real family. The one he deserved, the one who'd been deprived of him.

"When I found out, I wanted to call you," he says. "But…"

"But I was an asshole last time," I finish for him.

He sighs, rubbing a hand over his mouth, looking tired. "You were," he says.

"I'm sorry," I say.

"I know you are," he says. "Start the truck back up. We need to get going."

He's right. I turn the key and release the brake. "So you've been spending a lot of time in Hoopa with them?"

He nods. "It's beautiful in that valley. The Trinity cuts right through it. Everything's green, and the redwoods are bigger than you'd believe." He cuts himself off, smiling ruefully. "I love it there. I can't believe I'm half done with school. Or maybe not. My advisor wants me to think about becoming a nurse practitioner instead of just an RN. It would mean a few more years of school, but I'd have a lot more autonomy. Be able to prescribe medication and all that. Run a clinic on my own. Liana's been really encouraging me to go for it. She thinks it's a good idea."

"You'd be amazing at running a clinic," I say. "And, well, you've always liked school," I say, aware I sound slightly mystified. It makes him smile wider.

"You know, I'll never forget the reason I'm there is because of what you did," he says quietly.

I bite my lip, focusing on the dirt road. "We're nearly to the highway," I say, and he has the grace to let it go, to not push.

He made it to college all by himself. He'd filled out the applications, he'd written the essays, he'd gotten all the good grades. I just made

Duke let him go. And now he's found his family, all on his own. The pride I feel, the love and the flash of pain and worry tangle up inside me in a knot that can't be undone.

So I drive. And I pray that someday, I can find the freedom he's found.

# THIRTY-ONE

I turn sixteen on a beautiful day. There isn't a cloud in the sky as Uncle Jake and Miss Lissa set up the picnic tables and Duke stokes the fire in the barbecue pit, getting it ready for the pounds of meat in the fridge.

Sixteen is important in our family, the way eighteen is important for legit folks.

It means no more school.

It means I'm grown.

It means it's time to start working for Daddy.

I know he wants me to look forward to it like he is. The lessons that he'll be able to pass on, the empire he'll be able to give me.

Maybe there was a time I wanted it. But sixteen means I'm grown.

And grown means seeing things differently. My world is bigger than six hundred acres and Daddy's lessons now. In just two years, the Ruby will be mine legally, and while Daddy's been preparing me for his work, Uncle Jake's been preparing me for his, too.

I fear the day I might have to make a choice between the two. I'm not stupid enough to think it wouldn't happen.

My daddy drives hard bargains. Even with me.

Everyone comes to my party—all the cooks, everyone who works at the Tropics, the Sons of Jefferson, the waitresses from the Blackberry Diner, the Rubies, who bring three enormous sheet cakes with HAPPY

BIRTHDAY HARLEY written on them in blue frosting. Even Brooke is there, though I'm sure it was quite the conversation with her mother to get her to let Brooke come.

Kids run around the meadow, and Wayne picks at his guitar with a few of the Sons singing along, their voices floating above the crowd, joining the smoke from the barbecue. Miss Lissa's strung balloons and streamers all along the trees that line the far side of the garden, where the tables are set up, and I watch as Will kisses her cheek, snatching a piece of cornbread off the plate she's holding. She scowls at him, but he grins, ducking away to join the rest of the Sons, grouped around the coolers, drinking beer.

"Good party," Brooke comments, coming to stand next to me. She's got flowers in her hair—courtesy of some of little girls from the Ruby. They're making flower crowns and chains from the wildflowers.

"Yeah," I say.

Brooke shakes a red cup at me. "You want some?"

I grab the cup, sniffing it. "How much whiskey did you put in this?"

Brooke shrugs, snatching the cup back. "A lot."

I shoot her a look. "What?" Brooke asks. "Your family makes me nervous."

"They aren't going to start shooting," I say, but then I pause. "Well, not until later," I correct myself. "And just at the targets Daddy set up."

Brooke laughs. "C'mon, let's get some cake."

Sarah, Troy's wife, had taken charge of cutting the cake after I blew out my candles earlier. She smiles when she sees us, her hand resting on the bulging curve of her stomach. She and Troy are expecting twin boys any day now. "You girls having fun?" she asks.

"Yep," I say.

"Did your daddy give you your gift yet?" Sarah asks, dishing out a piece of chocolate cake onto a paper plate, handing it to me.

"Not yet," I say. "He says it's a surprise."

"I bet it's something big," Sarah says, with a conspiratorial wink.

"How are the babies?" Brooke asks.

"Good." Sarah strokes her stomach. "Almost here."

"We gotta talk about your baby shower," I tell Sarah. "Sal and Miss Lissa wanted to do something for you."

"Aren't you sweet." Sarah beams at us. "We'd love that."

"There you are!" Troy pounces on her from behind, wrapping his arms around her. He kisses her on the cheek loudly. "I want me some cake."

Sarah laughs, bending down to grab him a plate.

"C'mon, Harley," Troy says, jerking his head toward the bonfire, where Daddy and his men are grouped.

I look over at Brooke, whose eyebrows knit together. "I'm gonna stay here and help Sarah with the cake," she says.

"You excited?" Troy asks, as we begin to walk toward the bonfire. "Big day."

"Yeah," I say. "Of course."

I don't hesitate when we join Daddy and his men. I take my place at his right, where I belong. Buck shifts out of the way, and his shoulders tense, but I ignore it as Daddy hands me a beer with a smile.

They talk about everything and nothing as we stand there, everyone else around keeping their distance, knowing better than to bother Duke and his boys. Occasionally, their eyes go to me, their cheeks flushing when they say too crude a word, and Daddy just keeps smiling, smug, pleased. This is the new normal. This is my place, I remind myself. But I feel sick to my stomach, and it's not from the beer.

After the food's been eaten, the sleepy children are driven back home by their mothers. The cooks are the last to file out, hours past midnight. Cooper and Wayne hang back.

"We got something special for you," Cooper says as Wayne holds out a long, thin box.

I flip it open. Inside, nestled in black velvet, is a machete, like the one Wayne keeps strapped to his leg.

I look into his eyes, and his mouth quirks up. "I'll teach you how to use it," he promises.

I hug both of them tight. "Thank you," I say.

When they drive off, it's just me and Daddy left. Miss Lissa and Will

193

are back at the cabin, and Jake's gone into town, probably to visit the woman he sees, the one I'm pretty sure only I know about.

"Good birthday, Harley-girl?" Daddy asks.

"The best," I say. "Thank you."

"It's a big day," Daddy says. "C'mon. I've got something to show you."

He takes me out to the new barn, the red steel one he had built a few years back, to house the four-wheelers and Gators he kept on the property. He pulls the door open with a flourish, and inside is an old S10, painted a sandy gold.

My heart twists when I see the chunk of turquoise hanging from the rearview mirror.

Momma's truck. He kept it all these years, but it's been stored at the lumberyard for as long as I can remember.

"I fixed it up for you," Daddy says.

Part of me can't believe it. Even though he lets me off the property now, I'm never alone. I always have Jake or Busy or Will or him with me. A truck of my own means freedom.

"You're gonna need wheels now that you're working for me."

The elation floods out of me like air in a balloon.

This isn't about freedom.

This is about power. Everything is. And I understand it, I do.

But I don't know if I want it. But I don't have a choice, do I?

Daddy tosses something at me, and I almost miss catching the keys. I manage at the last second, and it makes him laugh, fondness shining in his eyes.

He's happier than I've seen him in a long time, and I want to keep it that way, so I get in the truck and smile, because I know it'll please him.

"Where are we going?"

"Drive up to the lookout," he says.

I pull the truck out of the barn, heading toward the forest and the back ways that weave up the mountain.

By the time we've made it up to the ridge that overlooks the valley the homestead's set in, dawn's cresting across the sky. Daddy gets out of the truck, leaning against the hood, and I follow.

From here, our place looks like a dollhouse, the meadow and the cabin that lies beyond it little patches of green and brown. The forest is bigger than you can imagine, even from this vantage point, where all you can see is acres and acres of old-growth pines as far as you can look.

"It's a beautiful sight," Daddy says.

I nod.

When it comes to this, home, I understand him fully.

"I have something else for you," Daddy says, digging in his back pocket, pulling out a folded piece of paper. At first, I think it's either a letter or some sort of makeshift birthday card, but when I unfold it, I see it isn't.

It's a list of women's names with dollar amounts next to them.

"What's this?" I ask, even though I think I know.

"Your job," Daddy says. "Every month, you'll collect those amounts from the women on this list."

"They owe you money?"

He nods. "Banks are bullshit, Harley Jean. Hardworking people get turned down for loans all the time. So men like me help them out."

I look down at the list and see the name *Haley Talbot* is third.

Brooke's mom.

I bite my lip. "And if they don't take me seriously?"

"You make them," Daddy says.

It's an order, and I know it.

Daddy puts his arm around me, drawing me close. "Sixteen," he says, squeezing my shoulder. "I can't believe it."

I lean my head against him and we watch the sun rise over the valley.

It's a new day.

It's a new life.

Whether I want it or not.

# THIRTY-TWO

*June 7, 12:00 p.m.*

When we get to Fir Hill, I help Will unstrap and unload his bike in the parking lot. We stand there awkwardly for a second, and I'm so aware that if things go wrong, I might never see him again. It makes me want to trash the whole plan. To just run away like he wants.

"Are you sure?" he asks me.

I nod.

He draws me close, pressing a kiss to my forehead. "Then be safe," he says.

He turns and walks into Fir Hill, and never once does he look back.

He knows I'll crumble if he does.

Will showing up had been a distraction from what was to come. What's waiting for me at the Tropics and how I react—how I sell my story—will determine everything.

I have to be focused. I have to make them believe me.

I drive away from Fir Hill, heading back west on 299. Coming into town, I take the off-ramp, drive down the main drag, and at Market Street, I take a left and pull into the Tropics parking lot. Cooper's old blue Dodge is already parked outside, along with Buck's Jeep and a few other familiar vehicles. They're all here.

My palms are sweating, and it's not from the heat. I know there's a hornet's nest waiting for me inside. I park next to Cooper and gingerly get out of my Chevy. My head and ribs ache, my black eye is throbbing, my nose is swollen, and I can still feel Brooke's sharp jabs. I pull the flannel shirt tighter as I walk toward the bar.

The neon sign is dark, there's a CLOSED poster on the door, and it's locked, so I knock. Once. Twice. Three times.

It slowly swings open, and for a second, all I see is Sal's silhouette, a shotgun in her hands.

"Jesus, Harley!" she says, stepping into the light when she sees my face. "Honey!" She grabs me, pulling me inside and snapping the door shut, locking it firmly behind us. "What happened?"

I sigh. "Bobby Springfield," I say. "He jumped me."

"Oh my God," Sal whispers. "The boys are in the back. Do you need anything?"

I shake my head. "I'll be okay."

"Go on, then," she says. There's fear all over her face.

I wish I could tell her it's gonna be okay. Sal's nice. She's always done right by the bar and by me.

I can hear the voices now as I move through the dark, empty space. Angry voices, coming from the back room.

I don't knock. I just push the doors open and step inside.

When the light hits me, a hush falls over the room.

"*Harley!*" Cooper's up off his feet, hurrying toward me. Wayne, his silent shadow, is close to follow. Wayne doesn't talk much, but when he does, it's usually worth listening to. The rest of the guys cluster around me too, worry and fear in their eyes.

"Who did this?" Cooper reaches forward, touching my bruised cheek lightly.

It doesn't hurt, but I fake a flinch, looking up at him, my eyebrows drawn together—the image of the helpless, scared girl that Duke trained right out of me.

"Bobby Springfield," I say again. "I was heading home last night, and he forced my truck off the road. He…" I trail off, waiting for his imagination take him there. Waiting for his heart to get seized with that murderous rage. "I got away before he could…" I say. "But he got me good." I wave at my face. "First Carl attacks one of the Rubies.

Now Bobby attacks me. The Springfields are up to something. I don't know what—"

"I do," Cooper cuts in. He whirls around, glaring at Buck, the only man who didn't leap to his feet when I came in. "How did you not see this coming?"

"Hey—" Buck protests.

"Duke put you in charge!" Cooper thunders. "And you fuck it up so bad that not only does Springfield blow one of our labs to kingdom come, but his piece-of-shit nephew put his hands on Harley!"

"Wait—*what?!*" I say, letting a shocked expression settle over my face. "What are you talking about?"

The other men look down at the floor, like they don't want to meet my eyes. Wayne sighs, walking over to sit at the table.

Buck glares at me.

"Springfield blew a lab?" I ask, letting my voice go dark and angry. I stalk over to the table, making sure I take a moment to look around the room, like I'm taking count. "When? Which one? Is everyone okay?" I ask Cooper.

He nods, grimacing in fury. "Last night. The trailer out east of Viola. Troy and Dale were lucky to get out," he says.

I look over to them. "Are you guys all right?" I say again.

They nod, looking scared and sheepish.

"We're so sorry, Harley," Troy says.

"I'm just glad you're okay," I tell him. It's the truth. Troy's got twin boys at home, and Sarah stays home with them because the littler twin has some problem with his legs. She'd be screwed if something happened to him. I turn to Buck. "What happened?" I ask. I wait a beat and then say, "Are we *sure* it was Springfield?" because they need to be sure for themselves, without me pushing them.

"Springfield set a fire," Buck says with a sneer. "And these idiots"—he jerks his thumb at Troy and Dale—"*both* went to deal with it. Left the trailer unguarded. Son of a bitch jacked the product and blew up the trailer. And spray-painted *Death to McKenna* on the fucking meadow. Who else but Springfield would have the balls to do that?"

"Jesus," I say, my shoulders slumping. I sit down, my eyes wide, staring at my hands for a long moment. "What did Duke say?"

"He hasn't called me back yet," Buck says.

There's a ripple in the air when he says those words. An almost invisible shifting of the men around me.

They're without their leader. They don't know what to do.

They're going to turn to either Buck or me. I gotta make sure it's me.

"He hasn't—" I snap my fingers. "Give me a phone. Mine's dead."

Cooper hands me his phone, and I dial Duke's number. It clicks immediately over to voice mail. Just like I knew it would, since it's turned off and sitting in my glove box.

"Duke," I say. "Call me back. We have a problem."

I hang up and hand the phone back to Cooper, zeroing in on Buck. "Okay. You know him when he's in Mexico. He disappears into some hole-in-the-wall bar and gets drunk off his ass. When he finds his phone, he'll call."

"That could be days," Buck says. "Springfield's just getting started. What if he hits the warehouse next?"

"What's your plan?" I ask, because I know it has to be a stupid one. I just need to draw him out, like a deer to a salt lick.

And then *bam*.

"Load up. Duke's still got the shipment of guns at your place, right?"

I nod, letting him dig his grave.

"I stopped by the warehouse and grabbed the guns there. Those plus the gun shipment should give us enough firepower. We go take Springfield out. He broke the truce. Duke would do the same thing."

Cooper snorts. As usual, Wayne is silent, but his eyes narrow a little, like he thinks Buck's stupid.

"I don't get why he's finally fucking stuff up now," Troy mutters. "It's been years."

"Who cares?" Buck says. "Point is, he did it. So he pays."

"We already have a plan in place for this," Cooper says. "When a lab gets blown, we lay low. We don't go start any fucking war. Especially when Duke's not here."

199

"Was the warehouse okay when you checked?" I demand.

"Everything was fine," Buck says. "No one knows it's there. He's not gonna find it."

"Are you kidding me? He managed to track the guys eighty miles into the national forest. You think he can't find the warehouse?"

Buck's frown deepens. "It's secure," he growls.

I ignore him. "Dale!" I bark, and he looks up at me, relieved that someone's telling him what to do. "Wayne is going to take you to the warehouse. Get all the finished product—if Springfield hasn't jacked it yet—and then call me."

"What about the chemicals?" Troy asks from the back of the room.

"He's right," Dale says. "The barrels—it'll have to be dark. We'd need one of the trucks."

"Just get the product out," I say. "We'll get the chemicals in the second round." I turn back to Cooper. "Where else are we holding?"

"Trucking yard," Cooper answers. "Shipment was scheduled to go out tomorrow."

"Pull it," I order him. "Send our apologies to our buyers down in L.A. Refund them the money plus ten percent. Tell them they'll get another ten off the next shipment because of the trouble. Be nice. Be apologetic. But don't be truthful. Tell them it was a bad batch or something. Quality control. Paint it like we didn't want a string of ODs on their hands."

"On it," Cooper says briskly, standing up. "I'll be—"

"Wait just a second," Buck interrupts. "We need to go after Springfield. We need to keep the product moving."

I move right up in his face and stare in his mean little eyes. "No, Buck. We need to lay low, pull all the product, and not draw any attention to ourselves." I spell it out slowly, like I'm talking to a little kid.

"We've got the sheriff controlled," Buck snarls. "He won't come after us."

"And what about the DEA?" I ask. "Law has to report the explosion. And even if Sheriff Harris buries the details, we still have the Forest Service to deal with. And then the firefighters—they'll make a report, so CDF's involved, too. And, if I remember correctly, my name was spray-painted on the grass for all to see. They'll come for us."

"We can strong-arm the Forest Service and the CDF," Buck says. "Buy them off."

"We don't own them," Cooper says. "They can go report whatever the fuck they want. And you know the Forest Service will because they're a bunch of tree-hugging hippies who care about pines and cottonwoods more than their own damn lives."

"Jesus," Buck swears, looking back and forth at Cooper and me. "It's like you don't *want* to fight."

"I don't," I say. "It's not the time. It's not the protocol." I turn to the rest of the men and take my chance. "Does anyone disagree?"

In the silence, I look around. Buck starts to say something, but then thinks better of it. The other men won't meet my eyes, but they shake their heads. I've got them.

For years now, we've been in a long stretch of peace, precarious, but holding up to now. Most of them started working for Duke after Springfield was sent to prison. They don't remember the world when Duke was still building his empire, brick by bloody brick. He's had control of North County for over a decade. They're not fighters—not the kind we'd need for the war Buck wants to start.

Luckily, I'm all I need for the kind of war *I'm* waging.

"Good." I nod. "I knew I could count on you. We need to secure whatever Springfield could steal. *Then* we figure out how to deal with him... after the heat from the blown lab dies down. If I sent that shipment down south, what's to say Springfield's not waiting to jack the truck?" I turn back to Buck, scorn written all over my bruised face. "We don't even know if he's hit the warehouse because you didn't bother to take the product out of there."

"I was busy!" Buck roars.

"You're a lazy motherfucker," I spit out. "And you're not thinking ahead. If Springfield wipes us out of product, it'll take a month to get back up running... longer if he destroys more of the labs. So we pull *all* the product. We'll keep it at the house, like Duke did last time a lab blew." I turn to Cooper. "That's what he did last time, right?" I ask, like I don't remember in perfect detail.

Cooper nods. "It's what he'd want us to do now."

I turn to Buck expectantly. The rest of the men are silent and tense, not knowing who to side with, but afraid to cross me. Afraid to cross Duke.

I go in for the kill.

"Duke could call back anytime," I remind Buck. "You think he'll be happy if you tell him you've gone after Springfield? You think you're gonna win points with him that way?"

Looking at him, at the low flush that starts at his neck and crawls up to his sweaty face, I realize that's exactly what he thought. If he wasn't so dangerous, I'd almost pity him. He wants what I have. What he can never have.

He wants Duke to give him the business someday, like a proud father. But he knows it'll never happen, because I'm in the way—Duke's child, the inheritor of all his training, his plans, his business.

That makes me Buck's enemy. If Duke hadn't gotten sick, it would probably be a few more years before Buck got fed up and tried to take me out. But it would've happened sometime. Which is why I have to take him and Springfield out now, to clear my path.

"Killing Springfield is something Duke decides when and how to do," I say. "You take that away from him, and you've got a big problem on your hands, Buck."

"You don't know that," Buck says, but it comes out weak. He's reacting without thinking, whipping it up in his head that Duke will be so grateful for Springfield's head on a platter that he'll give Buck anything he wants.

"Pull the product," I repeat, an edge to my voice. "All of it. Call me when it's done, and we can meet to transfer it."

"Where are you going?" Buck asks.

"I've got to go talk to Jessa," I say. "Springfield attacked her, so she might know something."

"Harley, you should rest," Cooper says. "Your face—"

"Is fine," I finish for him.

"We need to talk about Bobby Springfield," Cooper says, murder in his eyes, the tattoos beneath them twitching in anger—or maybe anticipation.

"We will," I assure him, reaching out and squeezing his arm gently. "Soon. But now, please go to the truck yard, get everything out. Take one of the guys with you."

Two men get to their feet at my words, and I feel a burst of triumph as Buck grits his teeth.

He's got no power here, not with Duke's original crew loyal to me. I am Duke's heir. His proxy when he's not here. And if I'm disobeyed during a time like this, it's as bad as them disobeying him to his face. As much as they like to dismiss me because I'm a woman, they can't deny my claim when Duke's MIA and everything's going to hell. There's a protocol Duke set up years ago, and my plan relies on them following it.

Duke is a man who doesn't leave things to chance. Cancer bit a lot of his careful plans in the ass, but no one needs to know that until I've got full control. And then I'll be the one making the rules.

"I'll see you soon," Cooper says to me.

He and Dale leave, along with Wayne.

Then it's just me, Buck, Troy, and the handful of underlings Duke keeps around for his dirty work.

"Go get a drink," Buck tells them.

The men scuttle out, their faces drawn. But Troy hangs back. There's a question in his eyes: Do you want me to stay?

He's afraid for me. Troy's one of the nice ones. Not a climber. Content to do his job, take his orders, not rock the boat. A follower, looking for a leader. And he found one in Duke.

He's always liked me, and he was nice to Will when we were kids, never made any nasty jokes about him, like some of the other cooks did when they thought Duke couldn't hear. And he's a good dad to his boys; he always brings them and his wife to the barbecues we throw at the Ruby in the summers. They're smiley kids, unburdened by the truth.

TESS SHARPE

"Go on, Troy," I tell him. I look back to Buck with a smile. "I'll be fine. Buck isn't gonna hurt me. Are you, Buck?"

Troy hesitates, but when I don't look back, when I keep staring at Buck, he leaves, the door swinging shut behind him.

Buck isn't a very tall man, but he's scarecrow skinny, with long, knobby fingers and arms. His skin is stretched tight all over him, like he's never had a decent meal in his life. His eyes are so dark they look black, and they shine like smashed beetles in the sunlight.

He's been around for almost eight years now. Duke brought him in when I was fifteen, and since then he's climbed his way up from lackey to second-in-command. I realized early that I had to watch out for him. He was smart enough to disguise his hatred of me around Duke, but the farther he climbs, the harder it is to hide.

"I want in Duke's shed," is the first thing he says.

"No fucking way," I spit back. My stomach flips in a slow circle at the thought of the damage he could do if he got this hands on the arsenal in Duke's armory. There would be a bloodbath. And then we'd have the DEA and the ATF on our asses.

Buck likes splashy. He likes to throw his power around, likes to make people feel it and see it. He has no talent for deception. He's a blunt weapon. Crude. Violent. Thoughtless.

"We need protection, Harley," he says, his beetle eyes squinting at me.

"We have plenty of guns already," I say. "And no one's gonna need them anyway, because we're gonna lie low."

Buck looks down at his phone, like he hopes Duke will call, give him leave to start a war, because violence is what clearly gets his dick hard. Fucker.

"This isn't a discussion anymore," I tell Buck, trying to sound as sure and steady as I can. "It's happening."

"I'm in charge while your father's gone," Buck says.

"You *were* in charge," I say. "And then our biggest enemy got the drop on you. So now I'm in charge."

Buck's fingers clench his phone so hard I'm afraid he'll break it. I can't see where his other hand is—it's hidden by the table, and that makes the hair on the back of my neck prickle.

I bet anything he has a gun pointed at me under there.

"Put it down, Buck," I say, and his shoulders hunch just the barest amount, telling me I'm right.

I don't raise my hands. I don't freeze.

I stare him down, even as I hear the unmistakable click of a safety.

"You shoot me, you're dead," I remind him.

"So are you," he counters.

My fingers twitch. My revolver's tucked into the waistband of my cutoffs, my flannel shirt hanging down long enough to hide it.

If I reach, he'll shoot for sure.

My eyes dart around the room, weighing the options, sifting through them like a dealer with a deck of stacked cards.

I could dive for the kegs in the corner. Use them as cover as we shoot it out.

I could stay where I am, reach for my revolver, and hope for the best. I know I'm a better shot than him because I'm a better shot than almost everyone. Duke made sure of that.

I've got six rounds. I can get off at least two before I bleed out from a gut shot. Unless he gets me in the head.

But that's giving him too much credit.

"The men, they won't kill you," I say. "They'll keep you for Duke."

When I say that last word, Buck licks his lips, a tiny movement of weakness, of nervousness.

*Find their weakness, Harley-girl. And exploit it.*

"You ever been around when he marks someone?" I ask, keeping my voice as casual as I can.

Buck doesn't say anything, but there it is again: his tell.

"You haven't, have you?" I take a tiny step forward. "Do you really want it done to you, Buck? It's not pretty. Burning flesh…it kind of smells like chicken. And the screaming…" I shake my head and prop my hand on my hip underneath my shirt. His eyes track the movement, but then snap to my other hand when I begin to swing it back and forth, just a little. The eye's drawn to motion over stillness.

"And that's just the beginning," I continue casually, and it's like I'm conjuring Duke's ghost between us. I can almost see him, the murder in his face. And I know it's all Buck can see too as I paint the picture with blood and guts. "You know what he does to men who cross him over a business deal. What do you think he's gonna do to a man who shoots his daughter? If you pull that trigger now, there's no running. There's no hiding. He'll find you. He'll tear you apart. And it won't be quick. It'll be slow, Buck. Slow and painful. Do you really think you could get away with it? Duke spent two years hunting Springfield. You weren't here for that. You didn't see the man he was."

"I know what kind of man he is," Buck says, but the red that crawls up his neck says otherwise.

"You have no idea," I laugh. "You know fluffy-bunny Duke. You know him at the top of his game. Not when he was clawing his way up there. Sure, he's killed men in front of you. He's hurt them. Ruined them. Tortured them. But you haven't seen Duke McKenna when someone threatens something he loves. And Buck?" I place both hands on the table, bending down so we're eye to eye. It's a calculated risk, but one I'm willing to take to drill in my point. "*I* am the only thing he loves."

There's a long, long pause.

"I'm his second," Buck says.

It's now or never. If I say the next thing, it's gonna make him stop or shoot.

"But I'm his family."

I can't see it, but I know the hand on his gun is trembling.

He has too much to lose.

Family trumps everything else for Duke. And he knows it.

"You won't win this way," I tell him. He won't win ever—his time's almost up. But I need one more day. One more day to get all the product. To lure Springfield out. To set them on each other. "So put it down."

One more impossibly long moment. His eyes on mine. And then I hear it: the click of the safety going back on.

He sets the .45 on the table.

For a second, I think about it—shooting him dead right then and there. I could tell the boys at the bar what he'd done. It'd be self-defense.

They'd stand by me.

But I need him. If my gut's right, he'll lead me right to Springfield.

It's a big county with miles and miles of forest—easy to get lost in. Easy to hide in.

I need to lure Springfield out. And Buck's my bait.

"Collect all the product we've got hanging around in the rental houses and motels," I say. "Cooper will text you with the meeting place."

He's grinding his teeth, his jaw working furiously. "Okay," he finally says.

"Good," I reply. "I'll see you later."

I turn around, half expecting a bullet in my back. But when that doesn't happen and I get to the door, I turn and look at him. "You ever point a gun at me again, I'll get the drop on you before you can pull the trigger. I let you off this time, but I've got a lot of reasons to shoot you—and no reason not to. You keep that in mind."

I close the door behind me, and I feel like I'm going to melt into the floor, but I have to stay upright. I have to be strong, because I've got work to do.

"You okay, Harley?" Sal asks as I walk up to the bar, grab a bottle of Jack, and pour out a shot.

I slam it, coughing as it burns my throat.

Jesus. That was close.

"I'm fine," I say.

And then I walk out of there like the queen he raised me to be.

# THIRTY-THREE

I'm twenty-one when I get the call in the middle of the night.

The sound jerks me out of sleep. It takes me a few seconds to read the screen, squinting at the letters.

"Mo?" I mumble into it. I rub a hand over my face with my free hand. "What's up?"

"I've got someone here," Mo says. "She says you told her to call if she ever needed help. She's got two kids with her."

I blink, trying to remember. "What's her name?" I ask.

"Jessa. Jessa Parker."

I'm suddenly awake, like I've had a bucket of ice water thrown in my face. "She's there?" I ask, my heart beating fast. She's there. That means...

My heart sinks.

"Yeah," Mo says.

"Is it bad?" I ask.

"Yeah," Mo says again.

"Is she tweeked out?" I ask.

"That's right," Mo says, because apparently she's playing morbid twenty questions. Or she's just trying not to let Jessa know she's talking about her.

Junkies and tweekers, they get spooked sometimes. They come to the Ruby when they want to get clean, but sometimes they bolt.

Sometimes I want to drag them back. But I know better.

Getting clean works only when you're willing to fight for it. Sometimes that kind of nerve is hard to summon up and even harder to keep up.

"How do the kids look?" I ask. She has a girl and a boy. No father. Not anymore, at least. My stomach twists. I need to concentrate.

"Okay."

"Good," I say. "I'll be right over. Don't let her leave, Mo. Promise me."

I can practically see Mo raising her eyebrow. "Something I should know?" she asks.

"Don't let her leave," I repeat.

Some secrets should stay buried. Just like some people.

The house is dark. I leave Busy in my room and head out into the night, my chest feeling tighter with each breath.

By the time I get to the Ruby, it's almost three in the morning. It's cold this time of year—on the edge of snowfall up here in the mountains. I pull my jacket tighter and head to the cottage that used to be the lobby when the Ruby was still a motel.

There's a little girl sitting on the floor, a puzzle in front of her, with her little brother by her side, who looks like he's more interested in chewing the puzzle pieces than anything else. They both look up when I walk in, and there's a wariness in the little girl's eyes that I recognize.

I smile brightly. "Hi, guys," I say. "Your momma in the back?"

The little girl nods.

"You two stay here, okay?"

I walk behind the front desk and push the office door open.

When I see her, everything in me goes cold. She's skinny—the scary, don't-eat-for-days-then-binge-and-crash kind of skinny. There are sores at the corners of her mouth, and when she meets my eyes across the room, her eyes fill with tears.

"Hi," I say, because I don't know how to start this. She doesn't know me well, but I know her.

209

"Do you remember me?" she asks.

I nod.

"You said…you said if I needed anything…"

"You want to get clean?" I ask, and I can't disguise the edge to my voice. I've had a few tweekers come to the Ruby pretending to need help but really looking to score.

I won't put that kind of temptation near any of the women who live here. Not in their home, where I've told them they're safe.

"Yes," Jessa says, and her voice is steady. "My kids…" Her face— so tired, still so pretty—twists, and more tears track down her cheeks. "Things were okay. But then they got bad. And now…" Her fingers clench together. "I don't have anyone," she says softly. "My kids don't have anyone."

I reach out, cover her hands with mine.

"You have us," I say.


Detox is the shits. Literally.

The Rubies set up a schedule so Jessa's kids are taken care of, away from the worst of it.

We look out for our own, always. Which is why I sit by Jessa's bed for a week and go home only at night because Duke makes me.

It's like watching someone die and be born at the same time. Messy. Foul. Painful. Even though I'm cleaning up after her, the room reeks of vomit and sweat. Jessa can't stand the light, so Mo and I draw the curtains and wait in the dark for her shivering fits to pass. The only sound is her moaning, and I try to close my ears to it, but it's hard, so hard.

By the third day, she's begging for a fix. *Just one hit. Please, please, please. I need to get my head right. Just one.*

I check the locks on the door and turn my head away from her pleading.

By the fifth day, she's swearing and hissing at me. She throws a full glass of water at my head.

I duck and Mo brings only paper cups from then on.

By the seventh day, Jessa just lies in bed and cries.

I smooth the sweaty bangs off her forehead and tell her it'll be better soon.

When I get home that night, Duke's in the living room, watching TV.

The house is so empty now, with Miss Lissa at Fir Hill and Will gone at college. It's just Duke and me, drifting in circles around each other, the space between us filled with the things we won't say and the ghosts of our mistakes.

Missing people—Momma, Miss Lissa, Uncle Jake, Will—it's a natural part of me now. I don't know where it starts and I begin. It's enveloped my life, and there's no running from it. No hiding.

I miss Duke, too. Even though he's right here. Even though he's the only one who hasn't died or taken off, he's disappearing in pieces right in front of me.

"Your Ruby okay?" he asks as I come into the living room and sit next to him on the couch.

"Better," I say. For now, at least.

He sighs. "You're always taking away my customers, Harley-girl."

It's a joke, a bad one. When I stiffen next to him, he knows it.

"It's our living," he says, because he can feel the judgment in me...the righteousness that rears its head from time to time, so fast and so hard I can't stamp it down.

There are so many things I can say. It may be our living, but it's others' dying. And it's not about survival, really. It's not even about getting Springfield anymore.

It's about power.

He's addicted to it, just as much as Jessa's addicted. Hooked on the fear and the authority, hooked on the way some men cower and others admire.

He'll never stop because he doesn't want to. The blood on his hands doesn't bother him, and the part of me that's his wishes I could feel the same. It would make things so much easier if I was all his.

But the shreds of Momma left in me, they hang on. They were nurtured by Mo, by Jake, and they grow stronger every time I'm at the Ruby. They wrap around my heart, whispering to do better.

To *be* better.

We sit there, side by side, but not on the same side, and I wonder how long he'll allow this.

How long until he decides to teach me another lesson.

How long until he understands I've learned all I need to.

How long until he realizes the student has outgrown the master.

# THIRTY-FOUR

*June 7, 1:30 p.m.*

Doc's house is the last one on the street, a shaky two-story deal that hasn't been painted in decades. I unlock the gate, white paint peeling off in strips as it swings open. Busy trots ahead of me, her ears perked, tongue out.

She's been here before.

I knock lightly on the door, and then, when there's no answer, a little harder. Doc finally yanks it open, reeking of booze, his hair going up in all different directions, his eyes bleary.

"Hey," he says. "Did I know you were coming?"

I shake my head, stepping inside. It's fucked up on the outside, but inside, he keeps things neat as a pin. Miss Lissa always used that phrase. It never made any sense.

He's a very orderly drunk, Doc is. Once upon a time, he was a surgeon. But he lost his license for drinking on the job. And he kept on drinking. If he hadn't, he probably would have a nice house and a nice wife and a nicely painted picket fence.

Instead, he's got this place, booze, and us.

"How's she doing?" I ask.

"She's in pain," Doc says bluntly. "As soon as she woke up, she wouldn't let me give her anything. What the hell happened to your face, Harley?"

"It's a long story," I say. "Can I see her?"

213

"You sure you don't want me to check out your nose?" he asks.

"I'd know if it was broken." It's been broken twice before. It's not something I'd forget. "Is she awake?"

Doc nods and leads me down a long, narrow hallway that has pictures of sad clowns lining the walls. He opens the door to the room off the kitchen and I go inside, closing it behind Busy and me. Doc gets the message, and I can hear his footsteps fade away down the hall. When I snap my fingers and point, Busy settles herself in front of the closed door.

I turn to Jessa, a smile on my face that drops when I get a good look at her. It's even worse than yesterday.

"Fuck, Jessa," I breathe. Her face is purple. Bruises everywhere, black around her jaw and neck. Her eyes are bloodshot, so many thin threads of red you can barely see white.

He'd strangled her.

My fists clench.

*Calm, Harley-girl. Control is key.*

I want to kill him. It's not a new feeling, but it's stronger than ever now.

"Hey," she croaks. She winces, swallowing a few times. "Hurts," she explains.

"I bet." I hurry over to the wicker side table, grabbing the water bottle there and holding it out to her. "The kids are okay," I tell her. "I don't know if Doc told you. Mo's watching them."

She took a few careful sips. "Better," she sighs. "Your face…"

"Don't worry about it."

I sit down next to her and she grabs my hand, squeezing it tight. "I'm sorry, Harley," she says.

"You don't need to apologize."

Her eyes fill with tears. "I broke the rules," she says.

"I know. I know about Bennet."

"You do? How…" She bites her lower lip, looking worried. "Did you hurt him?" she asks.

Her voice is so small, the worry in her, the worry *for* him, I can see it underneath her bruises.

Underneath what was done to her because of him.

Because of me.

"What happened?" I ask her. "Did you two get caught? Did Carl just jump you?"

"It was Bobby," Jessa says. "He got me outside of Bennet's place. I'd been going there so Bennet wouldn't have to come to town. We thought it would be safer. But Bobby saw me. He took me to Carl. They took turns."

I try not to squeeze her hand too tight, but it's hard, because I want to kick something. Maim something.

Preferably Carl Springfield.

"Do I need to get you the morning-after pill?" I ask her.

She shook her head. "They didn't rape me, they just beat me up. Big of them, right?" She laughs. It's that bitter laugh that all women understand. The one that's born out of years of fear, of waiting, of what-iffing, until it finally happens. Some man takes his anger out on you. Sometimes he yells at you. Sometimes he hits you. Sometimes he rapes you.

Sometimes he molds you into a weapon.

Different degrees of wrong. But they all leave wounds, some flesh, some fatal.

"Where did they take you?" I ask.

"I don't know," Jessa says. "Somewhere in a car. Bobby...he put me in the trunk."

I get up. I can't keep still. I can feel the walls closing in. The darkness of the trunk.

I remember what it's like.

"I'm gonna kill him," I say.

"You *can't*, Harley. He's Bennet's brother."

I close my eyes. How can I fight against love?

How can I take another person away from her?

"I love him," she says, like it needs to be said.

I want her to be happy. I do. I want all the Rubies to be happy and safe and loved.

215

But I need Bobby Springfield far away. As soon as Cooper's done rounding up the product, he'll start hunting for Bobby. And if Bobby isn't running scared, Cooper will find him. Bobby will get the better of him; he's too young and big and strong.

I need to use Jessa.

"Okay," I say. "Okay." I pull out the burner phone in my pocket. "Then you need to call Bennet. Tell him Bobby's in danger. He has to hide. I sent Cooper after him."

"Cooper..." Jessa's eyes widen and she scrambles for the phone, her movements clumsy and weighted with pain. She dials a number, breathing hard. "Baby?" she says into it. "It's me. No, I'm okay. Listen, no, babe, I need you to *listen*. Bobby has to hide. Now. They're coming for him."

Before she can say another word, I take the phone from her hand and hang it up, turning it off before he can call back.

She glares at me. "Why did you do that?" she asks.

"Because Bobby did that to you," I say. "And he did this"—I gesture at my face—"to me."

Her eyes widen. "What?" She sounds so much like a little girl in that moment. Disbelief all over her bashed-in face. Like there wasn't a world where someone got the drop on me.

I wish.

"I just gave you a gift," I told her. "I let you warn him. Now it's on him whether he lives or dies. And frankly, I'm hoping he dies. Because he's a woman-beating, racist asshole. Doesn't matter whose brother he is, Jessa. He deserves what's coming to him. He could've killed you. It's a fucking miracle Carl didn't."

"I don't want to hurt Bennet," she says.

"You don't think Bobby has hurt Bennet?" I ask her. The problem is that when it comes to men, Jessa never puts herself first. It's always them. What *they* want. What *they* need.

It's never about her.

"Bobby hurting you hurts Bennet. That's why he went after you, Jessa. To punish Bennet."

"We weren't doing anything bad," Jessa protests.

"Bennet broke the rules," I tell her. "There's us and there's them. We don't mix. They were raised to believe that, just like I was. And you're a Ruby, so that makes you a McKenna. It makes you Bobby's enemy." I need her to understand this, for her own sake. If she's going to keep seeing Bennet—and it's not like I can stop her—then she needs to be armed with more than weapons. She needs to know how they—how we—work.

"Would he hurt my kids?" Jessa asks, and a chill goes down my spine, because I don't know. Bobby's a wild card. And he's mean. He resents what Duke took away from his family. He'd be living a totally different life if my father hadn't killed his.

When Duke's gone—really gone, not fake-gone to Mexico—I guess I'll see the real measure of Bobby.

"I won't let him," I say firmly.

"Jayden and Jamie are okay?" she asks.

"They miss you. Which is why I want you to rest a lot. So you can come back home."

Surprise flickers in her blue eyes. "You're letting us stay?"

I grit my teeth against the sigh that wants to come out. I shouldn't. She broke the rules. She lied. She kept going across the river.

But it's Jessa.

"I'm letting you stay," I say.

By the time Busy and I leave Doc's, it's just after two. I'd charged my phone on the drive over and when I punch in the password, I see a missed call from Cooper and one from Mo.

I call Mo first.

"How's our girl doing?" Mo asks.

"She's up. In a lot of pain. Doc said she wasn't letting him give her any pills."

I could hear a vague rattle. Mo sucking in on another Camel. "At least she's not using again, then," she says.

At least Bennet hadn't gotten her to slide that far. But for how long? Worry snakes under my skin.

217

"How are the kids?"

"They're out swimming right now," Mo says. "Jayden's sweet. Always keeping an eye on Jamie."

She'd learned it early. Like Will learned to keep an eye on me while I learned how to keep an eye out for Springfield.

"Everything else okay there?" I ask as I turn off Doc's street and east toward I-5.

"More of the Sons showed up this morning. They're taking shifts. All quiet other than that."

"Good," I say.

"So…you gonna tell me what's really going on?" Mo asks.

My stomach tightens, my hands skid a little on the steering wheel. I could deny it. I could lie to her.

But it's Mo. We're partners. She's never done any of us wrong. Never slipped. Never wavered.

She'd die for each and every one of those women. And she knows that's a possibility.

There aren't many people willing to do that.

"It's better that you don't know," I say. It's weak, it's pitiful, really, considering all she's done for them and for me, but it's all I can give. A truth, but not *the* truth. Not yet.

I need more time.

I need those drugs the cooks are rounding up.

I have a plan.

"I'm getting a little tired of that excuse," Mo sighs.

"Just trust me," I say and it comes out more like pleading than I'd intended.

*McKennas don't beg, Harley-girl.*

"I do," Mo says. "Stay safe."

I say "bye" instead of "I will" because there's no point in lying more than I have to.

I hit the highway as I get a text from Cooper.

Meet at Folsom Hill 30 min.

218

I text back: On my way.

I drive north, and the gentle sloping foothills and grazing land fade into forest in a matter of miles. The truck's transmission complains as the highway begins to climb and twist, the trees thickening until there's nothing but green and shadow around me.

Duke's lived his entire life here in North County. Generations of McKennas—all of them crooked, from cattle rustling to claim jumping to making moonshine—have passed down the secret maps of the forest, back roads no one else remembered, landmarks only we can identify. Folsom Hill is one of those places—a spot deep in the Trinities that no one's getting to unless they know it's there.

I can't help but wonder about all the ways this could go down. Duke taught me to think of the what-ifs the way most fathers teach you to look both ways before you cross the street.

Best case, the cooks will hand everything over to me, no problem. Worst case, Buck's turned them or killed them and is waiting to pick me off, too.

I have to be prepared for both and everything in between.

The exit off Route 13 is quiet, no cars or trucks in sight. I pull over to the side of the road, hop out of the Chevy, climb into the bed, and unlock the toolbox.

There's a wooden box stashed sideways in the corner, and I pull it out, jump out of the truck bed, and set it on the tailgate. I flip it open. Nestled inside are my baby guns, the ones Duke taught me with when I was still small and breakable. The Glock 26 that he bought for me to put in a purse before he realized he hadn't raised me to be the kind who carried one; the five-shot revolver that has a bitch of a recoil; the sweet little .22 Magnum with the mother-of-pearl handle that had belonged to Momma.

After I make sure they're loaded, I take the Glock and the .22 and shove one into my waistband and the other in the pocket of my plaid shirt. Extra clips go in the pockets of my cutoffs.

My throat's dry. I need to get going. They'll all be waiting for me.

God, please let them all be waiting for me.

But my fear, that fucking paranoia, the endless *what-if* Duke drilled into me claws at my insides.

I take a deep breath and I drive, because there's no choice anymore.

I put it all in motion. Now it's time to follow through.

The dirt road through the woods is unmarked and narrow. I drive a good ten miles until I come to a tall oak, the trunk so old it's split in two. Just beyond it, there's a gravel road, and I turn onto it.

About three miles in, it gets rough, the gravel washed away with time, uncared for, giving way to dirt and rocks. You need a four-wheeler to handle the paths that pass for roads that branch off this one—and people like it that way out here. You choose a place like this because of that. As Duke always said, privacy to live your life the way you want it, with no interference from anyone, is priceless.

The switchbacks climb up the mountain, hairpin turns that make me grip the wheel tight. My gears are grinding by the time I get up to the clearing.

Relief rises inside me when I see Cooper and Wayne standing in front of their trucks, Troy next to them. The air's already shimmering with the heat as the sun climbs in the sky.

I park next to Cooper's faded black Dodge and hop out. "Buck's not here yet?" I ask.

Cooper shakes his head.

"He'll be here," Troy says. Wayne nods, but Cooper's mouth flattens.

"How was the warehouse?" I ask.

"Springfield hadn't hit it," Troy says. "We got everything out but the barrels. It's in the back." He jerks his thumb at Wayne's truck bed.

"And everything went okay at the yard?" I ask Cooper.

"Yep. We cleaned everything up," he says.

"You made sure there was nothing on the trucks already?"

He shoots me a look, disgusted that I even asked. I roll my eyes, but give him an apologetic shrug.

"Troy, can you start loading the stuff from the yard into my truck?" I ask.

"On it."

I jerk my head at Cooper, and he walks with me out of earshot, toward where the forest begins to thicken around the clearing.

"Any other places where we still have some product?" I ask. "Nothing stashed at the Tropics? Any storage spaces I don't know about?"

Cooper shakes his head. "We sent that big shipment down south right before Duke left for Mexico. Pretty much cleaned us out. My locals have been pulling in good quotas, too, so supply's low. I was gonna talk to Duke about bigger batches when he got back."

"What about the guns Duke got in January?" I ask.

"All the guns are at your place already," Cooper says. "Why?"

"Buck wants to get his hands on them," I say.

Cooper's eyes narrow. It makes the spider-web wrinkles at the corners deepen to grooves. "Like hell he will."

"That's what I said."

"I'm gonna put that motherfucker in his place," Cooper growls.

"No, you aren't," I say firmly. "I dealt with him. The only way he gets those guns is if I let him. And that's not gonna happen. So chill. I want this to go smoothly. Everyone's on edge for good reason. We need to lie low. We don't know what Springfield's got planned next."

Cooper's face kind of melts into an expression I don't recognize for a second. But when he hugs me, I realize it's pity.

"Oh, honey," he says, squishing me to him. "I know how scary this must be. But Springfield's not gonna do anything to you. We won't let him. You know that, right?"

I pat him on the back, trying not to tense up too much in his embrace, understanding that he means well. "I know."

I hear the sound of tires on dirt. I pull away from Cooper, looking toward the road. Everyone swivels, their hands going to their pieces, just in case.

Everyone relaxes when they see it's Buck.

Everyone but me.

"Finally you show up," Cooper says as Buck parks and saunters out of his truck.

221

"I figured I should obey the speed limit," Buck says. He doesn't even look at me.

"Come help me with the stuff from the warehouse," Cooper says. "We've been out here long enough."

I walk over to make sure Busy's okay in my truck cab. I've left it running with the AC on—gotta keep the old girl comfortable.

"Almost done, Harley," Troy says, setting another box in my truck. "It's gonna be okay," he tells me. "We'll make sure you're safe until Duke can get home."

I smile shakily and nod. What will happen when they find out Duke's never coming home? I can put it off for just so long. And I can only pray it's long enough.

"Wait—you said this was from the warehouse?" I hear Buck say to Cooper.

"Wayne, do you have extra bungees for the tarp?" Troy calls over his shoulder.

"Yup," he says.

"What do you mean it's light?" Cooper asks Buck.

"Hey!"

My head snaps toward the angry sound. Buck storms past me, grabbing Troy by the shoulder so hard he drops the box he's carrying. Full gallon-size Ziplocs spill onto the ground.

"What the hell, man?" Troy asks.

"The shit from the warehouse," Buck snarls. "I took inventory last week. The load you brought over is six bags short."

"Wait a second," I say.

"This fucker's stealing from Duke!" Buck yells.

"No, I'm not!" Troy says. He looks bewildered, running a hand over his ball cap. "Man, maybe you counted wrong. I wouldn't steal from Duke. I'm not fucking crazy!"

"Liar!" Buck shouts, and he raises his fist.

I move instinctually toward Troy. My hand closes over his arm.

It happens in rapid fire. Troy lunges forward, pulling me with him, blocking my view of Buck.

222

Someone screams my name. *It's Cooper*, my mind registers, right before it registers the gunshots.

One.

Two.

Three.

*Duck and cover, Harley-girl.*

# THIRTY-FIVE

I'm seventeen the first time I get rid of a body.

It's fall, just starting to get cold at night. I'm getting ready for bed, brushing and braiding my hair when I get the call.

"Hello?"

"Harley?"

It's Brooke. There's a long, hiccupping breath following my name, and something inside me goes very still.

But she doesn't say anything else, just breathes in slow, steady pulses, and then I hear something in the background.

Crying.

A girl.

"Where are you?"

Brooke whimpers. My heart picks up, sweat breaking out along my forehead.

"Brooke?"

She wouldn't have called me unless it was a last resort. She would've called her mom. Or her brother.

If she's calling me, something's very wrong.

I get up off my bed and shove my feet into my boots. Busy's head perks up from her place on the rug next to my bookcase, but I snap my fingers and she stays where she is.

"Brooke, tell me where you are. I'll come get you."

"Harley," she says again. "Oh, God, Harley." Her voice breaks, and she's crying too now. Big, uncontrollable sobs that make my heart kick up a notch.

"Tell me where you are." I switch my phone to speaker and go to the end of my bed, flipping open my trunk. I grab the stacks of folded quilts and the box that holds my grandmother's wedding dress and put them on the bed. Underneath are boxes of bullets and a slim black case.

"I didn't—she didn't—I couldn't—" Brooke's babbling. I open the case and pull out my single-action revolver, checking the chamber to make sure it's loaded before tucking it into a holster and fastening it to my hip. I get up and grab the phone again.

"Brooke, listen," I say. "Just tell me where you are."

"Off Route Twenty-Three. At the lookout."

"I'm coming," I tell her. "I'm coming right now."

"Promise?" Brooke's voice shakes on the word.

"Promise."

I mean it.

I mean it even when I get to the lookout, and Brooke is standing like a ghost at the edge of the forest, her hands covered in blood.

I get out of the truck and I see Molly, Pastor Evans's only daughter, head of the choir and of Youth Group and basically God's gift to good Christian men everywhere. She's sobbing, crumpled on the ground, her yellow sundress torn, her fingernails broken and bloody.

My eyes go to her right, a crumpled form lying under a pine tree.

It's Tripp. Brooke's ex-boyfriend. The one who liked to hit her.

Half his face is bashed in and bloody, and he's very, very dead.

I stare at him for a second, then I look at Molly, and finally I meet Brooke's eyes.

She looks back at me, and her chin tilts up.

"I didn't mean it," Molly mumbles. "I didn't. I didn't. I just—oh, God, oh Lord Jesus, save me!" She descends into mumbled prayer for a few moments before she takes a deep, shuddering breath and goes on. "He…he wouldn't stop…I had to make him. Please, please, please."

She's rocking back and forth on the ground, and for the first time, I realize she's holding something tightly in one of her hands.

A rock. Sharp, jagged, wet with blood.

The only weapon she could get her hands on.

My eyes widen, and I look at Brooke questioningly, and she nods once. There's blood all over Brooke's shirt, too. And streaked on her mouth.

She must've done CPR on him, trying to wake him up. I would've kicked his prone body a few times myself, but Brooke doesn't have a killing bone in her body.

Apparently, sweet little Molly does.

The world feels upside down. Never in a million years did I think I'd be standing here, looking at a man Molly Evans just killed for raping her.

"I didn't know who else to call," Brooke says under her breath. Molly's still on the ground, sobbing.

"You did the right thing," I tell her. I keep looking at Tripp's body out of the corner of my eye. I have a tarp and some rope in my truck. I'll have to stop somewhere for bleach.

"Okay," I say, my mind made up. I kneel on the ground next to Molly. I can do this. I just have to act like Mo or Will. Be nice. Comforting.

The feeling fits like a too-small T-shirt, cutting into me in all the wrong places.

"Molly."

She just keeps rocking back and forth, mumbling to herself and Jesus about how she had to do it.

"Molly." I grab her hand, the one holding the rock she killed Tripp with. She jerks under my grip, her wild, shocked glance flying up to meet mine.

"I had to."

"I know," I say. She won't give up the rock. So I just hold her hand over it. "It's going to be okay. I just need you to answer some questions. Can you do that?"

226

Molly nods, her fingers tightening on the rock like a vise.

"Did anyone know you were going out with Tripp tonight?"

She shakes her head. "My dad—he has rules about dating. I'm not allowed. I told him I was going to a girlfriend's house."

"What time did you leave?"

"Nine."

"Does anyone know you two were dating?"

She shakes her head again. "He wanted to keep it a secret."

Behind me, Brooke snorts. "I'll bet he did."

"So no one knew? No one at all?"

"Just Brooke."

I look over my shoulder at her. "You knew?"

Brooke folds her arms across her chest. "I saw them at church a month ago. I told him to stay away from her," she says. "And I warned her. I thought I had it handled."

I glare pointedly at Tripp's body.

"I realize now I didn't," Brooke says. "But I knew if I told you, you'd try to kill him."

My hands tighten into fists. She's probably right.

But I guess it doesn't matter now, since he's dead anyway.

"Okay," I say, trying to focus my thoughts.

"I—I should have believed you," Molly whispers to Brooke.

Brooke's eyebrows scrunch up. "Hey, no, Molly," she says, crouching down next to me. "You...it's okay. I know what people say about me. And he's..."

"A rapist who beats women," I finish her sentence.

My words just hang there in the night, the truth of it written on the hearts and bodies of the two girls next to me.

Molly looks up at both of us. "I don't know what to do." She looks so small.

"That's okay," I say. "I do."

I squeeze her hand, my fingers slipping a little in the blood. "It's time to let go of the rock."

Her breath hitches. I drop her hand.

227

"He can't hurt you anymore," Brooke says gently.

Her arm shakes, but finger by finger, her hand finally relaxes, and the rock falls to the ground between us.

"Let's get you up," I say. I grab her gently by the elbow, pulling her to her feet. "There's a bag of clean clothes and wet wipes and stuff in the toolbox of my truck. You need to clean up. Quick."

She takes a step toward my Chevy but hesitates, looking back at me. "But...what about evidence for the sheriff?" she asks, because she's a good girl, law abiding, and she just did what she had to, and she's programmed to think that's enough. That the sheriff's department will believe her.

Like they ever believe women, even when there's nothing riding on it.

And this? This has a whole lot riding on it. This is one of their sons. One of their shining examples. And he's dead. Killed by a girl half his size because they taught him *no* wasn't something girls said to guys like him.

Molly's screwed if anyone finds out.

"Molly." I feel like I'm holding a butterfly with a torn wing in my hands. I'm so scared to hurt her more. But I have to, to keep her safe. "You can't tell anyone. Ever."

"But—"

"Tripp's dad's a deputy," Brooke interrupts.

Blood is flaking off her hands in the moonlight as she steps toward Molly.

"They'd say you're making it up. That you were asking for it." Brooke's hands twist together, her voice flat like she's repeating something she's memorized. Something that's been said over and over...to her.

I can't help but be glad, so glad, that the bastard's lying there cold and dead, just a few feet away from me.

"That's what they said to me," Brooke continues.

"I—" Tears trickle down Molly's face. "But what's gonna happen?"

"I'm going to give you an alibi," I tell her. "Because even though you haven't told anyone about Tripp, he probably didn't keep his mouth shut. So go clean up. And hurry."

"I'll be right there," Brooke tells her. She turns to me, finally letting the panic fill her face. "Please tell me you have a plan," she says. "Because I'm freaking out right now."

"I've got a plan," I say. Really, I have half a plan. But I can't tell her that. My mind's clicking as I think it through. Neither of them will be any help in getting rid of Tripp's body. I need them out of here. Somewhere safe. Somewhere public, but not too public.

"You're gonna get cleaned up and change," I tell her. "There's some clothes in my bug-out bag. Take Molly to the Blackberry Diner, the one on Main Street. There's a booth in the back that has a RESERVED sign on it. Sit there. When the manager comes over to tell you to move, tell her that you're waiting for Jacob Green and that you've been there since eight o'clock. Can you remember that?"

"Who's Jacob Green?" Brooke asks.

"It's code. The diner is your alibi. When the sheriff comes 'round asking questions, every person working that night will tell him that you two were there. So will the regulars. You both stay there for an hour, try to get Molly to eat something. Then take her to your house and have her sleep over. Take her home in the morning, and make sure her dad sees you."

"Because that's not suspicious," Brooke says. "The choirgirl with the school slut."

"Tell him she led you to salvation. I don't care what you come up with, Brooke, as long as he believes she was with you and not out here killing Tripp. Because there's gonna be questions once he turns up missing. They will find out he was dating her. We need to make sure everyone thinks she was with you this whole night. There can't be any question to it."

Brooke sighs, scrubbing a hand over her face. "Christ," she says. "Is this really happening?"

"Yes," I say. "So get in gear."

Her eyes narrow. "You're such a fucking bitch," she says, and then her voice and mouth soften. "Thank you."

"Go get cleaned up. You guys need to go."

"What are you going to do with him?" Brooke asks.

If I told her, she'd never look at me the same way again.

"You don't need to know."

She doesn't want to know.

No one does.

I wait until the red glow of Brooke's taillights fade into the distance before I pull the phone out of my pocket. I punch in a number, waiting three rings before he picks up.

"Whassat?" Cooper mumbles.

"It's Harley," I say. "I've got a Man in Black, and I need some help."

There's a long pause. I can hear rustling, someone snoring in bed next to him. I know it's Wayne. No one ever talks about it. But everyone knows. They live on the same piece of land.

"You've gotta be kidding me," Cooper says finally.

"Nope. And I'd appreciate it if you don't tell my daddy about this."

He swears so loud and so filthy, I pull my ear away from the phone for a good fifteen seconds. "Holy shit, girl, you're worse than your old man," he mutters. "Fucking hellraiser, and you're not even legal yet. Where the fuck are you?"

"The lookout off Route Ten."

"I'm coming," Cooper says.

"Good," I say. "Bring bleach. Lots of it."

I hang up the phone and turn to face Tripp. I walk toward him; he's bathed in the beam of headlights from my truck, his cloudy eyes staring up at the starry sky, looking slightly surprised.

I should feel sick looking at him, but all I can feel is glad. Because it was either him or her, just like it is so much of the time.

Molly is my goddamn hero. It takes a lot of strength to bash someone's head in. Especially with nothing but a rock. And she's little.

I crouch down, wrapping my hand in my jacket so I won't leave any prints, and dig in Tripp's pocket, coming up with his phone. There are a few texts from his friends on his lock screen, but nothing else. I doubted his father enforces much of a curfew. Which is good luck for me and what I'm going to do.

I pull a bobby pin from my hair, bend it straight, and use it to pry the SIM card out of his phone. A few seconds with a lighter held under it, and bye-bye SIM card.

I'm just pulling the tarp out of my truck when I see lights in the distance. I drop the tarp, and my hand goes to my back, closing around my revolver. The brights hit my eyes, blinding me for a second.

I pull my gun.

But as the black spots in front of my eyes clear, I see the weathered blue of Cooper's old Dodge and his wild, fluffy white hair silhouetted in the cab like a halo. He's a funny kind of angel, not like the ones Molly's dad talks about, but he's the one I need right now. He pulls up next to my truck, flinging himself out of his own.

"What the fuck, girl?" he snarls, stalking past me and toward Tripp. He comes to a halt a few feet away from his bashed-in head.

"Isn't that one of the deputy sheriff's kids?" Cooper asks, staring down at the body.

I take a deep breath. I make my eyes wide. "He was gonna…" I don't finish the sentence. It's better to let his imagination take over.

But as my lie sinks in, Cooper doesn't look horrified. Instead, his head tilts and his eye tats twitch. "Who do you think you're fooling?"

The shock is cold, like ice water in my face. The reason I called him instead of Daddy was I was sure Cooper would fall for this. "What?"

Cooper looks down at Tripp. "There's no way you killed this boy. You wouldn't be this messy."

"Excuse me?"

"Oh, believe me, honey, I'll know your first kill when I see it," Cooper says. "But this is not it. So…who you covering for? Boyfriend?" He peers close at my face. "Nah, Will wouldn't be this messy, either." He makes a slow circle around Tripp's body, like he's a coroner or something. Though, come to think of it, he's probably seen as many dead bodies as a coroner. "A girl did this. He rape someone? She get the better of him?" He looks closer and whistles. "She did a number on him. Good for her."

"Are you gonna help me or just stand here spinning stories?" I spit out, pissed off that he's figuring it all out so easily. "You really think I'd get rid of a body that's not my fault?"

Cooper rolls his eyes. "Honey, you are your daddy's girl in many ways, but when it comes to a woman in trouble, you're just like your momma. One of the Rubies do this?"

"*I* did it," I say firmly.

"Mm-hmm," Cooper's enjoying himself, and my patience's wearing thin.

"Cooper: Dead body. Dead deputy's kid. And as much as the sheriff's department is in Daddy's pocket, I don't think they're gonna overlook me getting caught with one of their kid's body."

"Fine, fine." Cooper shakes his head. "Whatever you say, Harley. Pull the truck up. Go on home. I'll take care of the rest."

"No."

Cooper's eyebrows rise. "Don't think you want to be around after that. You want him really gone, no trace. We're talking chainsaw and lye, baby girl."

I lick my cracked lips. I could take the out he's giving me. It's a gift. It's because he loves me.

But it's also because he thinks I can't take it.

*Never show weakness, Harley-girl.*

"It's my responsibility."

Cooper looks back at me, respect mixed with pity in his blue eyes. "Okay, then," he says slowly. "Quit lying your head off and give me a hand. Grab that tarp, then go gather some leaves and branches." Jerking his chin at Tripp's body, he adds, "We've gotta get that thing out of here, ditch his truck, and cover up the blood in case somebody happens by." He looks back at me with a grin, and there's new respect in his eyes. "Big girls clean up their mess. Better get started."

Hours later, when the chainsaw is cleaned off with bleach and the chemicals are eating away at what's left of Tripp, I walk out of Cooper's barn and throw up in the bushes. Scarred, tatted hands pull my hair back, and when I straighten, wiping my palm across my mouth, he stares down at me and says, "You okay, honey? First time…it's hard."

It takes a few deep breaths.

"Any second thoughts?"

I meet Cooper's eyes. I harden my own.

"I warned him," I say. "He should have listened."

I walk away. Head high. Shoulders straight.

Cooper doesn't question me again.

I've made my point. I'm nobody's baby girl now.

# THIRTY-SIX

*June 7, 2:49 p.m.*

Copper. Bright. Bursting on my tongue.

Troy's blood is in my mouth.

Thick. Wet. Sliding in chunky drips down my cheek.

Troy's blood is all over me.

Weight. Suffocating. Pressing down on my chest.

Troy's body is on top of me.

Voices. Yelling. Coming into focus in a rush.

Cooper and Buck are shouting—*"Son of a bitch, you fucker, what the fuck were you thinking, shooting so close to her?" "Fuck you, he was skimming off the top!"*—their guns drawn and on each other. Wayne's got his hand on his hip at Cooper's side, seconds away from drawing that machete.

They're all gonna kill each other.

I push, gasping as the back of Troy's head drags against my cheek, and I twist under the weight until I've rolled out from under his body. Dazed, I struggle to my feet, my ears still ringing from the gunshots.

"Hey!" I call out, blinking hard, trying to focus. There's so much blood. I wipe at my face, and my hand's just red, so much red. Busy's barking like crazy in my truck, her paws scraping frantically at the glass. "Hey!" I yell this time, loud and clear.

They don't even look at me; just keep yelling while Troy's blood puddles at my feet.

234

I look down at his body.

What are Sarah and the boys going to do?

Fuck.

This is my fault.

This isn't how it was supposed to go.

My focus narrows.

*Think,* then *react, Harley-girl.*

I grab the Glock from my waistband. The second it's in my hand, I stop shaking.

The second I aim, I'm calm.

*No one.*

Bang, right between Buck's legs.

*Was supposed to.*

Bang, right over Wayne's shoulder.

*Get hurt.*

Bang, right above Cooper's head.

"Guns down!" I shout.

They're frozen, their full attention on me now, and it'd almost be funny except I'm spattered in Troy's blood and bits of his brain and skull, and I'm fully willing to add to the mess if I have to.

I shoot in the air and then point the barrel down to aim at them. *"Now!"*

One.

Two.

Three guns tossed on the ground in front of me.

I scrub at my forehead with my shirtsleeve. It just smears more blood on me. My stomach turns. I've never wanted to get clean so bad in my life.

I take a deep breath. I want to tremble. Break. Sink so deep into the ground I'll come out changed, with new growth. I want to be the kind of woman who can't handle this. Who doesn't know how.

But this is what I was raised for.

*A remote location, bleach, and tarp, Harley-girl, and you're golden.*

"Wayne, there's a tarp and rope in the bed of my truck. Put on the gloves that are in the toolbox before you handle them," I tell him. "Cooper, back your truck up so we can put him in the bed. Buck." I look at him long and hard, until the sweat springs up on his forehead. "Get out of here before I change my mind about shooting you."

He huffs out an indignant breath, opening his mouth to protest.

In a few strides, I close the space between them and me, and I level my Glock at Buck. "I have three bullets left," I tell him. "I'll put the first one in your foot. The second in your dick. And the third right here." I press the barrel against his forehead. "Go home. Don't leave."

"I—" Buck starts.

"You heard her, Buck," says a voice behind me. "Go."

It's not Cooper, though. It's Wayne.

His hand's on the machete he keeps strapped to his leg. I've seen him gut a deer with that thing, cut through tendons and joints like they're butter. And I know Buck has, too.

Cooper wears his threats tattooed on his face. Wayne keeps his voice and his violence to himself, because when he lets go, when he does what he does best, there are no survivors. Just rumors.

Buck's face pales as he looks back and forth at the three of us.

There's a beat, a moment where I'm afraid the ego that made him pull the gun on me earlier will get the better of him. But this time I'm not alone. Cooper and Wayne flank me like guards, and I feel safe, like it's the way it should be. Like it's what Duke always imagined for me. The queen and her knights.

"Fuck this," Buck snarls. "Call me when you're ready to fucking *do* something about Springfield."

I don't say anything. I don't even move. I just keep my gun on him as he backs up, gets in his truck, and drives off, spraying dirt and pine needles everywhere.

As soon as it's safe, I crumple to my knees. As soon as he's out of sight. The gun falls from my hands, and I stare at them as they start to shake again.

"Harley, honey." Cooper crouches down next to me.

But I can't. My hands are speckled in Troy's blood. All of me's spattered in Troy's blood. I need to get it off. I rub my hands together frantically, trying to get it off, but all that does is make the blood that's starting to dry peel up all over my skin.

There's this whimpering sound, and I realize it's me, and then Cooper's grabbing both my hands in his and going, "Okay, calm down, honey. Calm down."

I look up at him. His pale blue eyes—they're usually icy, but now they're kind.

I want to tell him. Duke's his best friend. If I don't tell, Cooper won't get to say goodbye. But if I do, he'll stop me. I can't let that happen.

Everything's already gone wrong. I promised myself no one would get hurt.

I lied to myself. I knew the cost. I was just pretending it wouldn't happen.

Now two little boys don't have a father and Sarah is a widow and she doesn't even know it yet. She won't even get a body to bury. Cooper will get rid of him. Put him somewhere no one can find him. Because that's what Cooper does.

Because that's what we do.

Because that's what my plan has wrought.

I have two choices. Crumble or rise.

My legs wobble as I get to my feet. The front of my shirt sticks wetly to my stomach. I stare down at myself. I look like I've butchered a deer and botched the job.

"I need a jacket," I say, pulling off my flannel shirt and handing it to Cooper. The tank top underneath it is black, so it's not as bad, but my arms are streaked with blood.

Wayne thrusts a jug of water and some napkins at me, and I use them to wash off my arms and hands and face.

"Is everything in my truck?"

Cooper nods.

I look over at Troy. He's half on his side, his face in the dirt. I can't leave him like that. I go over, crouching down, and roll him over on his back.

A good chunk of his skull's missing. I grit my teeth against the swell of sick that ripples inside me.

I reach out, hesitating, and then I press my hand to his chest. "I'm sorry," I whisper. "I'm so sorry. I'll take care of Sarah and the boys. I promise. They'll never need anything. They'll have a good life."

They'd have a better life if he was still alive.

I get to my feet and look at Cooper. "We need to get rid of him."

"I know," Cooper says. "Wayne and I will take care of it. You go lock up the product. Don't stop for anything."

"Sarah…"

"We can't tell her yet," Wayne says. His voice is always gravelly. I'm not sure if it's just that way or if it's because he barely uses it.

I know this, but it's still like a knife against my skin. "She'll get worried when he doesn't come home."

"I'll call her," Cooper says. "I want you to go home. Lock the gates and doors."

"Do you think he'll come for me?" I ask.

"I think we need your father," Cooper says. "We don't have just a Springfield problem. We have a Buck problem. He doesn't know his place. Never has."

"Tell me about it," I say.

"But we need to get this done first," Cooper says. "So go." He nudges my shoulder. "Be safe."

I get in my truck and make my way out of the clearing. Right before the final turn onto the road, I pause, turning back. Wayne's already got a tarp spread out next to Troy. Cooper's got an ax.

He swings it high.

I floor the gas pedal.

# THIRTY-SEVEN

I'm sixteen years old the first time I'm responsible for a man's death. I don't kill him with my own hands, but I'm the reason he's dead, all the same.

It all starts on a Sunday in February. Miss Lissa sends Will and me into town for groceries, and we stop at one of the gas stations on the south side of town before heading home.

Will's pumping the gas and I dash through the rain into the mini-mart because I want jerky.

I don't even look at the guy behind the counter beyond a quick glance as I do a 360 of the store, marking the exits in my mind like I've been taught to do.

There's no one else in sight, and I head over to the jerky rack, trying to decide between the jalapeño and the pepper when the bell on the door tinkles.

I look up to see Will frozen in the doorway. But he's not looking at me.

He's staring at the guy behind the counter, and the look in his eyes...

It makes the hair on the back of my arms raise.

It makes me reach for the knife in my jacket pocket.

The wrongness of the moment, the fear in Will's eyes, has me moving toward him swiftly. But I don't reach out and touch him.

There's something inside me that tells me not to. That tells me if I do, he'll flinch.

I focus on the guy on the counter, one hand hidden in my jacket, holding my knife tight. He's just a regular guy. Skinny. Tall. Dirty blond hair, light blue eyes, long nose.

"Will?" There's a hundred questions behind that one word, but I don't even know if he can hear me. He's so terribly still. It's not like him.

It's not who Daddy taught us to be.

Something changes in the guy's face when I say Will's name. There's a slow dawning of recognition, then a smile.

Something sick churns inside me at the widening of his mouth. The flash of his teeth. At the way Will stiffens next to me.

And then Will's grabbing my hand and yanking me out of the store. I stumble after him, letting him pull me. I look back at the man, who hasn't taken his eyes off us.

"Will—"

"Not now." He tosses me the keys, and I nearly miss them in my surprise. He never lets me drive.

I climb into the driver's seat, starting the engine up as he buckles himself in. The silence stretches as I pull out of the gas station and drive down the road, heading toward the highway.

My mind races, sorting out the scenarios, the possibilities, at a rapid-fire pace that comes only from being drilled, over and over again.

*Think of all the angles, Harley-girl. Cover all the possibilities. Always know more than your target.*

But Will isn't a target. Will is sitting next to me, horribly silent, his lips pressed together tight, and he looks like he's about to be sick.

"Do you want me to—" I start to say, and then I just pull over to the side of the road, right before the highway entrance. He jerks the truck door open, stumbling out. He throws up on the side of the road in the dark, and I don't know what to do. I scramble from the truck, going to stand next to him as he braces himself on his knees, panting.

"Fuck," he says.

Reaching out and touching him seems like a good and a bad idea all wrapped up together. But I do it anyway. I lay my hand on his shoulder, and his hand comes up, pressing over mine.

We stand there like that, the sound of the semis heading up the mountain in the distance.

"I need to get you home," he says finally.

"I need to get *you* home," I say. For a second, I think he's going to crack a smile, but then it's gone.

We drive home in silence. I don't ask, and he doesn't answer. Miss Lissa frowns at us when we get home, wondering why we're so late.

"They were training a new cashier at the store," I tell her. "She kept messing up the produce codes." The lie comes easy, and I walk into the kitchen with her to unload the groceries before she notices Will has slipped outside, heading toward the cabin across the meadow where he and Miss Lissa live.

I don't say a word to Miss Lissa or Uncle Jake, who ambles downstairs to help with the groceries. I wait until everyone heads off to bed, and then I grab one of the lanterns from the mudroom and hurry out into the night.

Out here, there's the pure kind of darkness that only comes from being far away from towns, from houses, from people. The sky's so clear it never quite looks real, the stars shining there like gold flakes at the bottom of a pan.

I am a lone prick of light as I move through the forest, my feet taking the path worn through the pines partly by instinct. The shadows stretch in front of me, forming shapes out of the corner of my eyes.

But I'm not afraid of the woods.

I'm afraid of what happens when I find him.

There are dozens of places he could've gone. But I get it right on the first guess: the deer blind closest to the creek. It's set high in an old oak, the trunk so thick it would take three men to circle it with their arms. I climb up the ladder, the handle of the lantern in my teeth.

I set it down next to him and push my back against the far wall of the blind, drawing my knees up like his. He reaches out and turns off my lantern, leaving us in darkness.

I wait, because pushing's no use with him. It just makes it take longer.

Will and I are good at silence. At being quiet. At things unsaid. At keeping a foot in the unknown.

We are made up of secrets: some we share, some we don't. And until I saw that look on his face in the mini-mart, it hadn't ever worried me.

I always told myself he'd tell me if it was important.

But now...

"You remember your momma, Harley?"

He's not looking at me, staring out the opening in the blind, out into the trees and shadows and rustles of the forest, instead.

"Of course."

"I mean *really* remember her," he says. "Not just stuff Jake or Gran filled in. Or Duke told you."

I frown, something twisting in me. I do remember. I do. But it's hazy.

"She smelled like lilies," I say. "I remember her bracelets. The turquoise ones. I liked to play with them. She read to me from this big book of fairy tales every night. And she didn't take shit from anyone."

His mouth twitched. "No, she didn't."

"You knew her longer than me," I say, and there's some sort of accusation in my words that I can't quite figure out or keep from leaching into my voice.

"She was nice to me," Will says. "Whenever Mom would call her, she always came. She always bailed her out of whatever shit-show Mom got in. I never understood why."

"They grew up together," I say. "Like us."

"They were *nothing* like us," he says, with a sudden ferocity that makes me sit up straighter. "Your Mom loved you. *I* love—" He stops, and it hangs there, the "you" he won't say. "But my mom..."

Will barely talks about Desi. The one or two times I asked Daddy about her, he got this disgusted look on his face and just shook his head, telling me to drop it.

"She loved you," I say, because it's hard to imagine anyone not loving him.

"She loved getting high more," Will says and it's one of those terrible, real truths that I can't deny. Because the things I do know about Desi aren't good. The longest time she stayed clean was when she was pregnant with him. She let Carl build a fucking meth lab ten feet away from her kid's bedroom. She was too beaten down by him to stop him when he burned those marks into Will's skin.

There's a line a mother crosses where she loses the title. When it becomes just a word instead of a bond.

"She kept a lid on it for a while," Will says. "But after she had me, Gran started watching her closer. Gran figured it out, so she promised to clean up. Rinse. Repeat. She cut Gran off when I was six. I never saw her after that until...." He picks at the hole in his jeans, twisting the fraying threads of denim around his fingers. "Things were bad when she didn't have Gran giving her money. She kept getting fired. We lost the apartment. Moved in with one of her boyfriends for a while, but he kicked us out when I was seven because he said I ate too much. And then we were at the Capri, renting by the week, picking cans and bottles out of the trash to take to the recycling center for food money."

He goes quiet. It's not a normal silence from him. Will likes to pick his words unless he's riled, and I'm used to waiting, but this feels different.

Heavy.

It's hard to find his hand in the dark without looking down; it takes me two tries to get palm to palm, our fingers threading through each other's. I squeeze, once, *it's okay*; twice, *you can tell me*; three times, *I'll stay no matter what*.

"She started turning tricks," he says. "For the drugs. And then..."

Something in the pit of my stomach turns dark and deadly as a horrible thought rises in me, urged on by his shuddering words and lost voice. My hand tightens around his.

"There was one guy," he says, hushed. I have to lean forward to hear, tilt my head into his shoulder. My ear brushes against the thin cotton of his T-shirt, worn soft from years of washing and drying on the line. "The guy from tonight. Dan. He always watched me, and I just…I *knew*. You know?"

I nod against his neck, and he lets out a shuddery breath.

"One night, I heard them talking. About how much."

I slip my hand that isn't holding his around his waist, tilt my body until it's a solid press of warmth against his side. I breathe against his neck, smelling green and fresh and *Will*, waiting for him to say more.

His hand squeezes back now: once, *I wanted to run*; twice, *I screamed and she didn't listen*; three times, *the cash was on the table in the morning*.

I rub my hand over his heart, wishing I could reach inside and fix it. I bury my face into the crook of his neck, and his hand squeezes mine, telling me all the things his mouth can't say.

I hold him and I keep the anger inside.

I press my lips to his forehead and I whisper it wasn't his fault.

I walk him home and I don't let the fury show.

I don't go into my house. It's late, but I get in my truck, praying that Uncle Jake's sleeping deep.

When I get back to the mini-mart, Dan's still there. It's nearly three in the morning; he must have the graveyard shift. I tick this off on a mental list I'm already developing in my head of the things I know. His name. His schedule. The fact that he's a fucking monster who buys little boys.

My fingers tighten around the steering wheel. I can't stop my eyes from going to the glove box.

It would be so easy. One shot. Right between the eyes. I wouldn't even have to get that close. He wouldn't be able to react.

I'm fast. And I don't miss.

*Stop and think, Harley-girl.*

There were cameras. I'd be seen. Even Daddy would have a hard time convincing the sheriff to look away from that sort of proof.

It's not just that holding me back. It's not just Daddy's voice in my head.

It's Mo's.

244

Daddy's raised me up a McKenna. But Mo and the Rubies are the women who've taught me what it is to survive. What it is to be a survivor.

Will survived this man. And if I just kill him, no one the wiser, if I take the choice of what happens to him from Will...

What does that make me?

Mo says there always has to be a choice. Choice is where the power is, that's why they try to take them from you. Getting your choices back is where healing comes from.

So instead of blowing Dan's head off right then and there, I sit in the truck and I watch. I wait.

And I try to figure out how to ask Will what choice he wants to make.

Will and I don't talk about it. I wait for him to say something, half-afraid he's waiting for me to do the same, but the next day, he shows up after school like normal, and we take Busy for a walk in the forest. It's raining, so lightly that the water gets caught in the canopy of the trees, in the leaves and needles and moss. The droplets never make it to the ground.

Spring's coming, glimpses of green shoot through the wet, soggy brown of late winter, as the snow melt rushes down the mountain and into the creeks.

I like this time of year, and I know it's Will's favorite. So we walk, on pathways through the forest that only we know, our breath and Busy's paws through the mud the only sounds for miles.

I act normal and so does he. But it's not like it didn't happen or I don't know.

There's this understanding suddenly, a warm branch of knowing that's twisted with all the others I've gathered through the years.

We keep walking, and somewhere along the way, he takes my hand and he doesn't let go.

A week later, I still haven't found the nerve to ask Will. But I've got Dan's schedule down pretty good. He pulls the graveyard shift on the

245

weekends, but the weekdays he's on the five-to-one-a.m. shift. He lives in a run-down house on Pine Street, near the jail and the Rusty Nail, one of the seediest of Salt Creek's six bars, which he visits for an hour or two after work most days.

He's a creature of habit, Dan is. He goes to work, then he either goes to the bar or he goes home. At first, I thought he was single. But then, ten days into my new stalking habit, I see her. And all those plans to talk to Will, to let him choose, go right out the window.

Because the first time I see his girlfriend, she's holding a toddler on her hip and her hand's pressed against the swell of her stomach. She looks about six months pregnant.

All those tentative plans of *maybe* turn to *definitely* in a second. My mind's made up, then and there. Even Mo couldn't fault me. I pray for Will's understanding if he ever finds out.

But kids in Dan's house means he has to die. That little girl is in danger, if he isn't already messing with her. And that baby will be, too.

So I continue to watch, letting my plan begin to fully form in my head as I do.

The toddler spends a lot of time at the girlfriend's mom's house. I tail them there a few times, because there's no way in hell I'm doing this in front of a kid. The kid spends Wednesday nights at Grandma's because Dan and the girlfriend's shifts overlap. She's gone until six a.m. He gets home at two or three, depending on if he stops at the Rusty Nail or not.

It's long enough.

So the next Wednesday, I park in the lot across the street from the mini-mart at five o'clock in the evening and I settle in for a long wait.

The sun sets at about six, fast like it does in the forest, and I'm grateful when it does. It starts raining around nine, and by midnight the parking lot's swamped with water. The rain falls in sheets against my windshield, a continuous patter of sound that'd be soothing if I weren't so on edge. When someone taps on my passenger window, I jump—and when I see who it is, my stomach drops.

Shit. I am in so much trouble.

I unlock the door, and Daddy climbs inside.

"I thought you were coming home tomorrow," I say.

"I decided I missed my daughter," he answers, slamming the door shut and shaking the rain off his coat. "Imagine my surprise when I get home and she's not in her bed where she's supposed to be. And her goddamn guard dog isn't with her."

"How did you find me?" I ask, partly to delay. Do I tell him? Do I lie? Which is better?

Which gets me what I want?

Am I even ready for what I want?

He shoots me a disgusted look, settling in the seat. "You think I don't have a tracker on your goddamn phone? I raised you smarter than that."

I glance out the window. It's nearly one. Dan's shift is over soon. He'll be heading home, and I need to follow.

"Start talking," Daddy demands. "You left Busy at home. You know the rules. You don't go anywhere without her."

"The thunder might've spooked her," I say. "I couldn't have her barking."

"And why not?" Daddy looks out my window, staring across the street, frowning. "You staking out the place? Planning a little robbery?" His voice is light, almost teasing, but his eyes are serious. He's pissed.

I don't disobey him. Or at least I don't get caught doing it.

I bite my lip, chewing on the chapped skin, trying to decide.

It's not my secret to tell. I know that. I'm better than that.

"Harley Jean," he says warningly.

Daddy understands me. I'm half his in nature and all his in nurture. Daddy will recognize this feeling inside me, the urge to lash out like a rattlesnake and strike until my prey's a bloody mess. I know he will, because he did the same thing to Ben Springfield.

That's what I want for Dan. But I won't get it unless I tell Daddy.

I need him. Because I'm not sure I can do it myself. But I know Daddy can.

"I'm hunting," I say.

247

"You're…" he trails off, his eyes going back to where mine are focused: on the mini-mart. "Who?" he demands. "The guy behind the counter?"

I nod. "He's a bad person." It's such weak words for what he is. *Monster* doesn't even cover it. I don't know if there's even a word that can hold that much evil.

"Did he hurt you?" Daddy's voice gets terribly low and thick, and instead of scaring me like it usually does, it spurs me on.

"No," I say. "I'm way too old. He likes little kids."

"He—" Daddy's head snaps back to the store's window, his eyes narrowing. I can feel the air in the truck change. It makes goose bumps pepper across my skin. There's one thing even the worst kind of men can agree on: Kid fuckers should die.

"How do you know this?" he asks.

"It doesn't matter," I say. "I just do."

I am caught up in my hate, and it swirls around me like dust clouds kicked up by truck tires. There's a vicious, hot churning in my stomach that I recognize, that I remember from the day I got Busy. But this is even more, a boiling sickness I can't rid myself of. All I can hear is Will's confession in my head. The way his voice broke.

I've been taught to make men pay when they cross me and mine.

"What are you going to do?" Daddy asks, and now he's looking at me instead of the store. He's looking at me like I'm a butterfly trapped in a water glass. Something fascinating, but too delicate to touch.

"His girlfriend has night shift on Wednesdays. He'll be alone."

"You've been tailing him."

"For a week," I say. "I'm not jumping into anything. You taught me better."

"I did," Daddy says. "And what are you gonna do when you've got him alone?"

I don't say anything. Admitting it makes it real.

"You're reacting, Harley," Daddy says gently. "Reacting, not thinking. What have I told you about that?"

*Think first. React smart.*

I glance out the window. A woman in the same red-and-black T-shirt Dan's wearing has taken his place at the counter. He's heading across the parking lot, toward his beat-up Ford, a six-pack of PBR in his hand.

It's time.

I start my truck.

"I've thought on it enough," I tell him as Dan pulls out of the parking lot, heading toward home.

I press on the gas, and we follow.

Daddy's silent the whole way to Dan's house. The light's on in the living room already, and I park a few houses down.

"So what's the plan?" Daddy asks.

He thinks this is another lesson. Maybe it is, to him.

But it isn't to me.

"Go 'round the back. Entry through the far door. Tread lightly. Double shot to the head. Use a pillow to muffle the noise. In and out in five minutes, tops." I rattle it off.

Daddy raises an eyebrow, radiating disapproval. "Sloppy," he says. "You'll end up with a murder investigation on your hands."

"The sheriff's an idiot."

"No body, no investigation," he says.

"No body means a dump," I argue.

"You scared of a little cleanup work?" He shoots back with a smile.

I glare at him because he seems to think that this is fun. That it's a time for teasing.

"I'm not scared of anything," I say, unbuckling my seat belt and reaching for the door.

Daddy's arm presses like a steel band against my chest, pushing me back into the seat with a bruising force.

"You do not go into that house without a plan," he says. "And you do not go into that house without me. Do you understand?"

I grit my teeth. "Yes, sir."

"You're gonna take your .38," Daddy directs. "We'll go through the back. You stay behind me until I give you the okay. You keep your gun on him."

"Yes, sir."

He pulls his arm away from me, flips open the glove compartment, and puts the gun in my hand. "Let's go."

This late, everyone who lives on Pine Street is asleep or still out at the bars or work. The only house with lights on is Dan's.

We cross the street and go down the driveway, slipping through the unlocked gate. The backyard's overgrown. I can feel weeds brushing up against my ankles as we make our way to the back door. Daddy tries the knob—it's unlocked, too.

He jerks his head, and I follow him inside.

The lights in the kitchen are off, and Daddy's beard shines silver in the moonlight coming through the window as he takes in the situation. The cabinets look like they're purple or maybe blue in the darkness, and there are dirty dishes in the sink, takeout containers on the counter. He points down the hallway, the one that leads to the living room. "Wait ten seconds. Then follow me."

I nod, adjusting my grip on my gun. My hands don't sweat or shake, but there's fear under my skin, lying still, ready to pounce. I breathe steady, counting in my head. One. Two. Three. Four. Five.

Six. Seven. Eight.

"Hi, there," I hear Daddy's voice boom out.

"What the fuck!?"

I pad silently into the room behind him. Dan's on the couch, facing away from the hall. Daddy's seated himself across from him, in a beat-up recliner that has a big rip in one arm. His gun's on his knee, not pointed at Dan, but a clear threat.

"I wouldn't move if I were you," I say, pressing the barrel of my gun against the back of his head.

Dan goes still, a whimper escaping his lips, his shaking hands going up.

Daddy smiles, all teeth and all business. "Now that I've got your full attention," he says. "You know who I am?"

I pull the gun a little away from Dan's skull so he can shake his head. He glances up at me as he does it, and his thin eyebrows scrunch together.

"You're the girl who was at the store with..." he trails off, his eyes widening as he stares back at Daddy. "Oh, God."

"You *do* know," Daddy says. "That's good. That makes this so much easier."

I move around the couch, so the .38's in Dan's face. So it's even more real.

He licks his lips, sweat pouring off him. "Look," he says. "I promise, whatever Will said happened, it isn't true."

My stomach quakes. Shit. I hadn't thought this through.

It wasn't mine to tell. It wasn't Daddy's to know.

Shit. Shit. Shit.

Daddy's head whips to me. "Will?" he says, and there's a horrible question there.

I look away, and it's the only answer he's gonna get, but it's the only answer he needs.

With one movement, Dan's lifted off the couch and hefted up against the wall, pinned by the throat. Daddy's hands wrap tight around his neck. He sputters, legs kicking out uselessly, his fingers scrabbling against Daddy's.

"You touched him?" Daddy hisses, right in Dan's face. "You put your filthy hands on my boy?"

Dan's eyes bulge, partly in terror and partly because Daddy's doing a real good job at cutting off his air supply.

"Harley. Explain." He grits out and there he is: the Daddy from the barn. The Daddy who punched holes in Ben Springfield like it was nothing and killed him even though he'd given him everything he wanted. The Daddy I need for this.

He's a weapon. My weapon. And I just need to pull his trigger.

He loves Will. I don't think he ever meant to. I think he brought Miss Lissa home to take care of the house and me, and he just saw Will as a bonus. A built-in playmate for me. Another tool to keep me content and trapped on the property, away from Carl Springfield's reach.

But Will has a way of getting to you. I loved him from the start. From the flip of a coin and a promise to have my back. It might've taken Daddy longer, but that didn't make it less real.

I know what he's feeling because it's exactly what I'm feeling.

When it comes to loving, we are the same.

"What did you do to him?" Daddy demands, and my heart breaks when his voice does. Daddy's fingers are so tight around Dan's neck that his face is bright red and his eyes look like they're about to pop out.

Daddy's on the verge of killing him. It would take just one word from me to stop him.

And it will take just one sentence to push him.

"His girlfriend's pregnant."

Daddy's shoulders tense. And right then his mind's made up, just like mine was the second I saw her and her daughter. Daddy's hands shift, lightning quick, and a horrible, thudding *crack* fills my ears.

Dan slides slowly to the ground, his head flopping to the side, his eyes bloodshot and blank.

I look down at my own hands and I think about how I'll never be able to do that. How I'll never have the strength in my fingers to crush men's windpipes and spines. It's scary that there's even a small part of me that wants that. But you think strange truths when someone dies in front of you. They spring into your head, and they're hard to ignore.

Daddy steps away from Dan's body and toward me. I can't meet his eyes until he reaches under my chin and lifts my face up. "Harley," he says quietly.

"I'm okay." My voice sounds strange in my ears. Breathless. Almost excited.

I should be upset. I was upset last time.

I was eight last time. I'm grown now.

Daddy's eyes search my face like it's got answers. But it doesn't, and

I don't. I just need to move. To do something. To avoid feeling…or not feeling. There's a strange blankness falling over me. When I look at the body, I don't feel anything.

I should feel something.

"Will?" Daddy asks again.

I bite my lip, crossing my arms. "You can't tell him," I say. "He can't know that you know. That we did this."

Daddy's lips press together tight, and he rubs a hand over his face. "Jesus," he sighs. "That *fucking* woman." I know he's talking about Desi. "I can't believe she let this happen. Goddamn junkie."

I don't tell him the whole truth, because if I do, Daddy will find some way to bring Desi back to life just to kill her himself.

"What do we do now?"

"You go home," he says. "I'll take care of this."

I open my mouth, because it's instinct to protest. It's instinct to want to learn the lesson.

It's instinct to finish what I started.

"Go home, Harley," he says, and it's a clear order. One I'm not going to defy. Not when I've already broken so many rules. He'll probably call Cooper. That's what you do when you want to get rid of a body. You call Cooper.

I take one step away, then another, and I don't pause when I hear him say, "You did good, Harley-girl," as I open the door.

I go home.

It's nearly dawn by the time Daddy gets back. He finds me in my room, wide awake. I'm curled around Busy on the bed, my back to him. I can feel the mattress dip as he sits down next to me, and the tightness in my chest uncoils when he strokes the hair off my face. It should make me flinch, those same hands that just hours ago were crushing the life out of someone, but it doesn't.

Like recognizes like.

And I am like him now.

"You okay?" he asks quietly.

I nod.

"I…" and then he stops, like he doesn't know what to say.

What do you say after all that training, all those lessons he's taught me, is finally put into practice?

This is what he wanted, wasn't it? This is who he raised me to be.

The kind of woman who can rule. The kind of woman who can kill.

"You love Will a lot," Daddy remarks.

I'm run down, frayed at the edges like a cut wire, because I can't control it—the laugh that bubbles to my lips, a sound that's all disbelief that he doesn't know this. That he hasn't seen it.

I turn over and look up at him, and I can feel the warmth trickle down my cheek, a single weakness, a single tear of truth.

"I love him more than anything," I say, and it's not meant as a warning, but he should take it as one.

But love makes you overlook the most obvious things sometimes.

I'm counting on it.


A month later, I walk into the diner where Dan's girlfriend works and take a booth in the back of her section. I order pancakes and coffee, and I try not to stare at the curve of her stomach.

She's pretty. Really pretty. Even in the ugly polyester dress from the eighties that the boss has the servers wearing. I sit in the booth, nursing my coffee, watching.

There are circles under her eyes, and the manager—some shithead with a patchy mustache and even patchier hair—keeps grazing her ass with his hand every time she passes by him.

"More coffee, hon?" she asks.

"Thanks," I say as she fills my cup. She has to brace her back with one hand, the coffee cup with the other. I can't imagine how much her feet must be hurting.

"How far along are you?" I ask.

"Seven months."

"Do you know if it's a girl or a boy?"

She smiles, but it doesn't reach her eyes. "Boy."

My heart thuds, a sound so violent and loud, I'm almost afraid she'll hear it.

*No regrets, Harley-girl.*

"Hey, Jessa." The manager brushes past her, his hand palming her ass again. "I need you to take table four."

Her jaw tenses. "I'm on it." She meets my eyes again, that false smile back on her face. "Can I get you anything else?"

"He always do that?" I ask, nodding toward the manager, who's now arguing with one of the cooks.

Her cheeks turn red. "Don't worry about him."

"You shouldn't have to put up with that shit," I say, grabbing a napkin and scribbling down my number. "My dad, he owns some restaurants. You call me if you ever need a job...or anything," I tell her, handing over the scrap of paper.

She tilts her head, looking puzzled, as she takes the paper. When she reads my name, her eyes widen, but she slips the paper in her pocket anyway before heading over to table four to take their order.

It'll take Jessa five years to come to me. She's stubborn like that. When she shows up at the Ruby with the kids, I don't look at her like I'm sorry because I'm not, even if I am guilty.

Even if I am responsible for this path she was put on.

She'll never know because I'll never tell.

It was the only way.

# THIRTY-EIGHT

*June 7, 4:45 p.m.*

It's almost five by the time I get all the drugs unloaded into the armory. Afterward, I go up to the main house and shower, trying not to look at the red-brown water that swirls down the drain.

When I go into my bedroom, Busy's sitting on my bed, looking relieved to see me. I pull a fresh pair of jeans out of my dresser and yank them on.

My phone rings. I look down, and my heart skips a beat.

It's Brooke.

"Hello?" I ask, when I really mean *Is he dead?*

"Where *were* you?" Brooke hisses. "You were supposed to be here at three to talk to the doctor. I called ten times."

"Oh fuck," I say. I'd forgotten. "Is he okay?"

"Harley," Brooke says, and her voice sounds strangled, like she's pushing down her frustration. "They said...it could be just hours. You really need to come."

"I—" I don't know what to say. I have to go. The warehouse is next on my list. I need to take care of it while the chemicals are still inside, before the cooks have a chance to get them out of there after it gets dark. If I don't, then they'll have all they need to start up again. And I'm not about to let that happen.

I have to finish this.

"Harley, I'm not saying this for him," Brooke says. "I'm saying it for you. You will regret it if you aren't here. I know you will."

She's right, of course. But I already have so many regrets. I've learned to live with them.

I might have to learn to live with this one.

"Will," I say. "He's coming. He'll be there. And I'll be there as soon as I can."

"Harley," Brooke sighs.

I know she's trying to look out for me, but can't she understand that I've already betrayed him? It doesn't matter if I'm there or not.

At least that's what I keep telling myself.

"It's the best I can do. I have to go."

I hang up before she can say anything else. I stand in the middle of the room for a second, staring at the phone in my hand, trying to convince myself it's the right thing I'm doing.

But blood's been spilled. I can't play the guardian angel in my head anymore.

I'm the devil, like him. I just have different priorities. Some noble. Some not so.

I text Will because I'm too cowardly to call him.

Because if I hear his voice, I'm going to unravel. And there's still so much to do.

Brooke is waiting for you at the hospice. I'll be there as soon as I can.

I hesitate before pushing *Send*. And then I tap out one more sentence: She says it's time.

I stare at the words, my traitorous mind screaming *no!* even now. But there's no miracle coming. And even if they do exist, Duke doesn't deserve one.

I press *Send* and put the phone in my pocket.

I finish getting dressed, and instead of staying put like I promised Cooper, I load up the truck with what I need and head south.

Duke's main warehouse is a big building on a stretch of land at the end of a dirt road about five miles out of town. There's a sheet metal place a mile up the road and a boat storage place on the other side of the high-

257

way, but other than that, it's secluded. Quiet. Remote.

Not somewhere a drug outfit operates out of. Which, of course, is why we use it.

There's no one around to see me after I dismantle the cameras. I unlock the doors, picking up the two gas cans I brought from home. Inside, it's a lot cleaner than the trailer was. Long stainless-steel tables with arrays of flasks and burners, and orderly shelves and barrels full of chemicals, ready to be mixed to fuck people up.

The drugs may be gone, but the real value is all this stuff, because once the threat's passed, they'll use it to start right up again. They'll cook up more. They'll sell it. I won't be able to stop it—or them.

So it's time to remove the resources. Once this is all gone, they'll be even easier to control.

I pick up one of the gas cans, pull off the lid, and walk the length of the warehouse, dumping the gas in a long, splattering line on the floor. I toss the can on the ground, letting it leak and pool on the ground. I splash the gas from the other can all over the tables and at the base of the shelves.

I cough; the smell's starting to get to me. With a hand over my mouth, I hurry outside, leaving a long trail of gas. I grab the can of spray paint from my truck. Busy watches me as I walk across the paved lot, to the very edge, and spray a MCKENNA where the fire won't get it, finishing with a bold red $X$ across the name.

I toss the can back in my truck bed and dig in my pocket for the box of matches. With shaking hands, I pull it out and step toward the line of gas leading to the doorway. I scrape the match against the side of the box, and the flame bursts free.

I drop the match, and fire leaps from the sliver of wood to the gas on the ground, spreading in a greedy line toward the warehouse.

I run to my truck, jump inside, and squeal away, my heart in my throat, terrified it'll blow before I make it out of range. Dust clouds in my rearview, and smoke will follow any second. I push harder on the gas, racing down the road, waiting, waiting…

*BOOM!*

The sound rattles the windows, and I can feel the blast of hot air even inside the cab. Busy yelps, then begins to bark furiously, staring out the back window at the plumes of smoke rising in the sky.

We're at the end of the road. I make a hard right, speeding off and away before anyone's the wiser.

"It's okay," I tell Busy as I turn onto the freeway heading back to town. "It's okay, girl."

The trailer. The warehouse. The house on Shasta Street.

Two down.

One to go.

By the time I make it back into town, it's dusk. Shasta Street's on the west side, where the little houses were cute once, but are run-down now. People try their best and they have some pride, but there's only so much you can do without any money.

I don't park right outside the house, but choose a spot down the street near the intersection, between a beat-up minivan and another truck, mostly hidden from view. I have a good visual of the house from here, which is what I need.

Buck's black F-150 is parked in the driveway.

He hasn't gotten the news yet. It's just a matter of time. Wayne listens to the police scanner like it's his religion. A fire that big is gonna bring everyone out.

Sure enough, ten minutes after I've started my stakeout, my phone buzzes. It's a text from Cooper.

Springfield just hit the warehouse. I'm dealing with it. You safe at home?

I text back: Safe & sound.

A few seconds pass, and then a new message: Stay there.

I'm not going anywhere. Not until Buck does.

The lights are on in the kitchen but all the blinds are drawn, so I can't see inside. That pink bike—the one with the training wheels—is on the front porch. It has streamers on the handlebars.

*This is for her, too,* I remind myself.

It's hard to believe that, though, when just hours ago, I was picking bits of another kid's dad out of my hair.

"Only way," I say, like it's a prayer.

There's movement on Shasta Street. I straighten in my seat as the door to the house opens and Buck comes out. He doesn't look around, just goes straight to his truck and backs out of the driveway.

"Stay down, girl," I tell Busy, pointing to the floor of the passenger seat. She jumps down, curling up, resting her chin on her tucked-in paws.

Buck takes a right off the street, and I wait a good thirty seconds before pulling out and following.

Tailing is always a risk. Following someone in a city is easier—there are swarms of cars and foot traffic and places to hide. But it's harder to hide in a small town or on a two-lane highway. I can only lag behind the sedan between us and breathe a sigh of relief when Buck turns left onto I-5.

The big rigs that wind up and down the freeway late at night and early in the morning are climbing the mountains, pushing the speed limit, trying to get their loads to Portland and meet their quotas. I pull behind one in the slow lane, keeping my eyes locked on the road ahead, where Buck's way up in the fast lane.

I've suspected his loyalty for a long time, but in the last year, I've seen things that have put me on edge. The first was when a bunch of red phosphorus went missing. Buck claimed he'd forgotten to reuse the phosphorus from the first batch and had to compensate. Duke believed him, but I didn't. He's been cooking for years—he knows how to recycle his chemicals.

Then he disappeared while he was on a run with Cooper—he was gone for hours. Cooper bitched about it for a week afterward, but Buck just rolled his eyes and said something about picking up someone in a bar. There was something in the way he shifted and looked away that made alarm bells ring in my head.

And the third time was the clincher: When Duke got sick and "went to Mexico," I was put in charge of the money. It was the first time I'd ever had my hands on Duke's ledgers. We were buying way too much pseudoephedrine and hydriodic acid for the yields the cooks were turning out. It wasn't apparent if you didn't do the down-and-dirty math, but I've always been good with numbers.

Buck was tipping the scale, and he'd been doing it for a while. He was either cooking up extra and dealing on the side or, even worse, selling off the chemicals to somebody.

There's only one somebody in this county who's willing to cross Duke like that.

And Buck's going to lead me right to him.

My phone rings, and when I look down and see it's Will, I let it go to voice mail. I can't be distracted.

My S10 weaves north through the Siskiyous, the tall pines so thick and the mountains so high they block out the sky and sometimes the moon. The higher we climb, the darker it gets.

We pass the exit that leads to my house. And then thirty minutes later, we cross the county line.

My phone rings. Will again. I let it go to voice mail. Again.

The Chevy's headlights hit a sign that says POLLARD FLAT, 1 MILE. Buck's turn signal flips on, and he merges into the slow lane in front of the big rig I'm hiding behind, disappearing from view.

This is it.

I scrunch down in my seat. "Stay down, Busy."

When I take the exit, he's already at the stop sign at the end of the off-ramp. I slow down, watching, as he turns right, and I count slowly to fifteen.

Then I follow.

Pollard Flat has nothing but a gas station and restaurant, and they're on the other side of the highway. Wherever Buck's going, it's in the backwoods.

I turn my headlights off, the darkness engulfing me. The only light I have is the fading red of Buck's taillight and whatever moonglow can make it through the trees. It's dangerous, it's a little crazy, but it's the only way he won't see me on such a narrow road. It's winding, the left side falling sharply into a long drop, and to the right it's studded with pines so tall they don't just loom, they tower.

They also hide the houses, set high up the mountain or deep at the bottom of the cliffs near the creek. I navigate the hairpin turns, glimpses of Buck's taillights spurring me on. And then suddenly I take a final curve, and he's gone. Nowhere in sight.

I slow the truck and spot the drive where he must have turned. I go beyond it a ways, then make a sharp turn around and pull over, partially obscured by a big oak, out of direct sight of the road.

"Stay here, girl. Quiet," I whisper to Busy.

I grab my Glock and flashlight from the glove box, get out, close the door quietly, and then hurry back down the road, heading toward where I saw the taillights disappear.

It's pitch dark now. But I can hear the rushing water from the creek down below. I stop at the side of the road, closing my eyes; listening, listening…

*There.* Up ahead, a truck door slams shut.

I run, tracking the sound. My feet are silent against the pavement, and then across the forest floor as I veer off the road, up the hill, toward a faint light I spot through the trees.

Duke taught me to be soft footed, to be quick, to be silent.

To be deadly.

I hurry through the trees, my legs burning as I climb. A few times I slip, but I dig in with my heels, grasping at rocks, branches, anything to keep myself upright. Now I can see the porch light on a beat-up mobile home, set deep in the forest, a rough dirt road leading up to it.

Buck's Ford is parked in the driveway. He leans back against the tailgate, his hands in his pockets.

He's waiting for something.

Some*one*.

I press myself tight against a pine tree, blurring my silhouette, watching as the door to the trailer opens.

And there he is.

My stomach clenches. My hand goes for my gun.

He looks like I remember. Slicked-back hair, dirty shirt, mean expression.

My trigger finger itches.

"What the fuck are you doing here?" Springfield snarls.

"What the fuck are *you* doing?" Buck shouts back. "We had a sweet deal going on, and you decide to get greedy on me?"

Springfield frowns. "What are you talking about?"

"What am I…?" Buck stares disbelievingly at him. "You're crazy," he says flatly. "One word of what we did gets out, my name even crosses your lips, I'm gonna kill you. You understand?"

Instead of looking cowed, Springfield smiles. "Well, someone's got you running scared, don't they?"

"Fuck you, Carl," Buck says. "Find another way to get your shit. Cook it yourself. I don't care. I'm out."

He turns, showing Springfield his back. He's either being brave or stupid—and I know he's a coward. But Springfield doesn't make a move—he just watches as Buck gets in his truck and drives away, kicking up dust and gravel as he goes.

Springfield moves to go back into the trailer, but then, suddenly, his head snaps toward the forest, staring through the pines in my direction. He senses something.

I push my back hard against the tree, holding my breath. Fear, the real, true, body-shaking kind, sparks inside me.

I need to reach for my gun. I'm afraid the movement will catch his eye.

But if I don't, and he sees me…

The eight-year-old inside me wants to run.

The fifteen-year-old needs to face him.

The eighteen-year-old would charge, firing without fear.

But I'm almost twenty-three, and I have been all those girls. I've made our mistakes and learned our lessons and felt our rage.

It's hardened me. Honed me.

I am smarter now.

I am patient now.

I wait, barely breathing, just a few yards away from his searching eyes. I stay still, frozen to the tree, praying the darkness will hide me.

The seconds tick by. It seems like forever, but eventually he turns around and walks back to his trailer, steps inside, and closes the door behind him.

I run. My heart hammers in my chest, and branches whip my face and chest as I stumble through the forest down the sloping, rocky ground. Twigs and pine needles crunch under my heels and I snag my feet against roots and rocks, but I keep going until I reach the road and my truck, pulled over to the side.

I can't catch my breath as I climb in. Busy's ears go straight up when she gets a whiff of me.

I smell like fear. She whines, pawing me, her claws scratching my arm.

I'm still panting as I start the engine and get the fuck out of there.

My phone's ringing again. I can't focus now that my suspicion's been confirmed: Buck's been working with Springfield. Or, at the very least, dealing whatever extra he'd been cooking up to him.

Is that where those missing six bags of product he accused Troy of stealing went?

My stomach swoops. Jesus. Of course it was. How fucking stupid am I?

That fucking bastard. He killed Troy just to cover his own bullshit.

My phone keeps ringing. I'm almost to the on-ramp. I want to put as much space between Springfield and me as possible. I need to think about this. If he and Buck have been in contact, if Buck's been selling drugs to him, that changes things.

I pull over to the side of the road, grabbing the phone, putting it on speaker.

"What?" I say into it.

"Harley?" Brooke's voice is frantic. "Is Will with you?"

I frown. "No. He should be with you." What time is it? I look at the clock.

It's been hours since I texted him. I look down at my phone.

There are three missed calls from him, but no messages. My heart tightens like a fist is closing slowly around it, testing its strength.

"He called me three hours ago, telling me he was on his way. He never showed up. I've been calling, but he's not answering his cell."

"Did you check the hospitals?" I ask. Maybe there was an accident. The road to Burney is twisty. He's on his bike. He could've gone too fast. Spun out.

My throat's dry as bone. The fist around my heart squeezes. Because I know. I know. I've always known.

*Loving that boy will get him killed, Harley-girl.*

My phone buzzes. Incoming message.

My hand shakes as I open it.

It's a picture of Will. His arms are yanked back behind him and his face is a mess of blood.

But he's alive. The relief bursts inside me like the water through the makeshift dams we used to build in the creek when we were kids. But it's there and gone, because I recognize that tattoo on the arm pushing Will's head forward.

It's Bobby Springfield's.

My phone buzzes again.

867 Butte Street. Come and get him, bitch. I dare you.

# THIRTY-NINE

I'm almost eighteen the first time I shoot a man.

It's summer, the second year that Will's been sent to work on the grow for the Sons of Jefferson. Daddy's in town that day, and Busy's at the vet because she'd tangled with a rattler, so it's just Uncle Jake and me in the big house.

I'm up in my room, and when I hear the front door opening, I don't even give it a second thought. I turn the page of my hunting magazine, thinking the footsteps I hear on the porch are Uncle Jake's heading out to the barn.

The gunshots that come a minute later make me think otherwise.

I roll off my bed and onto the floor, the years of Daddy bursting into my room at all hours to scare the instinct into me paying off. I stay flat on my belly, my back squeezed tight against the box springs. I yank out my Winchester .22 barrel first, searching blindly through the dust bunnies to locate the box of ammo.

I breathe in and out, loading the bullets, my lips moving silently as I count. I pull the bolt, the first bullet slides into place with a click, and I thumb the safety off.

I strain my ears, but there's nothing to hear. No more footsteps. No more gunshots.

No way in hell would Uncle Jake be shooting off a gun without good reason. And he'd have shouted for me by now if he wasn't...

I swallow and scramble across the floor, the rag rug in front of my window tickling my skin as I slowly raise myself up to peer out. I can see part of the porch from here if I angle my head right.

I spot the edge of a plaid shirtsleeve, and then Uncle Jake's arm comes into sight, hand scrabbling across the porch, trying to pull himself forward.

I watch in horror as he crawls into view, belly down and leaving a long, dark drag of blood behind him on the porch.

He's hit.

This is on me now.

My head whips around at the sound of the front door closing, followed by a steady thump of footsteps up the stairs.

I need to get to Uncle Jake. He'll bleed out if I don't.

My eyes track across the room as I put the pieces together. My door's half cracked open, and my bed's not gonna provide enough cover. I could maybe get off a few rounds if I needed to, but a .22 isn't exactly made for close quarters.

Window's my best option.

The shooter's footsteps are getting louder.

I flip the safety on, sling the .22's strap over my shoulder, open the window, and heft myself out feet first, my belly pressing against the pane. My feet dangle in the open air as I ease the rest of my body out until I'm hanging by my fingertips twenty feet in the air. The barrel of my .22 hits the back of my knees, and I grunt, swinging my legs *hard*, pushing off with as much might as I can, stretching.

I hit the porch roof hip-first with a thump, losing control of my roll halfway through and almost falling off the edge because of it. I grab for something—anything—to stop my momentum, latching onto the gutter pipe at the last moment. My muscles scream and pull, but I hang on. It takes me a few seconds to swing down onto the porch railing, trying to land as lightly as I can.

"Uncle Jake," I hiss, running in a low crouch to him. He's lying face-down on the porch, his shoulders rising and falling in horrible, jerky movements.

I kneel next to him and push at his shoulder, rolling him over. He moans, and if I didn't have to press my hands down on the gaping pulpy mess of flesh that used to be his stomach, I'd be clapping them over my mouth.

"Harley," he slurs, his eyes barely open. "Run, baby. Run."

"*No.*" Shit, his *stomach*. I pull at the tattered ends of his button-down shirt, trying to make some sort of bandage or compression or...

Oh God.

I strip off my T-shirt, spreading it across his middle and pressing down hard. The blood stains the white material a horrible rusty color, darkening by the second, until it's soaked through.

I can feel something slick and fleshy beneath my hands, like I'm just a thin layer of cotton away from touching his intestines. He smells like copper and shit, like burnt meat and bile, and I keep pressing down, trying to keep his guts from spilling out of him as his blood soaks my skin.

He groans, too loud.

"Shh, shh," I whisper. "He'll hear."

Something whizzes by my head, and I flinch, feeling something sharp striking my cheek. Not taking the time to press my hand to where warmth's spreading down my face, I throw myself down and back until I'm hugging the corner of the house, partly hidden.

Another shot lands in the porch railing. I peek my head around the corner just a sliver.

The shooter's sitting in my bedroom window. I can see his dark silhouette moving slightly through the curtains. He lowers his gun, the shot rings out, and a bullet sings inches above my head. I jerk back to safety.

Uncle Jake's still in range.

The next bullet goes into his leg. He doesn't have the energy to scream, he just jerks, and his breath stutters and wheezes in his chest at the impact.

I throw myself forward, grabbing his foot, the only thing I can reach and pull. He screams then, screams and screams, kicking out at me with his good leg as I yank at the bad one. His foot catches me in the stomach; it steals my breath, but I keep going until I've got him out of range, behind the porch swing.

"Harley," he pants again, but I can barely make it out, and then his head lolls against the swing, and for an awful second I think he's dead. Then he sucks in a sharp breath and coughs out blood.

"It's okay," I say, one hand on my gun, the other on his heart.

His hand reaches out to cover mine. I can't breathe. My throat hurts. All of me hurts.

He looks up at me, his eyes dim. "Look so much like your momma," he gasps out, and his fingers tremble, like he's trying to squeeze my hand but can't summon the strength. "But you've got his eyes. Never wanted this for you. Wanted more…better. Harley…"

"I'm here," I say. "I'm with you."

His gaze snaps to mine like it's the last thing he'll ever do.

*"Run."*

I've never been so close when it's happened before—but with that last word, his hand tightens on mine for a moment and then drops away. He's gone.

It's his dying wish. A command I can't ignore.

I run.

The paths of the forest are known to me like each wrinkle on Miss Lissa's face. They spiderweb out in all directions, through the hundreds of acres of trees and cliffs and valleys. They spread for miles, tangled and wild, twisting and turning until you don't know which way's back unless you walk them as much as I do.

This is my home. Jake was my family.

I will not yield.

But I run. The rifle slung across my back, I race across the meadow, toward the trees. My heels pound across the field so hard I can feel them sinking into the underbrush with each step. And then I hear the screen door bang open—he's coming for me.

Is it Springfield? I can't risk looking back. I'm almost to the trees.

I plunge inside the forest, dodging between scrub oak and digger pine, my bare feet slipping on the slick needles as I race up the old mining trail. My lungs feel like they're going to burst, but I keep running, faster than I ever have in my life, deeper and deeper into the woods.

My hand swipes a bush as I race past, smearing blood on the leaves. The trail rises, and my legs ache as I climb the slope. I strain to hear footsteps, branches cracking, anything to indicate that he's coming.

I stop at the top of the slope, looking around frantically.

*Find a perch, Harley-girl. Somewhere high.*

There.

The rifle bangs hard against the back of my knees as I scramble up the oak tree, my feet digging into the trunk and then scraping against the rough branches. Fifteen feet up, I hook my leg around the thickest one, gripping hard with my thigh as I pull myself up to settle on it. Tucking my legs out of sight, I push my back against the trunk for stability as I raise my rifle into position.

From here, I have a perfect view of the trail.

I'll see him coming—whoever he is.

And then I'll make him pay.

I can't catch my breath. I try to control it, calm it. But...

Uncle Jake. I feel sick. My stomach and my head swoop in a circle at the thought of him. I left him alone...

My fingers clench around my rifle stock.

*Focus, Harley-girl.*

I lick my lips, staring down at the trail. Unless he's stupid and doesn't see the puddle of blood I left behind, he'll be here any minute now.

Fifteen bullets. That's all I have.

But I need only one to kill him.

*Crack.* Someone's thrashing through the brush.

I peer through the scope, my heartbeat filling my ears.

He's short and stocky, with a shock of red hair that shines like a perfect target at me. I've never seen him before in my life, but that doesn't matter.

I'll remember his face until the day I die. He took the one good man in my family away.

He's walking slow, looking for clues—more blood, broken branches, anything to track me. I just need him to move a few more feet closer.

Something rustles to my right. Shit. My head snaps toward the sound, and so does he.

He starts to move, away from me...in a few seconds, he'll be out of range.

It's now or never.

My rifle's up and settled into the crook of my shoulder, nestling there like it's a piece of me that's been missing. I don't feel one lick of fear as my finger comes to rest on the trigger. This is where I fit, with a gun in my hand, pointed at the right person.

I breathe. One, two, *squeeze*.

I get him in the right arm. He yells, clapping his hand against it as blood spills down. He staggers in a circle, his gun swinging wildly, trying to find me.

My rifle moves with him: one, two, *squeeze*.

The bullet buries itself in his left thigh. He falls to the ground, swearing up a storm. He shoots in the air, blindly, enraged.

One, two, *squeeze*. Right thigh this time.

One, two, *squeeze*. Left arm.

Now he's screaming. It echoes through the forest, and I hear the rustle of birds flying out of the trees, up and away to safety. And it feels better than it should to hear him scream, to know that he's hurting, that he's in agony.

My eyes narrow as I peer through the scope again.

He's on the ground, flat on his back, but he's still got his hand on his shotgun. I think about those shells, the buckshot that shredded Jake's gut. How close he must've been to tear through him like that.

I flex my fingers around my .22, breathing in and out slow, just like Daddy taught me. I focus on his hand through the scope. It's a tiny target to hit. Tricky.

It'd be easier to kill him. I want to kill him.

But something stops me. Jake stops me. His words echo in my head: *Never wanted this for you.*

And just as clear, I can hear Daddy: *Killing a man changes you, Harley-girl.*

I'm already changed. So does that even matter?

If it's not this man, it'll be someone else. I already have blood on my hands. That is my life.

My finger settles on the trigger.

This is my gift.

One.

Two.

*Squeeze.*

I climb down the tree, my rifle trained back on him the second my feet touch ground. I kick his shotgun out of the way as he cradles what's left of his bleeding hand to his chest. His eyes are still open, and I stare down at him, holding the end of the barrel just inches from his face.

"Who are you?"

He just moans. I blew two of his fingers off. I can see the bloody stumps.

I jab the .22's barrel at him. "Who sent you?"

He shakes his head, his eyes widening as my finger goes to the trigger.

I want to pull it. I want him to pay for what he's done.

Jake is gone. The grief, it wants to swallow me. But I need to be smart.

I was raised to be smart.

My hands shift, bringing the rifle butt down hard on his head. He lets out a huff of surprise, and then he's out cold on the forest floor.

I wipe my hand across my forehead, smearing the sweat out of my eyes. Then I unhook the leather strap on my rifle and tie his wrists, looping the extra length of leather in my hands.

I take a deep breath and dig my feet into the dirt as I start to drag him through the forest, toward home.

If I can't get an answer out of him, I'll just wait until Daddy comes back.

Daddy always gets answers out of them.

By the time my feet hit the gravel of the driveway, I'm panting and covered in sweat. I leave Jake's killer lying there, and I run up the stairs of the porch to where I left my uncle.

His blood, a dark stain, has spread across the porch. It's dripping off the steps and Jake's staring up at the sky, his blue eyes cloudy and blank.

I say his name, I sob it, and I put my .22 down long enough to reach out and press his eyes closed.

It's not much. It's not anything. But it's all I can do.

No. It's not. Resolve hardens around the part of me that wants to scream and cry. I grab my rifle and march back across the porch toward Jake's killer.

He's still out cold. I push his bound hands out of the way and dig in his jeans' side pockets. Nothing.

I grunt as I push him onto his stomach, exposing the back pockets. I can see the outline of his phone.

I grab it and step away from him. He's beginning to moan softly. I bring the rifle up, circling around him so I can see his face, but his eyes don't open.

The phone's cheap, prepaid. I page through his calls received. There's only one number.

I press *Call* and raise it to my ear.

It rings three times, and then halfway through the fourth, a rough voice clicks on the line: "Are you coming with the girl?"

I'm acutely aware of the blood in my mouth. I know that voice.

"Andy?" Springfield asks. Then I hear his breath, taken in quick at the silence.

"Jake?" he questions.

I don't answer.

"Duke?" There's a tremor of fear in him now; I can hear it.

I don't answer.

I'm waiting.

I want him to know it's me. I want him to know he failed.

I want him to know that he hasn't taken everything. He's taken Momma. He's taken the man Daddy was.

And now he's taken Jake.

But he won't get me.

"Harley." It's never a question. It's half a breath, half a groan curled around his tongue, filled with a longing that makes me want to shove my knife in his gut.

I'm so glad he can't see me right now because I'm terrified, and keeping my trigger finger from shaking means letting everything else go.

"I'm coming for you, girl. Sooner or later. You're mine."

My trigger finger twitches. I want to put a bullet through Andy's brain, right between the eyes. I want to send his body back to Springfield, trussed up like a ten-point buck, to show him what's waiting for him.

"You best be ready."

He hangs up with a click.

I fall to the ground, my legs useless. My knees hit gravel and I don't even feel it.

Fifteen minutes later, that's how Daddy finds me. Crumpled on the ground, covered in Jake's blood, my .22 still in my grip, aimed at the unconscious wounded man in front of me.

He screeches up in his Ford, shouting my name and Jake's. He grabs me, yanking me to my feet as he spins in a circle. When he spots Jake's body on the porch, he lets me go. His gun's out, and the man—Andy— is dead before I can even blink.

Daddy doesn't notice the phone in the dirt. He runs up to the porch, and as he does, I bend down and pocket it.

I don't tell anyone about it. Not the sheriff's men, when Daddy calls them in and they ask me a few questions, before he tells them that's enough and they shut up real fast. Not Will, when he gets home and finds me on the couch and hugs me like he thinks it's the last time. Not when finally, finally, everyone is gone and the lights have stopped flashing and Jake…Jake…

Jake is gone, too. They took him away. The coroner did. I have to call the funeral home. Daddy's no good with that stuff, and Miss Lissa's memory isn't what it used to be…and he was mine. Jake was mine. So the responsibility is mine, too.

I curl my legs tighter underneath me on the couch. Will's palm settles on the back of my neck, squeezing gently, and I want so badly to let him take the weight of me away. I don't want to feel anymore.

Daddy's boots click on the wood floor, coming toward us. When I was little, before Momma died, it was a sound that made me think of him tucking me into bed and shooing the monsters from my closet.

"Will, why don't you go upstairs," Daddy says. It's not really a suggestion.

Will's hand falls from my neck, tracing down my back, between my shoulder blades, before pulling away. "I'll be in the kitchen," he says. "You should eat," he tells me.

He gets up, walking past Daddy without a word.

Every year that passes, the more Will grows into a man Daddy loves but can't control. It worries me.

"We need to talk about what happened," Daddy says. He sits down in his chair across from the couch. He hasn't touched me since he pulled me away from Andy earlier. It's like he's afraid. Like my grief's poisonous.

That would hurt me, but everything else hurts more. So it doesn't even leave a mark.

"I don't want to talk about it."

"We have to," Daddy says. "We have to figure out who sent him. He didn't say anything to you?"

I look at him. With Miss Lissa's memory nearly gone and Jake dead, he's the only adult I have left.

I know what will happen if I tell him it was Springfield. That he's broken the truce. That he sent a man to kidnap me and bring me to him for…God, I can't think about it. I won't.

I close my eyes, trying to block it out.

If I tell, it'll be war. Daddy won't be able to stop himself. He's been waiting for this my entire life.

Everything will burn.

Everyone will die.

Daddy will die.

It's that last thing, the primal fear inside me that's been there since the day Momma was killed, that stops me.

I should tell him because he loves me. He'd kill for me—he has before and he probably will again. I'm almost glad for it, grateful he's that man, even though that's the reason this all keeps happening.

How many men are rotting away in the wilderness, their blood on Daddy's hands?

I've lost so much. Springfield's taken Momma and now Jake from me. He's wiped out half of my family. I'm the last Hawes left.

It's never gonna end. Daddy will never give up. And neither will Springfield.

For the longest time, I thought it would end in one of them dying. I thought *that* was the whole point.

But now I see clearly. This didn't start with Momma's death. This started a long time before that. Before I was born, Momma was the prize. Daddy won her, but then Carl took her away.

Now I've become the prize. A chew toy gripped between two vicious sets of teeth, neither letting go.

Someone has to put a stop to this.

To them.

So I open my mouth and I lie.


We bury Uncle Jake that Sunday, next to his parents, the grandparents I never knew. I wear a black dress that buttons in the front, and it's a good day for Miss Lissa, so she helps me braid my hair, pinning it around my head like a crown. I don't let go of her hand the entire church service, and Will never leaves my side as we follow the hearse to the graveyard.

Long after the coffin's lowered into the ground, I stand next to my uncle's grave. Daddy has to take Miss Lissa home because she wears out fast nowadays. Will stays with me and we watch as they pull up the backhoe and start to cover Jake with the earth.

"Do you want to go?" Will asks when they're done.

I shake my head.

"Do you want me to stay?" he asks, because he always knows the right questions.

I shake my head again.

He sighs and pulls me close, pressing a kiss to my forehead. I close my eyes, my hand resting against his chest, over his heart for a moment, before I push away. "I'll come back at five?" he asks.

I nod.

He takes Busy with him and leaves me at the foot of Jake's grave. I'm grateful for the quiet.

I don't sit. I don't press my hand against his headstone and make promises to his body.

I stand there and I stare at the gravestone that I forced the funeral home to put a rush order on, and I wait.

I don't know how long it is—it could've been minutes, could've been hours—but eventually, the hairs on my neck prickle. Without even looking, I know he's standing behind me.

I knew he'd come. He wouldn't be able to resist.

He's finally shown his hand. This isn't about him and Duke anymore.

This has become about him and me.

He wants to hurt me. By any means necessary. Which means…well, it means it makes the woman in me shriek, the terror real and true, to even think on it.

I don't look at him, but my hands curl into fists as he comes to stand next to me.

"Such a shame," Carl Springfield says. "He was a good man."

He says it like it's a death sentence. And in our world, it is.

I have to bite the inside of my lip to keep from lashing out. My teeth grind down on my flesh, and I taste copper. It's the only way I can stop myself from going for him. From soaking Jake's grave with Springfield's blood and some of my own.

"I've been looking over my shoulder, expecting to find Duke there. So far, he ain't coming." There's a reedy note of joy in his voice. "You didn't tell him it was me, did you?" He laughs, the vicious delight rising to tangle with the branches of the old graveyard oaks. "That's a mighty big favor you're doing me."

"It's not a favor," I say. I keep my eyes fixed on Jake's headstone. BELOVED SON, BROTHER, AND UNCLE. OUR LOVE WILL CARRY YOU HOME. "If I told Duke, he'd kill you."

"And you don't want that? You getting fond of me, sweetheart?"

"No," I say. "This isn't about him."

Something in his face flickered for a second. It almost looks like pride. "So are you gonna do it? Gonna try to kill me?"

Finally, I turn and look at him, with my dead eyes and all my grief. I let him see it, I let myself feel it. I let it mark me and this moment. A promise that goes beyond blood or pain, into the pure, righteous kind of vengeance. "I guess we'll see, won't we?"

I walk away, my heart hammering in my chest.

Each step away from him is a relief.

*Only way, Harley-girl.*

Each step away from him is a burden.

*A life for a life, Harley-girl.*

Each step away from him is a step closer to the woman I'll become.

*Shoot to kill, Harley-girl.*

*Part Three*

# THE HOUSE ON SHASTA STREET

# FORTY

*June 7, 10:30 p.m.*

I stare down at my phone, numb. "Brooke," I say.

"What?" Brooke asks.

"Do you have the gun I gave you?"

I hear her take a sharp breath. "Yes."

Have they already tortured the information out of Will? Do they know Duke's dying? Do they know where he is?

Are they already on their way to Burney?

Heat sparks under my skin, an angry red crawling up my neck. I want to scream. But I grit my teeth instead.

"Listen to me carefully," I tell her. "You stay in Duke's room. Lock the door and don't let anyone in. Not even the nurses. Do you understand?"

"Are they coming?" she asks.

The guilt; it's overwhelming. I put her there, a sitting duck. If they find out Duke's dying, they'll come.

They'll come for all of us.

I'm not sure Brooke has it in her to pull the trigger. She's good. She's kind.

She'll get killed if they come. I'll get her killed.

Will might already be dead.

My entire body shudders. Everything's falling apart around me. I had a plan.

And it's failed. I've failed. Dread and fear, mixed together, rise in my stomach.

"They have Will," I say.

"Oh, God."

"Get the gun. Lock the door. Wait for me." Please, please, let it be enough. Please let him hold strong.

But you torture a man the right way, he'll crack open like an egg. I know this. I've seen it. I've been taught how to do it.

"What are you going to do?" Brooke asks.

I look down at Bobby's text.

"I'm going to get him back," I say.

It's a promise to myself. A vow that I won't go back on.

I'm not like Duke—Will isn't the only person I have left to love. But he is the one person I'd throw everything away for. Unfortunately, Bobby Springfield figured that out.

"I have to go," I say. "I'll get him back. And Brooke? If they come…"

"Shoot to kill," she finishes for me.

"I'm sorry," I say.

"Don't be," she responds. "I made my choice."

I know both of us are wondering if it was the right one.

"I'll call you as soon as it's safe," I say.

She hangs up. I close my eyes and picture her, huddling in Duke's room, lights off, waiting, unable to escape.

When I open my eyes, that photo of Will stares back at me.

I did this.

I scream. Busy scrambles away from the sound, and I can't even be bothered to soothe her. I lash out, punching the steering wheel with my left hand. My knuckles split open, and I don't even feel it. My hand bleeds, and I don't even care. My throat aches, and I just keep screaming.

*Calm, Harley-girl.*

I can hear his voice in my head, and all I can think is *Fuck you. Fuck you. Fuck you. You left me. You stranded me in a den of fucking wolves. You gave me no way out.*

My voice gives way, my hand goes numb, and finally, finally, I am still.

Busy whines next to me, nudging my side, lapping at my bloody knuckles.

I press my palms against my eyes, trying to breathe. I want to cry— if there was any time for tears, this is it—but they don't come.

My instinct is to find a way out rather than to feel.

Will might already be dead. If I just show up at the address Bobby gave me, I'm dead, too.

They know I'm coming.

I grab my phone, pulling up the address on the map. It's a storage facility.

One gated entrance and exit. Long rows of buildings, lots of paths and corners to hide, no one there late at night. They bribe security to look the other way, and it's the ideal place.

They have all the advantage. I can't change that.

That means I need all the leverage.

I get out of the Chevy and grab my box of guns from the toolbox, loading them methodically. I place two in the cab and two more under my seat. My fingers trace the barrel of my favorite revolver. It was Momma's. A twentieth birthday present from Duke.

It'll be fitting to use it now.

I am going to crush Bobby Springfield like a cockroach under my boot. Bennet, too, for going along with this insanity. Clearly, Jessa's love is not enough.

If they've left any permanent marks on Will, I'm going to wipe their entire family off the face of the earth, like Carl tried with mine.

But where he failed, I'll succeed.

I climb back into the truck, shutting the door, still holding Momma's revolver.

God help them if they stand in my way.

The house is small and gray, set down the road from the gas station. There are no other buildings around, no neighbors to hear.

It's perfect.

I park at the curb a few houses down the street, get my gun, and leave Busy in the truck.

There's a light on in the back of the house, and I crouch low, circling to the rear door.

She's in the kitchen. I can see her through the window, her dark hair falling down her face as she scrubs the dirty dinner plates.

I test the doorknob. It's unlocked.

Stepping inside, I can see the shadows of a washer and dryer. I'm in the laundry room. A shaft of light falls ahead.

Quietly, I move to the doorway, flattening myself against the wall, and peer around the corner.

Her back's to me, the water running. She's humming, a song I don't recognize.

I move fast. I close the space between us in two seconds. My gun barrel's against the back of her head before she even catches my reflection in the window.

She goes very still, her hands still immersed in the sink, hidden by the soapy water. Caroline Springfield's gaze rises to the window to meet mine in the reflection.

"Harley," she says. Her voice is steady.

I press the barrel harder against her head. "Caroline."

"You wanna tell me what you're doing?"

"You wanna let go of the knife and show me your hands?" I shoot back. I don't know how much she knows. Is she in on it, too? I want to say no. This woman is responsible for the uneasy peace between our families, and I've always admired her for it. For having the nerve to march right into the Tropics and barter for her boy's safety.

Except now her boys are fucking with my life. So I'm not taking any risks.

She slowly raises her empty hands out of the water. Soapsuds drip down her arm, but she doesn't shake.

She could go for me, try to knock the gun out of my hand, but she knows it's a bad idea. Caroline's smart—smarter than the rest of her family.

Which is why she just gets to the point. "What is this about?"

"Your boys," I say. "They took something of mine. You're gonna help me get it back."

# FORTY-ONE

I'm ten years old when Caroline Springfield walks into the Tropics. It's a bold move—most men wouldn't have the balls to do it—but she stalks in there like she's ready to do battle.

Daddy brings me along with him on his rounds a lot now. It's his version of school. So I'm there the day she comes, sitting at the bar with the puzzle Sal and I are working while Daddy talks with his men.

Everything goes dead quiet when Caroline comes in. Every pair of eyes is on her. The silence is so abrupt, it makes me look up from the puzzle.

I recognize her. I know what they all look like. Then the silence is broken by the sound of boots moving swiftly across the floor, and when I turn to look, I realize Paul and two other Sons have moved to guard me. Something sparks inside, the fear that Daddy's built into me, and it would fan to a full flame if they weren't there.

"You need something?" Sal asks. I watch as her fingers close around one of the biggest bottles of whiskey she's got, like she's ready to use it as a club if she has to.

"I want to talk to Duke," Caroline says.

Sal glances at Paul and then at me.

"I'll get him," Paul says. "You stay there," he tells Caroline.

"Go back to your puzzle, Harley." Sal smiles at me, bright and fake, like she thinks I don't understand what's going on. But I do.

Carl's been in prison for three months. He's not getting out for a long, long time. Caroline's got no protection—not the kind she needs against Daddy.

Carl may be locked up, but Daddy hasn't stopped targeting Springfields. Not when Caroline's got what he wants.

Daddy may take me with him on his rounds now, but he's trying to keep me away from the drugs the best he can. Which is stupid. I know he's cooking.

But Daddy wants North County. And Caroline's got most of it still, because the Springfields have been cooking since the dawn of time, it seems.

Or the dawn of meth, I guess.

"You've got some nerve coming in here." Daddy's voice booms through the bar, and I can feel everyone around us tense up.

He walks toward the bar, toward me.

"Come here, honey," he says, picking me up like I weigh nothing, like I'm still a baby. I don't like it, but I know better than to try to wriggle free. I loop my arms around his neck, and he turns to Caroline expectantly. "You wanna talk?"

"Yes," she says. Her face is like a mask, frozen and stern. I think she's scared, but I can't tell for sure.

Daddy pats my back. "Okay then."

He walks to the back room, and Caroline follows. Then he closes the door behind her and sets me down in a chair next to his at the head of the table. "Sit," he says to her, gesturing to a spot at the very end.

She does, pressing her palms against the table so he can keep an eye on her hands.

Daddy says you always have to keep an eye on their hands.

That frozen look on her face melts a little, nervousness trickling into her face like water through a rock dam. She glances at me and then at Duke, then back at me. "Should she be here?"

"We talk with her in the room or not at all," Daddy says. "I don't hide things from my child."

Caroline snorts.

"Don't try my patience," he says coldly. "Tell me why you came."

Her face pinches up, like she's sucked on a lemon. "I want you to stop."

"You're gonna have to be more specific, ma'am."

He's toying with her—even I can see that. There's a mean gleam in his eye that I've never seen directed toward a woman before. It makes the hair on the back of my neck rise.

"You went after Bobby," she says. "You *cut* him. But I haven't ever done anything to you or yours, Duke. You've made your point. You've won. Carl's in prison. It's time to let this go. My children stay out of this."

"Carl didn't keep Harley out of any of this," Daddy says.

Caroline gnaws on her lips. "I know," she says, shaking her head. "And I'm sorry. But I had no part in that. And neither did my boys. They're innocent."

"That older boy of yours is far from innocent," Daddy says, and that smile, knife-sharp and all teeth, flashes in the neon light. "He's not even old enough to drink and he's already dealing. He's got an entrepreneurial spirit, that one."

"Bobby made a mistake," Caroline says. "He knows that now."

"Damn right he does," Daddy says. "How many stitches did he end up needing?"

She goes white. If I were her, I'd be spitting mad, like a rattler that's been stomped on. But if she is, she holds it in.

She's too scared of Daddy to let it out.

"Please," she says, her voice low and pleading. My stomach twists, and I want to press my face into the softness of Daddy's stomach, hide from the desperation in every line of her face. "I am begging you. Leave us be."

Daddy strokes his beard. "You know it's not that easy."

"I need to provide for my family," Caroline says between clenched teeth.

"You still have the gas station," Daddy says. "Cooking's dangerous. It's not woman's work."

"Is that right?" she says, and she's looking at me and I don't quite understand why.

Daddy's head turns, so he's looking, too. "She's different," he says. "And she's not a part of this discussion."

"I thought you didn't hide things from her, Duke," she says.

His eyebrows draw together in a flat line. "You want to be left alone? Well, then, I want the equipment," he says. "All your product. And all your customers."

Caroline's fingers drum against the table. "You're a son of a bitch," she says.

"Your boys will be safe," he continues. "But you'd best keep to yourselves, across the river."

"They need to go to school," Caroline says. "Or do you expect me to keep them penned up like you've kept your girl there?"

"Careful," he warns.

"School and church," Caroline says. "We have to be able to go. And I've got to do shopping sometimes."

"You can go shopping in Trinity," Duke says. "But the boys can go to school here. As for church…"

"You've taken my husband," Caroline says, her eyes glittering. "You've taken my livelihood. I'm a Christian woman. Are you really going to take my church, too?"

He sighs. "Fine," he says. "But you keep your boys away from my girl."

"As long as you keep your girl away from my boys," Caroline says.

Daddy grins. "Agreed."

I tug on Daddy's sleeve. He turns to me, questioning.

"Will," I remind him. This is important, what the two of them are doing now. I understand that. They're creating a different world, with different rules to protect all of us. And if I'm safe from the Springfield boys, Will needs to be, too. Especially because Will goes to school with them.

I'm not stupid. I know people treat him different because he isn't white.

"Your boys need to stay away from Will, too," Daddy says. "I know that older boy of yours has already picked up on Carl's Aryan nonsense. I won't be having that Klan shit thrown at Will or any of the other kids. I don't know what you're thinking, letting him teach your boy that trash. But if your boys even look at Will funny, that lily-white skin won't be any help to them because I'll be peeling it right off them."

"They won't bother him," Caroline promises, fast and nervous. "I will keep them in line."

"All right then." Duke holds out his hand. She reaches out and takes it. They shake, but then he doesn't let go.

"You know what I do to people who go back on their deals with me," he says. "You don't want to be one of them."

She tugs her hand away and gets to her feet. "Call me with a time and place, and we'll set up the exchange. And after that...well, I guess I'll see you in church."

"Guess so," Duke says.

"It was nice to see you, Harley," she tells me, as if she'd just stopped by for a neighborly visit. Then she walks out of the back room, and Daddy sighs, leaning back in his chair, stroking his beard.

"Why did you do that?" I ask.

He had been winning. He could have run her down in the end. Like most mothers, her weakness is her children. He knows where to hit to make it hurt. To make her bow down.

"For you," he says. "I did it for you kids."

And just like that, our world is different. Caroline made it different, with her nerve and her love for her children and her gamble that Daddy loved his just as much.

She'd gone into the Tropics willing to lose.

But I wonder if really, she's the person who won.

# FORTY-TWO

*June 7, 11:30 p.m.*

I jerk open the truck door. "Go in the back, Busy," I tell her as I push Caroline forward.

Busy hops out of the passenger seat and into the Chevy's back cab. Her ears twitch, her blue eyes taking in the two of us.

I've tied Caroline's hands behind her—not the most comfortable position when being shoved inside a truck—but she'll have to deal.

"You try anything, Busy'll take a piece out of you." I press my free hand against her shoulders, and she steps up and into the truck. I circle around the front to the driver's side, my gun on her.

Caroline looks back at Busy nervously. Busy growls low in her throat, sensing her fear.

I climb into the cab, back the truck up, and turn it around, heading toward the freeway. The address Bobby Springfield texted me is on the edge of town.

He's breaking all sorts of rules today.

The tension in the car is so tight I'm afraid she'll snap at any second—Busy and my gun not being enough of a threat—but she stares straight ahead in silence.

I know better than to think she's resigned to her fate.

She's thinking it through. Looking for an out.

It's what I'd do.

"My boys aren't thieves," she says suddenly.

291

I raise an eyebrow. "Is that so?"

"You said they took something—what do you think they took?"

"What do *you* think?" I ask. I purposefully didn't tell her it was a person they took. I needed to know if she was in on it. Does she know?

Do they know? Have they cracked Will yet? Is Springfield already on his way to Burney?

My right hand's still on my revolver. I loosen my grip so the sweat won't make my fingers slip.

"They did not steal drugs from you," Caroline says strongly. She almost sounds like she believes it.

I snort. "You think I'd bother taking you if they stole some drugs?"

Her fingers twist together, her green eyes hardening. "Just fucking tell me what's going on."

"You've lost your hold on them," I tell her as we head across the river and pass the sign that says SALT CREEK 10 MILES. "You aren't calling the shots. Carl is."

"My boys listen to *me*," she says.

"Your boys kidnapped Will," I shoot back. "Unless you ordered that, they've clearly got other loyalties."

The shock on her face—it's too real. She doesn't know anything.

Carl's turned them, and she didn't even notice. Why did she even welcome him back after prison? How could she not see the danger?

I feel irrationally angry. Almost disappointed.

I expected more from her.

"Bennet's been sleeping with one of the Rubies," I continue. "Bobby found out. Told Carl. They beat the shit out of her and tossed her out on the edge of the tent city by the river. That sound like the boys you raised, Caroline?"

"You're lying," she says.

I look from the road to her, disgusted. "In a few minutes, you're gonna know I'm not."

The gate to the storage facility is open, but I don't drive through it. I park outside, hauling Caroline out of the car, my gun pressing against her skull again.

We walk forward, Caroline on my left, Busy on my right.

The storage units sprawl in front of us in neat lines. The second we step inside the gate, lights spring on, illuminating the pavement.

"Bobby!" I yell. My voice echoes, bouncing off the rows of steel buildings.

There's a rickety sound, a metal roll-top door being pushed up. They're in the unit three doors down.

My free hand goes to my back, pulling the .45 out of my waistband. My left hand has the revolver pressed against Caroline's head, and my right points the pistol toward the door.

Duke made damn sure I could shoot with both hands. No fucking point in being perfect with one hand and shit with the other.

Fifty feet ahead, Bobby steps out of the storage unit, Bennet close behind him. Bobby's got what looks like a .45 aimed sideways at me like a fucking idiot. Bennet's got a shotgun in his hands, but he's holding it instead of pointing it.

For now, at least.

"Believe me now?" I ask Caroline.

"Mom!" Bennet says, and when he steps into the light, his jaw drops in horror.

"Don't take a step closer," I say. "Or her head comes off."

Bennet freezes. It takes Bobby one more step to stop.

That tells me more than enough.

"Boys…" Caroline starts, but I press the barrel of the revolver into her head.

"No talking." I turn my attention back to Bobby and Bennet.

I don't see Will.

"Where is he?" I ask.

"We've got him," Bobby sneers.

"Get him. Now."

"You're not in charge, Harley," Bobby starts.

I shoot. Twice. One blast right after the other, making shards of asphalt dance at their feet.

Their guns are up and on me, but I step behind Caroline. She whimpers as my revolver skates across the back of her head. They can't take a shot at me without hitting her.

"I am not fucking around," I say. "I will kill her. Right here. Right now. Unless you bring him to me in the next ten seconds. Ten. Nine. Eight."

"Jesus," Bennet swears.

"Seven. Six. Five."

"You're bluffing," Bobby says, but his eyes shine, like he almost wants me to pull the trigger.

"Four. Three. Two."

"Please," Caroline begs.

"Goddammit!" Bennet turns and runs back into the storage unit.

"One."

And there he is. Bloody and busted up, but alive, alive, alive. The word sings through me, side by side with the voice that says *kill them, kill them, kill them*.

Bennet keeps a tight grip on his arm, and Will stares at me, like he's trying to tell me something.

"Let him go," I tell Bennet.

"Let her go," he counters.

I shake my head. "Not until he's next to me."

Bobby snorts. "That's not gonna happen."

But I keep looking at Bennet. Bobby may not care what happens to his mother, but Bennet does.

"Bennet," Caroline says, because she knows he's her best bet, too.

Bennet bites his lip, his eyes shifting from the two of us to Bobby and back.

*Come on,* I think. I don't want to shoot this woman.

He lets go of Will and then he lifts his shotgun, pointing it at Bobby.

"What the hell?" Bobby yells. He starts to raise his own gun, but Bennet pumps a shell into the chamber, the sound a clear threat.

Bobby freezes. "You fucker," he says. "This isn't Carl's plan."

"She's got Mom," Bennet chokes out.

"I don't fucking care!" Bobby yells.

"Well, I do," Bennet says, his voice steady now. "Drop it."

Bobby hesitates. The hairs on the back of my neck rise, and Caroline tenses, a low moan coming from her throat.

Bobby throws his gun down at Bennet's feet. "You fucking pussy," he snarls.

Bennet steps away from the gun, leaving it there between them, and I can see how Will zeroes in on it.

My fingers grip the handle of my gun tighter. I try to tell him with my eyes that he shouldn't…that he needs to run.

"Go," Bennet tells Will, keeping his gun on Bobby.

Will should run. A sensible person would.

But Will, he's wired to protect. He feints toward me, but I can see before he does it, the way his waist and legs twist. He drops to a roll, quick and smooth, reaches out, grabs Bobby's gun off the ground, and aims it at Bennet from his crouch before he can move.

"Hand it over," Will says.

Bennet wavers. I push Caroline down, and she falls onto the pavement, catching Bennet's attention.

I press the pistol to her temple. "Give him the gun, Bennet."

He shifts from foot to foot. Next to him, Bobby groans in disgust.

"Nice and easy," Will says.

"Let her go," Bennet demands.

"When you give me the gun," Will says.

One beat. Two.

"Bennet!" Caroline screams.

His face crumples. He hands it over. The second Will's hand is on it, he starts to back away.

"You good?" I ask.

"I'm good," he says.

I grab Caroline's arm and pull her onto her feet, and take a few steps forward. Without a word, Will and I fall into the rhythm Duke trained into us: *Always have her back. Keep him with you.*

We meet in the middle of the path, Caroline in front of us.

"Move," I tell her, raising the revolver and pushing her gently. She stumbles forward into Bennet's arms.

"You're not gonna get away with this," Bobby says.

"Move," I say again, walking toward them. The three back up until I've walked them right into the storage unit.

"Give me your phones," I say.

Bobby throws his hard, right at me. I sidestep it easily, glaring at him as Bennet chucks his on the ground between us. His arm's around Caroline's shoulder, and she just keeps staring at me like she knows I'm hiding something.

Bobby shuffles his feet, and the gun in Will's hand rises an inch, the barrel pointed at his head. "Don't even think about it," he says.

Bobby eyes him, disgust curling his mouth. "She's sure got you pussy-whipped."

Will grins, and I see there's blood still staining his teeth. "You're a fucking idiot for tossing a gun so close to me."

Bobby's hands clench into fists, and Caroline grabs his arm. "Not worth it," she says under her breath.

"I think it's about time you have a little talk with your boys, Caroline," I tell her. "I'm gonna give you three a few hours to discuss things. Then maybe I'll let you out."

I grab the top of the steel door and yank it down, trapping them inside. Bending over, I slide the bar lock into place as someone—Bobby, most likely—begins to pound on the steel.

I look at Will—really, truly look at him—and when his eyes meet mine I am more in love with him and more sure I'll be the death of him than ever. It's an enormous, terrifying feeling, and I can't face it—not now, maybe not ever. "You okay?" I ask, and my voice trembles like I'm eight years old again.

He nods. There's dried blood all over the left side of his head, and three fingers on his right hand are bent funny.

"We need to leave," he says.

He's right. But I find myself stepping toward him instead, my hands reaching around his neck as his slide through my hair. And I'm kissing him and he's kissing me. He tastes like blood and I taste like fading fear, but he's here and he's alive and we fucking *won*.

The steel door rattles as Bobby pounds on it, and we pull apart. I lick my lips, trying to chase away the copper tang.

There is so much to say. And still so much to do. So I bend down, scooping up Bennet's and Bobby's phones.

"You got a plan?" Will asks as we walk toward my truck.

"Always," I promise.

# FORTY-THREE

I'm nineteen when Will gets shot.

It's the fourth summer he's working on the grow for Paul. He's good at it, like he's good with the garden at home. He's strong and he works hard, and Paul sings his praises to Daddy.

But there's no future in it. We know that, but we don't talk about it. Because we both know what will happen when he stops working for the Sons: Duke will bring him into the business. He'll let him climb. And eventually, he'll put him in place to be by my side the day it all becomes mine.

He'll try to harden Will. Try to strip away his gentleness. Try to turn him into something he's not.

Things have changed since Jake was killed. I've changed.

Reality has hit. And it's cold and it's hard, but it's inescapable: Daddy tried his best to make Will into what he wanted, but Will is stronger than that. He's meant to take care of people, not hurt them. Caring is what makes him happy, what he's good at.

Daddy wants him to be able to shut it off. He wants to cut out Will's heart to get to some cold, rough core that Will just doesn't have.

It's something that gnaws at me late at night when I can't sleep. I walk the paths in the woods near the house and sometimes I see lights on in Will's bedroom in the guest cabin, but he never ventures out to find me.

Sometimes I want him to. Sometimes I want him to chase me, or maybe I want to chase him, pin him to the ground with my mouth and body, and kiss him until I figure out a solution to it all.

There's no good one, I know that for sure.

The Sons of Jefferson have a few parcels of land deep in the Siskiyous—off dirt roads that climb so high the clouds get tangled in the treetops. I drive up to an enormous wooden gate, honking my horn, waving at the security camera bolted to the top rail.

A few minutes later, Will swings the gate open, two mastiffs tagging behind him, their spiked collars gleaming against dark fur. I drive through the gate, down the steep hill that bottoms out into a large open space, sheltered by the pines. Will locks the gate behind me, whistling for the dogs as I park at the bottom of the drive.

I don't have Busy with me that day because the AC in my truck's broken and it's too hot for her without it. I'm grateful when I see the mastiffs; Busy's particular about other dogs.

I grab the bag of burgers I'd bought on the way and get out of the truck.

"Nutrients are in the cab," I tell him. "Want me to help you unload them, or do you want to eat first?"

"Eat," he says.

"I got you extra grilled onions." I hold out the bag as one of Paul's mastiffs noses at it. "No," I tell him sternly.

"Hunter, Bowie, go in the kennel," Will says.

The dogs trot off, Hunter casting one more longing look at the bag. Will follows and puts them in a fenced area that's less of a kennel and more of a pasture.

"How's the crop?" I ask as he leads me over to a set of battered lawn chairs next to one of the four trailers scattered around the clearing. They're loosely grouped around the four enormous hoop houses that house rows and rows of marijuana plants in hundred-gallon smart pots. The plants are lush and green, from what I can see, but I have a black thumb. I can't even get lettuce to grow, and that's supposed to be easy.

"Getting there," Will says, sitting down in one of the cracked white plastic chairs, digging in the bag and handing me my burger.

I unwrap it, taking a bite.

"Duke know you came out here?"

I shrug. "He doesn't need to know everything."

"You're gonna be in trouble if he finds out."

I start to say he won't, but there's a dinging sound. The motion censor on the gate.

Will's head whips toward the monitor set up underneath the trailer's canopy. There's a strange truck on the camera feed.

"Shit," Will says. "Harley, get the shotgun in the trailer."

I move, single-minded. There's a crashing sound: wood being rammed by an F-150 going way too fast.

They've breached the gate.

I clamber up the trailer stairs and grab the shotgun that's set against the rickety kitchen door. I look around frantically for shells, but I don't see any.

Shit. Shit. Shit.

I don't have time to look. I'll have to make do with whatever it's loaded with. I tuck the gun under my arm and head out. Will's crouched behind the trailer, a rifle in his hands. I join him, peering around the corner.

They haven't gotten out of their truck yet, but it's just a matter of time.

"You know who they are?" I ask, cracking open the shotgun's barrel. It's loaded, thank God. But it's an old one—it only has an eight-round capacity.

Will shakes his head.

The truck door creaks open. They're getting out. I flatten myself against the trailer, edging forward to get a look.

There are two of them. They're wearing leather vests.

I jerk back when one of them turns toward the trailer.

"They're bikers," I whisper. "Are the Sons fighting some other club?"

"Paul doesn't talk business with me," Will says.

"Well, maybe he should if they're busting in here when you're all alone!"

"Harley, this is not the time to get pissed at Paul," Will hisses.

He's right. Jesus. He's right.

I tilt my head against the trailer. One of the bikers is heading down the path that leads to the hoop houses; the other's heading toward us.

We need a plan.

"How many rounds do you have?" I ask him.

"Six."

"Fuck. Okay. I have eight. You head down to the hoop houses; I'll cover you. Take out the guy down there. I'll take out the one up here. Ready?"

Will nods.

I count it off on my fingers. One. Two. Three.

The shotgun's up against my shoulder, I aim, and blast the dirt at the biker's feet, making him dive for cover.

Will runs down the path, rifle in hand, and I pump the shell free, laying down two more shots in the guy's direction as Will disappears into the first hoop house.

I jerk backward, flattening myself against the trailer out of sight.

Five more rounds left. I have to make them count.

I'm straining to hear the sound of Will's .22, focusing on it. Later, I'll kick myself, because I don't hear the swish of grass behind me.

A hand grabs my braid and yanks me off my feet. I scream, bringing the shotgun up like a club, trying to hit the guy who has me. But he snatches the barrel, yanking it out of my hands. I twist desperately in his grip, dirt and twigs and rocks scraping my skin as he drags me down the path.

"I got a girl!" he shouts down to the hoop houses.

I dig my nails into his arm, but he just tosses me onto the ground in front of him, leveling a .45 at me. "Stop fighting."

I go very still, focusing on his face. Blond, with long hair pulled back in a scraggly ponytail, he looks like a lizard: thin, long features with a sharp nose and pale eyes.

"Hey, Spencer, you got the guy?" he calls.

"Yeah!" a muffled voice yells back.

Fuck. How are we gonna get out of this? No one even knows I was coming out here. No one's coming to save us.

We're gonna have to save ourselves.

Spencer—the blond one's partner—dumps Will next to me. He's got prison tats on his neck. "On your knees," he sneers, like he enjoys saying that a little too much.

Will glances at me. I nod, just barely, to let him know I'm okay.

"So what have we here?" the blond one asks. "Your boss Paul know you're riding your bitch on his time?"

"Fuck you," Will says. I press my knee against his in warning. He relaxes a little, but not enough.

"What do you want?" I ask. "The plants? Take them." I'll figure out a way to make it right with Paul. We just need to get out of here in one piece.

"Cory, isn't that cute? She's offering them up like they're hers," Spencer says, laughing.

Cory laughs, too, looking me up and down, his tongue between his lips. He sucks in his cheeks, leering.

I glare back, thinking about how nice it would be if I had my knife. I'd slice his tongue in two.

But then his leer turns into a frown as his gaze fixes on my face instead of my chest. Something goes very cold inside me when he says, "I know you."

Will's eyes widen. He shakes his head at me, just the barest of movement.

"I doubt it," I say.

"No, I've seen you," he says, a slow smile blooming across his reptile face. "You're the McKenna girl."

I grit my teeth, trying to figure out the best way to play this. Use the fear of Daddy to get them to let us go? Bribe ourselves free?

"Cory, we gotta get the pot," says Spencer.

"Nah, leave it for now." Cory stares at me, eyes shining with a greed I recognize. "We've got something even better right here."

"Leave her alone," Will says, tensing up next to me. He's gonna spring any second. I can feel it. I have to be ready to move when he does.

"Shut up," Cory says casually.

And then he shoots him.

My eyes track the arc of his gun like we're in slow motion. It swings toward Will and I'm screaming, wrenching, swearing as his finger squeezes the trigger.

Will jerks in a terrible, backward convulsion as blood spills down his shirt. He falls to the ground, and I'm kicking, fighting, punching; my nails sink into skin, into denim, into anything I can get my hands on. I'm going to kill them, I'm going to kill them, I'm going to—

Something hits the back of my head, hard. I stumble forward.

And everything's black.

I come to, gasping for air, a retching sound caught in my throat, my head throbbing. I roll to my side, blinking in the dim light. I gag, almost vomiting when I manage to sit up, the pain sharpening.

Flies crawl across my face as I probe the back of my head. My hair is clumped and sticky with half-dried blood. I breathe hard through my nose, clenching my teeth against the nausea that surges inside me.

I don't have time to throw up. I look around me. I'm in some sort of shed, a big wooden one. There aren't any windows, just a lone light bulb swinging from the ceiling.

I'm definitely not on the Sons' property anymore. There isn't a shed this big on their land. Those fuckers took me somewhere.

I need to get out of here.

I need to get back to Will. He's...He might be...

Alive, I tell myself. He's fucking alive.

He has to be.

I'd feel it if he wasn't. I'd know it.

*Don't be stupid, Harley-girl.*

It takes three tries to get to my feet. By the time I finally manage it, I'm drenched in sweat. I rub my eyes in the dim light, moving in a clumsy circle, taking it all in.

303

The floor isn't concrete; it's dirt. And it's scattered with straw. A half-used bale is stuffed in the corner. There's a four-wheeler with a flat tire and enough Coleman fuel, lithium batteries, and empty two-liter bottles for me to know these bikers don't stick to just growing pot the way the Sons do.

Cooking meth shake-and-bake style is easy, but it gets people killed. Or burned beyond recognition.

Fucking idiots. I have to get out of here.

But I need a weapon. I stumble over to the metal cabinet in the far corner of the shed. I have to yank at the door to get it open, and paint and rust flake off as the hinges groan at the movement. But it's empty.

I hear the click of a lock opening behind me. I turn my head so I can see him out of the corner of my eye.

Cory. He shot Will.

He's going to pay.

"You're awake." He closes the shed door behind him.

"You've made a big mistake."

He grins, strolling up to me like he doesn't have a care in the world. He's got surprisingly good teeth. Maybe he isn't a tweeker—just an opportunist.

The ambitious ones are the most dangerous. Either they're smart and they climb their way to the top, or they're stupid and they get people killed.

"Your daddy agreed to everything I asked for," he says with a smirk. He's all puffed up at the thought of getting one over on the boss of North County, I can tell.

"You've called him already? Wow, you move fast."

He shrugs. He thinks it's a compliment. God. He has no idea what's waiting for him. "I figured he'd want his daughter back." He steps forward, stroking my cheek. I can feel myself shaking. I can't stop myself. "Pity I told him I'd hand you over untouched."

I lash out, fast and precise, like Daddy taught me to. Gripping his wrist with one hand, with the other I wrench three of his fingers backward as hard as I can. The bones break with a satisfying crunch.

He screams, high-pitched, and I take advantage of the pain, jerking my knee up into his groin once, twice, three times.

Now he's on the ground. His gun's tucked in his waistband, and I've got it in my hand before he even starts writhing. It's a semi-automatic; a .45 with a bulky grip, and the weight's off. But it doesn't matter. I'm just inches away from him. I don't even need to aim.

I flick the safety off and level the barrel at him. "You don't get to offer up not raping me like it's a goddamn gift. Where's your partner?"

"He went to meet your father."

So the partner is dead. Or will be…soon. Good. That means one less problem.

"Hands in the air," I tell him as he struggles to sit up, still wheezing from the kicks I'd administered to his balls. I hope they turn black and fall off. He raises his hands, and I note with satisfaction that the fingers I broke are bent every which way and already swelling.

"The guy you shot," I say. "What happened to him?"

He snorts. "How the hell should I know? We left him there."

My legs start to shake. I want to kneel right down in that dirt and scream. I want to press the .45 barrel against his head and paint the shed walls with his brains.

Will might still be there. Bleeding out. Alone. The idea is so awful, so stomach twisting, I can't bear it.

The gun's against his forehead, I'm staring into his eyes, and I want to do it. I've never wanted to pull a trigger so bad in my life.

"I bet he's dead. Gut shots are nasty."

I know they are. I still dream about Jake's shredded stomach under my hands. Trying to keep everything inside of him as it spilled out. The smell. The blood. The pain.

He wouldn't want me to do this, I remind myself. Neither would Will.

But Jake's gone, and Will…

Will is *not* gone. He can't be. He can't.

The sound of tires against gravel twines through the cracks in the shed.

Cory smiles—the grin of a man who thinks he's won. "My partner's back."

I smile, because I *know* I've won. "That's not your partner," I tell him. "That's my daddy. And you're dead."

Daddy comes tearing into the shed like a bear looking for its cub. Huge, hulking, and savage, his gun drawn and his hands bloody.

And then Daddy sees me with the .45 pressed to Cory's head, and he stops.

He smiles.

"Well, fuck," he says. "Looks like you don't need saving."

"Did you get Will?" I ask. I don't know what I'm going to do if he says no.

If he says no, that means...

Cooper comes banging through the shed door, skidding to a halt next to Duke.

"Daddy." I look over my shoulder. "Did you get Will? Is he alive?"

His head tilts and he steps back, like he's taking in a pretty picture or a sunset or something.

"What are you gonna do if he's not?" Daddy asks.

My stomach sinks. Does that mean what I think it does?

"Duke," Cooper hisses. But Daddy cuts him off with a raised hand.

I stare at him, disbelieving. Is he playing with me? Is this another lesson? My stomach swirls, sick and heavy with dread and fear. Fresh sweat pops out along my forehead, trickling down my temple.

"Tell me if he's alive," I demand.

"Tell *me* why you haven't already taken this asshole out," Daddy counters.

"Fuck you," I say. It's comes out weak. My excuse is weak. Or maybe it's me that's weak.

"This trash shot your man," Daddy says, stepping forward. "He hurt you. He took you. And you put a gun to his head but you don't pull the trigger? That is not the girl I raised."

"Jesus, Duke," Cooper says, disgusted.

306

"Shoot this bastard," Daddy says. "And I'll tell you if Will's alive or not."

I don't bother to ask if he's joking. I know he's not.

He'll find a lesson in everything, my father. And he won't yield.

I step back three steps, steadying the .45 in both hands, grip firm around the heavy handle.

"There you go," Daddy says over my shoulder, and his voice is almost soothing. Familiar. How many times has he said the same exact thing, guiding me through target practice since I was a little girl? I've lost count.

But I'm not a little girl anymore. And I'm not looking at a target. I'm looking at a man. I may hate him and I may want to kill him, but I can't.

If I do, then I am all Daddy's. Whatever's left of Momma in me will be gone. Snuffed out like the life I've taken.

I know this. I've been running from it for years.

And now here I am. Will might be dead or he might be alive, I have a gun in my hand and a man I hate in front of me, and it would be so easy to kill him.

I aim, steady and sure. My eyes track to the target, my shoulders relax, my breathing slows.

One. Two. *Squeeze.*

He yelps, the bullet whizzing neatly against his arm, searing a good chunk of the skin, but embedding itself in the shed wall instead of his flesh. Just like I wanted.

I shove the gun into Daddy's hands, glaring up at him. The anger on his face should make me cower, but all I can think of is Will, and it makes me stronger. It makes me brave. "There," I snarl. "I shot him. Now answer my fucking question."

This isn't what Daddy wanted, but it's what he's got. And I did what he asked.

"He's alive. He's with Doc," he growls.

I can't stop the shaky breath I let out. I want to sag to the ground, but I won't do that, not in front of him. "I'm going there," I say, brushing past Daddy.

I hear the soft thud of his steel-toed boots making contact with Cory's ribs. He yelps.

"You're just gonna leave this mess behind?" Daddy asks.

I'm almost to the shed door when I turn back to look at him. Cory's whimpering on his knees in front of Duke, terror in every convulsion of his body. In a second, he'll be pissing himself.

"I'm not like you," I tell him.

I push the doors open, stalking out into the light and fresh air, away from the dark, away from the death, away from Daddy, back to Will.

Shots echo from the shed, but I don't stop.

I keep walking. And maybe, just maybe, I'm relieved to hear them.

There's more of Daddy in me than I'm willing to admit.

# FORTY-FOUR

*June 8, 12:30 a.m.*

By the time Will and I pull into the trucking yard, the late shift has left, and the next shift won't show up for a few hours. I drive around the back, toward the far corner of the yard, where a few of Duke's extra trucks are parked. We get out of the Chevy, and Will rests against the hood, staring out at the sky. Busy sits down at his feet, leaning against his legs, her eyes contented slits.

I walk over and stand next to him, and he puts his arm around me, drawing me close. There's just the barest chill in the air that'll be gone with the rising sun, but it feels good to be next to him.

"The keys are in the blue truck," I tell Will. "Where's your bike?"

"They chased me down on 299," Will says. "I spun out trying to avoid becoming roadkill. It's probably still on the side of the road if they didn't chuck it off a cliff into Nelson Creek."

"You sure you don't want to go to the hospital?"

"I'm fine," he says. "I've probably got a few broken ribs, but I can deal. Bobby's all rage and no plan, and Bennet pulls his punches."

"Of course he does," I say. "Did you see Carl at all?"

He shakes his head. "It was just the two of them. But Bobby spent a long time on the phone talking to him."

I'm grinding my teeth, thinking about all the ways I want to make him pay.

"Harley," Will says gently.

I close my eyes. I have to ask. "Did you break? Did you tell them anything about Duke?"

"God, no," Will says, surprised I'd even ask. "You think I would?"

"Bobby's a mean son of a bitch," I answer. "I was worried he was gonna cut you or burn you or something."

"Well, you rescued me," Will says, and any other guy, I think, would resent it just a little. But he's looking at me like he's proud, like he loves me, like he's grateful.

He's always been the bigger man.

"You helped," I say.

He grins, then winces when his lip splits farther, blood gathering at the corners.

"You need to get to Burney," I tell him. "It might not be too late."

Duke could still be alive. I have to call Brooke to tell her it's safe now. To ask her if he's still breathing.

"You should come," Will says.

"I can't."

I need to finish what I've started. I have everything I need to take both Buck and Springfield down, and I need to move before they stop panicking and start thinking.

"You still should."

He's right. But too much has already gone wrong. I have to set it right.

"Please go for me," I say. "I want him to have some family with him."

"I'm not who he wants," he says, and he says it gently. He doesn't want to hurt me, I know that, but it pierces all the same. Because Duke wouldn't hate me for not being there, but he would hate the reason why. "You gonna tell me what you've got planned next?"

I shake my head. I walk over to my truck and grab Busy's service vest and leash from the cab. "I need you to take Busy, too."

He swallows audibly because he knows what that means: Whatever I've got planned next, it's too dangerous to risk her.

I can't put her in the crossfire. She's done enough for me all these years. I want her with Will. With Duke. Safe.

"Come here, girl." I crouch down so Busy and I are eye to eye. I clip on her leash and I scratch behind her ears. She grins at me, licking my free hand. There's dried blood all over it. I don't know if it's mine or Will's.

"Hey," I whisper, petting her head compulsively. I want to bury my face in her side and cry. I want this to be over already.

But it's not, so I can't.

"You're gonna go with Will, okay?" I tell her. I know she can't understand me, but it makes me feel better.

She whines and nudges my elbow with her nose, leaning closer to me.

"You're such a good girl," I tell her, my entire face going hot and horrible at the idea of never seeing her again. "You're the best girl. I would've never made it without you."

I force myself to stand up, clearing my throat, and meet Will's eyes. "I need one more thing," I say.

And he must hear it in my voice, because his fists clench. "Harley..."

"No, listen," I say, the words coming out in a rush. "I made a will, at the start of the summer. It's in my trunk upstairs. It's all legal; a lawyer did it for me. Just make sure to do what it says, okay? Mo gets the Ruby and the lumberyard and the money to run everything. You won't have to worry about her. And I've paid for Miss Lissa's care. But the businesses, the house, the land..."

"Don't," he says.

"It'll be yours," I say. "If he dies and I die—"

"Stop." His voice cracks.

I stop.

He doesn't beg me to go with him because he knows I won't. Will's always operated better without words. He bends, and his mouth's on mine, and everything he can't say is in his kiss. Before he pulls away, his silent message is spread across my lips: *I understand, be safe, don't you dare die on me.*

"I love you," he says.

"I love you, too," I say. "Now go."

He goes. Because he loves me. Because he understands me. Because he knows it's my fight, not his.

I stand at the edge of the truck yard until his taillights disappear in the distance, and I know the feeling in my chest.

It's the feeling that comes only with the kind of goodbye that might be forever.

I breathe in the feeling. I breathe it out.

Then I turn, and get back to work.


The church is small—one little steeple and neat rows of pews that have seen better days. The choir has to cram in the corner each Sunday, and when it looks like a singer's about to fall down the steps, Pastor Evans is always saying "Just scoot over a bit more, please."

It's Thursday, a bit after nine a.m., so it's empty until eleven, when the Native Daughters of the Golden West have their meeting. I push the double doors open and walk inside.

Every Sunday of my childhood, I was here, right across the aisle from Caroline Springfield and her boys. But I haven't been back for a long time, not since Miss Lissa got sick and had to move to Fir Hill.

I walk to the doorway to the sanctuary, the air thankfully a few degrees cooler than outside. A young woman with curly brown hair is standing at the pulpit, her back to me.

I clear my throat.

Molly Evans turns around, her blue-gray eyes widening when she sees me.

"Harley," she says, with a wariness I can't blame her for.

She owes me. And I intend to collect.

I stay where I am, because it's been a while since I've been in church and I'm not a fan of testing God in His own house.

"Have you come to pray?" she asks.

I look up at the cross behind her. "Not sure God would want to listen to me."

"He's always listening," Molly says.

"He's always watching," I counter. "He knows what I've done."

Something flickers in her face, shuttered quickly, but I see it: concern.

We have never been friends. We have a kinship, though.

All this time, she's kept quiet about Tripp. His father searched for him for more than two years before he started losing faith, and Molly's held steadfast in her silence. She's lived with the blood on her hands.

It's the smart thing to do, but there are times I worried that her concern for her soul would get the better of her.

But God forgives. At least we hope.

"If you're not here for Him," she says, "you must be here for me."

"I need your help."

She bites her lip, crossing her arms and looking at her feet. For a second, I wonder if she's asking God for guidance. I wonder if He's answering her.

I've never been one for praying, even when I was little. I was brought up to believe—I think Duke felt like he owed it to Momma—but the Church of McKenna has always been my true faith. He's made sure of that.

"What do you need?" she asks.

"I need the church van," I say. "And I need you to drive it."

Molly relaxes just a little until she starts to spiral into the what-if. Because it sounds harmless. Until you consider who I am.

Until you consider what I know about her.

"Where exactly am I driving?"

"To a house on Shasta Street."

"And what am I transporting?" Molly asks, because she's no fool. She might've been naive once, but not anymore.

"Do you trust me?" I ask her. And I hate to admit it, but there's this burning in my chest, something like dread. I protected her once. Made her as safe as she could be, considering what she did.

"Yes," she says, and the relief is like aloe on a sunburn. "But that doesn't mean I don't get to know what we're doing."

Her face is steely—when did that happen? It's not like I've lost track of her since that night. I still saw her at church until I stopped going.

But we haven't really talked, because we had a dead body and tested faith in common, and that was about it.

"I need to move some product," I say.

Her mouth presses together, her pink lips turning white. She wants to say no. She's scared to say no.

"It's just taking it across town, Molly," I say. "I can promise you it won't be sold. Not one bit of it. No one will use it."

"Then what exactly are you doing with it?" she demands.

"That's my business," I say. "And you're better off not knowing."

She laughs, a short bark that robs the room of air with its bitterness. "That's what you said to me last time."

I pause, biting at my lower lip, trying to think of what to say. If she turns me down, I'm going to have to take on a whole lot more risk than I'd like. "Do you regret last time?" I ask her.

"I'm supposed to," she says. It's not an answer, and it's not *the* answer.

She's not sorry and I'm not sorry and I doubt Brooke's sorry, either. Molly did what she had to so she could stop Tripp, and Brooke did what she had to so she could get me there, and I did what I had to so I could keep them both out of jail.

"But do you?"

"No," and it's a confession, spoken to me instead of God, even though we're in His house. She knows I won't judge her. She fears He will.

"It's okay not to regret it."

"Says the criminal."

I shrug. "Doesn't mean it's not true."

"True and right aren't always the same thing."

"I think deciding that's His job." I point at the ceiling. "Not ours."

Molly closes her eyes, pressing her hand to her mouth. "You make things so hard, Harley," she finally says. "You are one of the scariest people I have ever met. But then you do things like taking care of the Rubies, and I know you keep the tent city by the river supplied with food, and you…just…you confuse me."

"It's not that hard to understand," I say. "I protect the Rubies because no one else will."

"But the sheriff—"

"Doesn't give a shit about domestic disputes."

"Then the church—"

"Has absolutely no power. Your daddy's harmless, Molly, but he's not exactly fired up when it comes to taking care of women. Most men aren't. Which is why we do what we do. Because your daddy, your people, they'll make sad faces if they hear a woman's being beat by her husband, but they'll say *it's none of our business*. Women come to me and Mo because they know we'll make it our business. And I intend to keep on making it my business because I've got enough power to share."

"But there are other ways than violence," Molly says.

"You're right. That's why I'm here. By driving today, you'll be helping me avoid a whole mess of violence."

Her eyebrows knit together. "I want to believe you," she says.

"Have a little faith," I suggest.

She rolls her eyes.

"Hey, it paid off last time."

"You saved me," Molly says. "It had nothing to do with faith."

This time, I'm the one frowning. Is that what she really thinks? It turns my stomach. It's not the kind of credit I deserve.

"I didn't save you, Molly," I say. "You saved yourself."

Her eyebrows knit together like that particular truth never occurred to her. "You—*you* got rid of him," she protests.

"Because you didn't know how." I need her to understand this. *She* stood on her own two feet and *she* took him out—because it was him or her.

And there's justice in that. There's honor in it.

"If I hadn't come along," I say, "or if you hadn't called Brooke, you would've found a way. You're strong. Anyone who survives something like that is strong."

Her eyes are wet. Her shoulders draw up. She takes a deep breath and goes over to the pulpit, grabbing a pair of keys on it. "Let's go."

# FORTY-FIVE

I'm twenty when I make Daddy let Will go.

It takes Will almost two months to recover from the gut shot. He doesn't have a spleen anymore, but there's no permanent damage to his kidneys, thank God.

I barely leave his side, and I know it's driving him crazy, but I don't care. I get nervous every time he's out of my sight.

It's weeks before we talk about it. And even longer before I ask the question that'll change everything.

I wait until it's night. Until Daddy's fast asleep. Until it's just me and Will, the house quiet, safe.

I sit on the edge of his bed, petting Busy as Will reads. He reads a lot, anything he can get his hands on. I've never been much of a reader, but sometimes he reads out loud, and I like that.

Tonight, though, I just lie back on the foot of the bed, my head close to Busy's, and listen to the soft *twhick* of the pages turning, building up the courage.

"What are we doing to do?"

For a second, I think either he's not going to answer me, or he's going to play dumb. But then I turn to look at him. There's a look in his eyes I've never seen.

A painful kind of hope.

"I don't know," he says.

And here we are: basking in honesty, in the unknown, in a future we were always too scared to plan.

"You have to go," I say.

"I can't."

Not *I don't want to*, but *I can't*.

*I can't leave Gran. I can't leave town. I can't leave you.*

I've heard it all before. I've let him convince me, every time.

No more. Not after this.

"Do you want to?" I ask.

His mouth flattens and his eyes glitter. "Don't," he says.

"Listen to me." I lean over and my hand's pressing against his stomach, where the bullets went in. "You are going to die if you stay. If you go to college—"

"He's never going to let me go to college."

"If he lets you, will you go?" I ask.

"He won't," Will scoffs, like the idea's absurd.

Before, I would've thought so, too. But now?

Now nothing will stop me. Not even Daddy.

"I'll make him."

"It won't work, Harley," he sighs.

It will.

It has to.

I wait a while. I convince Will to send in the applications. He spends hours on his essays, and he won't let me read them when they're done. I wonder if they're about getting shot, if they're about Desi, about growing up not knowing his dad or his tribe, about what Dan did to him. I hate that there's this endless slew of bad things heaped on him to choose from.

I wait. Until two big envelopes come. And then I knock on the door of Daddy's office, my heart in my throat.

Daddy's office is messy—Miss Lissa wasn't even allowed in here when she was taking care of the house. The walls are painted a dark red, with buck heads mounted side by side near the window. His big oak desk takes up most of the room. There's a picture of Momma and me in his top drawer, and sometimes I catch him looking at it.

"You need something, honey?" he asks, looking up from his desk.

He wears glasses now when he's at home, when he thinks no one's looking. It'd be sweet...if anything about him was sweet. I used to think there was, deep down.

I'm not so sure anymore.

I set the envelopes down on the desk in front of him without a word. He glances down. "What are these?"

"College acceptance letters."

His head jerks up. "For you?" he says, and there's that sharp, dangerous edge to his voice already.

I shake my head. "For Will. He's done here."

Daddy's still looking down at the envelopes. "And why isn't *he* here in my office talking to me if he wants to go so bad?"

My eyes narrow. We both know Will wants to go, he's always wanted to, but we—*me*—my fucking existence in his life made it too hard.

There are days I feel like I'm poison, the kind that kills you slowly.

"He's done," I repeat.

Daddy leans back in his chair, running a hand through his beard. "You don't give the orders around here, Harley Jean. You are not the head of this family."

I've reached a point beyond reason, and Daddy just hasn't realized it yet. The damage has been done. He pushed me too far that day in the shed and now he has to deal with the consequences. He raised me to rule—and I will rule him when it comes to Will.

"He'll leave for the spring semester in January," I continue as if Daddy hasn't said anything. "You'll pay for all of it. His room and board in the dorms or an apartment. His tuition. His books. I'll take care of everything at Fir Hill with Miss Lissa while he's away."

"Is that right?" he drawls.

I tilt my chin up and plant my hands on either side of his desk for support. If I don't grab onto something, I'm never going to have the strength to do this.

"You let him go," I say, "or I will run."

Now I've got his attention.

Now he won't treat this like a joke.

Now he knows how far I'm willing to go.

He sits up straight, his eyes glittering. "You're forgetting your place, Harley Jean," he warns.

I don't blink or move. "You have no idea what I'll do to get him away from you," I say. "I'm offering you the easiest way out. If you don't take it, I'm gone."

"You wouldn't dare," he scoffs.

"Try me."

Threatening Duke McKenna is a monumentally bad idea; I know grown men meaner than a wounded coyote who won't dare do it. But I throw it out there like a brand. I want to leave a scar, want him to know what he's done.

What—or who—all his lessons have hardened me into.

He doesn't laugh, like I half-expect him to. He doesn't hit me either, which is my second guess. There's no scary gleam in his face, that look he gets right before he slides his knife into flesh that parts like butter. But he looks at me like he's not quite sure who I am.

"I'd find you."

"You trained me to disappear. So how successful do you think that's gonna be?"

His mouth flattens as he realizes how serious I am.

I go in for the kill, hit him where it'll hurt the most, because in this moment, I am all his, through and through: willing to do anything, to hurt anyone, ignoring the consequences . . . because I have to be.

I have to keep Will safe from him.

"You'll never see me again. And he'll go with me, you know that. I want you to stop and think here. You won't walk me down the aisle at my wedding. You'll never hold your grandchildren. You'll have no heir, no one to inherit your empire. Think about that. Think about that long and hard, because if you push me, I'll do it."

"You're acting like a hysterical little girl," he growls. "I will not tolerate this kind of behavior from my own daughter. You will behave the way I raised you—do you hear me, Harley Jean?"

But the anger's too hot. It sears through everything else. My mind's full of it, my body's consumed by it, it burns and burns until I can't take it.

"You left Will with Doc," I spit out. "You didn't even take him to the fucking hospital when he needed to go! You risked his life so you wouldn't risk your own."

"I risked him for *you*," Daddy roars, springing from coiled and controlled to furious in seconds.

"He is *mine!*" I barely have the sense to feel anything at the way Daddy's eyes widen. Those words mean more than *I love him* or *I want him*. They mean things like *I'll kill for him* and *I'll die for him, because of him, with him.*

Daddy clears his throat, shaking his head, like he's trying to banish my words from it. "You're upset," he says slowly. "I understand. It's been a bad few months. You should go upstairs and rest."

"I'm not leaving until we have an agreement."

A muscle twitches at the corner of his eye. I can see it fluttering underneath his glasses. "I'm giving you an out," he says between gritted teeth. "Take it."

"You really want to push me again?" I ask. "You wanna see the woman you made, Duke?"

He doesn't say anything, just stares at me, like he hopes that if he's quiet enough, I'll just go away.

But I'm done playing his games. It's time for some of my own.

I pick up the phone on his desk—it's an old-school one with a handle and a cord and a rotary dial. "I could call the DEA right now," I say. "Give them the truck routes and schedules. I bet they'd be mighty interested in your cargo."

He lunges toward me, yanking the phone out of my hand.

"You…" He's so angry he can't even speak, his face turning a blotched red. I force myself to keep looking at him.

I can't save myself. I am who I am, and I'll do what I have to do. But I can save Will.

"You know if you were anyone else, you'd be dead on the floor right now," he finally says.

I've gone beyond anger at this point, settled into a strange calm. I walk around to his side of the desk and I pull out the .45 he keeps in his drawer right behind the picture of Momma and me. I place it on the desk so he can reach it easily. My palms are sweating as I dare him: "Go ahead. Put me down. Gonna bury me in the woods next to the others? Dump me in the river? A chainsaw, some lye, a little hydrofluoric acid, and there'll be nothing left but my teeth. Isn't that what you taught me?"

He lets out a sound, something between a groan and a snarl. I stare at the gun, waiting.

He doesn't move. Just looks at me, bewildered and miserable.

"Let him go," I beg. I hold out my hand, a peace offering, an apology, a plea. "And I'll never leave."

"Fine," he says. He grasps my hand, but instead of shaking it, he pulls hard, until I stumble into his chest.

"Who the fuck do you think you are?" he asks, his face right up against mine, staring at me.

Despite the fear that's thickening inside me like syrup, I stand my ground and stare back at him.

"I'm a McKenna."

He lets go and hits me straight across the face with the phone, knocking my head to the side.

I grit my teeth, dazed and tasting blood. I'm pretty sure my nose is broken. I can barely breathe.

My eyes tear up. I gasp, because I can't help it. But through the pain I raise my eyes to meet his. Blood trickles out of my nose and mouth, down my chin. I don't brush it away or swallow it back.

I want him to see what he's done.

"You ever do that again, I won't just bury you," I tell him. "I'll dance on your fucking grave."

# FORTY-SIX

*June 8, 9:30 a.m.*

I'm lying flat on my back on the carpet between the seats as Molly pulls onto Riverside Road and parks the van down the block so we have a clear view of Buck's house.

"Black truck's in the driveway," Molly says.

"Okay," I say. I flip over on my stomach, rooting around in my bag. I'm surrounded by cardboard boxes full of meth—a third of the product the cooks had collected for me. Four duffel bags full of guns sit on the backseat. I had to push a big box of Bibles out of the way to fit them all in.

I take Duke's phone out of my bag, pulling up Buck's name in the contact list, and start typing.

Just got into town. Harley's filled me in. Meet at Tropics. Now.

I bite my lip, my thumb hovering over the *Send* button.

He needs to be taken care of. This isn't the only way, but it's the best way.

If it works.

Please let it work.

I press *Send*.

"So we're supposed to just sit here and wait?" Molly asks.

"Give it a few minutes."

322

She sighs. "I can't believe I'm doing this."

"It'll be done soon." It's killing me that I have to stay down, but it's safer this way. Less chance of Buck accidentally catching sight of me.

The church van is perfect camouflage. No one thinks twice when they see it. Molly does regular routes bringing meals to the elderly, handing out clothes, and picking up donations. It's an ordinary sight— perfect to transport enough drugs and guns to put someone in prison for the rest of their life. No one's gonna pull it over or really even notice it. Not with sweet little Molly Evans driving.

"So why did you stop coming to church?" Molly asks.

"I was worried I was gonna get struck by lightning," I say. "Any movement out there?"

She shakes her head. There's a buzz coming from my duffel, and I look inside to see that the phone I took off Bobby Springfield is vibrating.

The idiot doesn't even have a lock code on his damn phone. I swipe it on. Text message from his uncle Carl.

Did she show up?

I tap my fingers against my mouth.

"Hey, Harley," Molly says, straightening in the front seat. "Someone's coming out."

"A guy?"

"Dark hair, skinny?"

I nod. "That's him."

"He's getting in the truck."

"Tell me which way he turns."

Seconds tick by. "Right. He's just turned right at the stop sign at the end of the street."

"Okay." We're in the clear. I sit up, grabbing the baseball cap and sunglasses. I stuff my braid in the hat and slip on the glasses. "Stay here."

I get out of the van and walk across the road toward Shasta Street.

There's an old lady watering the roses in her front yard next to Buck's house, and she squints at me as I walk up the path and knock on the door.

Buck's wife, Lindsay, is a tall blond woman who runs the beauty salon in town. She always has perfect hair and calls everyone sweetie. I've never seen her without full makeup on. Today, her lips are painted a bright red to go with her gel nails.

She frowns when she sees me. "Harley? Sweetie, what happened to your face?"

I look over my shoulder. "Can I come in?"

She steps aside to let me. "You just missed Buck," she says.

"Has Buck told you what's going on?"

"He said there was trouble, but didn't say what."

"It's bad," I tell her. "Springfield's attacked. I came to get you and Shawna. Carl's out of control. He sent Bobby to beat me up. I want you two to come stay at the Ruby just as an extra precaution. He's setting fires, and when I was little, he…" I trail off. It makes me feel sick to use Momma's death like this, but it's to save Lindsay's ass that I'm sinking so low.

"Oh, God," Lindsay says, horror in her heavily lined eyes. "Of course we'll go. Of course." She looks around, like she doesn't know what to do.

"Why don't you get Shawna?" I suggest.

"Yes, yes, good idea." She hurries out of the living room, into the hallway, calling her daughter.

Lindsay's purse is on the couch, and I go over to it, rummaging through the various makeup bags and receipts to find her phone. I turn it off and pocket it, grabbing the purse as Lindsay comes back into the room, Shawna clutching her hand.

Shawna's dark-haired like her daddy, but she looks more like Lindsay: pretty, big eyes, turned-up nose. She smiles when she sees me. "Hi, Harley!"

"Hi, honey. You guys ready?"

Lindsay nods.

I hand her the purse and her keys. "Drive straight to the Ruby. Mo will be waiting for you at the main office. She'll get you all set up and comfortable. I'll send Buck to you as soon as I can."

"Aren't you coming with us?" she asks.

I shake my head. "I've got to get back to the Tropics. Go now. Don't stop for anything. And don't leave the Ruby."

She and Shawna go out to her car and I watch from the window as they turn left, heading toward Main Street. Away from the house, away from Buck, and away from the trouble I'm about to cause.

As soon as they're gone, I leap into action. I text Molly: All clear. Back up into the garage.

As I walk through the house, I dial Mo's number.

"Hello?"

"Mo, in about fifteen minutes, a woman named Lindsay and her little girl will show up," I say, walking into Lindsay's kitchen, Shawna's half-full cereal bowl still on the red-and-white table. I head to the door that leads to the garage. "Put them in cottage number four. Keep a close eye on them. And Mo? She's gonna be looking for a phone. Don't let her find one. Not until I text you the okay."

"And if she gets her hands on one?" Mo asks.

I pull on my gloves before I push open the door to the garage and step down into it. "She can't. So make sure she doesn't. And don't let anyone in after her. Tell the Sons on guard duty. If anyone shows up…"

"You wanna tell me who *anyone* actually is?" Mo sighs, like she expects me to dodge again.

"It's Buck," I say. In a few days, if all goes right, she'll know anyway. "She's his wife."

"He beat her?"

"No," I say. "I need her out of the house."

"I'm not even going to bother to ask why," Mo says. "I'll make sure she and the kid are kept away if he shows up. You reckon that's gonna happen?"

"Not if I have anything to do with it," I say. "Call me if there's a problem."

"We're talking about a raise for me after whatever shit's going down wraps up," Mo says.

"Fair enough," I say. "Bye."

My phone buzzes. It's a text message from Molly: I'm here.

I find the button for the garage door, press it, and it rolls up. Molly's backed the van into the driveway, and I jog up to its rear doors and jerk them open.

"You got your gloves?" I ask Molly as she gets out of the van. She nods.

"Put them on and help me. We've gotta be quick." I lean into the van and grab the nearest box. "Mix them in with the stuff over there," I say, pointing at the far wall, where boxes are stacked on shelves.

We move fast. I fit one of the duffel bags of guns in the freezer that's half-full of venison. Another goes back in the house, in the master bedroom under the bed along with a few Ziplocs of drugs. I put the third up in the attic and jam the fourth behind a stack of boxes in the spare bedroom closet.

"This is the last one," Molly says, setting the box on the middle shelf next to one labeled BABY CLOTHES.

I grab the garage door remote from its place on the counter and then hop into the van, shutting the doors behind me. Molly gets in the driver's seat, starts the engine, and drives out of the garage. I hit the button on the remote. The door closes behind us and we drive away.

"Oh my God, oh my God, oh my God," Molly mutters under her breath as she turns off Shasta Street and we head back to the outskirts of town.

"You're freaking out *now*?" I ask. She'd been calm as hell in the garage.

"I can't believe I just did that," she says. "Oh my God. Harley, what did I just do?"

"You just made North County a little safer."

"You are so full of crap," she says.

"Not this time," I say. "Don't speed. It'd suck to get caught now."

326

She huffs hard through her nose, but she slows back to the speed limit.

I check the phones in my duffel. Daddy has three missed calls from Buck. I grab my own, dialing the number for the Tropics.

"This is Sal."

"It's Harley. Buck there?"

"He just left."

"Okay. Thanks."

"He seemed mighty pissed," Sal says.

I bet he is. He's trying to put it together. He'll come looking for me. But first, he'll stop at home to load up.

"I'll talk to you later, Sal," I say.

Molly pulls onto the road that cuts through the willows, leading to the back of the church where my Chevy is parked. As soon as she's brought the van to a stop, she leaps out and starts pacing up and down beneath the willows, nervous energy radiating off of her.

"Hey, Molly," I say. "It's okay."

"That was…that was…" She looks up at me, those baby-doll eyes of hers wide. "That was *exciting*," she whispers.

It's not what I expected. I raise my eyebrow. "Really?"

"I should not have liked that so much," she says. Instantly, the good Christian girl's back. She'll be mentally flogging herself by the next breath.

"Don't worry about it," I say. I start to head toward my truck. "I gotta go."

"Wait, Harley. Did…did you really mean it? That it'll make this place safer?"

"Yes," I answer, and she can tell I mean it.

"But why would you want that?" she asks, confused.

I pause, my hand on the handle of the truck door. "Because I want a better world than this."

She doesn't know it, but she's one of the people who make me think that.

"Bye, Molly."

327

She smiles faintly. "Bye, Harley."

I climb into my truck and drive through the willows, their long branches swaying in the wind. My skin's humming, and I flex my fingers a few times, trying to get rid of the feeling. I need to focus and get back to Shasta Street.

I've set my trap. Now I just need him to walk into it.

The street behind Shasta has an undeveloped greenbelt, and I turn onto it. I park the truck out of sight and head out on foot. An oak tree borders the place five houses down from Buck's. About fifteen feet up, it's got a clear view of his house.

I hoist myself up in the branches, out of sight, settle in against the trunk, and bring out my rifle scope.

Buck's truck is already back in the driveway.

It's time.

I grab the burner cell in my back pocket and dial 911.

"North County Dispatch, what is your emergency?"

"Oh my God," I say, breathing hard. "I was just jogging on Shasta Street and I saw a guy with this giant gun or rifle or whatever go into a house. The blue one! Um, number one-fifteen. There was shouting and then I heard a bunch of shots. Please hurry! I think there's a kid in there; there's a little girl's bike on the porch."

"Are you still in the vicinity, ma'am?"

I hang up, smashing the burner hard against the tree trunk. The cheap plastic shatters, chunks of screen showering onto the ground below.

It'll take the sheriff five minutes, tops, to get here. Faster if one of their patrols is in the area.

I lean back against the trunk, keeping one eye on my scope, and wait. It's so hot that sweat's trickling down my back within a minute, but I ignore it.

With Lindsay and Shawna far away when this goes down, I'll be able to keep the damage from blowing back too much on them. There'll probably be CPS checks, but Lindsay's a good mom; she just has bad taste in men.

Sirens. I can hear them in the distance.

It's time.

My heartbeat picks up as I focus back on Buck's house. There's no movement inside that I can see.

He's oblivious. Distracted. Just like I need him to be.

Fucking traitor. He should consider himself lucky that I'm the one dealing with him. Before he got sick, if Duke had found out Buck had been skimming off the top for Springfield, he would've torn Buck apart. Drawn and quartered, McKenna style. Instead of men on horses, Duke uses men on quads. More power that way.

The sheriff's cars screech down Riverside Road and turn onto Shasta, surrounding Buck's house.

They're moving fast through the gate, guns up and ready, and bash the door open.

Most of the windows have curtains, so from my perch I can't see inside, and the minutes stretch out as I wait, my heart in my throat.

They'll find the guns, I tell myself. They'll find the drugs.

Hell, Buck might even try to shoot his way out. That'd take care of everything.

I shouldn't want that, though. I've already taken one kid's father away.

But there's that voice inside me that tells me that maybe little Shawna's better off without him. And then it whispers something else: Maybe I would've been better off without Duke.

Movement ahead of me. The deputies are starting to trickle out of the house. My heart sinks. Their hands are empty.

Was it all for nothing? How could they miss the bags full of guns I'd stashed in there? Had Buck paid them off?

Goddammit, if he manages to weasel his way out of this...

I squint through the scope, and though I'm not one for praying, in that moment, I pray. Minutes go by.

Maybe it's God's answer...though probably just my smart planning—but there he is, cuffed, being marched out by two burly deputies. They push him down the path, and one crowds him hard against the squad car before shoving him inside. A bunch of deputies are still swarming around.

As I watch them drive Buck away, triumph rises in my chest. I ignore it, though. This isn't done yet.

Buck is slippery. I have to pin him down completely so he has no way out.

My phone rings. I pull it out of my pocket and answer.

"Hey, Cooper."

"I just got the strangest call," he says. "From Sheriff Harris."

"Oh, yeah?" I ask, staring down at Buck's front yard through my scope. They've got the garage door open, and they're going through the boxes. Excellent.

"Some of his deputies just picked Buck up. Harris is pretty upset. He was babbling about illegal guns?"

"You don't say."

"Harris is wandering around like a lost little lamb," Cooper says. "You know he's no good at taking charge. You might want to stop by. Give him some guidance."

"I'll do that," I say. There's a long pause.

"So the Buck problem's taken care of?" Cooper asks.

"That's right."

Another pause. "You're a damn smart woman, Harley."

It's the first time he's ever called me a woman. They—all of them—always refer to me as a girl.

For some reason, it makes my throat tight. I blink a few times, clearing my throat. "Thanks, Cooper."

"I'll talk to you later."

I hang up, tucking the phone and the scope back in my pockets. I swing down from the branches, scramble down the trunk, and head toward my truck.

I've got a sheriff to talk to.

The North County's Sheriff's Department is in a two-story brick building that's one of the oldest in Salt Creek. It has a little bell tower and a wide staircase that squeaks with every step, and the lights are always going out because the ancient wiring sucks.

Sheriff Harris's office is on the second floor, so I climb the steep stairs, creaking all the way to the top. I take a right and walk down to the end of the hall to the glass door marked SHERIFF in fancy gold letters that were painted almost a hundred years ago.

I knock lightly.

"Come in."

"Hi, Sheriff Harris."

He looks up from behind his desk, and when he sees it's me, sweat pops out on his ruddy face.

Harris has the unmistakable look of a long-term alcoholic—bulbous nose, red face, watery eyes. If he doesn't get a drink in him by noon, he'll get the shakes. His tan uniform is a little too tight, and his neck bulges around the collar.

"Harley, it's good to see you," he lies. "Sit down."

I take a seat in the thinly upholstered chair. It's uncomfortable, sticking me in the backs of my thighs. There are rows of antlers on the wall behind his desk—Harris likes his hunting and his booze. And his graft. I wouldn't want to forget that.

"I'm sorry to bother you," he begins. "But I couldn't get a hold of your father, and Cooper said it was best I talk to you."

"That's right," I say. "I'm in charge while Duke's away."

"So, we picked up Buck Riggs today. My deputies were responding to a 911 call; we weren't staking him out. But what we found inside his house was…not good." He pauses, trying to find a way to soften what's coming.

"Now, Harley, I respect your father and your family. He's been a good friend to me, and I value that friendship. But it's gonna take a lot to look the other way on this. My deputies found enough guns in there to arm a militia. And a few minutes ago, I just got a report back that they've found a large quantity of drugs on the premises, too."

I widen my eyes and wait a few beats, as if I'm absorbing the shock. "I…I understand the position you've been put in, Sheriff," I say. "And

331

I discussed this with my father before I came here. It turns out Buck's been stealing. Duke wants to make him an example."

Sheriff Harris frowns. "An example how?"

I don't blame him for being suspicious. If Duke was around, he'd be bailing Buck out of jail just to kill him himself.

But I don't want death; I just want safety.

"Duke wants you to splash this across the headlines and the evening news," I say. "Tell them you've taken down a major player. The Feds will be delighted. Hand over the guns and the drugs to them—and hand over Buck, too. And with such a monumental bust, when it comes time for funding next year, they won't forget you. And neither will Duke and I."

Sheriff Harris clears his throat, looking hugely relieved. "We could use a win," he mumbles.

"Perfect," I say briskly. "Then this works out for both of us. We really appreciate you and the deputies being so on top of it."

His chest puffs up a little at the ego stroking. "Well, it was pure luck."

"Knowing you, I'm certain it wasn't," I say, and he puffs up a little more. "Now, I do want to make sure Lindsay and her little girl aren't gonna be bothered with any of this."

"The wife?" Sheriff Harris asks.

I nod. "You know she's not involved with this sort of thing. In fact, she's been staying at the Ruby for the last few weeks."

"We'll have to interview her," he says. "But if her story lines up with yours, I doubt there will be a problem."

I smile, sweet as can be. "I'm so glad my father has a friend like you…and I'm sure he'll be showing his appreciation come election time. I just have two little things to ask: Did your deputies happen to get hold of his phone?"

Harris nodded.

"You mind if I take that off your hands?"

"It is evidence," he says slowly.

"Not if it's not logged in yet," I say. "If you're going to turn Buck over to the Feds, my father would be very unhappy if any of his business was exposed to the wrong people."

"Of course," Harris says, looking nervous. "I have it right here." He stands up, walks over to an open box stacked next to his desk, grabs Buck's phone, and gives it to me. I pocket it.

"You've been so helpful," I say. "I'll be sure to tell my father."

Harris's shoulders relax at the thought of Duke's approval.

"Anything else I can do for you?" he asks.

"Do you mind if I have a few minutes with Buck?"

He grins condescendingly. If I was close enough, he'd probably pat me on my head like a five-year-old. "You're not gonna kill him, are you?"

I laugh—I never quite learned how to giggle. "Oh, thanks to you, now I don't need to." He grins back at me conspiratorially at my joke, not realizing that for once I'm telling the truth. "I just want to give him a piece of my mind. My father raised me to believe in loyalty."

"Good trait to have. Sure, you can go back to see him," he says, because he's an easily swayed idiot, like the rest of them. In this whole department, Frankie Daniels is the only one with a brain.

I stand up and follow him out of his office. We go downstairs to the holding-cell area, where he unlocks the door and ushers me inside.

"Just tap on the door when you're done," he says.

Two of the cells are empty. Buck's in the one farthest from the door.

His eyes narrow when he sees me, and he gets to his feet. "You here to bail me out?"

I don't say anything as I walk toward his cell, coming to stand in front of him.

"Where's your father?"

I keep silent, staring at him.

"Where's my kid?"

"She and Lindsay are safe."

Buck wraps his hands around the bars, staring at me. "What did you do?" he asks, gravel and guts in his voice and murder in his eyes.

"What I had to," I say. "I know what you've been up to with Springfield."

He goes a sick kind of white. "I—"

"No excuses," I interrupt softly. "You're done."

"I can explain—"

"No," I say. "You'll listen. And then you're gonna sit here and think about what I said. You'll think about how many ways I can get to you in prison. About how many men in there know the McKenna name, how many owe my father a favor. Then you're gonna think about how I've got your wife in the palm of my hand and how I'll be the one to tell her how you've betrayed my family, but of course I don't blame her. The family will be there for her and her little girl. She's one of ours, and we take care of our own." I lean forward, smiling. "She'll choose us over you," I continue. "She's smart, and frankly, you're a shit husband who never deserved her anyway and now you'll be a felon. You're going away forever, Buck. There's no deal you can cut—no one you can betray. If you do, I'll have you killed."

His hands tighten around the bars. "What did you *do*?" he repeats.

The door opens. "Harley."

I glance over my shoulder. It's Frankie standing there, looking at me, all disapproving, as usual.

*"What did you do?"* This time he yells it. He slams his hands against the bars, and I smile.

I may look like my momma, but in that moment, I'm all Duke.

"You should've remembered," I tell him. "The first rule of North County: Never fuck with the McKenna."

I turn and walk toward Frankie.

*"Harley, goddammit…WHAT DID YOU DO?"* he screams.

The door swings shut behind me.

Frankie crosses her arms, her thin lips twisting. Sheriff Harris is nowhere in sight—he's probably retreated to his office to drink or nap or jerk off.

"You gonna tell me what that's all about?" she asks.

"Well, I'm sure the sheriff will fill you in…if he wants you to know," I say.

"You're up to something," Frankie says flatly.

"Then arrest me."

She glares, tapping her foot. "Just get out of here."

"Gladly."

"You're gonna get hurt," she calls behind me.

I'm fine with that. As long as no one else does.

# FORTY-SEVEN

I'm nine years old when Daddy teaches me how to kill.

We've been in the woods for almost two days, spending the night up in the deer blind, then the daylight hours tracking a buck I'd winged early the first morning, when we'd just started the hunt.

I hadn't listened to Daddy when he told me to hold my fire. I'd been so sure I had the kill shot.

I don't usually miss. It's not the way he taught me. But this time I did, and I'm ashamed.

I can feel the disapproval in his heavy steps ahead of me as he scans the area for the wounded buck's tracks. Daddy's light on his feet for such a big man, a natural hunter, with keen eyes and a steady hand. But right now he's thrashing through the underbrush like he's never been in the backwoods, and he doesn't need to say a word for me to know how angry he is. I bite my lip to keep the tears from flooding my eyes as I follow after him, scrambling up the uneven terrain fast as I can.

I'm a McKenna. McKennas don't cry.

Daddy stops ahead of me, his boots sinking into the red dirt trail as he bends down. "Over here, Harley-girl." He beckons me forward curtly. When I get close enough, I realize his fingertips are smeared with blood. "He's bleeding bad."

"I'm sorry, sir."

His mouth flattens, his lips nearly disappearing. "You should've listened to me."

"I know."

Daddy sighs. "You know what's coming when we find him."

My stomach lurches. "Daddy—"

He holds his hand out and I shut up fast. I can't stop staring at the buck's blood on his fingers. "You'll do as I say."

"Yes, sir."

"C'mon. I don't think he's far."

He walks slower now, so I can match him step for step. I'm getting tall like Daddy, but the rest of me seems to be taking after Momma, which I'm not sure is good or bad. Momma was delicate and pretty, with long brown hair and wide blue eyes, but she's gone, and sometimes I think I remind Daddy of her in a bad way. Sometimes he locks himself in his office with the whiskey, like he did right after she died. But other times, his face clears and he smiles at me, tugging the end of my braid and taking me out back for target practice.

We hike up the hill, where the ground's so steep I have to dig in with my boot heels to stay steady. I'm panting, and by the time we get to the top, my cargos are streaked in red dirt. I stop as soon as Daddy reaches out a hand in warning. I've learned my lesson today about disobeying orders.

"Right there." Daddy tucks his Winchester underneath his arm, pointing thirty feet ahead, where the buck's lying. Even this far away, I can see how he's struggling to breathe, his flanks moving up and down shallowly as he dies slowly and painfully from my bad shot. He's been in agony for two days, and it's all my fault.

Daddy moves toward the buck nice and slow, stepping over felled oak branches so the noise won't startle him. I follow in his footsteps, paying attention to his movements, trying to imitate them like I'm supposed to. It's the only way I'll learn.

The buck barely lifts his head as we close in on him, blood pooling and staining the dry leaves beneath it dark red.

Daddy kneels behind the buck, and for one dizzying second, I think

337

he's going to do it for me. That he won't make me, and I'll just have to watch.

But then he pulls out the knife and holds it out to me handle first. "Time to finish the job, sweetheart."

I take a shaky breath. His dark eyes shine at me above his silver-shot beard as I grab the knife and unsheathe it.

"I'm going to hold the antlers. You want one long, clean cut to the throat," he instructs quietly. "Press your hardest into it. He's gonna thrash."

My hand clenches on the knife as I stare down at the buck. His eye is half-closed, his head and neck covered in half-dried blood.

This is my fault. I missed the shot. It should've been clean. Quick. Daddy hadn't spent the last few years running me through hours of target practice for me to miss a shot like that.

"Harley," Daddy says. "This is the right thing to do. The humane thing. You understand that, don't you?"

I nod. I keep sucking in air frantically through my nose, because it's quieter. I don't want the last thing the buck hears to be me panting in his ear.

"Harley," Daddy prompts. "Please do as I say: one long, clean cut. You can do it, baby."

I grit my teeth and my knees grind into the dirt as I lean forward, the knife in my hand. Trembling, I raise my hand and summon all my strength to bring it down.

The second he feels the knife bite into his neck, the buck lunges. As he tries to rear up, Daddy holds onto his antlers hard, and I yank and yank, as hard as I can, pushing the knife through hide and skin, muscle and tendon. The blood gushes warm over my hand, and I can hear the gurgling sound before the point lands in the ground.

I'm done.

It's done.

I collapse backward. My shaking hands are covered in warm, wet red; my right one still clenched around the knife handle. I try to drop it, but I can't let go. It feels like a part of me.

"That was good," Daddy says.

I lick my lips. My mouth's dry. I don't think I can speak.

I don't think I want to.

"You did good," Daddy says. "You made a mistake. You fixed it. You took responsibility."

"I—I—" I can't breathe.

"It's okay to feel bad, sweetheart," Daddy assures me, rubbing my back. "That means you're human. No matter what, killing something's hard. If it isn't, if taking a life's easy for a man, there's something very wrong. You know that, don't you, honey?"

I nod.

He squeezes my shoulder, a little too tight, but I don't let it show in my face. I have to be tough.

"Sometimes, like right now, killing's necessary," he says. "You put him out of his misery. Sometimes you gotta do that. Sometimes you gotta do other things, for other reasons. It's always hard, baby. But sometimes it's the only way."

He gazes down at me, fixing me with a gentle look, a look that shows how much he loves me; how much I need to learn this.

"The only way," I repeat, because I know it's what he wants.

The smile lights his face like a jack-o-lantern, yanking me from misery into the warm glow of his approval. "That's right, Harley Jean."

I rub my fingers together. The buck's drying blood peels off my skin in little pieces.

I've learned my lesson.

# FORTY-EIGHT

*June 8, 11:30 a.m.*

As I walk out of the sheriff's department, I feel numb more than triumphant. Probably because I can't celebrate yet, not until I'm truly done.

I still have my final target. But to lure Springfield out, I need it to be dark.

So I drive out to Burney. I cross two county lines on my way to the 299. It's a curving road through the forest, the two-lane highway bordered by the thick tall pines and redwoods, following the path cut centuries ago by Cedar Creek.

I concentrate on the trees, on the road, on the cars and the trucks I pass by.

Anything but the fact that I'm driving to sit next to my father while he dies.

Am I supposed to hold his hand? Can he even feel it if I do?

In a way, he's already gone. But I haven't said goodbye, because I don't know how.

I've loved him and I've hated him. I've worshipped him and I've resented him. He put me in cages and car trunks and danger. He's taught me good things, useful things, terrible things. He's used me and I've used him, and I've survived...and he won't.

That's the awful, twisted truth of it: People like us, we find true freedom only in death. Because I can burn what he built to the ground, but

340

I have to make something from the ashes. And that means alliances. Compromise. Violence.

That's what's waiting for me ahead.

But Duke gets to be done. I tell myself that has to be some sort of relief for him. Some sort of freedom.

I pray that it is.

When I pull into the parking lot of Pathways, fear sweat is crawling down my back. Is he gone already?

I hurry into the building, nodding to the nurse in charge. When she sees me, something in her face shifts, and my stomach falls. Am I too late?

I pick up my pace down the hall, jerking open the door to Duke's room, my heart beating too fast.

Will and Brooke look up when I step inside, but I'm not looking at them, I'm looking at him.

His chest, it's rising and falling.

He's still alive.

I sag against the wall, the air whooshing out of me like I've been punched. Busy gets up from her spot next to the bed and trots up to me. Brooke follows, to help me.

"Come sit down next to him," she whispers. She guides me over to the chair closest to his bed. "I'm going to let you two have some time," she says.

I squeeze her hand. "Thank you."

She closes the door behind her, and then it's just Daddy and Will and me. Family.

"I've been playing him some music," Will says, gesturing to his phone.

I take the damp towel, using it to dab at Daddy's dry lips, moistening them. "What's up next?"

Will looks down and he lets out a breath that's almost a laugh. "If I Were a Carpenter."

My throat burns. Daddy's favorite. I sandwich his hand between both of mine, pressing lightly, hoping he can feel it somehow. I think I feel an answering pressure…did I imagine it?

Will presses *Play*, and Johnny and June's voices wrap around us, singing about the kind of devotion and sacrifice that either fixes or breaks us—or both.

The minutes tick by. The songs change from Johnny and June to Loretta, singing about being free. I reach out to moisten his lips every few minutes, holding his hand the rest of the time.

I don't know how much time has passed, but it seems like we've been sitting together like this forever. The nurses come in once to check on him, and they have that knowing look in their eyes when they look at me.

I just keep holding his hand and watching him breathe. And then it changes, suddenly, horribly. It goes from peaceful and quiet to a rough gasping, like he's struggling. Like it hurts. My hand tightens around his.

"I'll go get the nurse," Will says.

He hurries out, and I just hold on to Duke, resting my other hand against his heart.

I know what this is. He's holding on. Some part of him knows it's not done yet.

Some part of him knows it's not safe yet.

I lean forward. "It's okay," I whisper in his ear. "You can go to Momma now. I'm fine here. I'll be okay. I promise."

But he's stubborn. Even in death.

*Gotta do it for me, Harley-girl. Gotta kill him.*

I close my eyes. His heartbeat is so weak beneath my fingers. He keeps struggling to breathe, struggling to hang on, and I don't want him to hurt anymore.

Fate left him with this: the long, painful months of decay and now the struggle as his stubborn soul hangs on, unfinished, unable, unwilling to leave me.

I'd been selfish.

I hadn't wanted him to go.

"I'm sorry, Daddy. I'm so sorry." It doesn't sound like my voice, but it is, I know it has to be. "Please, everything's all right. It's okay to go. I'll do it…I promise I'll do it. I'll finish it."

I bow my head, pressing my forehead against his palm. "I promise," I whisper.

His chest rises and falls, suddenly quieter. Did he hear me?

Will's hands are on my shoulders, holding me. I don't know when he came back in the room, but I'm grateful.

Duke takes a breath in. Lets it out.

And he doesn't draw another.

Busy, who's been quiet this whole time, starts to whine. She jumps up on the bed, curling in a ball at his feet, her nose resting on his leg.

For a long time, neither Will nor I say anything. Out of the corner of my eye, I can see the nurses in the doorway, but they stay out. I close my eyes, pressing my lips to my father's hand.

I want to stay. I want to cry and scream and grieve. But I can't. Not now.

I made a promise. I have a job to do.

When I finally let go of him, it's like letting go of a part of myself. Like I just reached inside and handed over my heart.

But I get up. I stand tall, the way he would've wanted.

"I love you," I tell him. I smooth his hair back. This will be the last time I touch my father. This will be the last time I see him.

I don't want to remember him like this, sick and wasting away. Do I remember him healthy and deadly instead? I don't have the answer.

When it comes to him, I never do.

"Harley," Will says softly.

"I have to go," I say.

Will frowns. Tears are rolling down his face. But I'm not crying. I should be.

I cried when Duke was diagnosed. It'd been the first time in years. But I haven't cried since.

It feels like a boulder is slowly pressing down on my chest. Pound by pound, the pressure increases, so now I can barely breathe around it.

*Gotta do it for me, Harley-girl. Gotta kill him.*

I turn, staring at the door.

If I leave him now, I never see him again.

So I look back. Once more. He's so thin. So still.

But he's not him anymore. He's gone.

And I promised.

"Harley, don't," Will says, because he knows me. "Please."

But I'm backing away. Away from Will, from Duke, from all the love, from all the lessons.

It's on me now.

It's just me now.

"I'm ending this," I say.

It's time.

# FORTY-NINE

I don't know how old I am. Young. Young enough that there's a fuzziness to everything, to the sound of his voice, the smile in his eyes.

He's chasing me through the garden. My bare feet slap against the brick path he laid between the raised beds, and I'm giggling, my little legs pumping as I run from him. There's this giddy feeling in my stomach, *run, run, run,* and I shriek with delight as he swipes at me and I dodge out of the way.

"I'm gonna get you!"

I run, and run, and run, and I'm laughing and I'm happy.

I am safe. I am loved. I am innocent.

I am not me yet. Not really. I am barely formed and soft at the edges. Living in a world where Mommas don't die and Daddies don't kill.

Eventually, he catches me. Swings me up on his shoulders. I'm higher than anyone's ever been, high enough to touch the clouds, and I chant, *Higher, Daddy, higher.*

I grab for the sky.

I'm sure I can reach it.

# FIFTY

*June 8, 9:00 p.m.*

The house is silent and dark as I approach. The tall weeds—a mix of foxtails and cornflowers that have overgrown what was once a lawn—swish against my legs as I come at it from the north.

Whoever owned the lot built this place a few years after the rubble from the first house was cleared away. Rye grass was planted over the scorched earth, and the charred remains of the trees blasted in the explosion were replaced with saplings.

I bought it a few years ago, with some of the money Uncle Jake left me. I never told anyone because I knew it was kind of ghoulish, especially because I didn't do anything with it. I just left it empty. The sycamores and mimosas are tall now, and the yard has returned to the wild.

Whenever Duke had to get to this part of town, he always took the long way. He couldn't drive past the street.

Even before I bought it, the house never stayed occupied for long. I don't really think she's haunting it, but when you walk through the rooms, there's something unsettling in the air. Maybe it's true that some places, they just hold the pain that came before.

I walk up to the back porch, find the key I taped under the railing, and let myself inside. There's no power, so I flip on my flashlight and set the two gas cans down so I can close the door behind me.

I'd originally planned to use Buck's phone to lure Springfield out, but Bobby's is even better. I take it from my pocket, scan through the contacts, and find Carl.

I tap out a message: I got her. 2360 Meadow Lane

When I hit *Send*, there's no hesitation. I toss the phone on the kitchen counter and head to the living room. It starts ringing almost immediately, but I ignore it.

He's gonna have to come and see for himself.

In the living room, there's a ragged couch and an old wooden chair left by the former tenants, and I set my duffel down in the corner, where I can reach it easily. I take out the two guns, one in a holster that I fasten to my waist. The other in my hand, I walk the rooms of the house methodically. Bedroom. Bathroom. Second bedroom.

I decide to start in the second bedroom. It has fading flowered wallpaper and a bare curtain rod above the window.

Am I near the spot where she was standing when she died?

My body tightens up, and I force my muscles to relax. I can't think about it.

It's all I can think about.

They're both gone now. Momma being gone so long ago is a natural thing, a hurt that simmers, boiling over only once in a while. But Duke…

I don't know how to grieve for him. I don't know how to live without him. I don't know how to do any of this without him.

My legs start to shake. Leaning against the wall, I grit my teeth and breathe. In. Out. One. Two.

*Gotta do it for me, Harley-girl. Gotta kill him.*

I lock my knees and straighten up. I can do this.

I have to do this.

I walk quickly back into the kitchen and grab the gas cans. I dump half of one in the kitchen, then head to the second bedroom, which I douse, too, and then dribble a long line down the hall leading to the living room. By the time I'm done, both cans are empty. The sharp smell of gasoline fills the house, and I open the windows and unlock the front door before going to lock the back one.

I tuck the cans behind the couch and then grab the motion sensors out of my duffel. They're the basic model, with loud chiming alarms. I fix one to the wall next to the front door and the other to the back of the couch.

Then I retreat into the doorway of the first bedroom, careful not to step on the line of gas in the hall, and I wait.

Eventually, Bobby's phone on the counter stops ringing. I check mine for the time—there are four texts from Will and two from Brooke, but I don't read them. I can't be distracted.

I promised Duke. My whole life's been leading up to this moment. So I wait.

The house is set far down the street, away from anything else, so I can hear his truck rumbling down the road and turning into the driveway. It slows to a stop; the truck door opens and then slams shut. He's coming.

My hand tightens around my .45.

The porch stairs creak. I try to keep my breathing normal, flattening myself against the bedroom wall, hidden from view in the darkness.

*Hands steady, Harley-girl.*

The door swings open. He steps inside, triggering the first motion detector.

Set at the highest volume, it goes off, and the sound makes him whirl around to face the open doorway, backing toward the living room as he fires, the trigger-happy bastard. Glass shatters as the bullet hits the front window.

As he moves into the living room, he sets off the detector on the couch, and it blares on, filling the air with chimes. He spins toward the sound again, and *there*, he's in position, his back to me.

I rush through the darkness toward him, the sound of the detectors covering up my footsteps. He senses my presence a second too late: Just as he starts to turn, my gun's at the back of his head.

"Don't even think about it."

He freezes.

I reach around, grab the gun out of his hand, and pat him down, making sure he's got nothing else on him.

I pull a knife out of his back pocket and toss it into the hall.

"Sit in the chair," I say, pivoting to face him, and I drag the barrel of my .45 across the back of his skull, up to his temple, and between his eyebrows, before I pull back.

I can't quite see his expression in the darkness, but when he sits down, a shaft of moonlight falls across him.

He's smiling.

It sends chills down my spine. My teeth grind together, trying to stamp out the wrongness as his head tilts, looking me up and down.

I grab the zip ties out of my duffel. "Hands flat," I direct.

I tie his hands and legs to the chair, punishingly tight, and then I back up, taking the LED lantern out of my duffel and setting it to the side. I flip it on, and the room's glowing with light, stretching out the shadows across the room.

I sit on the couch across from him. My heart's beating fast, but my hands are steady.

I can do this. I have to.

I look at him, now that we've got light. Now that he can see me.

It's been a long time since we were face-to-face. He looks older—much older, since last I saw him close up. There are deep lines around his eyes and mouth, grooves carved into his forehead. His hair's thinning like crazy, and he tries to hide it by slicking it back.

But he's still smiling, like it's all a joke.

He has no idea. But soon, he will.

"You got hold of my nephew's phone," he says.

"I did."

His fingers flex, and I'm not stupid—I know he's testing his bonds.

No way he's breaking free of those zip ties. They're the ones the cops use.

I'm quiet, staring at him, waiting.

"You got him somewhere?" Carl asks, and he's trying to sound dis-interested, but I can hear the worry sneaking in.

"Maybe."

"He alive?"

I shrug, holstering my gun and pulling out Duke's antler-handled knife, the one that's been passed down for years in my family, from father to son, and finally, from father to me. I pluck the lighter out of my shirt pocket, flicking it on.

He doesn't flinch—it's not as obvious as that. But the second the flame spurts out, glowing orange and blue, his eyes fix on it like he can't stop them. When I move the lighter toward the knife, his eyes follow, widening just a little.

"What are you playing at, girl?" he asks.

I stay silent and run the flame back and forth under the knife, just like I've watched Duke do. I think about Uncle Jake's screams in that motel room. I think about his blood on my hands as he lay dying, begging me to run. I think about Momma, shining so bright, loving so hard, and getting snuffed out because she chose the right man instead of the wrong one.

The knife blackens with soot, and slowly it begins to redden. To glow. Just at the tip at first, and then spreading farther down the blade.

I blow on it gently, and it turns a ruddy orange. Then I stand up and circle around him, knife in one hand, lighter in the other. When I bring the blade an inch away from his left eye, he jerks back so hard it might've toppled the chair if my boot wasn't firmly pressed against the leg. I know he can feel the heat against his skin. I hope he's remembering those burns he got from killing Momma. I hope they're aching like a bitch right now. I hope he's scared.

"I'm not playing at anything," I say. "We're going to talk. And then," I flick the lighter next to his right eye, "I'm going to set this house—and you—on fire."

# FIFTY-ONE

I'm five years old when I catch Uncle Jake and Momma arguing in the barn.

I'm supposed to be inside, but she didn't lock the screen door like she usually does. I want to run in the meadow behind the barn and pick the wild sweet peas that grow along the edge of the forest.

I'm heading down there when the voices stop me. I turn around and circle back, peeking in at them through the doorway.

"I'm not talking about this with you!" Momma says.

"We need to," Jake says. "This is dangerous."

"I am so sick of you saying that," Momma snaps. She's pacing back and forth, her long paisley skirt swirling around her ankles. She has silver rings on her toes. One has a moon with a face; it always makes me smile. "He's *not* dangerous—not when it comes to me. And not when it comes to Harley."

"He's a criminal, Jeannie."

"I love him," she says. "He loves me. He would never hurt me."

"You sure about that?" Jake asks, and there's something in his voice that makes my stomach hurt. That makes Momma go white and reach out and slap him, hard across the face. My eyes go wide. I've never seen Momma hit anyone before. She doesn't even spank me—and she doesn't let Daddy, either.

351

"You keep your mouth shut," she hisses. "Or you'll be getting more than the back of my hand."

Uncle Jake touches his fingers to his mouth. His lip's bleeding.

Her face, twisted with anger, relaxes into sorrow. "I'm sorry," she says immediately. "Fuck, Jake, I'm sorry. I just—" she sighs, pressing a hand to her forehead, staring up at the ceiling of the barn. "I don't like thinking about it. Her and him…" She sighs.

"Eventually you're gonna have to deal with it."

"I—" Momma starts to say, but then she catches sight of me in the barn doorway. "Harley," she says. "Honey, what are you doing out here?" She hurries forward, scooping me up. She looks over her shoulder at Jake. "I've got it under control," she tells him. "I promise."

"I want to pick flowers, Momma!" I tell her. And she laughs and we walk through the meadow to the edge of the forest, gathering armloads of sweet peas and lupine and golden California poppies.

I don't think to ask her why she looks worried. I don't ask her why she was mad at Jake. I forget about it almost immediately, my full focus on the rainbow of color in my arms.

Momma laughs and claps her hands as I thrust a fistful of flowers at her.

"That's my sweet girl," she says, reaching out her arms and holding me close. "That's my sweet, sweet girl."

# FIFTY-TWO

*June 8, 10:58 p.m.*

I sit back on the couch and I look at him, this man who had set my life on its path. It's strange to be so close after this long. I should be more scared than I am. But instead, it feels like I'm finally standing still after years of spinning.

"You're not gonna kill me," he says, and he almost sounds like he believes it.

I set the knife—starting to cool down now, on the floor next to the couch, keeping the lighter in my hand.

"Killing takes balls. You don't have any. If you did, you would've sent Duke after me when my guy shredded up Jake's guts." His mouth tilts up at the memory. I bite the inside of my lip, trying to stay calm.

He's just seeing how to get to me.

"You kill me, your daddy will be so pissed," Carl continues. "He wants to be the one who does it."

I fold my hands together around the silver lighter with the wolf's head engraved on it. I can feel the etching against my palm. "It doesn't matter what he wants."

Carl snorts. "It's all about what Duke wants. Always."

"It doesn't matter what he wants, because he's dead," I say. And it's the first time I've said it. *He's dead.* The words are strange on my tongue, the sound of them like hail on a tin roof, it sets your teeth on edge.

For a second, Carl's mouth drops open; then he snaps it shut, trying to recover. He laughs shakily. "Bullshit."

"Before he died, he made me promise him something," I continue. "See, at the end, he was so fucking weak, so sick, he knew he wouldn't be able to get you. He made me promise I would. So I did. And now"—I throw my arms out wide—"here we are."

He shifts as best he can bound to the chair. "You're fucking with me," he says, but there's doubt in his eyes.

Real soon, it's gonna turn to fear.

I picture him in my mind…my daddy. A man with bloody hands and a shady heart. He had loved me. He had terrorized me. He had made me.

I look across the room to Carl.

So had he.

"Duke ain't dead. He's in Mexico," Springfield says.

"Where'd you hear that?" I ask. "Buck?"

The look on his face tells me that's exactly where he heard it. I smile. "Buck got it wrong because I wanted him to. He won't be working with you anymore, by the way. He's gonna be busy, what with the Feds taking him in."

He sucks in a shaky breath, tensing in the chair. "What did you do?" he asks.

"Funny, that's exactly what Buck asked me when I visited him in jail this morning."

He jerks against the zip ties, making the chair jump, but it holds. "What the fuck are you up to?"

"You know, my entire life's been about you," I tell him, my head tilting as I take him in. He seems so much smaller now. So much less terrifying.

He shifts again, sweat trickling down his forehead.

"Even when you were locked up. He could never let go, never rest. You were always coming for me. You were the bogeyman, really. But now…" I look him up and down. "I'm starting to think that fear was misplaced. You failed every time you tried to get me. And the first time I tried to get you, I did it in three days with nothing but a smile, a gun, and a little creativity. Really, Carl, what are you other than a murderous, racist fucker who thinks he's a lot smarter than he actually is?"

"Smart enough to kill your Uncle Jake," he says. "Smart enough to kill Jeannie. She was a hot piece, your momma," he says. "She had a tight little ass." He licks his lips for good measure.

My stomach clenches. He doesn't have the right to say her name. To even think about her. But I'm not going to give him the pleasure. "It's not going to work," I tell him. "Trying to get me angry. You've hurt or killed every single person I've ever loved. There's no getting angry after that—there's just getting even."

"Were you close enough to hear the screaming that day?" he asks, and I go very still, because I wasn't. Because this is something new from the day that defined me. That ruined me.

"I was," he says, and the lantern light paints his face in long shadows as he leans forward as much as his bonds allow. "She must've burned for a good minute before the flames got the better of her. Screaming her head off the whole time." His smile stretches, gaping, cruel. "If I remember right, it was your name I heard."

I get to my feet, the knife in my hand and against his throat, pressing there hard. It's still hot enough to sear, and his flesh peels and bubbles up in blisters instead of bleeding.

He laughs, a choking sound that's all triumph. "You can't do it," he says.

I jerk the knife away from his neck. The long burned spot shines red.

Goddammit. My skin feels too tight for my body. I want to stab him. Shove my knife as far into his heart as I can.

It's what Daddy would do.

It's what a McKenna would do.

I turn back to him, the knife still in my hand.

"You wanna know why you can't kill me, Harley Jean?" he asks, and that smile is back, and I hate it. I hate him.

"Not really," I say.

But he keeps on going, because I haven't shot him yet. I need to shoot him.

I need to end this. I grit my teeth. But I don't grab the gun.

"You can't kill me because there's some part of you, deep inside, that's telling you not to. And you don't know why, but you keep listening to it. Over and over. I knew it the first time I saw you, in that parking lot. You didn't scream. You just sat there and took it. Let me tear the hair right out of your head. But you never told anyone you saw me, did you?"

I shake my head.

"You should've," he says. "He raised you to be a vicious little bitch. But you didn't tell him. Why's that?"

I try to keep my face blank, but it's hard. "I was seventeen. I was stupid."

"Last time, you were grown," he says. "I waited till you were grown before I sent Andy for you."

I shudder. I can't stop it.

"I as good as killed your uncle, and even then you didn't tell. Duke would've gone after me in a second if he knew the truth. But you spun some other tale, didn't you?"

"I was trying to prevent a war," I say.

"Bullshit," he says. "You could've tried to kill me when I came to the graveyard. Every time, baby girl, I leave myself wide open for you, and every time, you don't take advantage of it. You gotta be asking yourself why."

"Are you really complaining about all the times I've stopped myself from killing you?" I ask.

"Once is luck. Twice is a coincidence. Three times? That's a pattern. What keeps stopping you?"

"You seem to think you have the answer," I tell him.

He leans forward, the lantern light filling his face, and it's like looking into the darkest part of the water, where the things you don't want to see lie. "You can't kill me, because deep down, there's a part of you that knows the truth."

My hand slips in my pocket, closing around the lighter. The cool metal feels good against my skin. "What truth?"

"That you're not Duke's daughter. You're mine."

He leans back, and it's like he's the cock of the walk. He smiles, because he thinks he's won. He thinks it's gonna destroy me. That I'll crumble.

But I am a McKenna. We're always two steps ahead.

We always win.

I pull the lighter out of my pocket, flicking it on, and I raise my eyes to meet his. "I have your blood," I tell him. "But I'll never have your heart."

I drop the lighter onto the line of gas.

The flames leap high.

Springfield screams.

# FIFTY-THREE

I'm eighteen when I find out.

It's an accident, really. Right after Christmas, we move Miss Lissa to Fir Hill. She needs round-the-clock care, and it's for the best; we all know that.

But Will's quiet for weeks after the move, and Miss Lissa is so confused—even more than usual. It's awful leaving her after each visit because she doesn't understand why she can't come with us.

The nurses tell us it's normal, that she'll get used to her room, to the other patients. *She'll think of it as home soon,* they reassure us.

But it isn't home. Half the time, Miss Lissa may not know who she is or where she is, but she knows she's not home.

I throw myself into making it better for her. I bring her quilts, her pictures, the worn paperback mysteries she liked to read. I read them to her now, and she keeps her eyes closed most of the time, but whenever I pause to flip a page, she opens her eyes, like she doesn't want me to stop. So I don't. Sometimes we spend hours reading.

I cook every single recipe she's ever taught me. I win the nurses' devotion with her snickerdoodles, and the food seems to cheer her up the most, so I start bringing it every day for dinner. Will meets me after work as much as he can, and we all eat together, but a lot of the time it's just her and me.

One day, when I walk in the door carrying her favorite fried chicken and biscuits with star-thistle honey, she beams and says, "Jeannie!"

It's not the first time she's mistaken me for Momma, but it's the first time I don't correct her. Whenever I do, she either gets confused or she starts to remember, and it's like she's finding out Momma's dead all over again. So this time I decide not to put her through that anymore.

Instead, I play along. I smile and hold out the basket of chicken. "It's your recipe," I tell her.

"Did you soak the chicken in buttermilk?" she asks.

It'll never not be weird how she can't remember who I am but she knows I'm supposed to soak the chicken. Why is it that the important stuff gets scrambled and the random stuff stays in reach?

"Just like you taught me." I set the basket down on the tray over her hospital bed and make up a plate for her. I tuck a napkin in the neck of her housecoat, smoothing it down her front.

"Have you talked to Desi lately?" Miss Lissa asks, taking a bite out of a biscuit. A smile lights up her face. "You did a good job on these, honey."

"I haven't seen Desi for a while," I say carefully.

Miss Lissa snorts. "I worry about her," she says. "She has Will to think about now. I was hoping once she had him..." She trails off and sighs.

My stomach clenches.

"Try the chicken," I prod gently. Despite all the meals I bring, she's lost weight since she moved to Fir Hill.

"I don't know what I did wrong with that girl," Miss Lissa sighs.

"You did your best," I say, because I know she did. Miss Lissa had made her mistakes, but she raised Will up into a good man despite his nightmare of a mother. But Desi's demons, they just ran too deep.

Miss Lissa falls silent, concentrating on the meal. And when she's done, I clean everything up and read to her until I think she's drifted off.

But when I stand up to gather my stuff and go, she reaches out and grabs my arm.

I look down at her, and my stomach drops, like I've slipped while climbing and am about to fall.

Her brown eyes are suddenly alert, serious. Her fingers clutching my arm are strong.

"Jeannie, what are you going to do about the baby?"

I think for a second, trying to figure out the best answer. Earlier she thought Will was a baby. So if she's still at that time in her head, that means I haven't been born yet. Is she remembering Momma telling her about being pregnant with me? She must be.

"I'm going to keep the baby," I say, thinking it'll soothe her. It's what happened, after all. "I love Duke. We'll get married."

But it doesn't calm her. Her grip tightens around my arm and suddenly, she pulls hard. It takes me off guard and I stumble forward, settling on the bed next to her.

"What if he finds out?" she hisses, and there's fear in her face, in the way she's holding me, looking at me. Something cold and clammy starts to form inside me.

I frown. "Finds out what?"

"This is dangerous, Jeannie," Miss Lissa says. "You're playing with fire."

"I'm being careful," I respond, because I don't know what else to say. What is she talking about? Is she just mixing up the timelines? Did she just not want Momma to marry Daddy? I can't blame her for that.

"What if the baby looks like him?" Miss Lissa asks, every line of her wrinkled face is written with concern, with genuine fear.

Fear for Momma.

Fear for *me*.

Oh, God.

I jerk backward.

"Looks like who?" I ask shakily.

But I know. I know. Oh, God, I know.

"They're dangerous men," Miss Lissa says. "I know you love Duke, but tricking him like this…"

My entire body feels like it's on fire. She's confused. She has to be confused.

Duke is my father. Momma wouldn't…

"And what if Carl finds out?" she continues, shaking her head.

And there it is. A scream's rising in my throat, but I can't let it out. I can't scare her like that.

So I force myself to keep my face neutral. "Don't worry," I say, trying like hell to keep my voice from shaking.

"But…" Miss Lissa frowns. "Duke's not the kind of man who'll raise another man's child. Especially *that* man. If he finds out, Jeannie…" She wrings her bony hands.

"I've got it all figured out. I promise. Everything will be fine." I lean down, kissing her on the forehead. "I'll be back tomorrow, okay?"

She's got that lost, worried expression on her face, the one she gets when she's swimming in the confusion, unable to latch on to anything real. "Okay," she repeats softly, uncertainly.

"I love you," I tell her. "I love you a lot."

"I love you, too, Jeannie," she says.

I want to cry. I've never wanted to cry so hard in my life. She's broken my heart, she's torn my life apart, and she doesn't know it and she'll never know it and I thank God for that, because if she knew, she'd hate herself.

She kept this from me. All these years. She kept Momma's secret. She protected her.

She protected me.

But now I know.

Now I have to protect myself.

# FIFTY-FOUR

*June 8, 11:15 p.m.*

The fire speeds down the hallway toward the second bedroom, filling it with fire and smoke.

Springfield jerks backward in the chair, crashing to the floor just inches away from the fast-spreading flames. He's not laughing anymore. His eyes are wide and terrified, sweat pouring off him, panting like he's running a race. He pulls against his bonds, but he's not going anywhere.

He's trapped, and the fire will get him in the end.

I crouch down, so we're level.

"Goddammit, Harley!" he yells. "Let me free!"

There's a whooshing sound. I look down the hall. The fire's climbing up the walls of the second bedroom—the flowers on the wallpaper are turning black.

It's time to go.

I grab my gun and knife. The smoke's growing thick, billowing up around us.

"Harley!" he screams.

I look down at him, at the terror in his face, at the way he's struggling, fighting, still, to survive.

Is that where I get it from?

Is this what Momma felt, this terrible heat, sweat rolling down her back in bullets, as she screamed for me?

He coughs violently, his body convulsing. The flames are only inches away now. If I just give him a little push...

It's what Duke would do.

But I am not Duke.

I am not Momma.

And I am not Springfield.

So I bend down, slip the knife under the zip ties, and cut him free. He tries to rise to his feet, but the smoke's too much for him. Coughing, he falls to the floor.

I grab his arm and pull him away from the fire, out of the house, onto the grass near the fence. He rolls over onto his side, choking, spitting, trying to clear his mouth and suck in some air.

I stand tall over him, my lungs burning from the smoke, my heart split in two from the hurt.

He stares up at me, bewildered, coughing.

"I want you to remember this moment," I tell him. "I am not him. I am not you. I am *better*. That's the only reason you're still alive. You remember that while you're rotting away in your cell. You remember how I spared you. Not because of blood or any of that shit you think matters. But because I chose to be better than you and him and all of this."

He struggles to his elbows, panting. "I'm in you, girl. You can't outrun me. I'm your father."

"I'm a goddamn woman," I say. "And Duke McKenna's my father."

I lash out, the butt of my gun smashing against his temple. He goes down like a sack of rocks.

I loom over him for a second, half-sure he's going to leap up, like he's playing possum or something. But he stays down.

I put him down.

Smoke is pluming in the sky, and I can hear sirens in the distance. Someone's called the fire department.

I need to move.

I sprint to the shed behind the house, pull out the boxes of drugs, and cart them over to Carl's truck, where I open them and stuff the Ziplocs in the toolbox and under the seats. I grab the bottle of spray paint from one of the boxes, and along the fence, where Carl's lying unconscious, I paint DEATH TO MCKENNA on the grass. Then I press the can into his hand.

The sirens are getting louder. The fire's leaping and climbing. I can see flames soaring out of the kitchen window now.

It'll reach the gas line any minute. Then it'll blow.

I run. Across the meadow, the star thistle pricking my legs as I cut a path through it. I'm almost to the tree line where my truck's hidden when I hear it, that terrible *boom* from my childhood, and the blast of heat washes over my back.

I don't look back. I just keep running.

It's time to focus on the future.

The storage place is empty, like it was the night before when I locked them up. The gate's still wide open, and I drive through it, pulling up to the unit.

There's no banging on the door as I unlock it, heaving it above my head. I step back immediately, my .45 in hand.

Caroline squints in the bright light. Her boys are in the corner—Bennet's asleep. Bobby glares at me, but he doesn't move.

I toss two bottles of water near them. "You." I point the gun at Caroline. "Come with me. We're taking a drive."

She steps out of the unit, and I lock Bobby and Bennet up again. She gets in the truck, watching me warily. And I drive us through the gate and toward the west side, where there's a bluff that overlooks town.

That's where I park the truck, the headlights shining off the cliff, the lights of the town flickering in the night. It's a beautiful sight. Peaceful.

I look over at her, my gun still on her.

"You gonna shoot me?" she asks.

"I could've done that in the storage unit." I let out a long breath. The weight on my chest keeps pressing hard, but I keep breathing. I keep moving.

If I stop, then it'll really hit me.

He's gone.

Keep moving. Keep talking. Don't think about it.

"Carl's been arrested," I say. "He's going away for good, Caroline. I made sure of it."

Her eyes narrow; she sucks in her lips, hate written on her face. "You little bitch. You and your daddy—"

"Duke's dead," I interrupt her.

She sputters, her mouth hanging open like a dead fish. "What?"

"Duke's dead," I repeat. "And I've taken Carl out of the equation. No more men telling us what to do. So now you and I are going to talk. About your boys. And about your future."

She shifts on the bench seat of my truck, angling toward me, still in shock, I can tell, but already calculating as the new reality starts to click into place in that head of hers.

Caroline's smart. She knows how to play the game. I'm pretty sure the only reason Carl managed to hide out from Duke for more than two years was because of her quick thinking. Not that it would've ever occurred to Duke she was the mastermind behind it—she played him, too.

But she won't play me. Because Caroline and me? We're alike. Out to protect ourselves and our own. At any cost.

"The truce holds," I say.

She snorts. "You locked me and my boys up in a storage locker for over a day."

"Your boys kidnapped Will," I countered.

"You framed Carl," she hits back. We're just airing our grievances now. Laying them out, so we can see: who has more, who has the leverage, who has the upper hand.

"Carl needed to be framed," I say. "Jesus, Caroline. He's a fucking anchor around your neck. He made you a target. He's useless. Nothing but trouble. You really telling me you're gonna miss taking his bullshit? Weren't you better off when he was inside? I know your boys were."

"Your father took the business away from us," she says between clenched teeth.

"And I've taken the business away from him," I say. "Catch up. The past is the past. It's a new world. *My* world."

"And what does your world look like?" Caroline asks.

"No more meth," I say.

She laughs. "Girl, I knew you were crazy, but I didn't think you were stupid. People are always gonna be cooking up that shit. Hell, I bet they'll be moving in before your daddy's cold in his grave."

"They won't get far," I say, and she laughs some more.

"You gonna be your daddy?" she asks. "Be the McKenna? You can't—they never take women seriously."

"They'll take me seriously," I say, because I have to believe it. I burned it all to the ground, and the only way to atone is to build something better—safer—from the ashes.

"Good luck with that," Caroline says, sarcasm dripping from her words like honey off a spoon.

"I don't want to fight you," I tell her. "You've never done anything to me."

"My boys have," she says.

I know I have her then. She needs to keep them safe.

And with me around, they won't be—unless the truce holds.

"I'm willing to overlook that," I say. "As long as you stay out of the business. Run the gas station. Be happy you have that. No cooking. No dealing. Not even weed."

Her eyes narrow. "Is that what you're doing?" she asks. "You taking up gardening, Harley?"

I ignore her and turn the key in the ignition. The engine purrs to life.

"We should be getting back." I look over at her. The lines of her face tell a story I can't quite read, her eyes full of anger, but I think I see a hint of resignation.

"So, what do you say, Caroline?" I ask. "Truce holds. Your boys walk away free, unhurt. You stay out of my business, I stay out of yours."

She gnaws on her lower lip, her pride warring with her logic. "Fine," she says finally.

I hold my hand out, and she takes it.

I squeeze her fingers, too tight and too long. "If your boys put one toe out of line, I will kill them," I tell her, my voice serious. I let it show on my face, how much I mean it. How I could put Bobby or Bennet down like a rabid dog—a necessary act, for the greater good. "You make sure Bobby understands that especially."

I can hear Caroline's teeth grinding, holding back what she wants to say. "I'll do that," she says.

I let go of her hand. There are red marks on her fingers.

I remind myself it's necessary. I think about the Rubies. About Brooke and Will and Cooper and Wayne. About the kind of damage Bobby Springfield could do with his violence and his neo-Nazi bullshit. About how Bennet had already drawn Jessa into the Springfield crosshairs unwittingly.

I won't allow that to happen again.

We drive back in silence. I pull up to the gate of the storage space and unlock the truck door.

She gets out, but she turns back to me, staring through the open window with an expression I can't quite place. Bitterness? Regret? Both?

"You have his eyes, you know," she says.

And there it is, out in the open. An acknowledgment of a truth we both know but won't ever speak of again: that when it comes down to it, she and I are family. Not just through blood, but through experience. We've weathered the storms of the men who came before, and now we're both free.

"I know."

I press on the gas. And I'm gone before she can say another word.

# FIFTY-FIVE

*June 9, 1:00 a.m.*

I want to go home. To sleep. To do anything to escape the ball of grief in my chest that's growing with every breath.

I drive home on autopilot, barely aware of what I'm doing until I get through the gates. When I turn the final curve of the driveway, the house comes in sight and my body relaxes.

This is what I fought for, I remind myself as I unbuckle my seat belt. This is what I betrayed Duke for.

Home. The Rubies. Will.

Safety. Family. Sanity.

There's a light on in the living room and a motorcycle parked in front of the porch, and I should have expected he'd be here.

He's always chasing after me.

I walk up the porch steps and through the door.

Busy starts barking when she hears me and stops when she sees me. She leaps forward and plants her front paws on my stomach, smiling like she knows I need it.

There's a creak from the third stair from the top. I look up, and Will's there, his eyes red and tired. He hasn't shaved; there's rough stubble on his chin. It makes him look older.

Or maybe losing Duke made us older.

He doesn't say anything and he doesn't touch me, which I am so grateful for. If he touches me, I'm going to cry. I have years of tears to make up for, and if I start, I don't think I'll ever stop.

I can't think anymore. I've been stamping it down, planning, moving forward, getting shit done, ignoring, ignoring, ignoring it.

But now he's dead.

And now I'm alone.

I'm all that's left of the McKennas. Of Momma and Jake.

It's a strange feeling, being lost. It's not one I'm used to. I always know where I am. Where I'm going.

It's how he raised me.

He was true north and I was the compass, so now I'm just spinning in circles with nothing to point to.

"I just want to go to sleep," I say.

"I'll lock up," he says, and it almost hurts to breathe around how grateful I am that he's here. I don't know what I would've done if I'd come home to the dark, empty house I expected.

I make it up the stairs, Busy at my heels. I'm so tired it takes almost all the energy I can summon up. But when I pass Duke's bedroom door, I pause, my hand hovering over the knob.

I know it doesn't look the same. The antique brass bed he and Momma slept in every night is gone. I packed it up and put it in one of the barns for storage. In its place is the hospital bed I bought the second month when I still thought I could do it—give him his peaceful death at home.

If I open the door, I'll see it, taunting me. Reminding me what kind of daughter I am. Reminding me that I don't deserve that title. Reminding me that I don't even have his blood.

I force myself to move past the room into my own. Busy hops on the bed, her tail wagging back and forth against the quilts Miss Lissa stitched.

My entire body aches as I pull off my clothes, leaving them in a pile on the floor. I know I should shower—I reek of sweat and smoke—but I can't bring myself to move. I just stand there, frozen, exhausted, spinning, spinning, always spinning, with nothing to grasp on to.

I hear his footsteps coming up the stairs, pausing to turn off all the lights but the ones in the hall, and then my bedroom door swings open, and he's there, in the room.

A wash of warmth goes over my bare back as he comes to stand behind me. "Wait a second," he says. I force myself to stand still in the middle of my room, the cool air hitting my back as he steps away. I hear the scrape of my dresser drawer opening, and then he's behind me again. I shiver, I can't help it. He presses his forehead against my shoulder before he drapes the folds of the flannel shirt over me.

I button the shirt—his shirt—over my chest, and when I turn around, he's stripped down to his black boxer briefs.

Busy jumps off the bed, trotting over to the rag rug next to the bookcase she likes.

I walk to my side of the bed and pull back the quilt and sheet, and he does the same on the other side. I slide in first, lying on my back, and he brings the quilt over the both of us before settling on his side facing me.

I've slept next to him dozens of times. In the back of trucks and high up in deer blinds. Snug in a tent, side by side in sleeping bags. Drooling on his shoulder on the couch after watching those old musicals Miss Lissa likes. Out in the backwoods, with nothing but a blanket between us and the sky.

Never in a bed. Never like this.

"Hey," he says softly. His palm stretches over mine, but he waits until my fingers thread through his to pull me toward him. We're lined up together, shoulder to shoulder, chest to chest, a tangle of thighs and calves, my always-cold feet pressed between his. Our noses brush. His legs are scratchy with hair; it tickles. His arm drapes over my waist, his hand settling at the small of my back, and I tuck mine over the curve of his hip, where cloth meets skin.

"You did so good," he murmurs. "You are so good, Harley."

I press my face into his neck.

"He'd be proud," Will whispers. "I know you don't think so. But he would be."

"He'd hate me," I say.

"No." He brings me tighter against him. "Never."

I wish I could believe it. But that's not the woman he raised.

I close my eyes.

And finally, the tears come.

# FIFTY-SIX

*June 16, 10:00 a.m.*

We bury Duke on a sunny Friday morning.
I walk through the graveyard like I've done too many times. I've taken this walk to bury Momma, to bury Jake, and now to bury Duke.

It's strange, being the last one.

It doesn't matter whose blood is in my veins. I am a McKenna. The only one left.

Will walks next to me, Cooper and Wayne close behind. We walk down the main path of the cemetery in silence, crossing the lawn to stand in front of my family's line of graves, where his headstone already sits.

The service is private, just the four of us and Pastor Evans. He says lovely things. Pretty lies and half-truths, about Duke's loyalty to his family and his entrepreneurial spirit. It's nice of him. And when it's over, he hugs me and tells me he's here for me.

As he walks away, I think about Molly, wondering what he'd do if he knew what a fighter his daughter is under her sweet surface.

Fathers underestimate us. Duke and Springfield underestimated me.

And now here I am: the last one standing and free. I have control.

I just have to hold on to it.

"Do you need a ride to the Tropics?" Cooper asks me.

I shake my head. They're throwing Duke a wake. Something noisy

372

and loud, with too much whiskey and too much weed and not-so-exaggerated stories about the mean old son of a bitch. He'd love it.

"I'll be there later," I tell them. "I just need some time alone."

"Of course," Cooper says. "Honey." He pulls me forward, hugging me tight. "I'm so sorry," he says. "It's gonna be okay. I promise."

I nod, pulling back. Wayne hugs me, too, but he doesn't say anything. He just presses his palm against my cheek, and it says everything necessary. I cover his hand with my own for a second.

They head down the path toward the Tropics, where they'll celebrate Duke's life in style. If there isn't a fistfight by the end of the night, it'll probably be considered a failure.

I turn back to Duke's grave. Now it's just Will and me.

His arm goes around me and I lean my head against his shoulder. "Do you want me to stay?"

I shake my head. "I need some time."

"I'm going to head to the house, then," he says.

"You're not gonna go to the wake?" I'm not really surprised, though people—Paul and Mo in particular—will miss seeing him.

He'll be gone soon. Back to college. I try to push it out of my mind.

"I'll pour one out to him at home," Will says. "Build him a fire in the fire pit."

He would've loved that, too.

"Thank you," I say.

Will's eyes glint as he presses a kiss against my forehead. "You don't have to thank me for anything. I loved him. And I love you."

I kiss him, a quick meeting of the lips; it's there and gone, but it eases the tightness in my heart just a little.

"I'll see you at home," Will says.

And then I'm alone. Just me and Duke.

Like it should be.

I sit cross-legged at the foot of his grave, the black dress Brooke went out and bought me drifting up my thighs like cobwebs. I pull the silky fabric down over my knees, staring at the blank headstone.

They'll take it away to engrave it soon. And then it will be back for good. My father's final mark on the world.

I press my hand to the dirt the backhoe had piled into the grave. It'll be covered up with sod, and grass will grow above him, flourishing while his body fades.

If I'm to believe the god Momma believed in, he's probably burning in hell.

If I believe Duke, the god of my childhood, he's sneaking into heaven, looking for her.

If I look too deeply in myself, I'll have to face the fact that it's probably neither of those. That there are pretty lies or hard truths and little room between for a woman like me.

So I don't look too deep. Not yet. I close my eyes and I press my hand into the dirt and I think about the two of them, meeting up in some bright place. Her smile, his relief.

Even if it isn't real, the truth remains: He is finished with the world—or maybe it was finished with him. No more revenge. No more pain. No more anger.

It has to be a relief. Even if he isn't wrapped in some white light and Momma.

I should get up and leave. But getting up and going to the Tropics means saying goodbye to Duke, and going home means saying goodbye to Will, and if I just sit here a little longer, I don't have to do either. Just for a few more minutes.

A branch cracks behind me. I tense, my hand going for my purse. I have Momma's little pearl-handled pistol in there.

"I'm sorry, Harley," says a voice.

Frankie Daniels steps into place by my side, and I rise to my feet, brushing off my dress, leaving the purse—and my gun—on his grave.

"Thank you," I say. It should get easier every time I have to say it, but it seems to get harder instead. It's like trying to swallow gravel.

"He loved you very much," she says.

It's the truth she can offer, and it's sweet of her to do it. I look at Momma's headstone, next to his now. I didn't know the Momma Frankie knew. Maybe I would've liked her.

Maybe we wouldn't have gotten along at all.

She was a woman led by her heart instead of her head, my momma. She was made up of secrets. I'm not sure I want to unravel the woman she was more than that. There are so many stones I could turn, but I don't think I want to.

I could forgive her, but there's nothing to forgive.

She made a choice. She did her best for me and for her. She didn't know what was to come. How the father she chose for me and the man who never deserved the role would both shape my life with their war, hatred, and greed.

"You know, I haven't quite figured it out yet," Frankie says, jerking me from my thoughts.

"Figured what out?"

"How you did it," she says. "You wiped the playing field in North County clean. Everyone who was a threat to you is out of your way, and now there's a Duke-sized hole in the market. I'm guessing you'll be filling it."

My mouth twitches. I could lie to her—the instinct trained into me tells me to.

But some things should be fought. And some fights need allies.

I guess that's the question, isn't it?

Am I Duke's daughter? Am I my momma's girl?

Or, deep down, am I Carl's?

McKenna? Springfield? Am I both?

Or am I better?

I turn to her. "The next election's in, what, six months?"

Her pale eyebrows—almost white against her freckled face—scrunch together. "Five, I think."

"Sheriff Harris is running unopposed."

"He always runs unopposed." It's unspoken, the bitterness there, but it's also the truth.

Or it *was* the truth.

I zero in, like Frankie's my target. A beer bottle set on a fence rail. A red circle painted on a tree.

"You should think about running," I say.

Her eyes widen. "You're crazy," she says.

"No, I'm not," I say. "People like you, Frankie. You just need money for a campaign. For posters and buttons and commercials and all that shit. And you need enough dirt on Harris to ruin him."

"I don't have any of that," Frankie says firmly, shaking her head.

"Well, I do."

She props her hands on her hips. "You trying to buy me, Harley?"

I shake my head. "You can't be bought, and I'm not stupid enough to try."

"Damn right," Frankie says, that iron note of pride in her voice betraying exactly why she'll be good at this.

"Harris is lazy *and* dirty," I say. "It makes him easy to manipulate. The whole damn county knows it. It would just take some proof to topple him."

"You can keep Harris in your pocket easy," Frankie says. "Why do you want me?"

"Because you'll actually do your job."

She fixes me with a glare. "My job is to catch people like you, Harley," she says bluntly.

I smile. "But you and me, we want the same things," I say. "We don't want someone organized moving in. And you know the Aryans will come sniffing around too when they hear Duke's gone. You won't be able to keep a lid on it by yourself. That's where I come in."

"So you hand me over your competition and I look the other way while you keep peddling your shit?" Frankie asks, disgusted.

"We work together, from both sides," I explain. "If we team up, we can at least keep out anything organized like the Aryans and the cartels. Or another man like Duke springing up, crowning himself the new kingpin. Think about it: No more men powerful enough to buy off your deputies. Just tweekers with labs in their car trunks and cooking it shake and bake in the motels. Think about how much easier that would be."

"So you…you don't want to take over the trade," Frankie says slowly, skepticism fading as the realization hits her. "You want to destroy it."

"I have other business pursuits," I say.

She sighs. "I'm not crooked."

"Then be smart," I say. "My family's kept control over the county for decades, and Duke had a hold on it that no one else ever did. Now that he's gone, there's too much opportunity, not just for weed, but much worse: for meth, for pharmaceuticals, for heroin, for trafficking—drugs and girls. Hell, give the small-time dealers a month, and they'll have half the town hooked on Oxy. Three months, and it'll be half the county. Unemployment rate spikes again, and it'll be heroin because pills are too expensive. You'll have people OD'ing all over the place."

"I can handle it," she says, but we both know that's a lie.

"You've got no power, Frankie," I tell her. "You're a good cop, but you're never gonna make any kind of difference unless you start playing the game."

She's looking closely at me, like she's searching for something. The lie in my words, maybe?

But she's smart. She knows I'm telling the truth.

"That's not the way it's supposed to be," she says.

"But that's the way it is," I say. "You want some fairy tale? You're never gonna get it. You want to actually make some change? Then put your black-and-white bullshit aside and *work* with me. Become sheriff. Get some fucking power. And use it."

"And what happens when I use it to do something you don't like?" Frankie asks. "I disappear?"

"You talk to me," I say. "We compromise. We figure out a solution. We trust each other."

Frankie snorts. "You don't trust me," she says.

Maybe she's right. Maybe she's wrong.

It doesn't matter. I'm on the edge, and I can step back or I can leap.

"You really want to know how I did it?" I ask her. "How I got the better of those men no one's ever been able to touch? How I did it without killing any of them or letting them lay one hand on me?"

She nods.

"I was smart. I waited. I listened. And I learned. I learned the most important lesson: Even the man who loves you, who's dedicated his entire life to raising you up into something powerful, that man will underestimate the hell out of you just because you're a woman. And the man who hates you? Who's scared of you deep down in places he'll never acknowledge? That man will work even harder to dismiss you. There was no way I could've won a full-out war against any of them. So I conned them. Every one of them. Even Duke on his deathbed. I blew the lab in Viola. I burned down the warehouse on State Street. And the house on Meadow Lane. I framed Springfield for all of it, and my guys bought it, hook, line, and sinker. They handed over all the product, and I used it to trick Harris and his boys into arresting Buck and Springfield. Now the Feds will take over, and my hands are clean. Because I'm just a woman. I'm not capable of such violence."

Frankie stares at me like I've grown another head. "Fuck, Harley. Why tell me all this?" she asks, her eyes wide with horror, like she thinks I'm about to off her.

This could very well be the end of me. For a second, we just look at each other, and it's a dare and a threat wrapped up together.

She knows there's no proof. That I'd just recant if she brought me down to the station.

She knows she can't catch me. I'll be two steps ahead, always.

She knows I'd be an asset. That she and I, we could do something good.

"I'm trusting you," I say. "So trust me. And become something powerful."

I've extended the olive branch. Now it's up to her to take it.

I leave her there, and she doesn't hold me back. But I can feel her eyes on me, all the way down the path through the cemetery.

One down.

One to go.

It never ends.

# FIFTY-SEVEN

By the time I get to the Tropics, the parking lot's full. I pull around the back, park, and walk in through the delivery door. Sal's office is at the end of the long hallway, and when I see her inside, I knock lightly on the open door. Her tiny office is crowded, stacks of papers scattered across her big metal desk.

She smiles gently when she sees me. "How you doing, Harley?"

"I'm okay."

She stands up and envelops me in a hug. "Is there anything I can do for you?"

"Can you get Cooper and have him meet me in the back room? I need some whiskey. Top shelf. A few glasses, too."

"I'll go get him," Sal says.

I walk through the hall, slipping into the back room. Duke's domain.

The long oak table's the same as it was a week ago, but the room feels different. Like it's missing something. Missing him.

There's a light knock on the door, and Cooper ducks his head in, bottle and glasses in hand.

"Don't ask me how I'm doing," I tell him.

His mouth quirks up as he sets the bottle and glasses on the table. "They're all waiting for you."

I lean on the edge of the table instead of sitting in one of the chairs. "I didn't make up a speech or eulogy or anything." I wouldn't know what to say. How do you sum up a man like Duke? He was loved. He was hated. He was kind. He was terrifying. But mostly, I think he was scared. Scared of losing me. Scared of losing anything.

I'm so tired of being scared.

"They're not here to listen to you speak," Cooper says. "They're here to see if you're up to snuff."

Of course. Everything's a test.

I look to the red steel door, listening to the strains of music—someone's brought a guitar—that leak through. "Who showed?"

"Paul and the rest of the Sons are out there. Our friends from Shasta and Trinity counties came. And Oregon and Washington. The hippies from Weaverville who bought protection from him last harvest. L.A. also showed. They sent two men."

"What about our friends from Mexico?"

Cooper nods his head. "Everything's settled with them. They sent their condolences. And some very nice tequila. Sheriff Harris also made it known to me he'd like to speak to you."

"That won't be happening."

Cooper raises an eyebrow. "Harris is easy to deal with."

"I'm looking for more than that," I say. "We can talk about it later."

"Who do you want to see first?"

"Paul," I say. He's the only one who matters.

"I'll send him in," Cooper says.

"You can stay," I tell him.

Cooper shakes his head. "It'll come off stronger if you do it alone."

I bite my lip. I can't help the slight hesitation in me, and I know he sees it because he smiles encouragingly at me. "You can do this," he says. "It's a good idea."

"You have what I asked for?"

He hands me the tiny brown glass bottle, which I pocket.

"I'll tell Paul you're ready for him," he says.

He leaves me alone, and I get up, pacing a little. I should have changed. The dress keeps swishing against my knees and I don't like it.

The red door slides open, and Paul steps inside. He's in a black shirt and jeans, and he's even replaced his normal red bandanna with a black one.

It's a nice gesture. I appreciate it.

"Harley." He smiles sadly at me, holding out his arms. I step into his embrace, letting him kiss me on the cheek. "I'm so sorry."

"Thank you," I say, pulling back.

"He was a hell of a man," Paul says. "One of a kind."

"He was," I agree.

"It's an end of an era."

I don't know if I'm just reading into the warning in his voice or if it's really there. But I'm not taking any chances. Cooper's right, of course: They're all here to see if I'm up to snuff. It's time to make my claim.

I go over to the bottle of whiskey, pouring out two fingers in each glass, handing one to Paul.

He raises his glass. "To Duke."

"To Duke," I say, clicking my glass with his.

He downs his whiskey in one toss, and I do the same, my eyes tearing up a little as it burns down my throat.

I sit down at the head of the table, in Duke's chair. If I close my eyes and breathe in, I can almost smell his tobacco.

"Cooper said you wanted to talk," Paul says.

"Will you sit?"

He pulls up the chair next to me, settling his elbows on the table. His bandanna covers most of his head, but that thin silver braid swings down his back. "I'm not sure how much Duke told you about the business—our dealings," he starts.

"I know everything."

"That makes things easier," he says.

"Oh?" I lean back in Duke's—no, *my* chair.

"We've never expanded," Paul says. "Out of respect for your father."

"You mean out of fear of my father."

Paul smiles, but it's not affectionate now. There's a sharpness to it. "Duke was a fair man. He provided good transport for my product. I have no complaints."

"But you have plans to expand and renegotiate the terms of your deal," I say. "Now that he's gone."

Paul shifts in his seat, looking uncomfortable. "You're very young, Harley."

"Duke was running guns at my age," I say.

"You're not your father."

It's the first time anyone's ever said that to me. I don't know if I should take it as an insult or a compliment.

All I know is it's the truth.

"No, I'm not," I say. "My father was a smart man. A dangerous man. But he didn't think about the future. I do."

Paul's mustache twitches. "And what do you think the future's gonna look like?" he asks.

It's now or never. Either he's going to go for it or he'll reject it, and then I'll be going down a very different path than the one I've planned.

"I'm done with cooking," I say. "I'm done with guns. I'm done with shit that kills people. And don't think you're gonna fill that hole I'm leaving in the market, because you're not gonna to start with shit that kills people just because I'm stopping."

Paul raises an eyebrow. "Is that right," he says flatly. His anger's barely coiled. The nerve of me, telling him what to do. I can almost taste his rage.

In that moment, I know the fact that we're at my father's wake is the only reason he isn't laying me out on the ground for my presumption.

But I've got a trump card.

*Find their weakness, Harley-girl. And exploit it.*

"Your little girl," I say.

He goes very still. "You touch Rebecca—"

"I wouldn't," I say sharply, and I mean it. "I don't hurt children. I will, however, hurt the people who hurt them. How old is Rebecca now?"

His eyes narrow warily. "Ten."

"I remember when your wife passed away," I say. "I helped Miss Lissa make casseroles."

"Everyone made casseroles," he growls.

"I've always admired you for how you've dealt with it," I tell him. "Rebecca was, what? Only two when Karen got sick? You were so strong for both of them."

"That's what a father does."

"That's what some fathers do," I say pointedly. "Does Rebecca know what you do?"

"She doesn't need to know."

"She'll find out," I say. "Especially if you expand. She won't be safe otherwise."

"I can keep her safe."

"You're fooling yourself if you really think that," I say.

"So what do you say I should do?" Paul asks. His fingers tap the table. My eyes keep skittering to them. "Stay under your thumb, like I was under Duke's? You don't scare me, Harley."

"I should," I say, staring him down. "I mean, the two men who posed the biggest threats to me both got arrested within a day of each other. That's very convenient for me."

Paul's mouth drops. "You didn't," he says.

I fold my arms, leaning back. "Maybe I didn't," I say. "But maybe I did. And maybe you should think about what I'm capable of. Because I may be young, but unlike your daughter, I was raised for this."

"But you want to stop dealing," Paul says.

"No. I said I wanted to stop making and selling shit that kills people. Huge difference."

Understanding filters into his face, followed by anger as he jumps—fucking leaps—to the wrong conclusion. "You want to take over the pot business."

"You built it. I respect that. But like I said, we need to focus on the future." I reach into my pocket, pull out the bottle, and set it on the table between us.

Paul looks at it. "What's that?"

"Organic, top-shelf cannabis oil," I say. "I've seen the honey oil your guys have been churning out. It sucks. And using butane and other shitty solvents can be just as dangerous as cooking meth."

"This is better?" Paul snorts.

"This is the gold fucking standard," I say. "You grow great weed, Paul. But when they finally legalize it, that won't be enough. The tobacco companies are already buying up all the free land and mills in Humboldt. They're just waiting to take over and they'll gobble up the market for plain old weed—they can grow more of it and sell it cheaper. But the specialty stuff—organics, vaping oils, edibles—all that hipster nonsense—and the medicinals?" I shake the bottle a little. "That's the answer. Plus, it's not gonna kill anyone. It might even help some of them."

He eyes the bottle. "Where'd you get it?"

"Cooper makes it," I say. "He has this new compression method. No solvents."

Paul frowns. "At all?"

"Not necessary. He's got this big heat-press machine. He'll be able to explain it better than I can. But he's agreed to work with your guys."

"In exchange for what, exactly?"

"You need cash," I say. "It takes a pound of bud to make an ounce of this stuff. You'll need more land, more guys, more equipment, nutrients, seeds, clones, lights, soil—all of it."

"So you're just gonna finance all of this?"

"I have money," I say. "This is a good investment."

"What's the catch?" he asks.

"I finance the oil side of your business. We still use the truck yard to transport the bud for the same percentage as you gave Duke. But when it comes to the oil, we're equal partners. And partners help each other out."

"You need muscle," he says.

"I can buy muscle," I say. "What I want is loyalty. I want to know that if I snap my fingers, the Sons will be there. I want the Rubies to live without being afraid their asshole exes will come and mess with them. I want a better fucking world."

He's silent, and then he reaches over and picks up the bottle, unscrewing it and pulling out the full dropper, holding it up to the light.

"Sixty-forty on the oil."

I shake my head. "Fifty-fifty."

"I'll be assuming more of the risk," he counters.

"Bullshit—it'll be my trucking company transporting it. And Cooper's production method."

He squeezes out a drop onto his hand, smells it, and tastes it, considering the possibilities. "My guys will need to test this stuff. Talk to Cooper. And I'll need to run the numbers."

It's more relief than triumph that floats through me, like leaves scattered on still water.

"Of course," I say.

"And I need to talk to my club," he says.

"And if they agree?"

Paul sighs. "You really gonna ban us from running guns?"

"The Sons have never run guns before," I say. "Why do you want to bring in more trouble now? The ATF's a nasty enemy."

"It's not an easy rule to enforce, Harley. What you want to do..." He sighs again.

"You've got two paths in front of you, Paul. You take one, you become Duke. And Rebecca? She'll become just like me. Because you can't become Duke and keep your child out of harm's way."

He looks down. I'm getting to him. I lean forward.

"But you take the other path, and Rebecca keeps her innocent life with her biker daddy. Sure, he's a little tough and he grows weed, but in a few years, it's gonna mean shit-all that you grow. By the time she's old enough to really understand, it'll be legal, and you'll be a legitimate businessman, respected in the community. You can send her to college. She's smart, Paul; you know that better than I do. She could become a doctor or a lawyer. She could grow so far from our roots that she'll be at the top of the tree. She could have everything—be anything. Don't you want that for her?"

"Yes," he blurts out, and it's more of a confession than either of us expect. I can hear it in his voice.

"You don't want her to become like me."

"No," he says flatly, his eyes hard.

No one wants their daughter to become like me.

"Then it's an easy choice," I tell him.

He leans back in his chair, folding his arms as he stares at me across the table. He looks at me like he's never seen me before, like I've taken off a mask he didn't know was there.

I am the McKenna now. And he knows it.

"You really are your daddy's girl," he says finally.

He holds out his hand and I shake it.

"Let's go celebrate the old man's life in style," he says.

Even before the sun sets, the party's raging. Sal's pouring whiskey like it's water, and the Sons are getting along with the hippies from Weaverville like long-lost brothers, trading growing tips and downing beer and harmonizing with the Merle-and-Willie duet pounding out of the speakers. The guys from L.A. keep asking for vodka, and Sal keeps pouring them beer instead, but they're already too shitfaced to notice.

I stay by the end of the bar where Duke used to sit, and I watch. People come up to me, and I hear "I'm so sorry" a hundred times, give or take a few. I manage a smile and say *Thank you for coming* and *Please, have something to drink.*

I wait until they're all drunk enough not to notice that I'm slipping out. I kiss Sal on the cheek and hand her a thank-you envelope stuffed full of three thousand in hundred-dollar bills. The moon's high in the sky and the streets are silent as I step out of the bar and into the alley behind it.

"Party too hard?"

I turn, waving away the cloud of Camel smoke. "I'm gonna make you stop smoking those things," I tell her.

Mo snorts. "Over my dead body."

Anyone else, they'd probably catch themselves or look shamed. But instead, Mo chuckles. "He would've liked that one."

He probably would. Duke wasn't a terribly funny man, but when he cracked jokes, they tended to be dark.

"Things are gonna change," Mo comments, puffing out another lungful of blue smoke. It hangs in the air for a second, obscuring her face.

"I know."

"They're gonna come," Mo says.

My stomach clenches. "I know," I say again. It's all I've been thinking about. Duke's gone, and so is the invisible barrier that protected the Ruby for so long.

The ex-husbands and boyfriends. The Fathers Who Didn't Approve. The men who bruised and broke and kicked toddlers down stairs. They'll come for the women and children they think belong to them.

Now Duke is gone, they'll think that it's safe to come. That we won't be able to stop them.

I look straight ahead, out at the town stretched out over the valley, the mountains sheltering it, protecting it.

"What are we gonna do?" I ask Mo.

"This time," she says, "I think we do it your way."

# FIFTY-EIGHT

*July 16, 11:45 p.m.*

It's dark. The porch lights are shut off, the cottages silent. The pool, usually shining a ghostly blue, is engulfed in the blackness.

The only light comes from the moon rising high in the sky. It provides enough shadows to hide in.

I wait, eyes to the front. It's almost midnight. The cottages are locked shut, the curtains drawn, the women and children inside.

They're waiting, too.

In the distance, a car door slams shut. My head turns toward the sound, and my fingers stay steady on my sawed-off shotgun, the kind that's easy to carry. A few minutes tick by, and then I see it out of the corner of my eye: movement coming from the south.

He's circled around back.

I rise from my crouch, padding with light feet across the roof to the edge that overlooks the back field the Ruby butts up against. I can see him in the moonlight—a stocky man in a big jacket, coming to claim what he thinks is his.

He walks between two of the cottages, and I follow, silently dropping onto the porch roof as he passes by.

He moves toward cottage seven with unhurried steps. Like he's got all the time in the world.

Sam and her kids live in cottage seven. So it's Sam's husband, then. Luke.

It figures. She's the newest Ruby. The pain and anger of her leaving him is still fresh. When I helped her move her stuff out, he almost went for me. The only reason he didn't was because I'd called in Cooper to stand watch.

Luke hadn't just broken Sam's arm that last fight. He'd gone for one of their kids, too.

And, as it goes with so many women, trained to take so much, guilted into being so forgiving, raised to be so nice, that was it—she finally broke free. She called her mom for help, and her mom called me, I showed up with a gun and guys, and we got them out. She and the kids were safe at the Ruby.

Until now.

Until he got it into his head that because Duke is gone, the rules don't apply anymore.

I swing down from the porch, landing on the ground softly. He doesn't notice. His back is to me. He thinks he's safe. That it's gonna be easy pickings.

He's wrong.

I move forward, silent and quick, until I'm just a yard away. I raise the shotgun into position, up against my shoulder.

"Hey, Luke," I call.

He spins, his hand going for his waistband when he sees me.

"Don't even think about it," says another voice. Mo steps out from the shadow of the pool shed, her bolt-action hunting rifle pointed right at him as she stalks forward.

"There's nowhere to run." Jessa darts out into view, her hands steady as she points her Winchester at the back of his head.

"Hands up," I order.

Slowly, his hands rise.

We form a loose triangle around him, Mo and Jessa at his back, me at his front, pointing the shotgun dead at his chest.

"You're breaking the rules," I say.

"McKenna's dead," he says, with a lot more bravado than he should have, considering he's got three locked-and-loaded, pissed-off women pointing guns at him. "There aren't any rules."

Mo snorts. "Can I pepper his ass with buckshot yet?" she demands.

"Go ahead," he says. "Doesn't matter." He looks straight at me, a mean smile twisting his lips. "I may be the first, but I won't be the last. You think you can take a man's woman from him? His children? And he'll let that lie? A few women with guns ain't nothing."

"We got the drop on you, asshole," Jessa says.

"You can't get the drop on everyone," he says, staring at me like he's won. Like he thinks I won't blow his fucking head off, right here, right now. "You can't protect all of them all the time."

"No," I say. "I can't. But they can protect each other."

Mo raises her hand. "Come on out!" she calls.

The porch lights on each cottage flick on, the doors open, and the Rubies step out, each one armed and ready to protect her home, her children, her friends, herself.

We defend our own. To the death.

His gaze darts back and forth, taking in the sight, taking in Sam standing there on her porch, hunting rifle in her hand like she can't wait to use it. And I see it in his eyes, the moment he realizes that he's screwed.

That he's nothing. That there's nothing stronger than a woman who's risen from the ashes of some fire a man set.

"You've made a mistake," I tell him quietly as Jessa and Mo move forward, closing in. "How could you think we wouldn't arm our women? That we wouldn't give them every advantage to protect themselves against men like you coming for them? Stupid."

Mo grabs the gun still tucked in his waistband and kicks it far from his reach. She grabs his arm, Jessa takes the other, and they zip-tie his hands behind his back as the Rubies watch and wait.

"Get the car," I tell Jessa.

She glares at Luke for a second. "Sure I can't shoot him?" she asks. I shake my head and she sighs, slinging the rifle strap across her back and heading off.

"Bastard," Mo growls. When she spits at his feet, he flinches at the anger in her eyes.

I glance over at Sam. She hasn't left her porch, but she and Luke are staring at each other.

"You want your say?" I ask her.

She shakes her head. "I want this to be the last time I ever see him."

"Sounds good to me," Mo says.

"Sam!" he yells.

*"No!"* she yells back. And that's all she says.

That's all she needs to say.

She turns and walks back into her cottage, shutting the door firmly behind her. Leaving him behind.

Leaving him to us.

Jessa pulls the car—one of those big, boat-like Buicks from the nineties—up behind Mo. She gets out, popping the trunk, and the two of them wrestle Luke into it while I keep my gun on him.

I close the trunk with a thud and look up at the Rubies, all standing in silent witness.

"We'll take care of this," I tell them. "I promise."

Jessa tosses the keys to me, and I catch them in midair. "You'll hold down the fort?" I ask her as I get into the car. I can hear Luke thumping away in the back, yelling his head off. I should've gagged him.

She nods. "I've got it," she says.

Mo hops into the passenger seat, and I back the car up out of the Ruby's courtyard and head out of town.

Mo lights a cigarette, and when I make a face, she rolls her eyes, stubs it out, and flicks it out the window. "You think this is gonna work?" she asks.

"It has to," I say.

"It's risky."

"It's the best chance we've got."

"And if they don't show?"

That's the question that's been gnawing at me. My fingers slip against the steering wheel, and I wipe the sweat off on my jeans. "They'll show," I say.

\* \* \*

North County is a big place; it takes quite a while to get to the county line. By the time we get there, Luke's gone quiet in the trunk. I'm not stupid enough to think he's knocked himself out or anything. He's probably lying in wait, thinking he'll be able to get away from me somehow.

He's just full of bad ideas, this one.

I slow the car down, pulling over to the side of the empty road right in front of the sign that says NORTH COUNTY LINE.

No one comes out here this late, not on this dinky one-lane road, far from the highway, in the middle of nowhere. There are no houses out here. No rest stops.

Just forest for miles around.

I get out of the car and lean back against the quarter panel. Mo comes to stand next to me, lighting another cigarette. She has the grace to blow the smoke away from me.

"What time is it?" she asks.

I look at my phone. "One. They'll be here."

The words are barely out of my mouth when I hear the rumble of the first engine. And then the air's filled with them as the Sons of Jefferson come roaring up, their headlights cutting through the dark, flooding the road with light and sound and menace.

They stop in a loose circle in front of us, blocking the road. The rest of the Sons stay on their bikes, but Paul gets off his, coming toward us.

"Mo," he says, and there's a fond expression in his eyes that almost makes me laugh.

"Paul," she says back, flicking the ash of her cigarette at him. For Mo, that's practically flirting.

"Harley," he nods to me. "Heard you had some trouble tonight."

"We handled it," I say. "You talk to your boys?"

"I did," he says, crossing his arms. His leather jacket rustles a little at the movement. "We're in."

I smile. "I'm glad," I say, holding out my hand.

He takes it in a bone-crunching shake. I squeeze back just as hard as

I can. Partners. I take a deep breath in relief right as the loud thunking noise from the car trunk starts back up again. Paul raises an eyebrow.

"Something you want to tell me?" he asks.

"More like *show* you," I say. "All of you, in fact."

His lips twist, considering it. "Go ahead, then," he says.

He steps back to join the Sons, and suddenly, I'm terrified. Cold-sweat-down-my-back, heart-thumping a-million-beats-a-minute kind of terrified.

This is it.

I have to prove it, here and now, who I am.

It'll decide everything. If I'm weak. If I'm strong.

If I'm fit to rule.

I take a deep breath, and then I flip open the trunk.

I drag Luke out by the scruff of the neck, onto the road, shoving him onto his knees in front of the half-circle the Sons have assembled in. They watch, silent, judging, as I step forward.

Luke's eyes rise to take in all the men, and he gulps, his throat working furiously.

"All of you knew my father," I say, my voice ringing out, sounding stronger than I'll ever feel. "And most of you have known me since I was a little girl." I pull out Duke's knife from my pocket, flicking it open, my gaze spanning the half circle. "I am not a little girl anymore."

Something in the air changes, and the Sons seem to straighten up on their bikes, like sharks sensing blood in the water.

"This man"—I point the knife at Luke—"came to the Ruby tonight. He thought that because my father is gone, there's no danger. No rules. He thought he could take his ex-wife and his children against their will, and I'd just let it happen. He was wrong."

I nod to Mo. She steps forward, grim-faced, grabbing Luke's head, jerking him back by his hair, exposing his left cheek to me. He fights her, but Mo's strong, she's determined, and she's got fifty years of rage to fuel her.

"I want to make things clear," I tell the Sons. "You and I are in business. We are partners. I respect you, I respect your organization. But if

393

any of you look the other way when a man lays his hand on a woman? Rapes her? Hurts her children? I will blame you." I carve a line into Luke's cheek, blood bubbles up as I dig in with the tip of the blade, and he screams. "And if you do those things to any women or children in your own life? I will find you." I carve a second line into his cheek. He screams again, and blood pours down his chin. "And I will hurt you." Then I carve the final line deep into the skin and wipe off the blood.

There it is, on his face. A bloody *H*.

My mark.

My choice.

My world.

"I am not my father," I tell the Sons, circling around Luke so I'm at his back. "You broke his rules, he'd blow your head off. That's a quick, painless death. You break my rules? I'll cut your dick off and make you eat it before you bleed to death, nice and slow."

A collective intake of breath breaks through the silence. A few of the Sons look at Paul in alarm, but he doesn't seem to be bothered. He's just sitting there, staring at me, a half smile on his face.

"This was my father's county," I continue. "But now it's mine. You will abide by my rules. And if you don't?" The knife skates down Luke's stomach, resting on the outside of his fly. I can feel the Sons take in a collective breath. I raise my eyes. "I'll spare you the sight this time," I tell them. I draw the knife away, flipping it in my hand, and then sink the blade into Luke's back with the precision of a surgeon. He screams again, this time an animal howl. He thinks he's going to die, and so will the Sons. Perfect.

But I know exactly how deep to go so I won't nick anything important. He'll live.

He'll just wish he hadn't.

I draw my knife out of him, shiny with blood. As the red blooms across Luke's gray T-shirt, he pitches forward and passes out with a muffled groan. I wipe the knife on the ground and sheathe it. Then Mo and I grab Luke by the arms, drag him across the road, and toss him on the other side of the county line.

I turn back to the Sons of Jefferson, my hands bloody, my eyes steady as I stare them down. They stare back, some of them shifting on their bikes, wide-eyed and unsettled, some of them grinning like I've just given them a show, some of them frowning, not sure they like this.

I have their attention now.

"First rule of North County," I say. "Never fuck with the McKenna."

# FIFTY-NINE

I'm twenty-two years old when I inherit what's left of Duke's empire. Time passes slowly now that he's gone. Will stays with me the rest of the summer, lending a hand, an ear, and anything else I need. But when summer leaves, so does he. It's just until Thanksgiving—I've promised to spend Christmas with him and his family on the coast—but his absence makes me ache, all the same.

At first, everything's hard. Like slogging through knee-deep mud. Running the legit businesses is almost as difficult as keeping a hold on the darker side of North County. But day by day, week by week, month by month, I learn, I manage. Cooper and Wayne are by my side, and I rely on Mo more and more until it becomes clear Jessa has to take over most of her duties at the Ruby. The Sons of Jefferson keep to their promise, and Paul's more of a help than I expected, more of a business-man than I realized.

It's almost November by the time I relax enough to think this might work. That I can do this.

Then I get a call in the middle of the night. It's not on my regular cell, but the one whose number is given out to women who might need help.

I'm still awake because I don't do much sleeping still, so I pick up on the second ring and leave Will, who's come for the weekend, asleep in bed. I step over Busy snoring on the rug and walk out into the hallway.

"Hello?"

There's a long pause, but I can hear breathing.

"This the McKenna?"

I don't recognize the voice. It's a woman's. "Yes."

"Exit six forty-eight on the Three. If you take the main road north ten miles, you'll come to a dead end. Go east on foot. You'll see the tracks. Follow them."

I frown. "What am I looking for?" I ask.

"You'll know it when you see it," she says.

Another long pause. There's a rustling sound. Is she running? She doesn't sound out of breath.

"Who is this?" I ask.

"A friend," she says. "They're moving in. You need to take care of it."

The line goes dead. I stare down at my phone.

"Harley?"

Will's up. I look toward the bedroom.

"Coming," I say.

I wait a day before I go searching. The first snow comes early this year, and when I get off on exit 648, I see that the road ahead hasn't been plowed.

I take the road carefully—I never did like driving in the snow—and sure enough, in ten miles or so, there's a dead end. I park my Chevy, shoulder my pack, and hop over the long chain that's strung across the end of the road.

The forest is white-tipped and quiet, the sun filtering through the pines, making the snowy forest floor sparkle. My boots crunch as I move east, deeper into the forest.

I walk for hours, my legs and lungs burning from the effort of slogging through the snow. I'm just about to give up when I spot something in the distance—a disturbance in the smooth, untouched whiteness. I crest the hill at a jog, stopping dead when I make it to the top.

Tire tracks on a makeshift road, leading west.

My hand goes to my revolver tucked under my shirt in its holster, and I start to move slower, more cautiously. It takes another mile of following the tracks, but eventually the rough road they've cut through the forest opens up to a natural valley between the mountains.

I stay hidden behind the timberline, scrambling up one of the pines for a better vantage point. I pull my scope out of my pocket and focus it on the valley below.

And there they are: three trailers grouped in a triangle, with blacked-out windows and at least four sets of footprints in the snow.

I wait there, high in the trees, patient, gaining energy from the cold bite in the air. I start sketching it out in my mind: a new plan. To catch the runners, I'll need guys stationed at all four corners of the valley and more on the road through the woods.

The triangle formation of the trailers makes it a little tricky. When they're ambushed, the cooks might use the trailers as cover. But that's risky, using meth labs as armor. One spark in the wrong place, and you're done for.

One of the trailer doors bangs open, and a man steps out.

He's wearing a gas mask and those white coveralls that zip up over your clothes.

My stomach clenches. This is organized.

Professional.

"Take off the mask and let me see you," I whisper under my breath, staring at him through the scope. His arms are covered; I can't see any tats.

He pulls the mask off.

White. Shaved head. I focus in and see it: the 88 tattoo on his neck.

Fucking neo-Nazis. Looks like they're moving in.

And looks like my mystery woman on the phone—whoever she is—isn't too happy about it. I don't blame her. They're the worst kind of scum. You steep yourself in that kind of hate, there's no redemption.

Duke used to say they should be put down like rabid dogs, and my fingers itch to do just that. I bite my lip hard against the urge.

I wait until he pisses and goes back inside the trailer, then I slip down the tree and head back to my truck. I'm mindful of my tracks, worried they might see them when they head out.

When I reach my Chevy, I'm sweaty and I've got my jacket tied around my waist. I slick back a strand of hair that's fallen out of my braid, climb into the cab, and grab the bottle of water I left there, guzzling it down.

Turning back to the highway, I head toward home. I should call Cooper and Paul, let them know what I've seen, but I wait. For now.

I'm halfway home when red and blue lights flash in my rearview. Before I pull over onto the shoulder, I gun the engine, just to be an ass.

I roll down my window and stick my arm out, waiting for the telltale crunch of boots on snow.

"Deputy," I say.

"Harley," she replies.

I look up at Frankie. Running for office looks good on her. Gone are the bouncy ponytail and fluffy bangs. Nowadays, she's all sleek braids and strong shoulders.

"Heard Harris was thinking about dropping out of the race," I say in a conversational tone.

"That's the rumor," Frankie answers with a shrug. "I'll believe it when I see it." She pauses, her voice lowers even though there's no one around to hear us. "Was that tip you got solid?"

I nod. "It's the Aryans. I didn't recognize the one I saw. I don't think they're from around here. But they're pros."

"Sacramento branch?" Frankie suggests.

"Maybe. Or Southern Oregon. I tracked them to a spot about eight miles east from the trailhead, deep in the pines. Three trailers set up. Not that big, but not that small, either. And winter's almost here. The rangers have already cut hours so they'll have enough left in the budget to pay for fire watch this summer. So these people aren't gonna have anyone bothering them out here for a while—and they know it."

"They'll have all winter to expand and train their guys." Frankie taps her fingers against the edge of my window.

"Not if we let them know how unwelcome they are."

She raises an eyebrow. "Do I want to know how you're going to do that?" she asks.

"Do you ever?"

She sighs. It's taken her a while to come around. But she has. And so have I.

In some ways, at least.

"No killing," she says.

"No killing," I agree.

"Let me know if you need anything." She turns back to her patrol car.

"Let me know when Harris drops out," I call back.

"He's not gonna," Frankie says.

Even if he doesn't, she's going to beat him. I don't know how to fix a ballot box, but I do know how to play the people, which is just as good, maybe better.

She drives off, heading toward town, toward that bright future and all that power I'm gonna make sure she has waiting for her.

It'll always be risky having her around, because I can't control her, not really.

But she can't control me either. So we'll circle…and sometimes we'll be on the same side; sometimes we won't.

She's the best for the county, for the town. She can keep the law there.

But in the backwoods, she can't, and we both know it. The backwoods never forget and rarely forgive. It was Duke's domain, and now it's mine.

As I pull back onto the highway, I keep my window rolled down. The temperature's dropping each night as we head into winter. The cold air's crisp in my face, and I breathe in deep, the smell of the forest in my hair, on my skin.

Will and Busy are waiting for me at home. It makes me smile just thinking about it. Him and home. Someday, there's gonna be the sound of little feet to match the scratch of paws on the wood floors. There'll be picnics at the park with the Rubies, where punch and the smell of tri-tip fills the air, and the kids run around in the grass, laughing. There'll be holidays in Hoopa with his family, and Will's hand will be at my back, always near.

I'll get Frankie elected because McKennas don't lose, and together we'll build something new. It won't be all good and it won't be all bad, but it'll be better than Duke and Springfield's world.

There'll be nights when I don't come home when I'm supposed to. Nights when Will has to wonder if I'll make it home at all. Nights when I can't talk about what I've done as he helps clean off the blood.

I will become a troubled whisper on the wind. A rumor only the brave seek out. A shadowy figure in the woods who protects her people, who guards the land.

I will love the good parts of Duke I remember and hate the bad parts that haunt me and mourn all the parts of him and Momma and Jake that are dead and buried.

I will keep Duke's lessons close to my heart, but never in it.

I will move forward: Eyes on the target. Hands steady. Aim true.

*Only way, Harley-girl.*

# A NOTE FROM THE AUTHOR

The neo-Nazi characters in this book play into society's stereotypical view of white supremacy: the uneducated, poor, criminal, and rural man. While these characters are true to Harley's world and the area I grew up in that North County is based on, it would be irresponsible if I didn't acknowledge that these characters and their portrayal are just one facet of the evil of white supremacy, which is deeply entrenched in our country and society in covert and overt ways.

It is not just rural white men with swastika tattoos who espouse and act on these hateful beliefs. It may be a coworker. A neighbor. A family member. The politician you voted for. The well-dressed kid next door who mows your lawn. This hate is not restricted to the South or to the rural, poverty-stricken parts of the country. It is everywhere, a poison knit into the fabric of this country's founding, past, and present. And it must be fought, denounced, and stamped out everywhere, especially if you benefit from the power of white privilege, like I do.

The organizations below are working to make sure that this hate isn't part of the future:

**NAACP:** http://www.naacp.org
**Southern Poverty Law Center:** https://www.splcenter.org
**Native American Rights Fund:** http://www.narf.org
**Black Lives Matter:** http://www.blacklivesmatter.com
**Anne Frank Center for Mutual Respect:** http://annefrank.com

Much of *Barbed Wire Heart* is centered around surviving many forms of abuse. If you, or someone you know, is being abused, please know that it is not your fault and there are people who can help.

*National Domestic Violence Hotline*

1-800-799-7233
Online chat also available at
www.thehotline.org

*National Dating Abuse Helpline*

1-866-331-9474
www.loveisrespect.org

*National Sexual Assault Hotline*

1-800-656-4673 (HOPE)
www.rainn.org

*National Child Abuse Hotline*

1-800-422-4453 (4-A-Child)
www.childhelp.org

*Women of Color Network*

1-844-962-6462
www.wocninc.org

*National Indigenous Women's Resource Center*

855-649-7299
www.niwrc.org

*Casa de Esperanza*

Linea de crisis 24-horas/
24-hour crisis line
1-651-772-1611
www.casadeesperanza.org

*Deaf Abused Women's Network (DAWN)*

VP: 202-559-5366
www.deafdawn.org
Email: Hotline@deafdawn.org

*NW Network of Bi, Trans, Lesbian, and Gay Survivors of Abuse*

1-206-568-7777
www.nwnetwork.org

# ACKNOWLEDGMENTS

Every book is a ride, but this one took longer than expected. I started this novel as a college dropout and chipped away at it all through my twenties and never really thought it'd come to be. But through the hard work of the following people, it did.

Lindsey Rose, my editor, who took a huge chance on this dark piece of my life and heart. Your wisdom, enthusiasm, and understanding truly carried me through.

Jim McCarthy, my incredible agent, who always has my back, who saw the possibility in this when all he had was the first 100 pages, a very long synopsis, and my promise to finish it in eight weeks. I will never be able to properly thank you for taking a leap with this book and me.

Lori Paximadis, whose eagle eye and attention to detail when it came to copyediting this monster of a book was so needed. Thank you for fixing all my timeline discrepancies!

Jarrod Taylor, who created an absolutely beautiful cover.

Luria Rittenberg, managing editor extraordinaire, and the rest of the Grand Central team. Thank you all for your hard work.

Rebecca Roanhorse, whose honesty and insight enriched this work and these characters so much. Thank you for everything.

Elizabeth May, the best person a woman could ever have on her side in the wilds of publishing—and in life. I owe you for pushing me to finally finish this damn thing.

Lisa Yoskowitz, who saw a partial draft of this years ago and whose notes led me to create the Rubies and therefore something for Harley to really fight for.

Red, who didn't sell Arden for a year despite other offers, because *I promised that writer girl I'd sell it to her.* Thank you for giving me the homestead I needed to finish this book. Rest in Power.

My mother, Laurie, who took a risk and a leap and brought me to the place that would become the inspiration behind North County when I was a child. I know it hasn't been easy, but it shaped me and my work in ways nothing else could have, and I am grateful.

My wonderful writer friends: Charlee Hoffman, Kate Bassett, EK Johnston, Dahlia Adler, Jess Capelle, Jessica Spotswood, Sharon Morse, Kelly Stultz, RC Lewis, Paul Krueger, and the entire Fourteenery. Thanks for seeing me through the very rough year that came before this book's sale. I know I was a pain, sometimes.

The old guard who helped grow a mountain girl into a writer: Arnie, Ellen, Georgie, Michael, Carol and Ted, Kitty and Paul, John and Antonio. Thank you for being a part of my raising up.

And my husband, the city boy I lured to the backwoods with promises of good food, good books, and the love of a (mostly) good woman. This piece of my heart, just like the rest of them, is yours. I love you.

# READING GROUP GUIDE

## Discussion Questions

In order to provide reading groups with the most thought-provoking questions, there are some major plot spoilers included in the questions below. We strongly suggest that you finish reading the book before looking at this discussion guide.

1. In the opening scene, we see Duke kill Ben Springfield in revenge for what happened to Jeannie. Do you think Duke's actions are justified? After all, the Springfields knew what they were risking by attacking Duke's family. Or is killing wrong, no matter the circumstances? Does the fact that Ben has two young children change your answer?

2. How does the violence Harley witnesses throughout her childhood affect her? How long do you think children should be sheltered, and what do you think is an appropriate age to begin teaching a child about some of the horrors that exist in the world?

3. Should Harley be punished for her role in Dan's death?

4. The McKennas love "hard and fast and only once." Do you think this is a realistic depiction of love? Are there people in your life you feel this fiercely about? Are there crimes that are forgivable, if they're committed in the name of love?

5. *Barbed Wire Heart* has many strong and complicated female characters: Harley, of course, but also Mo, Jeannie, Brooke, Jessa, and Molly, to name just a few. How do you feel about the portrayal of women in *Barbed Wire Heart*? Is there a character you particularly identify with?

6. And what about the men in the novel? Do you feel that Duke, Carl, Will, and the other men are realistically portrayed?

7. Harley and Duke have an incredibly complicated relationship. Do you think they love each other?

8. Duke believes he's doing the best he can for Harley by raising her to be tough and by teaching her to defend herself. Do you agree? Do you think Harley agrees? If you were in Duke's position, would you have made different choices? Is Duke a good father?

9. One of the most heart-wrenching scenes in the book is the one where Duke "kidnaps" young Harley as a test, forcing her to escape from the locked trunk of a car. What do you think Harley learns from this experience? Do you think she learns the lesson Duke meant to teach her?

10. Do you think Harley would have had a better life if Jake had been successful in his attempt to take her away from Duke?

11. At one point, Harley threatens to run away. Why do you think she never does? When Jake tries to rescue her, why doesn't she let him?

12. If you were born into the McKenna family, would you participate in the family business? Or would you leave town, abandoning your family?

13. Why do you think it is so important to Will to find his birth family?

14. What do you think Carl Springfield wants from Harley? Does he want to kill her, or is there something else he wants from her?

15. Carl Springfield attacks Harley three times, and she doesn't tell her father that it was Carl. Why do you think she remains silent?

16. Is a person's personality governed by their genes or by how they've been raised? Do you believe in nature or nurture?

17. Does Harley take after her father or her mother? Both? Neither?

18. In choosing to remain in her hometown rather than escape and forge a new life for herself, Harley feels the weight not only of her father's expectations but also of her responsibility to protect the Rubies and to prevent an even more violent group from coming in to take control of the town. Do you think she makes the right choice in deciding to stay?

19. As Harley gets older, she doesn't always behave the way Duke would like her to—notably, when she insists that Will go to college. How do you think Duke feels about the woman Harley has become?

20. Why do you think Harley chooses to rescue Carl from the fire? Should she have left him inside the burning house?

21. Were you satisfied with the book's ending? Would you call it happy?

22. What meaning did you take from the title? Is a barbed wire heart, ultimately, something to aspire to? Or something to rid oneself of? What is *your* heart made of, would you say?

23. If *Barbed Wire Heart* were to be adapted into a movie, who would you cast in the lead roles?

# A Conversation with Tess Sharpe

**What inspired you to write this novel?**

I started writing this book after I dropped out of college and moved back home. I was working as a maid and listening to a lot of Lucinda Williams and Steve Earle while I cleaned houses. The book was born out of those times I was scrubbing toilets and listening to Lucinda and Steve. Lucinda's work, especially, was very influential. Her voice, her lyrics, the messiness and anger and glory that she captures always carried me through.

It's been so long, I can't pinpoint the moment it all clicked. I do remember that the first scene I wrote was the flashback when Harley is locked in the car trunk. It told me everything I needed to know: about her, about Duke, and about what he was willing to do to his child to prepare her for the life he'd thrust her into. In those first few years, I spent most of my time working on Harley's past—her present took a lot longer to come together.

**How long did it take you to write it?**

A little less than a decade. I started writing it just after I turned twenty-one, and it was published a handful of days after I turned thirty-one.

**What is your writing process like?**

I'm pretty settled into my routine. I write full-time and work in several genres and age categories, so I'm usually mid-project on something, revising something else, and in copyedits for a third thing. Most days, I draft for two to four hours, and I spend a lot of time walking in the woods I live in, running dialogue with myself to get scansion and character voice right.

I don't write in order. I like to assemble the book like a puzzle once I feel I have enough pieces. I write thousands of words of backstories and different points of view that I know will never end up in the book but give me the full picture of each of the characters. It's a time-consuming process, not terribly practical, but it's what works for me.

**You've also written a novel for young adults—*Far from You*. How was the process of writing a young adult novel different from writing one targeted toward adults? Which one did you enjoy writing more?**

Writing books for teenagers is my calling in life—and YA fiction is the reason I managed to survive my difficult teen years. When I write a book for teenagers, the teen audience is what's always at the forefront of my mind, as well as my responsibility to them. Also, teenagers are great bullshit detectors. You can't risk any moments of falseness in books for them. They'll call you on it. That's the great challenge of teen fiction: to be authentic for an ever-evolving group of individuals that's forever changing because teens age out of the category and new teen readers age into it constantly.

Writing an adult book is very different. It's not more difficult, but I view it as a more singular pursuit—something I do first for my own enjoyment. I'm able make narrative choices that I wouldn't make in a YA book, and that can be such a wonderful challenge.

I like challenges, so I feel really fortunate to write for both adults and teens.

**The setting of *Barbed Wire Heart* is so vivid, it feels like another character in its own right. Why did you decide to set this book in rural northern California?**

NorCal has always played a huge role in my work. It's where I grew up, and what made me the person and writer that I am. When you say you're from Northern California, most people associate it with the Bay Area, as if the state stops there, and all of NorCal is this progressive haven—but really, the territory north of Sacramento can be very different. When I describe where I grew up—the politics, the poverty, the racism, the remoteness—it surprises a lot of people. But in these mountains and small towns, and in the people who live in them, I've found a wealth of untold and diverse stories that should be told. And I'm very lucky I got to tell this particular story about this particular piece of Calabama.

**Harley McKenna is a force to be reckoned with: strong, driven, and full of grit. What inspired her character? Is there anyone in your life you would consider a "Harley"?**

Harley is the kind of resilient I wanted to be as a kid. So later on, I invented her. I know that's not the most writerly of answers, but the source is basically this childhood longing that grew up. But over twenty-five years, I've watched the north state suffer as meth took good people down, and the wrong side of the tracks got even meaner, with no end in sight. And now the opiate invasion's in full force, too.

So the communities just get poorer, angrier, and more desperate. And though you put in the work—you donate, you organize, you protest, you try to right wrongs, you help your neighbors—there's always a new goalpost down the road.

No matter what, I always come back to the words, to the story, for comfort and strength. So I created a girl who was powerful enough to save a fictional version of it all.

*Barbed Wire Heart* plays with concepts of freedom and justice— Harley strives to attain both. Do you feel that she succeeds? Is she free at the end? And how about the other characters in the book—do they get justice?

I think Harley accomplishes what she sets out to do—though there are consequences she didn't quite bargain for. I'm not sure you can ever be free when you're the McKenna. Her life is tied to the county, to the Rubies, to the people. But Harley has control in the end, which is safer than freedom.

What's next?

I have some thriller projects in progress. They're still in the early stages, and I can be a bit superstitious about sharing at this point, but I'll be coming back to NorCal, to the more mountainous regions up near the border, where secrets run deep and when they finally surface, you'd best watch out.

In my YA life, it's all dinosaurs and witches: A *Jurassic World* prequel called *The Evolution of Claire* will be out this summer, as well as my first anthology, *Toil & Trouble*, a collection of feminist short stories about witches by a group of incredible authors that I had the pleasure of co-editing with the amazing Jessica Spotswood.

# ABOUT THE AUTHOR

Born in a mountain cabin to a punk-rocker mother, **Tess Sharpe** grew up in rural Northern California. She lives deep in the backwoods with a pack of dogs and a growing colony of slightly feral cats.

She is the author of the critically acclaimed young adult novel *Far from You* and the co-editor of *Toil & Trouble*, a feminist anthology for young adults. This is her first novel for adults.